DREAMDARK

Silksinger

ALSO BY LAINI TAYLOR:

Dreamdark: Blackbringer

Lips Touch: Three Times

DREAMDARK

Silksinger

LAINI TAYLOR

ILLUSTRATIONS BY JIM DI BARTOLO

G. P. PUTNAM'S SONS
PENGUIN YOUNG READERS GROUP

G. P. PUTNAM'S SONS A division of Penguin Young Readers Group.
Published by The Penguin Group. Penguin Group (USA) Inc.,
375 Hudson Street, New York, NY 10014, U.S.A.

Penguin Group (Canada), 90 Eglinton Avenue East, Suite 700, Toronto, Ontario M4P 2Y3, Canada (a division of Pearson Penguin Canada Inc.). Penguin Books Ltd, 80 Strand, London WC2R 0RL, England. Penguin Ireland, 25 St. Stephen's Green, Dublin 2, Ireland (a division of Penguin Books Ltd.). Penguin Group (Australia), 250 Camberwell Road, Camberwell, Victoria 3124, Australia (a division of Pearson Australia Group Pty Ltd). Penguin Books India Pvt Ltd, 11 Community Centre, Panchsheel Park, New Delhi—110 017, India. Penguin Group (NZ), 67 Apollo Drive, Rosedale, North Shore 0632, New Zealand (a division of Pearson New Zealand Ltd). Penguin Books (South Africa) (Pty) Ltd, 24 Sturdee Avenue, Rosebank, Johannesburg 2196, South Africa. Penguin Books Ltd, Registered Offices: 80 Strand, London WC2R 0RL, England.

Library of Congress Cataloging-in-Publication Data Taylor, Laini. Silksinger / Laini Taylor. p. cm. — (Faeries of Dreamdark) Summary: While journeying by dragonfly caravan over the Sayash Mountains, warrior-faerie Whisper Silksinger, hunted by devils, meets a young mercenary with an ancient scimitar and secrets of his own. [1. Fairies—Fiction. 2. Fantasy.] I. Title. PZ7.T214826Si 2009 [Fic]—dc22
2008047981

ISBN 978-0-399-24631-9
1   3   5   7   9   10   8   6   4   2

for those who will grow up
to build the new age

List of Plates

DREAMDARK

Silksinger

PRELUDE

"The Tapestry of Creation is failing," hissed the Djinn King.

Looking up at him, Magpie Windwitch could see why the few humans who had ever glimpsed fire elementals had mistaken them for devils. With his flaming horns and his immense bat wings of hammered gold, he was magnificent and terrifying. Sparks leapt from the eye slits of his golden mask as he said, "My brethren must be found, little bird. Do you understand?"

"Aye, Lord Magruwen," Magpie said. "I understand."

This was her second task as his champion: to find the remaining fire elementals and bring them back to Dreamdark, so they could reweave the Tapestry before it was too late.

"If we do not begin soon," said the Magruwen, "blackness will seep through its threadbare weave and the world will drown in such a torrent of nothingness as will make the Blackbringer seem no more than a bird's shadow falling across the land."

A chill snaked up Magpie's spine at the memory of the

1

Blackbringer, the greatest foe her folk had ever known. Capturing him had been her first task as the Djinn King's champion and she had done it, though she had nearly lost herself to darkness in the process. Now she paused to imagine a tidal wave of that same gnawing blackness swallowing the world she loved.

"I'll find the Djinn," she vowed, her eyes glinting like sunstruck steel. "I promise."

ONE

Whisper Silksinger knew two kinds of death. There was the peaceful kind, quiet as eyelids fluttering shut, and there was the kind with teeth, sudden as a spurt of blood, a devil pounce, a scream. She had seen both. Of her whole clan only three faeries remained, and now death had come for them too.

And it had come with teeth.

"Whisperchild, fly faster!" her grandmother cried, perched behind her on the flying carpet. Whisper clutched the carpet's edge tight in both hands and looked over her shoulder. The devils were closing in, a rampaging, winged swarm of them too great to count.

She faced forward again, her black eyes wild with panic. The magical glyph for speed was already burning bright in her mind; she didn't know how to make the carpet fly any faster!

Beside them on a carpet of his own, Whisper's grandfather was conjuring fistfuls of bluefire and hurling them at the horde, striking the devils again and again. They lit up like torches in the night sky. Some kept flying, fully ablaze. Others plunged like meteors into the bay below and hit the water with a hiss. But there were still more devils, and more. They were so close now that when Whisper glanced back again, she could see the moonlight shining on their slaver.

"Faster, Whisper!" her grandmother cried again.

"I can't go any faster!"

They were scamperers all three, as Silksingers had always been. Their wings were small as cherry blossoms and couldn't lift them in flight, so their only hope of escape was the flying carpets. But these were works of beauty, not of battle, and they weren't spelled for speed.

The devils gained.

Whisper's grandfather drew up close beside her. "Whisper-child," he said urgently. "Take this." He thrust a battered copper teakettle at her. Besides the carpets, it was the only thing they'd taken when they fled the devils. Whisper clutched it close and stared at her grandfather.

"But Opa—"

"Keep it safe," he said. "I love you, child. Blessings fly with you."

His words struck a sudden terror in her. "What are you going to do?" she cried.

But he didn't answer. He reached out and clasped his wife's hand and said, "Plum, my love, be brave."

4

"Blessings, my husband," she said, clasping his hand hard. "And you."

Whisper gasped, "Nay!" as her grandfather whipped his carpet around to face the oncoming devils. In an instant the swarm was on him, wings and teeth, tails and talons, slashing, shrieking. As her carpet scudded away through the skies, Whisper's concentration failed. "Opa!" she cried. The glyph for speed fell from her mind and the carpet began to slow as she looked back in horror.

"Whisper, fly!" Plum commanded.

But Whisper couldn't take her eyes off the clot of devils. No two were alike—scaled and slime-slicked, horned, spined, beaked, and barbed. She could see no trace of her grandfather through their rotten feathers and hides. As she stared, stricken, she saw shapes peel themselves away from the frenzy and wheel in the air on jagged wings. And she saw . . . a sparkle inside the swarm.

"Look away!" Plum cried.

And then the night sky bloomed daylight.

A blast of white radiated outward, and too late Whisper squeezed her eyes shut. Strobing light blinded her; a quaking silence filled her head. Light and dark clashed and she didn't know if her eyes were open or closed, if it was day or night. An instant after the flash, a wave of heat rolled past; it prickled Whisper's skin and stole her breath. As she reeled in shock, her grandmother visioned the glyph for speed and got the carpet racing through the sky again, over the dark waters of the Bay of Drowned Dragons, away from the heat.

Away from the ash.

"Dragonfire," choked Whisper. A sob was building in her chest. She knew what her grandfather had done. He had visioned the twelfth glyph for fire and it had consumed him. It was a dragon's glyph, a magic too powerful by far for a faerie, as her grandfather had known it would be. He had incinerated himself and taken all those devils with him so that his wife and granddaughter might escape and keep safe their precious burden. Whisper clutched the teakettle tight to her belly. The sob escaped her throat.

"Hush, child, and look back," Plum said. "Did it take them all?"

Whisper turned to look, but she was still half blind. She couldn't see what lay behind her, but she heard it. A scream shrilled forth and was quickly answered by another. She remembered the shapes that had peeled themselves away from the swarm just before the blast. They had survived. Squinting, she could just see them coming. "There are two!" she said.

"Speed. Quickly!" Plum snapped.

Whisper summoned the glyph. She faced ahead and felt the wind quicken against her face. Her vision was clearing, and she saw they had nearly reached the mainland. The bay's hundreds of islands lay behind them now in all their strange and scattered shapes. One of those islands was their home, and this was the farthest Whisper had ever been from it. How had the devils found them? For four thousand years her clan had lived in secrecy, believed dead by the world, and now they were flushed from their island like songbirds from a thicket, to be devoured in flight!

Whisper concentrated. She knew that if she let the glyph slip, the devils would be on them in a flash. She would die, and the unthinkable would happen: they would take the kettle!

Behind her, her grandmother conjured bluefire and threw it, but her aim was poor and the devils dodged the blasts, drawing ever nearer. They came so close that Whisper could smell them, putrid as fish festering on a rock. And then Plum hit one—it went up in a blaze but kept coming, its wing beats fanning its own flames until it was a ball of scalding blue light, somehow still flying. It reached out with its talons, hooked the fringe of the carpet, and yanked.

The carpet lurched, and the other devil caught up. It descended on the faeries, squalling, and battered at them with its stinking wings. Claws grazed Whisper's cheek—it was groping for the teakettle! She curled around it as if her own slender body could keep it safe, but it was no use.

Pain knifed into her bare shoulders—talons, sinking in, clamping down. The devil had her. She screamed and held the kettle tight as the beast dragged her off the carpet.

This was it. This was death.

Her grandmother grabbed her around the waist. For a sickening second she hung suspended between them, the talons ripping at her shoulders, Plum tugging her back. Their eyes met. Whisper knew her own were wild, but Plum's were cool as agate stones. Keeping one arm around Whisper's waist, she reached up and grabbed the devil's foot with the other and wrenched it away. Flesh tore and pain lashed through Whisper's body like lightning bolts. The devil released her and she dropped back onto the flying carpet, but Plum didn't release the devil. Still hanging on to it, she looked into Whisper's eyes and said, "The clan's duty is yours now, Whisperchild. Blessings go with you."

And she pushed her off the flying carpet.

Whisper fell. Above her, hot white light flared and night once more turned to day. She hit the ground hard. She hadn't even realized they'd reached the mainland. She lay gasping for breath while overhead, dragonfire blistered the sky.

Blindness and silence pressed in on her, and it was many long moments before her vision cleared enough that she could see. She was on a beach, the water only a few yards off. The sky was empty and silent, and ashes were sifting down like black snow and settling on the sand. The ashes were devils, and they were carpet, and they were her grandmother.

Tears glistened in Whisper's lashes but didn't fall, and

ashes caught there and clumped. She was too stunned even to grieve. The teakettle had rolled onto its side in the sand and she stared at it, unblinking.

Inside it burned an ember. It didn't look like much, a small seed of fire, but devils would kill for it, her grandparents had died for it, and the world depended on it. And now it fell to her to keep it safe.

What would she do? She couldn't go home—the devils had found them there. Where could she go? She knew nothing of the world beyond her island. She couldn't fly, and she was no warrior—she had no weapon, and she wasn't even brave. Ever since the day many years ago when she'd seen a sea serpent's jaws close over her parents, she had lived with a chill at the nape of her neck, wanting always to glance over her shoulder.

Shakily, Whisper drew herself up to her knees and gathered the kettle back into her arms, feeling the low pulse of warmth from within.

"Please," she whispered to the ember. "Please wake." But it had not stirred once in all the millennia that the Silksingers had guarded it. Nor did it now.

Whisper knelt on the beach, pale and trembling, shoulders torn and bleeding. She hugged the warm kettle close, but it did no good. She was alone now, and she was as cold as a pit of ash after a fire has burned out.

TWO

"This should be interesting," said Magpie, perched in the entrance to a cave. Within, the darkness was total, and it was *alive*. Casting an orb of faerie light into the gloom, she could make out thick clusters of bats hanging from the ceiling, thousands of them, jostling each other and quarreling like peevish biddy aunts. Down below, the cavern floor rustled with life too, but Magpie did not float her light down for a better look. She knew what was there.

"Cockroaches," said Talon Rathersting, listening to the scuttling.

"Aye, and don't forget the pythons."

The cockroaches fed on the bats' guano, and the pythons on fallen bats. A bat cave was a world unto itself, and they were about to fly into its stifling darkness to hunt.

"Ready?" asked Magpie.

"Ready," said Talon.

Casting their spelled lights before them, they flicked

open their wings—Magpie's dragonfly and Talon's feathered ones—and plunged in.

They were deep in the land of Ifrit, in the wild, jungled foothills of the Mountains of the Moon. The cave, upslope from a blue lake, was huge. It even had its own weather—a constant pitter-patter of rain made up not of water but of sticky bat droppings. The faeries were agile fliers and dodged these as best they could, navigating through the syrupy dark. On the far side, the bats thinned as the ceiling sloped down, and they had no choice but to descend nearer to the living carpet of roaches.

"There," said Magpie, pointing to the mouth of a small tunnel. Unfortunately, it was blocked by the sleek curve of a python. The snake's head protruded from the hole; its body receded down the tunnel, filling it.

"Think you can get him to move?" asked Talon, hovering in the air.

"What, ask nice?" said Magpie. The snake was a giant; if it yawned, she was sure she could stand up inside its mouth without slouching. Not that she had any plans to do so.

"Well, we can't get around him," said Talon. "We'll have to lure him."

"Aye. You want to be bait or should I?"

"I definitely look more delicious," replied Talon.

Magpie chuffed. "Mouthful of feathers, you are."

"Tastier than a mouthful of scales," said Talon, indicating Magpie's tunic of precious firedrake scales.

He had a point, thought Magpie, tapping one of the diamond-hard scales with her fingernail. "Okay, you can be bait this time, but don't go thinking you always get to have the fun."

"Neh, sure," said the lad, giving a hard backbeat with his wings that carried him higher in the air. He paused a moment, and Magpie watched to see what he would do. She couldn't help smiling at the sight of him. Just three weeks gone from his home forest of Dreamdark, and he looked nearly as wild as the jungle faeries here in Ifrit. His pale hair, always a mad thatch, had a leaf stuck in it and needed to be cut, his arms were smudged with dirt, his trousers frayed. And of course there were the Rathersting tattoos aslant his cheekbones that could make even a gentle soul look ferocious. And Talon was a gentle soul, but he was a warrior too.

He made his move, launching himself at the python, flipping in a graceful blur before landing in a crouch on the snake's head, right between its eyes. "Blessings, serpent," he said cordially.

The python didn't return the greeting. Instead, with furious speed, it reared its head, dislodged Talon, and struck like a hammer at where the faerie should have been. But Talon was no longer there. Pythons are swift, but Talon was swifter. He darted back from the strike and hung in the air, taunting,

Magpie and Talon

"Come get me, slithermeat!" The snake slid after Talon, and Magpie watched in awe as it kept coming and coming, the tunnel disgorging a seemingly endless length of snake flesh.

"Jacksmoke," she murmured. It had to be twenty feet long!

Talon lured and coaxed, letting the python get near again and again before spinning clear of each strike, and Magpie watched like it was a show. Talon had been quite the acrobat even as an earthbound scamperer, but now that he could fly—on crow wings he'd crafted himself out of magic, spidersilk, and dreams—he was a sight to behold. He led the snake across the cavern, its body plowing through the soup of guano and roaches like a ship cutting through a sea. Then he cast a lifelike magical phantasm of himself for it to chase, and darted back to Magpie. "Come on, before it gets wise," he said, and they made for the small tunnel. Magpie went first, her orb of light flickering ahead of her, and Talon followed close behind.

The tunnel was narrow and dank, and as the cave had been, it was teeming with life. Dodging scorpions big enough to ride on, quivering clumps of maggots, and weird eyeless troglobites, they darted left and right as the passage turned. At length they came to a forking of the way, and Magpie veered left without even pausing to consider. She was guided now by a pulsing, unseen power. It drew her onward, and she knew that they were on the right track.

All her life Magpie had felt this pulse, and she had never known what it was, nor ever met anyone else who felt it. But her time in Dreamdark had changed all that. Now she knew it was nothing less than the thrum of the Tapestry of Creation, that mystical fabric dreamed into being aeons past by the seven Djinn who had made the world. The Tapestry *was* the world, its essence and its power, and Magpie could *feel* it. So could Talon, and their friend Poppy Manygreen, and this sensitivity gave their magic a power that faeries had not known for thousands of years.

In Magpie's case, it gave her a power *no* faerie had ever known, not even her heroine, the great Bellatrix. Though Magpie was just a twig of a lass, small enough to ride crowback, there wasn't a creature in the world—the Djinn excepted—who had more raw power than she. Of course, she hadn't even begun to master it.

"Talon, look," she said when the passage funneled into a small cavern. Here were no unsightly troglobites, no maggots or bats. As if some magical boundary kept them at bay, the cave was empty of all but a burning ember upon a dais of stone. Magpie dropped down to her feet and approached it. It was a beautiful sight, an orange glimmer in this deep, dark place.

"The Ithuriel," she breathed.

Talon cocked his head and squinted at it. "You sure?"

"I'm sure," said Magpie. To anyone else, the ember would

seem nothing but a dying fire. But to Magpie's eyes, which could *see* magic, it was alive with arabesques of light. This was no common thing, but a fire elemental deep in slumber. It was a Djinn.

"If you say so," said Talon.

Once the Djinn had ruled the world they made. But four thousand years ago, they had forsaken their creation and vanished without a trace. Some believed they'd returned to the blackness beyond the world, others that they'd died, still others that they had never existed at all and were naught but stories. But here in this cave was the truth: the Djinn had retreated to deep places to sleep and dream.

"One down, four to go," Magpie said, pleased. The Magruwen, of course, was already awake, and the Vritra had been murdered by the Blackbringer. That left five to find, of which the Ithuriel was the first. She cleared her throat and prepared to wake him. "Blessings, Lord Ithuriel," she said.

Nothing happened. She repeated herself. Still nothing. The ember just lay there like . . . an ember. Chewing her lip, Magpie cocked an eyebrow at Talon, who shrugged. For the next half hour she visioned a variety of glyphs, raised her voice, and even tried blowing on the Djinn, but he did not stir from his deep sleep.

"I guess we'll just have to carry him out," she said at last.

"How?" asked Talon.

"Good question." It hadn't occurred to Magpie to bring a receptacle. When a search of the cave turned up no vessels, she realized there was one thing in her possession that would work: her tunic. Firedrake scales, like dragon scales, were fireproof. She unbelted it and pulled it off over her head. She was wearing a homespun shift beneath, but she had gotten so used to the feel of Bellatrix's ancient armor in the last few weeks that she felt a little bare without it.

She visioned a glyph to make the ember float up from its dais, then she caught it in mid-air and wrapped it in the tunic. "Let's go," she said. And with Talon behind her and her orb of light ahead, she sped back down the tunnel, anxious to emerge once more into the fresh air.

In her hurry, she rounded a bend and flew right into the python's waiting mouth.

THREE

"Skive!" Magpie hollered, and only a sharp backbeat of her wings saved her when the serpent's jaws snapped shut like a trap. Reeling backward, she crashed into Talon and they both collapsed to the tunnel floor.

"Hoy, slithermeat!" cried Talon.

The python filled the tunnel. In this tight space there could be no luring him away and no going around him. They could only go back, and they did. *Fast.* Like a blur, the snake pursued. Magpie thought she felt its forked tongue flicking at her heels and put on a burst of speed. At the split in the tunnel, she shot right this time, knowing that to the left lay only a dead end in the Ithuriel's dreaming place.

They discovered soon enough that the right was a dead end too. The passage dwindled until none but cockroaches could have squeezed through, and the snake came on, plowing scorpions out of its path. Magpie and Talon stood side by side and faced it, and the snake's head was massive before them.

"Er," said Talon. "Can't you do something?"

Magpie had been wondering the same thing. She didn't want to *kill* the snake. It wasn't her business to kill—not even devils, let alone magnificent creatures such as this that were just filling their niche in the Djinns' wild world. But neither did she plan to let those fangs come any closer. Surely she could do something. She did have the magic of the Tapestry at her fingertips.

The problem was, she didn't quite know how to *use* it yet.

"Inept meddler" was what the Magruwen had called her after his most recent effort to teach her. But she couldn't begin to control her power! It was elementals' magic, and she was just a lass; it blurted from her and ran rampant in the Tapestry's radiant threads, tangling them and wreaking unpredictable magicks. Just the other day, she had accidentally cast a spell that made all the apples in the world taste like *blood*. The Magruwen had hastily unworked that one, muttering all the while. Now Magpie felt a familiar tingling building in her fingertips as the snake prepared itself to strike, but instead of clenching her hands into fists to stem the magic's flow, she raised them and willed it forth. Curls of light loosed themselves from her fingertips and spun toward the snake.

There came no magician's sparkle or poof of smoke. Simply, one second the giant python filled the tunnel, and the next second it lay wee before them, diminished to the size of a worm. Magpie breathed a sigh of relief and said, "That'll do."

"Aw, look how cute he is," said Talon. "I want to put him in my pocket."

"Ach, leave him be, poor meat. Imagine how long it took him to get so big, and now he has to start all over. Guess he shouldn't have tried to eat us."

To the bewildered python, Talon said, "Let that be a lesson to you, bully."

"Come on," said Magpie. "The crows'll be in a flutter if we don't get back soon." Bypassing the serpent easily now, they flew on their way.

As they emerged into the huge bat cavern, they saw it must be twilight. The bats were rousting themselves from the ceiling and swirling in a veritable tornado of wings, out the small rock opening and into the world beyond. The faeries had to hover and wait as the exodus went on and on, thousands of bats winging their way into the night. By the time they were all out and Magpie and Talon could exit behind them, the moon had risen over the forest. By its light, the bats looked like a twisting river in the sky, streaming away into the distance.

The faeries found the crows where they had left them earlier: perched on the fat arm of a fig tree downslope from the cave.

"Jacksmoke, 'Pie!" croaked Calypso, the crow chief, whose chipped beak made him seem always to grin. "There ye are! I was getting mad anxious. Did ye find him?"

"We did!" she announced proudly. Holding her wadded tunic in the crook of one arm, she lifted the edge to show the birds the ember. Its glow lit their black eyes orange and they oohed and aahed over the sight of it.

"Good on ye, darlin'," said Bertram, the bespectacled one with the ebony peg leg. "It's a fine beginning!"

"Aye," agreed Pigeon. "Won't the Magruwen be pleased!"

"Four more to go now," said Swig.

Four more Djinn, hidden like treasure around the world. They were the Iblis and the Ashmedai, the Sidi Haroun and the Azazel. From here, in the center of the huge Ifrit continent, Magpie could choose to fly either east or west to continue the hunt. She was leaning toward east because that's where her folk were, still oceans away on the island of Anang Paranga, and she dearly wished to see them.

"Mags!" came a piping squawk, and the crow Pup descended on her, excited. "Mags! Talon! I want bat wings too!"

Magpie and Talon shared a perplexed look. "What?" Magpie asked Pup. "What do you need with bat wings? You *have* wings."

"But *he's* getting bat wings," said Pup, pointing with his feather tip up at a higher branch.

"Ah," said Magpie. "Bat wings now, is it?"

"I thought it was eagle wings," said Talon.

On the branch, with his hands on his haunches and his great nose lifted haughtily in the air, stood Batch Hangnail, the scavenger imp. He was watching the recession of bats into the distance. "I changed my mind," he said. "I want bat wings."

"Me too," said Pup. "Can I too?"

Magpie put her arm affectionately around Pup's neck and said, "Neh, feather, you cannot. Your wings are perfect. Why else would Talon have made himself wings exactly like yours?"

Talon's wings were indeed identical to the crows' own, and he was surely the only faerie in the world with feathers. Faeries had butterfly, dragonfly, and moth wings most commonly, and more rarely those of other insects, but never bird wings. Pup brightened at this thought and said, "Jacksmoke, for true!" He looked at Batch and said, "I *have* wings already," and then he spread and fluttered them gloatingly.

Batch sniffed. "Crow wings! I'd never want them ugly things."

"Call *us* ugly, gobslotch?" demanded Pup, puffing up his feathers. "Look who's ugly with that great lump of nose . . ."

"Enough, Pup," said Magpie, turning to Batch. "Imp, you may change your mind as often as you like till we've searched out all the Djinn. After that, Talon will knit you whatever wings you want. Neh, lad?"

Talon nodded. Alone of all faeries, he had perfected the art of knitting magical skins such as those crafted by elementals. He said, "Aye. Bat, eagle, moth, any kind, any color, just like we agreed. *After* we find the Djinn."

"Sure," sniffed the imp. "And in the meantime I get to go on being a faerie slave."

"Slave?" hooted Calypso. "Slaves *work*, ye mad miscreant, so clamp yer moanhole. All ye do is point that twitchy finger of yers, eat all our food, and fart up yer caravan!"

Magpie pressed her lips together to keep from laughing. What Calypso said was true. Batch did fart more than any creature she'd ever known, and as such he had won a caravan to himself, the crows choosing to sleep outside rather than share with him. That well bespoke the foulness of the imp's bodily humors, since the crows were far from dainty, and among the many risks of sleeping outside in the jungle were leopards, prankster monkeys, and fat, bristled spiders hunting through the trees.

"Fart?" repeated Batch with a sneer. Then, turning himself around and thrusting out his rump, he cried, "Do ye mean like this?" and Calypso squawked in disgust and flapped his wings furiously to fan the wafting odor back at Batch.

Talon said under his breath, "Behold the dignity of the Magruwen's delegation," and Magpie couldn't help but snort.

23

All things considered, she knew they were lucky to have Batch along. Among her many talents, she was not so fortunate to possess the "serendipity"—that uncanny gift that allowed scavenger imps to find hidden things—so they were forced to endure Batch's company.

They had come upon him by chance a week after leaving Dreamdark, when they had stopped over to camp on the rooftops of Rome at the start of their expedition around the world. The falcon skin that Talon had traded to the imp had fallen apart, and though he had acted horrified to see them, Magpie thought he had secretly planned the meeting.

Batch Hangnail loved to fly, and there wasn't anything he wouldn't do to get wings of his own. He had once tried to peel the very wings off Poppy Manygreen's shoulders, and Magpie didn't doubt he'd try it again if he thought it would work. But for the time being, she trusted him to behave. That is, she knew never to *trust* a scavenger imp, but as long as the key to his greatest desire was Talon Rathersting's unique artistry, she believed Batch would do as he had agreed and help find the Djinn.

"Well," she said. "Let's get back to camp. Maniac and Mingus'll have supper ready."

They flew back through the forest canopy, past giant pendulums of green bananas, bursts of birds, and a family of chimpanzees bedding down for the night. Soon they came to their camp. The five colorful gypsy wagons were not on the ground among the leeches and rooting bush pigs, but drawn up side by side on a massive vine-wrapped tree branch.

The crows had been towing Batch by his long pink rat tail, all strung with diamond rings. They let him go and Magpie released her floating glyph with care to set him gently down. If he noticed the gentleness, he didn't appear to appreciate it. He was regarding her with a touch of malice.

"What?" she asked.

"I'm still waiting for a *thank ye,* missy faerie," he said, his rodentlike face pinching into a pout.

"Ach, well, thank you," she said. "You did real fine, Batch, like the king of scavengers you are." She didn't mind buttering him up, not if it meant a smooth journey, unearthing the rest of the Djinn as easily as they had the Ithuriel. If things continued like this, they'd be round the world and back to Dreamdark in no time, with all five fire elementals in tow.

She looked down at her bundled tunic and, turning to Calypso, asked him, "Where do you think we should put the Ithuriel?"

"Cook pot?" the crow suggested.

It didn't seem quite respectable, but it was iron and it would hold him without catching the wagons alight, so she agreed. They settled the ember into one of their spare pots, put on the lid, and tucked it away safely in the stage caravan near Magpie's little bunk. She shook out her tunic and slipped it back over her head.

"You going to go tell the Magruwen the good news?" Talon asked in a low voice, making sure Batch couldn't hear him.

Magpie nodded, likewise whispering. "I'll go right now. He'll be mad pleased."

It wouldn't do for the imp, or anyone else besides the crows and Talon, to find out about Magpie's "shortcut" back to Dreamdark. The fact was, though they were thousands of miles away, she could be there in a moment. She simply had to pass through the Moonlit Gardens. Her old hedge imp nurse had blessed her with the gift to travel to the land of the dead and back. Using it as a shortcut, Magpie could get almost anywhere, so long as she'd been there before and could picture the place in her mind.

"Ye going to bring the Ithuriel through with you?" asked Pup, his whisper a loud rasp that the imp could easily have overheard. Luckily, Batch was now deeply involved in exploring his nostrils with his toes and wasn't paying attention.

"Neh," Magpie said. "I can't bring anything living through with me, blackbird. You know that. If I could, I'd bring you all and we could feast at Rathersting Castle with Talon's folk. As it is," she said, giving the lad a sly look, "I'll have to go on my own and eat for us all. I hope there's chestnut pudding tonight."

Talon looked pained. "No fair! Sure we're just having mush again here."

She laughed. "Skiffle, I'm joking. No time for pudding. I need to stop in the Moonlit Gardens on the way and tell Bellatrix and Kipepeo too."

As the lady Bellatrix had been the Magruwen's champion in the Dawn Days, her husband, Kipepeo, had been the Ithuriel's, and Magpie knew both faeries would be very glad to hear the Djinn was found. "Save me some mush, neh?"

"Course, Mags," said Mingus.

Then Magpie went into her caravan, where she visioned the glyphs for moonlight, threshold, and garden, and vanished into the air. An instant later she was standing beside the river in the calm, silver land of the dead.

But it was not calm. Not now.

She found herself in the eye of a battle.

FOUR

Slomby hated plucking leeches off the firedrakes. There was only one place on their tough, scaled bodies soft enough for the bloodsuckers—a little spot in the folds of their wattles—and when the leeches were full and fattened, he had to reach through the bars of their cages and pluck them off. His pappy, who had done the job before him, had said it was like picking fruit—the ripe ones just sort of dropped off into your hand, and that was true, but the firedrakes hissed at him and flickered out their long, forked tongues, and of course, there was the matter of them breathing *fire*.

His pappy had taught him a sack of tricks for not getting scorched, but none of them were foolproof. Slomby's strange anatomy was his best protection: he bore upon his thin shoulders a big, spiral snail shell, and he could suck his whole narrow body up inside its cavity—arms, rubbery face, and all. But there was nothing he could do to protect his hands when he reached for the leeches, and his knuckles were always blistered and sore.

"Blessings, my beauties," he said to the drakes, and then, walking in the shambling, shackled way of all the snag slaves in Master's dungeon, he went from cage to cage with the leech bowl. Ryawy the queen drake was sleeping, and, holding his breath lest he wake her, Slomby reached in and groped in the folds of the soft wattle under her beak. The leech dropped into his fingers. He pulled it out and set it in the bowl, then held a new one in place and waited for it to grab onto Ryawy with its nasty sucker mouth. After, there were Therys, Zheper, and Stryth, the young drakes, whom he bribed with small blind fishes from the underground lake, still wriggling.

Last of all, with heavy feet he turned to Vesrisath's cage. The king firedrake was peering over his curved beak at Slomby, and the intensity of his baleful, golden eyes was enough to make the snag withdraw half into his shell. A ruff of crimson feathers framed the drake's head like a mane, brilliant as flames, and everywhere except that one small spot beneath his chin he was armored with impenetrable rust-colored scales. He was an elegant blending of lizard, sinuous and sleek, and rooster, regal and strutting. Today, Slomby thought he looked very weary.

Vesrisath said, "One million, four hundred and fifty-seven thousand, one hundred and eighty-six."

"Never lose count, do ye, king," said Slomby, nervously easing his face back out of his shell.

"Do you not count the days of your own captivity?" asked Vesrisath.

"Neh. I can only count as high as fourteen," Slomby admitted. "Anywhich, I was born here, and I didn't think to start counting when I was just a snagling." He paused, and then with a tremor in his voice he asked, "Ye going to char me today, king?"

The firedrake sighed and, to Slomby's surprise, lifted his chin and remained still while Slomby reached in and plundered his wattle for the fat bloodsucker hidden in its furls, switching it out for a fresh one. As he laid the leech in the bowl with the others, Vesrisath gave a shudder. "I hate them," he said quietly.

"Me too, king," said Slomby, looking down at the throbbing parasites. "I'm sorry. I am."

"You could set us free."

Slomby's eyes popped wide open. They were globed and red, set far back on either side of his face like fish eyes, and they swiveled around in a welter of anxiety. "I couldn't," he said quickly. "En't I a slave too, king?" He did a little dance to rattle his ankle shackles.

The firedrakes too wore shackles—anklets of iron chained to the bars of their cells—as well as iron collars around their necks. Slomby at least was free to move about the dungeon, but the drakes were held nearly immobile so that they couldn't harm themselves or gouge out the leeches with their long, sharp claws. "B-besides," said Slomby. "Only Master's got the key."

Vesrisath regarded the fretting snag through half-lidded eyes, and then he said something that frightened Slomby even more than the thought of freeing the firedrakes. He said, very softly, "You could kill us."

Slomby's breath rushed raggedly out of him. He whispered, "N-neh—"

"We'd have done it ourselves long ago if we could. You know that without our blood he would die, and all here below would be free."

"But ye'd be dead. . . ."

"Aye. *Free.*"

Slomby couldn't bear the pressure of those luminous eyes another moment and he squeezed his own tight shut. Snag though he was, Slomby was fangless and clawless. He had never slain a thing in his life but little fishes. The firedrakes, even at their scorching worst, were the only beautiful things he had ever been privileged to see. "I couldn't do it," he whispered, backing away. "I could never hurt ye. I'm sorry, king!"

As he scuttled away down the long row of prison cells filled with many more wretched creatures, he heard Vesrisath give a sigh that was nearly a sob, and the sound was one of such despair that Slomby felt his heart twist inside his chest like a wrung rag. He knew that twist well. It was misery.

31

When he reached the dungeon kitchen, the she-snag Num gave him a scornful look, and he realized he was crying. "What ye blubbering about now, snivelskin?" she asked, rolling her single cyclops eye.

A third slave, the froglike Mogorm, was fishing through a trough of rotten fruit. He paused and asked sympathetically, "Feeling sorry for the drakes again, Slom?"

"It's all wrong! They en't blood fountains," Slomby cried, his thin voice rising. "They're *creatures*—"

"Ach, dry yer snot and do yer job!" barked Num. She'd been polishing a silver spoon with a rag, and she slid it into the leech bowl. "And don't be trying any more of yer fishwit tricks this time. He'll know. If ye think he can't tell the taste of yer own sorry blood from firedrake blood—"

"I know, I know," Slomby muttered. He'd learned his lesson about trying to fool Master. The one time he'd given the firedrakes a break by leeching his own self in their place, Master had tasted the difference at once, and while he usually used a bone to beat his slaves, that time it had been an antler. It was a beating Slomby would not soon forget.

Num added, "Ye'd best not foul up again or Master'll feed ye to the army for a snack. And it en't like we got any slaves to spare."

Slomby knew she was right. Life in the dungeon was a constant peril these days. The main cave was overflowing with a ravenous devil army, and it was by no means certain a slave would make it through the day. Hadn't his own pappy been one of the first to go? As of now, there were only himself, Num, and Mogorm left to do the work of twenty.

"Slom, look!" cried Mogorm. In the mass of slimy mango peels and banana mash that was the fruit trough, he had found a single, perfect raspberry. He held it out like a jewel.

Slomby's mouth watered. It wasn't often they found fruit that hadn't turned to pulpy sludge, and when they did, he and Mogorm always shared it. But before he could claim his half, Num snapped her rag at him. "Get on with it, snailbrain," she said. "Ye want to keep Master waiting?" She was an expert snapper and landed a good sharp sting to his belly.

"I'll save yers for ye, Slom," Mogorm assured him, and Slomby slouched away. He knew Num was right. It wasn't good to keep Master waiting. When he wanted blood from the firedrakes, he wanted it bad.

As Vesrisath had said, it was the blood that kept Master alive. Without it, he would shrivel to his true, ancient age. Of all the things that had ever lived and never died—of all *immortal* things—only these five firedrakes had blood that he could drink to draw out his own unnatural life, day after month after century. Dragons were extinct, and all the rest of the world's firedrakes were long dead too. There were only five left in all the world, prisoners these four thousand years, and it was Slomby's job to get their blood.

Well, that was *half* his job.

With a shuddering sigh he turned his mind to the other half. It was even worse than the leeching. Now he had to carry the leeches to Master, through the whole horde of the devil army and up the long black stair. With a whimper, he retreated into his shell, sucking his arms in tight and folding himself up so that only his eyes were visible, blinking, above his shackled feet, and he shuffled on his way.

FIVE

Even before she had fully materialized in the Moonlit Gardens, Magpie was drawing her daggers. Winged devils were everywhere, shrieking, darting, clogging the sky. She had never seen so many devils!

"Jacksmoke!" she cursed, and launched herself into the air.

Somewhere in the world, someone had been killing devils, and here the snags were now, just as bloodthirsty dead as they had been alive. Snags were to be captured, not killed, and this was why. When they were killed, they just ended up here to terrorize the afterworld.

Fortunately, the Moonlit Gardens had two great warriors to defend its border: Bellatrix and Kipepeo. She saw them on the far riverbank, blades flashing in the swarm of snags, and she raced to join them. "Lady!" she called out as she drew near.

Bellatrix wielded a slim sword in each hand. She gave a quick glance toward Magpie without slowing the rhythm of her blades, and called out, "Ah, Magpie, good!" She drew slightly to one side, which Magpie took as an invitation to join her.

With a powerful thrust of her wings she rocketed toward the cluster of devils, rolling forward at the last minute to somersault heels over head. Visioning the glyph for strength, she met the attackers feetfirst with all the force of her momentum. She collided with a devil that resembled an airborne shark and sent it reeling into its fellows, temporarily scattering them.

She got a good look at them then, and what she saw sent her thoughts into a spin. In this horde was a mad variety of devils. There was a beetlelike snag with flickering wings, another with antlers that branched into knife-sharp points, and a warty one oozing yellow slime—and that was just the start. It was as if a devil zoo had thrown open all its cages and spilled out this terrible multitude.

Flummoxed, Magpie couldn't begin to imagine where in the world they'd come from. She lashed out at them with her daggers. Skuldraig, her djinncraft blade, made a sound like a chime as it paralyzed her foes and temporarily dropped them out of the air. Beside her, Bellatrix's body whipped and her long braid whirled as she defended herself from all sides. Further on, Kipepeo was doing the same.

Long swords would have been better than daggers, Magpie saw as she fought to keep the ever-shifting swarm at bay.

In all her hunts and all her captures, she had never fought more than three devils at once, and usually just one. Fighting a mob like this required entirely different tactics, which she had never had occasion to master. She had to spin wildly, lashing out with both her knives to prevent the beasts from coming together into one brute clump of deviltry that might be able to overwhelm her. But how to capture so many? She could paralyze them briefly with Skuldraig, but that was little help with so many all around her.

It wasn't just in sheer numbers that this battle differed from all others she'd fought. She had never fought the dead, and she was about to learn that it wasn't like fighting the living.

Bellatrix called out to her. "Magpie! You must slay them!"

"*Slay* them?" Magpie spun round just in time to see the lady plunge her swords simultaneously into two devils. She skewered one through its gaunt torso, the other through the soft underside of its beetle body. They pitched back their heads and screamed in unison, and Magpie felt a shock of horror to see her heroine *kill*—champions didn't kill, they captured!—but the screams bit off suddenly. In a glimmer, the devils vanished as if they had never been.

Confounded, Magpie had to twist to fend off an assault from a vulture beast. On instinct, she still didn't stab it but only paralyzed it with the edge of her blade. It went limp and fell out of the air, but it quickly rebounded—Skuldraig's paralysis was only temporary—and she saw it take wing and break for the trees.

"Nay!" cried Bellatrix as the devil fled. Powerfully she hurled one of her swords and harpooned it between the wings. With a squawk, the snag vanished as the others had, and Bellatrix's sword fell unfettered to the ground. The lady swooped down to retrieve it, and as she swung her blades back into battle, she said, "Magpie, trust me. When devils come here, it's too late for capture. We must slay them before they can slay us. If you're killed in the Moonlit Gardens, you are *unmade*."

Unmade? That could only mean that your spark—your very soul—was snuffed out of existence. A chill gripped Magpie. She thought of the tranquil dead who were usually here picnicking on this riverbank—they must have fled into the shelter of the trees. They were almost all elderly faeries, waiting for their loved ones to come and join them. Magpie had never thought the dead could *die*. Or worse—be unmade. If that vulture devil had reached the trees, even now it could be savaging the helpless folk who hid there.

Bellatrix was right. The devils had to be stopped.

But Magpie had never killed before. She gripped her dagger hilts tight and hesitated. A devil lashed out at her with a tail like a whip and caught her around the ankle. Slashing down with Skuldraig to hack it off, she momentarily left her face vulnerable and had to jerk back from the snap of jaws that came close to shearing the nose right off her face. So close, the snag's death-reek breath stung her eyes.

She did what she had to do. She stabbed it. The sensation of her blade sliding into flesh was one of the worst things she had ever felt. The devil convulsed and then in a glimmer, it was simply gone. Unmade, it left no corpse behind, nor even any blood on her dagger.

It was her first kill and she hated it, and it was only the beginning. She, Bellatrix, and Kipepeo fought like furies, relentless and grim-faced, unmaking snags in a blur of blades, working desperately to thin the swarm. It was slow going; there were just so many! The shark devil rolled in the air, swinging its tail to bat a pair of smaller snags at Magpie like projectiles. She dodged them just as another snag's long tail lashed out at her.

The creature had the look of a winged badger with a mat of spines on its back. The tip of its tail was a heavy club of flesh, bristling with more spines, and though Magpie deflected the brunt of the blow with Skuldraig, one spine pierced her hand. It sank deep into her palm and broke off there, and a flush of numbness radiated out from it at once. Poison!

Magpie could feel it beginning to spread through her blood. It worked fast. Her fingers went numb and she couldn't hold on to Skuldraig. She dropped it and used her remaining dagger to slash the devil's throat. She didn't know what manner of snag it was, but she'd heard stories of devil venom that killed almost instantly. As the numbness climbed to her shoulder, she felt a flutter of panic.

Remembering the champion's glyph, she conjured it up at once in her mind.

The Magruwen had given it to her when he had first named her his champion. It was fused of all the Djinns' sigils, and nothing but the Djinn themselves could breach its protection. It would halt the venom's spread. Holding its complex pattern bright in her mind, she fought on left-handed, her right arm limp, until at last there were just a few devils left. Kipepeo dispatched one, Bellatrix another, and then only a small, scabby specimen remained. It had a head like a poorly worked lump of clay, and small wings it had to beat furiously to stay aloft. Kipepeo was raising his sword to finish it off, but Magpie said, "Kipay, wait! Grab that meat!"

The Ithuriel's former champion sheathed his swords and seized the snag by its thin shoulders.

Magpie demanded of it, "What is this horde? Where did you lot come from?"

The devil leered at her, and a queer, quivering sound burbled up from its throat along with a froth of spittle. She wondered if it was even capable of speech—some snags were, some weren't—and then she realized that the sound it was making was *laughter*.

"If you haven't noticed yet, you *lost,* meat," she growled at it. "You're dead! So why are you laughing?"

"Because you're dead too, faerie," it answered in a wheeze.

"In fact, I'm not."

"You will be. You all will be. I'll see to it this time!"

"And how are you going to do that?" Magpie asked. "If you haven't noticed, all your fellows have been unmade, and you're about to be too."

"You think this is all I am?" It rasped out more laughter, and Magpie began to get the uncomfortable feeling that something was speaking *through* it. "Neh, faerie," it said. "I am so much more. I am armies."

"What?" Armies? A terrible suspicion struck Magpie. "Who is that?" she demanded.

"I am Ethiag!"

"Ethiag!" she gasped. She knew that name. No record of the Devil Wars was complete without it. Shock registered on Bellatrix's and Kipepeo's faces too, and the devil took advantage of the moment to twist its arm free of Kipepeo's grip. Crowing in exultation, it darted for the trees. This time, it was Magpie who flung her blade. She caught it in the back and the snag ceased to exist. The silence that followed was eerie, broken only by the placid shush of the river and the heaving breath of the three weary warriors.

Magpie retrieved her knives. Such a glut of devils—all

species, and fighting together like comrades. With the ancient name Ethiag attached to it, the swarm made terrible sense. "Did you hear that?" she asked Bellatrix and Kipepeo as she landed between them.

They nodded, their faces grave.

"Do you think that means—" she began to ask.

"Magpie," said Bellatrix, cutting her off. "What's wrong with your arm?"

Magpie was cradling her dead arm to herself. "Oh," she said. "One of them got me." She reached down and plucked the spine from her palm. It was slender and black, its tip red with her blood. There was no feeling at all in her arm now. "I been visioning the champion's glyph, in case it's bad. Do you know what—?"

"It's a fugu quill."

"Oh," said Magpie, her eyes widening. Fugu venom was among the deadliest of all devil poisons.

Bellatrix said, "Sit down, Magpie. Keep hold of the champion's glyph and vision this one beside it." By touching her finger to Magpie's brow, she passed a new symbol into her mind. "It's a powerful healing spell. It will purge the poison from your blood."

Together the three of them visioned the spell with their heads bowed over Magpie's pinprick of a wound. She soon felt the numbness subside. She wiggled her fingers, wrinkling her nose at the pins and needles, and when she was satisfied that she was well, she let both glyphs fall from her thoughts. No one spoke. All around them, the quiet continued. High overhead, dragon silhouettes passed before the moon. The dead remained hidden in the trees, and though the devils were gone, their stench still hung in the air, mixing with the fragrance of nightspink blossoms that scented the Moonlit Gardens.

Magpie found she was trembling. All that stabbing and slashing . . . Though there had been no blood, she felt as if her hands were stained with it.

Bellatrix asked her, "Are you all right, child?"

Magpie nodded and said in a small voice, "Aye, I'm fine. It's just . . . to kill all of them . . ."

"They were dead already," said Bellatrix.

"To unmake them, then. Why not capture them instead?"

"For what purpose? Magpie, they're devils. The reason you don't kill them in the world isn't because they deserve to live, it's only to prevent something like this from happening. They're abominations."

Magpie chewed her lip and said, "I . . . I just didn't like it."

Bellatrix said gently, "I know."

"We don't like to kill either, child," said Kipepeo. "But the devils do. You mustn't pity them. Given the chance, they'd slaughter every soul in this world. Just try to remember that."

Magpie nodded. Looking up at the two faeries, she couldn't help seeing them in a new light. She'd always known that they and the other five champions had led faeries to victory in the Devil Wars, but she'd never seen them fight before. The ballads of the Dawn Days were all about great deeds, but now Magpie imagined what it must have been like growing up when the world teemed with devils. How much carnage they must have witnessed! It was they who had brought about the long peace that faeries had known ever since—a peace that might now be coming to an end, if what the devil said was true.

Magpie said, "I almost forgot why I came. I brought good news."

"Good news?" Bellatrix asked.

"Aye. We found the Ithuriel," Magpie told them.

Kipepeo's eyes brightened. He was a tall, handsome faerie, a prince of Ifrit with skin of the darkest, richest brown, set off magnificently by huge white moth wings that sparkled in the moonlight. His voice husky with emotion, he asked, "He's safe?"

"Aye," said Magpie. "Asleep, but safe."

"Blessings," he whispered.

"That *is* good news," said Bellatrix. "Thank you, child."

"But I think we better talk about the bad news," Magpie replied.

Bellatrix nodded. "Ethiag."

Magpie felt a tightening in her chest. She knew the legend. Until Ethiag, devils had been lone hunters, at worst chaotic mobs as likely to turn on each other as on faeries. The champions had hunted them down, facing them in one-on-one fights that invariably ended with the snags shoved into bottles and sealed away. But Ethiag changed all that. A devil himself, he exerted some unfathomable power over the nightmare creatures, and he united them. He shaped them into armies fit to devour the world—and they very nearly had.

The Devil Wars had raged for years. It was only when the Azazel's champion, Manathakkali, finally captured Ethiag that the tide of the war had turned. With Ethiag gone, the troops had fallen back into chaos and the faeries had at last prevailed.

Twenty-five thousand years had passed since then, and now the dread general of the Devil Wars was back.

"I suppose it was only a matter of time and chance," said Kipepeo.

"Aye," agreed Magpie. "Mannies open enough bottles, he was sure to get out sometime." She gritted her teeth and swore. "Skive, though! What am I supposed to do now?" The Magruwen had given her strict orders to find the Djinn. That was her task. But she couldn't very well leave Ethiag loose, could she?

Bellatrix laid a gentle hand on her shoulder. Her eyes

were troubled. "Magpie, I wish we could come back into the world to help you."

"I wish you could too," she replied. With her hands on her hips and her eyes narrowed, she said, "But what I'd like to know now is, who killed all those snags?"

Kipepeo nodded. "It's a good question."

"It had to have been some wild battle, neh, to kill all those? But weren't any faeries killed in it too?" She turned and scanned the riverbanks to look for any new dead. But she saw no warriors, only a biddy and codger clutching each other as they crossed the bridge. Bad time to die, Magpie thought. To come here expecting calm and find a battle instead? She noted with fleeting interest that the biddy and codger were both scamperers. It was rare enough to see one scamperer, let alone two together.

She turned her attention to the forest. The dead were emerging cautiously from hiding. Wide-eyed and shocked, they approached to cluster around the three champions. "Terrible," they muttered. "Just terrible. . . ." They too were elderly faeries, among them no warriors who might have moments ago been slaying devils in the world.

"It was probably some mercenaries who did it," Magpie said uneasily. When a devil was killed, mercenaries were often the culprits. They were the closest thing faeries had to warriors in these times. Magpie had traveled through the mountains with their caravans and she knew their type:

gruff, swaggering, and reckless. When they met a devil, they slew it first and asked questions later. After the awful battle she had just fought, she was all the more keen to prevent devils from reaching the Moonlit Gardens. "I'm going to have to teach those brutes to capture snags instead of killing them," she said.

"If Ethiag is back . . . ," Bellatrix began, and trailed off.

She didn't need to finish her sentence. Magpie was thinking the same thing. If the devil Ethiag was building a new army, a few companies of mercenaries weren't going to stand a chance against them, capturing *or* killing.

SIX

"I'd better get on to Dreamdark to tell the Magruwen about all of this," said Magpie. "The bad news and the good." She was powerfully glad that she had tidings of the Ithuriel to balance out this news of Ethiag's return.

"Give the old scorch my love," said Bellatrix.

As Magpie nodded, a shout broke the subdued hush of the riverbank. "Papa!" someone cried. "Mama!"

She saw some of the dead rushing to greet the old scamperers on the bridge. It was a common enough scene. The dead waited at the riverbank for years for their loved ones to join them here, only then giving way to the natural evolution of the afterlife and becoming seraphim, those crystalline beings of pure spirit who dwelt in the upper realms of the sky.

Soon, Magpie knew, Bellatrix and Kipepeo would go that way too. Now that they were reunited, there was nothing to hold them here at the border of life. They would begin to change, they would lose their grasp on worldly concerns, and one day they would join all the others up in the ether. It was the way of things, but it made Magpie very sad to think they wouldn't always be here for her. At least, she thought, the dragons would never go away. She tipped back her head to see them soar, high overhead.

Looking down again, she watched the dead greet each other with hugs. Then, thinking it just another happy reunion, she started to turn away. But something stopped her.

There were four or five dead greeting the codger and biddy who had just arrived. Among them were a couple she had noticed before for being younger than most on the riverbank.

They were speaking urgently. "Nay!" the young lady cried, as if she had just received dreadful news. She dropped to her knees and moaned, "Whisper! My child!"

The gent knelt down and wrapped his arms around her, and the older faeries began to weep openly. Sad news from the world, Magpie guessed. She exchanged a sympathetic look with Bellatrix and Kipepeo. It was then she heard her own name uttered.

"The Windwitch lass!" the young lady said suddenly. "She's the Djinn King's champion! Surely she can help Whisper!" She rose from her knees and made straight for Magpie, who bit her lip.

Skive, she thought. All the dead knew who she was. They

witnessed her comings and goings and knew that she could slip between the Moonlit Gardens and the living world, and they often asked her to bear messages—sometimes even recipes, and once even a curse!—back to the living. And though she was moved by the lady's grief, she had no time for such errands now. But what could she do? The dead were upon her.

"Please," the lady implored, reaching for Magpie's hands. "Little champion, you have to help our lass. She's all alone." The lady was delicate to look at, but in her wild state she gave Magpie's fingers a ferocious squeeze.

Magpie asked, "Goodfolk, what has happened?"

"Those devils . . . ," said the newly dead codger, his voice shaky.

"It's okay," Magpie assured him. "They're all gone. Some eejit's been killing them in the world, but you're safe here now."

The codger looked even more distressed. "Well, I'm sorry for it," he said, "but it couldn't be helped. They were hunting us—" He faltered and looked to his wife for reassurance.

"It was the only way," the biddy said decisively. "We had to kill them!"

Magpie gaped at the two elderly faeries. "*You* killed all those devils?" she asked. She had scarcely believed a whole company of mercenaries could have done it. But a biddy and a codger?

"I'm sorry for it," said the codger again.

"Neh, it's all past now. But good uncle . . . *how* did you kill them?"

"Dragonfire," said he, his voice dropping to a rasp.

"Dragonfire! But . . . that's a dragon's glyph! No faerie can vision it without—"

"Without burning up, aye," said the biddy. "And aren't we here, dead? We killed ourselves killing them. We had to do it, to give our lass a chance to get away!"

Magpie glanced at Bellatrix and saw her own surprise mirrored on the lady's face. "Goodfolk," said Bellatrix. "It sounds as if you've quite a tale to tell, but you've been through a shock. Please, come to my house and rest."

"Nay," interrupted the young lady. "It's no time for rest. Please." Again she squeezed Magpie's hands. "You must find Whisper."

The biddy continued, "She's all alone without a flying carpet now, and more devils will come hunting, now they've found us out."

Dragonfire, flying carpet, devils. All these unlikely things swamped Magpie's thoughts so that for a moment she could only stare. "Wh-what?" she managed to ask. "Goodfolk, who *are* you?"

"Ah, forgive us," said the codger. "We are the last of the Silksinger clan but one. Now only Whisper remains—"

"Silksinger!" exclaimed Magpie. "But the Silksingers died out ages ago! At the Battle of Black Rock—"

"Forgive us for letting the world believe that. We had to. Indeed, many died that terrible day, but not all. Those who survived took a sacred oath. My own great-great-grandparents were there through it all. For four thousand years we've lived in secret, and our numbers have dwindled by the century until only we two and Whisper remained. But somehow the devils found us out, and now our lass is alone in the world. You have to find her."

"Where is she?" Magpie asked, wondering how, with devil armies and lost Djinn to worry about, she could possibly find time to search for a lass.

"'Twas the Bay of Drowned Dragons where it happened," said the biddy.

The codger nodded. "Aye, but she'll try to get to Nazneen. She'll try to set him on his throne."

Magpie felt the pulse of the Tapestry quicken around her. "Who, good uncle?" she asked, trying to keep her voice calm. "Set *who* on his throne?"

He blinked at her and said, "The Azazel, lass. That's what the devils are after. Whisper's his only guardian now."

SEVEN

Dazed, Whisper stood in the market pavilion of Shark Fin Peak. All around her was a blur and scurry of flying and shoving and a ruckus of mingled cries.

"Magic string to hold up yer britches!"

"Honeycakes, two for a tink!"

"Cures for lice and lightning strike!"

Everyone had something to holler, something to sell, something to buy. Faeries and imps seethed together, and though Whisper stumbled among them mustering up faint "pardon me"s and trying to catch someone's attention, all eyes slid right past her, as if she wasn't even there. She couldn't understand why no one seemed to see her.

Growing up in isolation on her clan's little island, Whisper had never before been in a marketplace, nor ever in a crowd. She'd heard tales of the dragonfly caravans of the Sayash Mountains. She had conjured images of dragonflies loaded with goods, tusked hobgoblins driving them on, and ancient stone halls like these where they stopped to trade.

There would be spice and silver, she had imagined, and silks billowing in the mountain wind. And here was all of that. But in her daydreams there had never been anything like this pandemonium.

Music jangled and merchants sang. Clouds of smoke billowed from cook fires, and imps beckoned folk into a gambling den with cries of, "Liar's dice and whirl-the-snake!" There were huge mice foraging for crumbs, and up in the eaves, bats hung by their toes with their wings wrapped snug as cocoons. The great dome of the pavilion rose so high over Whisper's head she almost got dizzy looking up at it. It was the first true building she had ever been in, having lived her whole life in a series of cozy caves, and she was overcome with awe. For all its grandeur, though, she saw the walls were lichen-streaked and spidered with cracks, and there was a general reek of mildew and soot.

As for the faeries, they were so fine and fancy she could scarcely stop staring at them. The gents wore colored turbans and great twirled mustaches, and the ladies had jewelry pierced right through the edges of their wings. Their garments were caftans and capes, and around their necks they wore, each and every one of them, coins with holes in their centers, strung on long silver chains.

A lady paused beside Whisper, so heavily laden with these coin necklaces that she had to catch her breath. "Pardon me, mistress—" said Whisper in the feather-soft voice that was the reason for her name. But the lady just turned away, flicking her wings right in Whisper's face.

Exhausted and light-headed from hunger, Whisper swayed on her feet. In a passing instant of delirium she found herself wondering if she had somehow gone invisible. But then a tall faerie trod on her toe, and when she gasped in pain he looked down at her just long enough to hiss, "Don't stand where I step, mudlark," and she knew she was not invisible.

Tears sprang to her eyes as she stood on one foot and rubbed her bruised toe against the back of her ankle. Those were the first words ever spoken to her by a stranger. *Mudlark*, he had called her. She looked down at herself. Her feet were bare and her soles black with trudging. Her pajamas were so torn and stained that no one would notice they were of silk finer than any in this market. Her long, black hair draped in lank clumps around her neck and arms and stuck to the crusting claw wounds on her shoulders, concealing them.

A wave of shame washed over her and she hugged her kettle tight to keep from shivering in the mountain chill. This was her first venture ever into the world, her first glimpse of strangers—and their first glimpse of her. And that she should look like a . . . *a mudlark!* She wished she had clean clothes, combed hair, slippers on her feet, but it was no use wishing. She had nothing but the pajamas on her back. That, and the old dented teakettle.

Of course, the ember inside it was worth the life of every soul in this market a million times over—her own included—but that would hardly serve to buy her food or a cloak, not if she couldn't tell anyone about it, and she didn't dare. The Azazel was a secret too precious for strangers.

Blinking back her tears, Whisper spotted a codger with a tuft of cottony hair who reminded her of her grandfather, and she summoned the courage to make her way toward him. He sat astraddle a backward chair, whittling a chess piece with an overlarge knife. "Pardon me, good uncle . . . ," she whispered. "I need to get on a caravan for—"

He glanced at her without curiosity and went right back to his whittling. "I en't uncle to thems that know me, and nither am I to thems that don't," he said.

"Oh." Whisper blushed. She'd been taught that "good uncle" was a term of respect. "I'm sorry . . . I . . . I'm trying to get on a caravan for Nazneen, sir. Could . . . could you please tell me where to go?"

But he didn't look up again and didn't respond, so Whisper slowly backed away.

Thrice more she stoked her courage like a little fire and tried to ask for help. Twice she was ignored, and the third time a lass drawled, "No tink, no talk," and gave her own coin necklace a shake. It finally dawned on Whisper why nobody would speak to her. She wore no necklace of coins around her neck, and in the world of the trade outposts, apparently, that was the same as being invisible.

Panic seized her. She had come so far, to the only place she could think to come. Shark Fin Peak was a southerly outpost of the great caravan routes of the Sayash. It was the nearest one to the Bay of Drowned Dragons, but still a perilous journey for a scamperer. In the course of two days, Whisper had crossed the waterlogged levees of rice paddies, dodging mannies and their half-starved dogs. She had climbed into the foothills on bleeding feet, cowering when winged shapes hove overhead, swinging in great searching circles.

They might have been birds, but she was certain they weren't. They were devils, and they were hunting the Azazel. Sometimes the wind had carried their stench down to her, and sometimes she'd heard their ghastly cries volley back and forth, like questions and answers in some fell language. She wondered if she would be safe here in the midst of all these folk, or if no place was safe for her now, and she was only bringing danger to others.

"Watch it, ragdoll!" a lad snapped at her, rumbling past with a wheelbarrow full of pearls. Startled, she leapt out of the way and bumped into an imp, overturning the tray of fritters balanced on his reptilian head.

"Plague! Look what ye done, feeblewing!" he snarled at her.

She whispered, "I'm sorry," and knelt to help him pick up the fritters, but he chased her back, and she was nearly trampled by a saddled weasel carrying a row of faeries astride its back. Heart thumping, Whisper struggled to get free of the crowd. She found her way to the arched doors of the pavilion, and it was only when she was through them into the relative calm of the outer courtyard that she realized she was still clutching one of the imp's fritters in her hand.

She had stolen it.

She had never imagined she would steal. A wave of shame washed over her, but it was quickly overpowered by her hunger. She hadn't eaten in days. Glancing around to see if anyone was watching her, she took a furtive bite of the little pastry. It was both sweet and salty, filled with persimmon jam and white cheese, and as soon as it touched her tongue she forgot her shame long enough to wolf it down.

When it was gone, she looked around. The big stone hall was ringed by courtyards, which were in turn surrounded by a rampart. The courtyards, she guessed, were where the dragonfly caravans landed when they arrived each evening from the sky.

Outposts like this one were spaced all across the Sayash Mountains, each a day's fly from the last, and between them the caravans were ever on the move, stopping to sleep, eat, buy, and barter. Cocoons for gold, saffron for tea, nectar, rare herbs, silk. The hobgoblin traders hauled anything and everything that faeries sought or sold.

Once upon a time, they had even carried Silksinger carpets—they had been a wonder of the ancient world, more sought after than emeralds or ice mirrors, and the Silksingers had been a great and celebrated clan. But that was long ago. It had been four thousand years since the world had seen a Silksinger or a flying carpet. Whisper wondered if anyone remembered them. She peered around the courtyard at the hard-eyed folk who would as soon step on her as look at her, and she pictured what would happen if she started to sing.

How stunned they would be if her voice poured forth and swept aside all their noise like dead leaves on a great wind, if their turbans and capes suddenly rippled and changed color. Green to gold, plum to pink, blue to orange! And it wouldn't just be the color of their cloth that would change. Her voice could uncurl their grand mustaches and weave their hair and beards into patterns and pictures!

Her voice could do a lot more than that.

It *could,* but she held her tongue. She wouldn't sing. She would hold her voice to its careful whisper and hug her kettle close—she would keep her secrets to herself.

She looked up into the sky and saw a shimmer of wings— dragonflies, hundreds of them, flying in long glittering rows. Here were the caravans, coming in to land. A tremor of hope and terror went through her. In the morning, when they flew on their way, she needed to be with them. She had no tink to pay her passage, but she had to reach Nazneen. Once there, in the Azazel's ancient temple, she would set his ember burning on his throne. There, he would do what no amount of whispered pleas on her part could make him do. Restored to his throne, the Djinn would wake. Four thousand years ago, he had promised it.

Whisper just had to get him there.

From the edge of the courtyard, she watched the dragonflies land. They were not at all what she expected.

For one thing, they were massive. They were nothing like the dainty insects that skimmed across the lagoon back on her island! Their carapaces were as thick as the bodies of birds, their wings at least three times longer than she was tall!

And they were vicious. They came down two by two and landed heavily under the weight of their burdens. Imps dashed about grabbing their reins to lead them to the stables, trying to clear the courtyard in time for the next pair to land. There were collisions, and dragonflies reared and snapped at each other with their fearsome teeth as the imps dragged them apart.

Whisper trembled to imagine riding such a creature, and then she saw something that made her tremble even harder, and she realized *why* the dragonflies were so huge. They had, after all, been bred to carry hobgoblins on their backs.

At her first sight of a hobgoblin, her courage quailed. She watched the creature leap off its dragonfly's back and land on all fours like an animal. It was a big, hunched beast with short legs, long arms, and a massive head and shoulders. Its fingers were tipped with tough, yellowed claws, and from between its lips sprouted four tusks—two upcurved and reaching nearly to its own narrow eyes, two down, their points lost in its beard. It tossed its head and lashed its tufted tail, bellowing orders to the imps.

Several more hobgoblins landed and dismounted, and armored faeries dropped down too, not riding dragonflies but flying with their own wings. They carried swords and had messy tattoos on their knuckles and necks. Mercenaries, Whisper thought with a shiver.

Dragonflies, hobgoblins, and mercenaries! Could she really travel in such savage company?

But she had to. Between here and Nazneen stood the Sayash, the greatest mountains in the world. Even if she could fly, attempting to cross them alone would be madness. The caravans were her only hope.

EIGHT

"Lad, catch!" growled a low, animal voice, and Hirik looked up just in time to see an ashcake spinning toward him. He caught it, and crumbs cascaded down the front of his tunic. It was not a noble way to get one's supper—to have it flung through the air by a hobgoblin—but Hirik didn't care. He'd have eaten it even if it had overshot him and he'd had to fish it out of the murky pool behind him. He was that famished.

"Thanks!" he said to the hob before biting into the disc of dough. It might have been baked in the ashes of a hob's fire, but it wasn't bad, really. Anelka the hobmarm had even put a little salt in it, which, according to the other mercenaries, was unusually generous in a hob. There were horror stories among the "murks," as the mercenaries called themselves, about hob cooking, but Hirik's only complaint was that there wasn't enough of it—he could easily have devoured three ashcakes, salted or not. He wasn't finicky.

"Ye finished watering the skimmers?" asked the hobgoblin. It was Zingaro, the caravan chief. He was a hulk of a hob with gold rings on his tusks and a tidy braid down the center of his beard. Whenever Hirik saw that beard he couldn't help imagining Zingaro fumbling it up with his big, blunt fingers.

He swallowed his mouthful of ashcake and answered, "Aye, fed and watered." The "skimmers" were the dragonflies, and Hirik had sloshed water into their troughs back in the stables before flinging himself down beside this pool to rest.

"Good, good," said Zingaro, grudgingly offering, "Ye en't half bad with 'em, for a greenwing."

"Thanks," said Hirik. He was inexperienced, at only a week on caravan, but he was beginning to learn the ways of things. Or at least, he thought he was.

As Zingaro turned to go, he paused and said over his shoulder, "And lad?"

"Aye?"

"I wouldn't sit there if I was ye."

"Why?" Hirik asked. Then he heard a splash behind him. He whipped round. The surface of the pool fragmented and gouts of water erupted into the air. It all happened in an instant. Something surged up from under the water and all Hirik saw of it was a mouth gaping open, and teeth. Its lower jaw unhinged and shot out, and before he could leap away the jaws snapped shut on the edge of his wing. He cried out and the thing fell with a slap back into the pool, taking a mouthful of his wing with it.

"That's why," grunted Zingaro.

Hirik stumbled back, dripping wet and stunned. He fanned out his wings to get a look at them. They were the broad, furred wings of a hawkmoth, dark brown streaked with rust and black, with large blue eye spots on each hindwing. And now the right one bore a distinctive half-round chomp mark at its edge.

Zingaro examined it and said, "Green as a curled leaf ye are, faerie, letting a nymph get its jaws onto ye."

"Nymph," repeated Hirik. Of course. This pool was where the dragonfly young were bred—nymphs, as they were called. All the outposts had pools for raising up new stock to replace older skimmers mid-route.

Had he really let an insect sneak up on him? It was absurd. He blamed his accursed disguise—it muffled his senses. But it couldn't be helped. Hirik couldn't very well let folk see who—*what*—he really was.

"Tummies with teeth is all they are!" said Zingaro. "Ye're blessed lucky it didn't get yer whole wing." With another shake of his head, he lumbered toward the arched entrance to the market pavilion where he would do his trading.

Morosely, Hirik traced the edge of the bite with his finger. It wasn't big. He didn't think it would affect his flying, and it didn't hurt. Wings had very little sensitivity. But the other murks would have quite a smirk about it when they found out. They gave him a hard enough time as it was, being the greenwing.

With a sinking heart, he realized he'd dropped his ash-cake in the water. Several nymphs were attacking it from beneath, and he watched, stomach growling, until even the crumbs dissolved. Then he turned slowly and went inside the hostelry, where the travelers were setting up their evening camps.

This was Hirik's first journey as a mercenary, and his first time away from his own forest. Zingaro had taken him onto his crew just a week ago at the remote outpost of Fishsplash, but only after raking him up and down with a critical eye. He'd declared him "a scrunty job of runtmeat," though he was tall for his age, and "about as fearsome as a biddy with a butter knife," though he wielded a scimitar far finer than any of the other murks' weapons. And it was true Hirik was only a lad without real battle experience, but after plenty of grunting and grousing, Zingaro had agreed to give him a trial.

It turned out that a "trial" meant doing all the heavy work, rising earlier than anyone else to wake the skimmers, being the butt of every joke and the blame for all bad luck, and on top of it all, not getting a single tink of his wages until they reached Nazneen. *If* he lasted that long.

He would last. Hirik was determined to get to Nazneen, and that would mark the end of his brief career as a mercenary. He'd told Zingaro that the murk's life was his dream, but that was a lie. He had a dream, but it was a far finer one than this, and it was his secret.

In truth, it was but one of his secrets. And only one of his lies.

The hostelry at Shark Fin Peak was much the same as the others he'd seen so far: a long, barrel-vaulted hall with alcoves scooped into one wall where travelers could have some privacy. He saw Zingaro's wife, Anelka, and his mother, Old Neyn, building a fire in one alcove, and he headed toward them to fetch his satchel from the pile of baggage off-loaded by Zingaro's son.

"Moonshrive!" someone called out, and it scarcely registered in Hirik's tired mind as he kept walking. A few seconds later the same voice cried, more insistently, "Moonshrive!" and he remembered that *he* was Moonshrive, or at least, that was who he'd said he was. He turned.

It was Stormfoil, the caravan's lead murk. He was in the next alcove with the other four murks, and he had a dancing look in his eyes as he called, "Come here, greenwing! Join us for a guzz of the old throatfire."

Hirik thought throatfire was the last thing his empty stomach needed, but he knew the murk wouldn't stand for a refusal, so he went over.

Stormfoil was a lean, sly-eyed faerie with thorny vines tattooed around his neck, and butterfly wings the color of dried mustard. Though fairly young at two hundred and six, he held a high position on the caravan, coming as he did from a weatherwitching clan. It was his job to fly ahead to divert any rogue winds that might upset the skimmers, a task Hirik thought he performed poorly. Aside from that duty, Stormfoil took it upon himself to torment the greenwing, and that was a job he did very well.

"What happened to you, scrunt?" Stormfoil asked, looking at Hirik's wet clothes. "Washing day? Maybe your mammy never told you, but if you take your clothes *off* to wash them, you don't have to sit around in them wet."

"I'll try that next time," Hirik said, hoping Stormfoil wouldn't notice the bite in his wing.

He didn't. "Good lad," he said, handing over a bottle. "Blessings! Go on, then. Tip it in."

"Blessings," Hirik replied without enthusiasm, and he took what he hoped looked like a long "guzz" of the searing liquor, though he blocked the bottle neck with his tongue so only a trickle reached his mouth. It was enough to make his eyes water, and he forced himself to cough, as expected, as he handed back the bottle with a muttered, "Thanks."

"My pleasure," said Stormfoil, watching him with a keen interest as if waiting for something to happen. And just as Hirik registered his interest with alarm, something *did* happen. His lips and tongue began to burn, and it wasn't the burn of liquor but a low, vicious fire in his skin that he recognized at once. Chili pepper. The burning on his lips was joined at once by a blaze of anger.

So Stormfoil had rubbed a chili on the bottle neck. Nasty joke. Once when Hirik was a sprout, he had eaten a dried chili on a dare and he had thought in the agony that followed that his face was going to blacken and peel open like a roasted pepper. What he felt now was nothing to that pain, and his anger muted it further. He resisted the urge to wipe his lips and tried to keep his face impassive, but he couldn't keep his eyes from watering.

"Sad about something?" Stormfoil asked brightly.

"Nay, not at all," said Hirik, giving him what he hoped was a withering look, though he thought the effect was likely diminished by the tears shining in his eyes.

"Sad or not, I call that weeping, gents," Stormfoil declared, slapping his leg. "Pay up!"

Serefrost, an older murk with iron-grey whiskers, drawled, "Doesn't count, Stormfoil."

"Doesn't count? What do you mean, it doesn't count?"

"He isn't really crying, is he?" said Merryvenom, who after Hirik was the youngest murk in the company.

"What? Aren't those tears I see?" demanded Stormfoil. "Great glubby ones. Look!"

"You know it's a cheat, you blackguard," said his crony Reaveroot with a smile, punching Stormfoil on the shoulder.

"Aye," agreed Gladprowl, taking a guzz out of another bottle. "Let it drop."

"I won't!" Stormfoil said, indignant. "I win fair and square. Look at him cry for his mammy. Now pay up, you snivel-hearted gaggle of biddies!"

And Hirik understood. The murks had been wagering over how long it would take before he, the new lad, broke down and wept. Stung, he glanced from one windburned face to the next, and they looked back, nonplussed; to them he was clearly just another thing to wager on. He turned and walked away, leaving them to their argument. In seven days of weariness, hunger, and—he had to admit—homesickness, he hadn't once come close to crying. They could bicker amongst themselves whether these were real tears. He knew it would take a lot more than chili to make him weep.

But Stormfoil wasn't finished with him. With a grunt of laughter he cried, "Look at his wing! He got a bite taken out!" Several of the others began to laugh as if this were outrageously funny, and Stormfoil said between guffaws, "Reckon he tried to feed himself to the nymphs? That's no way to end it, Moonshrive. Cheer up! Sure the life's not so bad as all that."

Hirik entered the hobmarms' alcove, skirting round where they crouched by the fire baking the next day's ashcakes, and he found his satchel. Crouched over it, he dug for his extra set of clothes. He wiped his lips on his wet sleeve, but they just kept on burning.

"Moonshrive," said a voice behind him. He looked around and was surprised to see Merryvenom. "That was badly done," the other young faerie said.

Poor apology though it was, it was more than Hirik had expected. He replied, "It's nothing. But I'd hate to see Storm-foil win a wager by cheating."

"He didn't win. The cheat was too plain. He couldn't expect that to be the end of it."

"So the wager stands?"

"Aye, but don't take it to heart. Every greenwing gets it. It was me before it was you. You might want to just squeeze out some tears and let him win. That'd be the end of it."

Hirik narrowed his eyes. "What, is that what you did?" he asked.

"Unlikely," replied Merryvenom with a lazy smile.

"And I'm not likely to either."

Merryvenom shrugged. "Suit yourself. Just understand, there aren't many lads fit for the life, and there's even fewer who fall in it if they have any choice." With bitterness, he added, "I should know."

Hirik knew almost all murks came from fallen lands, their forests felled by human axes, their clan homes and livelihoods destroyed. He well knew that this was a life of last resort for a faerie.

Merryvenom went on. "There's lads who dream on the adventure of it, and they're the ones who get glubby a few days in when they learn just how *uncozy* adventure can be. Those with any home to go back to . . . they *go*. You get my meaning?"

It was more than any murk had said to him all week, and Hirik did get his meaning. They thought that he was an adventurer, that he wouldn't last. Well, they were right, but not for the reasons they thought. For one, *this* wasn't his adventure. This was only a means of making his way over the vast mountain wilderness to Nazneen. But once they reached the city he planned to get on to his real dream. Of course, he didn't say this to Merryvenom. He only nodded and told him, "Aye, I get your meaning, but I wouldn't advise you lay any tink on my tears. There won't be any."

Merryvenom said lightly, "We'll see," then gave Hirik a nod and walked back to the murks' alcove. Hirik watched as Stormfoil flung something that looked like a rat turd at him, and Merryvenom drew his sword quick and sliced it in half in mid-air. Hirik turned his back on them and took his dry clothes into a shadowy niche to change. While he was there, he shook his head hard to spin the water from his hair. He had a broad sash tied round his forehead, and though it was soaked through, he didn't remove it, but just pushed his black hair down over it. His bangs reached nearly to his eyes.

He was a handsome lad, brown-skinned and strong-boned. His eyes were set deep and sharply shadowed, and

71

the liquid brown of them could take on a golden gleam in light that gave him a watchful, wild look, like a bird of prey. His lower lip was split down the center by a thin white scar, and his knuckles bore their share of scars too, from training in swordplay with his uncles back home. They'd used bamboo staves until he was ready to wield the scimitar he now carried.

Hirik rested his hand on its hilt. It was a wondrous thing, this blade—one of his clan's two great treasures. He carried the other treasure with him too, sewn into a secret pocket inside his tunic. It was such a thing as would make the hobs' and murks' eyeballs bulge if they should see it, but he hoped they never would.

The scimitar made them curious enough about him already. Of course, if they'd known history a little better they'd have recognized the sword at once, and that would have been the end of Hirik's disguise. But he didn't really worry. They didn't know history, and they wouldn't guess who he really was or why he was headed to Nazneen. Hirik wasn't a mercenary any more than he was a Moonshrive.

He was going to be the Azazel's champion. But first he had to find him.

NINE

With her teakettle clutched to her chest, Whisper approached a hobgoblin chief. "P-p-pardon me . . . ?" she stammered in her feather-soft voice.

"Eh what, maidy?" the hob growled, swinging his great head around to look at her. Behind his tusks, the features of his face were blunt, his nose flat, eyes mere slits for squinting into the wind, and his beard was as wild and coarse as a briar thicket.

Whisper felt herself shrinking under the slab of his massive shadow. She said, "Please, I . . . I need to go to Nazneen—"

"Speak up!" he rumbled. He'd been standing upright but he slouched abruptly forward, settled his weight on his big fists, and knuckle-walked closer to her.

She backed away. "I need to go to Nazneen," she said again, whispering a little louder. "Are . . . are you going that way, goodhob?"

"Nazneen, eh?" said he, his eyes skimming over her

grimed feet and torn clothes, taking in the absence of coin about her neck. Whisper's cheeks grew hot, knowing how she must look to him. "Aye," he told her. "All caravans get to Nazneen sooner or later. But it en't cheap. Fifty and not a tink less."

Whisper said, "I . . . I don't have any tink, but I—"

He snorted. "No tink? Well, ye best have a diamond hid in yer ear, littlething, 'cause hobs en't known for charity! Eh, then?"

Whisper shook her head. "Nay, I've nothing to pay you with, but I *must* reach Nazneen. *Please.*"

The hob roared a laugh and his breath gusted in Whisper's face. It smelled like brandy. He reared up and stood over her like a great bear. *"Please?"* he repeated, still laughing. Turning his head, he called out, "Hoy, Fanggrin!" and caught the attention of another hob chief, who was squatting nearby with some faerie merchants.

"Hoy what, Grismal?" growled Fanggrin, looking over. One of his tusks was broken off, giving him a mad, snaggletoothed look, and on his big head was a helmet from which two tiger fangs jutted like horns. The devilish look of him gave Whisper a shiver.

They were in the market pavilion. After the caravans had landed, the hobgoblins had unloaded their dragonflies and shouldered the bales in here to do business with the merchants, and Whisper had followed. In all, three separate caravans had come to Shark Fin Peak this evening, with some hundred dragonflies apiece. That meant, Whisper thought, she had three chances to find one who would take her. She couldn't help hoping it would not be Fanggrin.

Grismal asked him, "Ye taking *please* for payment these days, ye great goatloaf?"

"Plague!" cursed Fanggrin. "Who in hollerbelly's asking?"

"Little priss here asks nice as sugar," said Grismal.

Fanggrin squinted at Whisper. "That tangle-haired feeblewing?" he asked. The scorn in his voice made her wilt. With a smirk, he said, "Tell her she can fly behind and try to keep up!"

Grismal laughed heartily at that and slapped his knee. "Fly behind! Ach, that's rich. Ye get that, littlething?" he asked Whisper, as if the joke might have eluded her, then he turned to share the humor with the third and last of the hob chiefs. "Zingaro! Ye hear that? Fanggrin told the maidy she can fly behind, but she can't, can she, being as she's a scamperer!"

Zingaro was squinting at an enormous emerald through a jeweler's glass and didn't even look up as he said, "Aye, he's a clown, is Fanggrin. Ought to run away with a circus."

Grismal stopped laughing and muttered, "Grouch. Maybe *ye* want to carry the waif, if ye're too good for a joke."

Zingaro lowered the jeweler's glass and looked over at Whisper. She straightened up hopefully. This hob, she saw, was neither snaggle-tusked nor muss-bearded. In fact, his beard had a neat braid right down its center. On tiptoe she went closer, her heart thumping hard as she whispered, "Please, goodhob, I need to get to Nazneen. I won't be any trouble—"

"Neh, and ye sure won't be. Not to me, anywhich," he replied, and then he turned away and tossed the emerald back at the faerie merchant beside him. "That's got a flaw as big as yer dastard nose, Charlock. Ye want me to spread the word ye're sly?"

"Ach, Zingaro," said the faerie. "A fellow's got to try, neh?"

"Try it on some dimwick, then, like Grismal. Ye ought to know by now I won't take yer junk jewels. Now, got anything fine to show?"

Whisper was still standing there. Was that all the hobgoblin was going to say to her? A frantic thrill went through her. This was her last chance. After him, there would be no more hob chiefs to beg for passage. She was just parting her lips to speak again when Zingaro turned to her. "Eh, maidy? Is there aught else?" he asked impatiently.

"Goodhob, *please*," she implored, and in her desperation her voice rose above its accustomed whisper. It was still scarcely more than a rasp, but it was enough to let magic slip into it, and she saw at once that the hobgoblin felt it.

His narrow eyes went even narrower. "What was that?" he demanded. "That . . . *wishy* feeling?"

Zingaro the hobgoblin

Wishy feeling? Whisper bit her lip and tried to look innocent. She wasn't sure what glyph she had let slip. A Silksinger's voice was a powerful thing, and hers far more powerful than even her elders' had been. But it was wilder too—that was why she rarely spoke above a whisper. She had no mastery of her voice except in singing, when she felt the pulse of some great power guiding her to translate *glyphs* into *sound,* as only Silksingers could do. Now her rasped "please" had hit the hob chief with a thrum of sudden feeling. Maybe she had accidentally sent the glyph for desperation at him, or hope.

Whatever it was, it didn't help her. Zingaro's heavy brow furrowed as he regarded her with suspicion. "Skiddy out of here, maidy. I need a charity lass like I need a typhoon tied to my tail! Git." He turned back to the merchant and reached for another emerald.

And that was that.

Whisper backed away. Everywhere she looked, she saw fine things spread out on cloth: gems and velvet, bricks of golden palm sugar, pyramids of precious spice. All this wealth, yet no one would help her.

Hollowed out of all hope, she fled the pavilion.

TEN

"Ow! *Oowww* . . . ," Slomby moaned, squeezing shut his big red eyes. The king firedrake had been in no humor for leeching today, and had spewed a torrent of flame at him while he groped for the bloodsuckers.

"He got ye good this time," observed Mogorm, carefully dabbing cool beetle butter onto Slomby's sore hand.

"Ooh!" Slomby winced. Mogorm's touch was gentle, but Slomby's raw knuckles were starting to blister. Only when Mogorm blew on them lightly did the pain ease some.

"He asked me again to . . . to kill them," Slomby confided in a squeaky whisper. "Then Master would die too. Vesrisath said he'd meet him in the Moonlit Gardens without his shackles on, and then Master would be sorry!"

Mogorm clucked his tongue and whispered back, "If only there was some way to kill Master without the drakes dying too."

Unlike Slomby, who was stringy and lean, Mogorm was a thickset snag with flesh on his bones. He had the haunches of a frog and a round tummy with a deep belly button dimple that curved like a smile.

The two slaves were sitting side by side on the floor of the dungeon kitchen, and that's where the cyclops she-snag Num found them when she came in. "What now, sobfish?" she asked Slomby. "Get yerself scorched again?"

Slomby and Mogorm both shrank under her withering one-eyed glare. Mogorm tried to hide the crock of beetle butter, but Num saw it. "Hoy!" she cried. "Give me that!" She snatched it away and snarled, "How many times do I have to tell ye not to steal from my kitchen!"

"But Slom's hurt—"

"If the quiverlip's stupid enough to get hisself burnt, he can just live with the sting and not use up my butter. Now get up, ye moony pair of snivelskins!" She swirled her dishrag into a tight whiptail and delivered two sharp snaps, catching them both on their bellies.

"Ow!" Slomby squealed, jumping to his feet.

She wound up for another snap and Mogorm cried, "Quit!"

Unexpectedly, Num did quit. She dropped her rag and staggered back, her face turning pale. For an instant Slomby and Mogorm thought she was retreating from them, but only for instant.

Behind them, a thick voice said, "Slaves."

They whirled around. A figure was coming down the long passage from the devils' cavern.

"Neh!" squeaked Slomby.

Huge, restless, and shambling, the thing emerged from the darkness. First, a leg edged forth into the light. It was bristle black, many-jointed, and hairy, and it was followed swiftly by another leg, and another, and another. . . . Eight legs moved with a nasty rhythm. At first, that was all the slaves could see of it—the legs of a giant tarantula, rising and falling—but their eyes, rolling in terror, traveled up to behold the rest of the beast.

Ethiag.

They huddled together, quaking. As many times as they saw him, he never got any easier to look at.

His powerful torso rose centaurlike off his spider thorax, so that he seemed to be two creatures torn in half and pieced together—part spider, part man. His chest was a thick slab of muscle scored with battle scars, and his arms were as hairy and bristled as his tarantula legs. As for his head, it was a ghastly rendition of a spider's, with mandibles opening to unfold deadly fangs. For eyes, he had no mere spider's eight but dozens—beady, black, and clustered together like insect eggs glistening on a leaf—and all of them were fixed on the slaves.

Flexing open his fanged maw, Ethiag asked, "How many slaves are left in the dungeon?"

Paralyzed with fear, none of them could find their voices to answer.

"How many?" Ethiag roared.

Knees knocking, Slomby blurted, "Three!"

Ethiag grunted. "So few? Then I suppose I'll only eat one of you."

"Eat?" gasped Slomby. Mogorm seized his hand and held it tight. It was his sore hand, and his friend's grip was bursting his burn blisters, but that pain seemed a very small thing at the moment.

"But which one?" said Ethiag, glancing between Slomby and Mogorm with his pitiless clusters of eyes. Shrinking away, Slomby felt a pressure against the small of his back, just under the curl of his snail shell, and he realized it was Num. The she-snag was crouched behind them, hiding.

He tried to push her out where Ethiag could see her, but she bit him hard on the thumb and he swallowed a yelp. He wanted to hide too. He wanted nothing so much as to draw himself up inside his tough shell, but to do that, he knew, would be as good as shoving Mogorm into Ethiag's fanged mouth—it just wouldn't be fair. Mogorm had no shell to hide in.

So Slomby did the hardest thing he had ever done. He forced himself to stand before the devil with his long white arms and legs and his stringy body all revealed. While Num nudged them from behind, trying to push them closer to the devil's mouth, Slomby gripped Mogorm's hand hard and waited to learn if his life was over.

It wasn't.

"Fat one," said Ethiag wetly, pointing to Mogorm. "Come here."

Mogorm made a frantic, hopping attempt at escape, but Ethiag seized him and dragged him away wailing.

"Neh!" cried Slomby, and he scampered after them. He kept ahold of Mogorm's hand for as long as he could, his rubbery arm stretched out taut, but he couldn't keep up. Mogorm's hand slipped from his grasp and his arm snapped back to him.

Ethiag swept back up the passage, bearing Mogorm away. Slomby followed, sobbing, to where the passage spilled out into the devils' cavern with the army all arrayed before him, and there he stopped, too terrified to go any further. There was nothing he could do to save Mogorm.

He sucked himself into his shell and sobbed and sobbed. First Ethiag had eaten his pappy, now his only friend. Slomby's heart felt as raw as his poor burnt knuckles.

In his nest, Ethiag finished his meal and tossed the slave's bones and shackles atop a growing pile. The dungeon's slaves—lowly snags all—were unsuitable for soldiers. But what made a poor soldier—a lack of spines, claws, horns— made for a tender meal. Not as sweet as some meats, but better than the diet of bats he'd been feeding his devils until they could have a proper feast.

Out in the main cavern, Ethiag's army was growing. Next to the force he had raised in the Dawn Days, these hundreds of devils would be reckoned as almost none at all, but these weren't the Dawn Days. There were no warrior clans in the world, and only one champion. He didn't need a vast force to take on the weak folk of this dying age.

His hundreds would do just fine.

Most of his soldiers were hunkered right out in the cavern, waiting, but not all. At large in the world were a half hundred more, hunting. And though Ethiag lurked here in his nest of gnawed bones, he knew the precise location of every single one of them. He didn't merely *know;* he felt, saw, smelled. Their senses belonged to him. He watched through their eyes as they circled like vultures in the skies. He tasted the flavor of their prey even as they tore it apart. Every furious, ravenous, black, and bitter thought of his hundreds of soldiers was enfolded in his own.

He had ensnared their minds. It was what he did.

The force of his will was like a fist clamped over their own; he had never encountered a devil who could resist his commands. The pathetic slaves in the dungeon, he didn't bother with but let them scuttle about their work with their meek heads down. Low snags such as they could scarcely be called devils at all. But the others needed constant controlling. He held their natural chaos at bay, and like vile puppets, they did as he willed. And now, he willed his hunters to find the faerie and her treasure.

Incredibly, the Silksinger had gotten away!

She would be somewhere in the foothills of the Eastern Sayash. She couldn't have gotten far, not after those old fool elders had unleashed their deadly magic, incinerating not only their attackers, but themselves and their flying carpets too. The lass was on foot, and even now Ethiag's second wave of hunters scoured the land for her.

His first wave was, of course, dead. Fifty-nine soldiers, dead in a flare of dragonfire! And a few minutes later, two more. Ethiag had felt himself scorched to ash and he had thrashed in his nest, screaming as if he were being burnt from the inside out. But it had passed. He had endured many soldiers' deaths in his day, but he himself always lived on to get revenge.

He would find the Silksinger and the ember she carried.

A new age was coming, the faeries were right about that, but Ethiag didn't think they'd like it once it was upon them. There would be no place in it for Djinn and champions, and faeries would only be fodder for his armies.

The age ahead belonged to devils.

"Find her," he said, and his will flowed into his many hunters, though they were all the way on the far side of the Sayash. They were watching the faerieholds and outposts. The Silksinger wouldn't be able to elude him for long.

ELEVEN

The dragonfly courtyard was nearly deserted. Night had fallen, and the only soul Whisper could see was an imp lighting the colored lanterns that dangled from the parapet. She could hear voices inside the hostelry, and she imagined all the travelers hunkering down around fire pits, snug for the night. She would not be snug. It was her third night away from home; the last two, climbing up into the foothills, she'd spent pressed into crevices in the rock, chilled to the bone and haunted by nightmares. She'd thought that once she reached this outpost the worst would be over, but it wasn't.

In fact, she felt even more desolate than she had before, because there was nothing left to hope for now. No one was going to help her.

Overhead, she spotted a nook recessed into the mossy wall. She had to climb up to it, and it was small, but by tucking herself up tight she managed to fit inside with only her dirty toes poking out into the night. This had been an incense niche back in the days when faeries had still worshipped the Djinn; she could smell the faint hint of sandalwood, and it reminded her of home, of the Silksinger caves and the narrow stair that wended down to the Azazel's deep dreaming place.

It was empty now, all of it. The dreaming place, the kitchen, her little curtained bed, her grandparents' rocking chairs. The thought of her grandparents brought a fierce pain to her heart. Never again would they call her Whisperchild. Indeed, she realized, there was not a soul in the living world who even knew her name. The thought was so desolate it brought tears to her eyes, but they didn't last long. She was too wrung out to make tears, and she just hunched there, thinking darkly how if she died, no one would even know. She'd turn into a skeleton in this tiny niche and no one would ever find her but the wasps who came and built nests in her bones.

It would be easier, she thought, with yearning—easier to die now and join her folk in the Moonlit Gardens. They were all together there, even her parents. She'd been very young when they died, and she had seen it happen, the huge head of the sea devil that reared out of the water and seized them between its teeth before sinking swiftly out of sight. It had been so quick there had been no screams, only a sudden silence. A terrible, sudden absence.

Whisper had believed she knew death. She had seen her parents eaten, and she had held the hands of her last great-aunts and uncle as they passed calmly to the Moonlit Gardens. Now she was beginning to see that death could come in a way that was neither violent nor peaceful, but only a long, hopeless skid into the dark.

Fiercely she thought that she'd rather be carried off by devils than die of hopelessness in a hall thronged with her own kind!

It was just then, as if her thought had summoned it, that Whisper saw a shape glide down out of the darkness and come to land on the rampart. It had wings, but it was no bird. Prowling, it moved on many restless legs, weaving around the pools of lantern light and keeping itself in shadow. But when it paused and lifted its head to sniff, Whisper saw it clearly—its hard, segmented body and its terrible mouth, black pincers as long as the blades of mercenaries' swords, scissoring open and shut.

A devil, as ugly as anything that had plagued her nightmares.

Paralyzed by fear, she stared across the courtyard at it. She desperately wanted to pull her toes tighter into the incense niche, but she dared not stir for fear of catching the monster's eye. And then it began to move again. It went up to the nearest lantern and, with a snip of its pincers, severed the wick so the flame was snuffed to smoke. It went on to the next and did the same. One by one the lanterns blinked out, and soon the moonless black of night prevailed.

Whisper huddled in the dark and listened to the skirr of the devil getting closer.

In the hostelry, Hirik fished a tin of clove oil out of his satchel, along with the soft cloth he used for polishing his scimitar.

The hobgoblins had settled themselves around the fire in one alcove and the murks in the next. He didn't feel welcome with either group, so he sat by himself in the corridor with his back against the wall. Stormfoil still wasn't through with him, though. Just as Hirik unsheathed his scimitar to clean it, the murk called out, "Hoy, scrunt! When that wee baby dragonfly attacked you, did you slay it with your fancy sword?"

Into their second bottle of throatfire, Stormfoil and Reaveroot were finding themselves terribly funny. Hirik knew he'd have no peace, so he got up and set off further down the hall to find a quiet spot where he could be free of their taunts.

"Neh, greenwing, where you off to?" Stormfoil slurred after him.

Hirik didn't look back. He passed more alcoves, across some of which the travelers had rigged curtains for privacy. He could hear snores and soft laughter, and even the muffled sound of weeping. He reached the end of the hall and was about to settle into a quiet corner when another sound came to his ears. It was flute music, rising in soft but intricate trills.

If he were back home with his clan, Hirik thought, it would be time for fireside music. He could picture his uncle carving out a tune on his whisker fiddle while sprouts grew drowsy in their mothers' arms and courting couples sneaked kisses at the outskirts of the firelight. The thought of his folk made him ache with homesickness. He pictured how his mother had looked, worried but trying not to show it, when he'd gone away. She'd always known he would leave, she'd said, since he was a tiny sprout. His dreams were too big for their small hamlet.

Feeling like a sneak, Hirik paused outside the last curtained alcove to listen in on the music. There was something hushed about it, something haunting, and when he heard murmurs and then a collective gasp from within, he couldn't stop himself from peeking through a gap in the curtain.

What he saw there was like something out of a story.

The alcove was dim, with no proper fire to light it but only glowing coals in the hearth. Some faeries sat on the ground watching a turbaned gent playing a triple flute. His eyes were closed and his fingers flew deftly over his instrument. Before him, smoke drifted off the coals. But it was no ordinary smoke.

It rose in a thickening wisp, sinuous as a cobra, and Hirik sensed at once that the smoke was *answering* the music. Here, hidden in an alcove at Shark Fin Peak, was a smoke charmer.

He knew of them only from tales, this rare breed of fortune-tellers from the deserts west of the Sayash. Quite forgetting his homesickness, he watched, mesmerized, as the smoke whirled in time to the fluting and began to gather itself into a form. It grew wings, stretched out arms, took on the diaphanous drift of a skirt . . . and then, there above the fire pit floated a faerie biddy—or rather, the phantasm of one. And though she was no more than fume, she was so perfectly rendered she looked like she might breathe.

"Arisaema!" choked a rough voice.

Hirik looked to the audience. Amid the half-dozen faeries was a codger, staring at the phantasm with wide, wet eyes. Hirik didn't have to be told that the phantasm was a vision of the old faerie's dead wife.

Her smoke hair drifted as if on a breeze, and her lips curved into a gentle smile. Then, amazingly, she *moved*. She extended one smoke arm, and the codger reached for her hand. But as soon as flesh met phantasm, the smoke broke apart. The biddy's arm dissolved up to the elbow, and the codger drew his hand hastily away. "Arisaema . . . ," he whispered. "Are you well there . . . in the Moonlit Gardens?"

The biddy's lips parted and she spoke a soundless message, and then, with a final smile, she melted dreamily away. The little cluster of faeries murmured amongst themselves for a moment, and then a lady turned to the smoke. "Please," she asked. "Tell us, how can we live now? Where should we go?"

Hirik thought they must be refugees—some of the many weary faeries fleeing ravaged forests. He'd seen their like in other outposts, and heard their tales of mannies and axes and sad slave elephants forced to uproot trees with their trunks. They told of elders too weak to flee as their ancient trees were hacked to pieces, whole forests laid waste, and dryads left to wither and die gasping. He imagined his own clan and his own forest meeting such a fate, and he shuddered.

The fluting was low as a moan now, and the smoke didn't move to answer the question, but from behind the smoke charmer something unfurled itself from the shadows. It was a chameleon; Hirik hadn't even noticed it there. It sidled forward, held out a tin cup, and shook it with a crude clatter of tink. Clearly, the smoke's wisdom was not to be had for free.

The faeries groped for their tink chains and unstrung some coins. No sooner had they dropped them into the cup than the charmer trilled a breathy riffle through his flute and the smoke leapt to answer, taking the shape of a city.

Hirik knew it at once, though he had never been there. There were the domes of Rasilith Ev, the Azazel's ancient temple. It was Nazneen, the golden city of Zandranath. How beautiful it was! As the faeries whispered together and pointed at the smoke, Hirik was struck suddenly by a notion.

If he were to ask where the Azazel was, could the

smoke show him? Could it lead him to the Djinn's dreaming place?

No sooner had the question formed in his mind—*where is the Azazel?*—than the smoke suddenly churned. The vision of Nazneen evaporated and something else began to take shape. Hirik's heart gave a thud. Had the smoke heard his thoughts? Was it going to show him where the Azazel was? He held his breath as it swirled and eddied and finally settled into a form.

Disappointed, he let his breath out as a sigh.

It was only a lass. Her long hair was all mussed and coiled about her arms and she wore a haunted look on her face. In spite of his own disappointment, Hirik felt a deep pang of sorrow for her, whoever she was.

"Who's that?" a sprout asked.

"I don't know," murmured a lady.

They didn't know? Hirik had assumed the lass was of their clan, like the biddy before. He was just thinking that he ought to back away and quit his spying when suddenly, the phantasm moved. She turned above the coals and looked straight at him, and the urgency of her gaze sent a jolt surging through him, all the way down to the soles of his feet. He nearly gasped.

She was only an illusion. But for all that she was colorless and sculpted of smoke, she was also somehow *real,* and the jolt was real. Her face was as delicate as a doll's, her eyelids as smooth as wind-sculpted dunes. She held something tight against her chest—a teakettle—and Hirik saw that her wings were small. Scamperer's wings. Her clothing was ragged, her arms and feet bare. She parted her lips to speak and Hirik held his breath, gripped with anxiety to know what she would say, as if her words were for *him*. But there were no words or, at least, no sound.

Of course there wasn't. She was only an illusion!

Nevertheless, he found himself straining to read her smoke lips for whatever message she might be trying to pass on.

And then several things happened at once.

The smoke charmer caught sight of Hirik spying at the curtain. He ceased piping and cried out, "Hoy there, sneak!" just as someone shoved Hirik from behind and sent him crashing into the alcove. The curtain pulled loose and tangled around him as he skidded forward. The refugees gasped and fluttered back, and Hirik heard familiar laughter.

"Getting a peep show, greenwing?" jeered Stormfoil.

Hirik shrugged off the drape, furious. Twice in one day, he'd let himself be surprised! He wanted to push aside his feeble disguise and get full command of his senses. Then let Stormfoil try to creep up on him! He spun toward the murk, but before he could retort, the smoke charmer's chameleon loomed in his way. It stuck its tin cup right in his face and gave it a rattle.

Behind it, its master demanded, "Think you're sneaking a vision for free? Pay up!"

"What?" asked Hirik. He glanced at the phantasm that drifted over the coals and saw her eyes were still staring right at him with desperate intensity. "Nay," he protested. "She's not *my* vision!"

"Then whose is she, I'd like to know?"

"Who? *Her?*" asked Stormfoil, peering at the smoke.

Reaveroot squinted at her too. "Pretty. Bit peaky though, neh?"

Stormfoil gave Hirik a little push. "You got yourself a little bridey someplace, Moonshrive? You scamp! I'd never have guessed!"

"I've never even seen her before—" Hirik tried to say, but he was caught between Stormfoil's guffaws and the rude clatter of the chameleon's cup.

"A sweet little smoke bridey," chortled Stormfoil, slapping him on the back.

"Maybe it was *her* bit his wing," suggested Reaveroot, and the drunk murks nearly collapsed with laughter.

Despite all the commotion, Hirik found his eyes drawn back to the lass, and again her gaze hit him with a jolt. She looked so real! Seeing him looking, the smoke charmer crashed his arm through the phantasm, cutting it in two. Hirik flinched as the lass dissolved right in front of him, those haunted eyes of hers seeming to hold his gaze even as she melted back to formless smoke. There was something terrible about it, and a cold fury danced through him. He almost felt as if he'd seen her murdered! But he hadn't. It was madness. Magic.

Again, the rattle of tink. "I'll be paid—"

"Nay, you won't!" he snapped. "I've nothing to pay you with, and it wasn't my vision anyway. I'm telling you, I've never seen that lass before!"

The smoke charmer took an uneasy step back and Hirik realized he'd half raised his scimitar, his knuckles white on its hilt. He felt wild, and guessed he must look it too. Taking a deep breath, he sheathed the sword. Turning to retreat, he glimpsed the refugees huddled together in the corner and felt a pang of guilt for his spying and his temper. Grabbing their curtain off the floor, he muttered, "Pardon, goodfolk," and strung it quickly back in place.

So much for peace and quiet, he thought as he stalked back down the hall with Stormfoil and Reaveroot at his heels.

"Come on, Moonshrive, tell us," wheedled Reaveroot. "Who was she?"

It was no use repeating that he'd never seen her before. Stormfoil made a wet smooching noise and crooned, "Smoke bridey, who *are* you?" and Hirik felt anger building in his fists. His eyes went narrow and he turned. He knew he shouldn't tangle with the murks, but there was some strange fury still pumping through his veins and he couldn't stop himself.

But before he could do anything, someone pushed him hard, right into the stone wall. It was Zingaro. The hobgoblin scowled and demanded, "Problem here?"

"Neh," said Stormfoil, all innocence. "Not here. Right, greenwing?"

Still glaring at him, Hirik said, "Nay, none."

"Glad to hear it," said Zingaro. "I won't tolerate fighting. Now, ye two eejits—" he said to Stormfoil and Reaveroot, "go sleep off that throatfire. If ye're still drunk come morning, I swear I'll leave ye here!"

Stormfoil smirked with disbelief and Zingaro cut him a sharp look and added, "Weatherwitch or neh, mind?"

"Aye," the two grudgingly conceded, and as they slunk away, Zingaro turned to Hirik. "As for ye, go and sleep with the skimmers. That ought to cool yer ginger."

Hirik did as he was told. The hob may have meant it as punishment, but he was happy to pass the night in the skimmer stalls, well away from Stormfoil. He pushed through the heavy door of the hostelry and emerged to find the courtyard in total darkness.

He heard a faint scuttle receding over the stone and thought it must be a beetle of some sort. It was of no importance, surely, but it gave him a pang of almost unbearable frustration. He ought instantly to have known what shared the darkness with him. His clan's unique senses were . . . extraordinary. But they were bound and muffled, leaving him half blind, with naught but his eyes to guide him just like any other faerie—and after all, what use were eyes in such darkness? Putting one hand to the stone wall, he made his way by touch around the perimeter of the courtyard and let himself into the skimmer stalls.

It was comfortable enough within, with fresh grass strewn over the stone, but he was a long time falling asleep. He kept thinking about the lass in the smoke, and the desperate look in her eyes. Who was she, and why had the smoke shown her? It had been a fluke, surely, and nothing to do with him. He wished he could have seen the Djinn's dreaming place instead, so he might know where to start searching once he reached Nazneen. Still, though he tried to dismiss the memory of her, the lass's face kept returning to him, and each time he recalled those eyes of hers, he remembered the jolt and felt it anew.

TWELVE

Whisper's eyes were wide and wild in the dark. Below her on the wall, the sinister skirr of the devil was getting louder. Nearer. Her toes still jutted over the little stone ledge, and she knew that at any second she would feel the jab of pincers against her bare skin. The monster would find her. Her breathing had gone shallow; a film of icy sweat clung to her skin.

And then the door to the hostelry swung open. Weak light spilled across the threshold, and the devil spun into a scuttling retreat.

As if some key turned in Whisper's mind and unlocked her, she sprang from her hiding place and swung down to the ground. She landed silently on her toes, kettle hugged to her chest, and in the instant before the door closed, she glimpsed the silhouette of a faerie. Backlit, he was just an outline with hawkmoth wings and a long, curved sword—and, she saw, a bite mark scalloped into one hindwing.

But she was concealed by the darkness, and he didn't see

her. The door shut, and all went dark again. Never had the chill at Whisper's neck been icier than at that instant when she found herself standing exposed in the courtyard at Shark Fin Peak, knowing a devil was near. She darted forward, her bare feet making no sound, and the expanse of stone seemed to stretch endlessly before her until at last she came to the door.

And then she was through it and closing it behind her. She had no delusion that she was safe now, but the lamplight was some comfort, and the low drone of voices in the hostelry made her feel less alone.

A hobgoblin lumbered into view, and she crouched down in the shadows until he was gone again. She watched and waited, her skin still clammy, heart still hammering. Perhaps a half hour later, the last murmurs in the hall died away. There was a long stretch of silence, and by the time snores rumbled up to fill it, Whisper knew what she was going to do.

She had to get away from here, and whether they wanted to or not, the hobgoblins were going to take her.

She moved down the hallway, pausing at each alcove to peer inside. Some were curtained, others weren't, and all were dim, lit only by dying fires. She could make out which sleeping forms belonged to hobgoblins, but that was all. Among their snoring shapes would be Grismal, and Fanggrin, and Zingaro, but which hob company was which, she couldn't tell. Choosing one alcove at random, she crept inside.

The bales of trade goods were piled against the inner walls, and Whisper saw she'd have to navigate a landscape of bodies to get to them. Her heart beat fast as a hummingbird's as she tiptoed among the sleeping hobgoblins, here and there having to leap over a meaty, outflung arm. The darkness seethed with the noise of grinding tusks and phlegmy snores, with mutterings and gobblings and whipcrack snorts.

Just as she slid through a narrow gap between two bodies, one hobgoblin roared a snore so great its draft blew her hair back and she nearly leapt out of her skin. Her little wings made a tremulous show of fluttering, and in her panic she stumbled over a tufted tail and froze as a hob turned himself over with a heave and a snort. But he only muttered, "Mouse tails," smacked his lips, and slept on.

Whisper took the remaining few steps at a frantic tiptoe dash, and then she was through the maze of sleeping bodies to the bales stacked neatly against the wall. Finding one that was packed with silk, she scaled the side of it and slipped silently down between parcels, leaving a slight gap in the canvas cover so she could breathe. She curled around her kettle and listened to the hobgoblins' wild snore symphony. At dawn they would begin the next leg of their journey, with her and the Azazel along for the ride.

Cramped as it was, the silk bale was still more comfortable than a rocky cleft or an incense niche, and Whisper dozed.

She woke at dawn to the first sounds of the hobs yawning and growling orders to each other, and heard them smack down their breakfast and roust the mercenaries. By and by, she felt her bale lifted and jostled as it was carried out to the courtyard and settled onto a dragonfly's back. She could even hear the whir of the insect's wings warming up and then the hob's steps shuffling away.

She held her breath, waiting.

There were shouts and grunted orders, all muffled by the silk that padded her on all sides, and then at last, she was moving. She felt a lurch, a lift. There was a heart-stopping moment when it seemed the dragonfly would not rise under the weight of its burden, then it surged, and she was flying away.

THIRTEEN

Magpie and company made landfall at dawn after two days' flying without rest. They still had far to go. Between the Ifrit continent and the Bay of Drowned Dragons lay an ocean and two seas. And though Magpie might deny *herself* much-needed rest, it was altogether different to deny it to her crows. They were frazzled, and when Swig fell asleep in flight and plunged halfway to the ocean before waking up, Magpie knew it was time to land. They diverted to the teardrop island of Serendip and towed the wagons down into the trees.

"Jacksmoke! I never been so weary in all my life," said Swig, collapsing in a heap.

"I'm sorry, feather," said Magpie. "I hate to push you so far."

"Aye, Mags," said Pigeon. "We en't albatrosses, ye know. We can't find the Azazel if we die of exhaustion."

"Nobody's dying," said Calypso, though rather unconvincingly, Magpie thought, as he punctuated his words with a wheeze.

The door to one of the wagons banged open and Batch Hangnail appeared. "Why'd we stop?" he demanded. "We en't near there yet."

"We're taking a rest if you don't mind," said Magpie.

"Rest? Flotch! I en't even tired."

"*Ye're* not tired, irkmeat?" snapped Maniac. "Sure and ye been napping for two days straight!"

"Not only," said Batch, offended. "I also been polishing my diamonds." He gestured to his tail, and sure enough, his diamond rings dazzled like sunbursts.

They set up camp amid satinwood and ebony trees, and Magpie went into her caravan to make sure the Ithuriel's cook pot had not shifted during the journey. She lifted up the lid to peer at the ember and watched the glyphs flickering in its fiery heart. She wished there was a way she could spirit the Djinn straight to Dreamdark, but since she couldn't carry him with her through the land of the dead, the only choice was to bring him along on their journey. Satisfied that all was well with him, she set the lid back on and went outside.

The crows had tossed out cushions around the fire, and she dropped onto one and felt a wave of weariness roll over her. Feebly she said, "Somebody feed me quick before I expire." She opened her mouth like a baby bird and Talon dropped a leaf into it, which made her sit up quick and spit.

"I'll make a stew, Mags," said Mingus.

Dragging herself to her feet, she said, "I'll help."

"Neh, sit, sit," he insisted, and so she did, and slumped over and stayed put until the stew was ready. It was a savory concoction of chickpeas and tomatoes, and she ate ravenously, then announced, "That was good, Ming. I'd lick out my cup if my tongue was long enough."

"What, like that?" asked Calypso, eyeing Batch. The imp had gotten stew all over—and *in*—his huge nose and was giving his nostrils an exploratory licking with his long, pink tongue.

Magpie grimaced.

It was Pigeon's turn to wash the dishes, and while he did, Calypso made tea and Bertram got out his sewing box. Magpie watched as he opened the lid with caution, as if afraid something might spring out at him.

"Any pixies, Bert?" she asked him innocently.

"Neh," he said. "I never can catch 'em. But look!" He held up a threaded needle. "They been at it again!"

"The sneaks!" said Magpie.

From across the fire, Calypso gave her a disapproving look—as disapproving as he could manage with his permanent cracked grin, anyway. She winked back at him. She supposed that someday she'd have to tell Bertram it wasn't pixies that kept his needles threaded, but for now she still had too much fun with the prank.

It had begun eight years ago, not long after he'd lost his

foot to a croucher devil's second mouth and she'd carved him the ebony peg to replace it. He'd taken it upon himself to learn to sew, and was getting on rather well except when it came to threading needles. He was nearsighted after all, on top of having only one good foot to hold the needle while he fed the thread through with his beak. How he'd cursed!

The first time Magpie threaded his needle for him, she'd simply forgotten to mention it, but he was so surprised to open his sewing box and find it done that she'd invented the pixie story then and there. Pixies were no taller than acorns, and were so swift most eyes couldn't catch their movements. They were notoriously elusive, which was how the prank had gone on this long.

Besides slyly keeping Bertram's needles threaded, every once in a while Magpie slipped some subtle "evidence" into the sewing box, such as a hibiscus petal with tiny bite marks taken out. And now that Talon had taught her how to cast a phantasm, she occasionally made a tiny figure appear out of the air, seeming to dart from the box as soon as Bertram lifted up the lid.

"Give me yer slippers to mend, Mags," said the crow, and she handed them over. All Magpie's clothes, heavily patched and darned, were a testament to Bertram's skills. She thought with a wry smile that her wardrobe was in the same sorry shape as the Tapestry of Creation—but it was Bertram, not the Djinn, who kept it from falling apart.

"Skiffle," he remarked, examining one of her slippers. "For a flying creature, how do ye wreck yer shoes so? It's not like ye ever *walk* anyplace!"

"Well, skive, I don't know," she replied. "Anywhich, I need new ones. Those are getting too small."

"So stop growing," said Calypso, who hated the thought of his lass growing up.

Magpie snorted, lay back in the cushions, and propped her bare feet up by the fire.

At her side, Talon unspelled his magical wings. They turned back into the shimmering expanse of knitted spider-silk they really were, and he slipped it off from around his shoulders and pulled it into his lap. Magpie watched him flex and flutter his own true moth wings—scamperer's wings—then take up his djinncraft knitting needles to reinforce some stitches in the silk.

As he set to work, he asked, "So, are you ever going to tell me about the Silksingers?"

"What, you never heard of 'em?" Magpie asked.

"Sure, but just the name and the flying carpets. I used to wish I had one."

"I still wish it," said Batch. "Then I wouldn't need to be sitting here with ye lot."

Ignoring him, Magpie propped herself up on her elbows and asked Talon, "You heard of the Battle of Black Rock, neh?" When Talon shook his head, she said, "Whatever happened to storytelling in Dreamdark? That's one legend I never thought folks could forget. It's how Fade died."

"Fade!" said Talon.

"Aye, the great dragon himself. He was murdered in the sky over Nazneen. You can still see where his breath melted the cliff face to black glass. That's where the name comes from, Black Rock. It's like a scar on the city."

"What happened?"

"It was when Fade was the only dragon left alive; all the others had been murdered by mannies. The Magruwen had kept Fade safe by hiding him in Dreamdark, but when he saw the dragon's spirit was dying from captivity, he knew he had to let him go. Fade flew out into the world, and he never came back."

"Why'd he go all the way to Nazneen, though?" Calypso asked.

"That's a good question, feather," said Magpie, pausing a moment to consider it. Why *had* Fade flown all the way to the Sayash Mountains? "Must have been some reason," she mused. She would ask him next she saw him in the Moonlit Gardens, though she didn't relish the idea of reminding the great dragon of the day he died. "Anywhich, he was ambushed by witches in the sky above Nazneen and he fought fierce, but there were so many. They were human, but they were flying and they were winning. The faeries should have helped him, but more than twenty thousand years had passed since the Devil Wars, and faeries weren't much in the way of warriors anymore. They just watched out their windows and cowered while he died."

"What?" said Talon. "None of them fought for him? But . . . wasn't there a guardian clan, like the Rathersting?"

"There was indeed. Mothmage, they were called, but only one clan flew to fight for Fade that day, and it wasn't the Mothmage. It was the Silksingers—"

"Silksingers? But weren't they all scamperers?"

"Aye, and they flew into the battle on their flying carpets, brave as warriors but *not* warriors, and Fade was near dead already, crazed and blinded. The legend says it was Fade's own dying breath that incinerated them, right along with the humans. Then he fell out of the sky and crushed half the city under him. Any Silksingers who weren't killed in the battle were crushed in their palace, and they weren't the only ones. Hundreds of faeries died that day."

"Jacksmoke," said Bertram with a shiver. "That's drear."

Talon said, "But now we know the Silksingers *didn't* all die."

"Aye," agreed Magpie. "Now we know there were survivors. They swore an oath to the Azazel and went away with him to guard his dreaming place. It should have been the Mothmage who went, but—"

"But they died too?" guessed Bertram.

"Neh, but the opposite," said Magpie. "They *lived*. They didn't lift a single sword to fight. After the dust and ashes settled, and charred scraps of flying carpet drifted down out of the sky, and the rivers of dragon blood stopped flowing in the streets, the folk who survived went to Mothmage Castle. The Mothmage were all there, safe and snug, and in the keep was the pile of rubies the witches had paid them not to fight."

"Jacksmoke!" cried Talon. "How could they do it?"

She shook her head. "Flummox me. Better a thousand times to die in battle than turn traitor, but that's what they did. And they'd been a great clan back in the Dawn Days too. Faeries could never have won the Devil Wars without them, but after the Battle of Black Rock, it was like everything great the Mothmage had done before was forgotten. The mob even wrecked the statue of Manathakkali, who'd been the Azazel's champion."

"The Azazel's champion was a Mothmage?"

She nodded. "You heard of the insect armies of Zandranath?"

Talon shook his head. Magpie snorted and said, "When this is all through and we've found the Djinn, you got to go live in a library and read the old legends! See, the clan magic of the Mothmage was communion with insects, and they used it to marshal armies of 'em during the Devil Wars.

Wasp regiments and mantis battalions and moths and drag-onflies and even ant brigades! It's all that kept Zandranath from being eaten up by devils when Ethiag's army was on the warpath. And it was Manathakkali who captured Ethiag! He was a true hero. Sure he'd have died of shame if he knew what his clan would come to later."

"Well, what happened to them, after Fade died?" Talon asked.

"They were exiled."

There was a little more to it than that. Magpie had read about the revenge that had been taken on the Mothmage, but she didn't like to think about it. The idea of bloodthirsty faeries taking vengeance on their own, it shivered her, no matter how great the crime that preceded it. It just seemed devilish behavior unworthy of faeries. But in all her travels, she had never known a clan name to inspire such violent hatred in faeries as Mothmage still did throughout Zandranath. No matter how great they'd once been, after the Battle of Black Rock they were doomed to be history's villains.

A thought came to her, and she sat up on the cushions.

"What is it, 'Pie?" asked Calypso.

"I was just thinking about the timing," she said. "It was right after Fade died that the Djinn vanished, neh?"

"Aye."

"Well, remember how the Magruwen talked about a

faerie betrayal? Do you think that could be it? Do you think it could be why the Djinn forsook the world?"

"You mean because the Mothmage let Fade die?" said Calypso, puzzling.

"Maybe."

"Forsake the whole world for what one clan did?" asked Talon, unconvinced. "That's hardly fair. Do you think that's really why?"

"Flummox me," said Magpie, flopping back again. She wasn't convinced either. She wished the Magruwen didn't have to be so mysterious—she knew only that it was a faerie betrayal that had driven him from the world. Whether the Mothmage treachery might be the reason, she couldn't guess.

"Do you think the Mothmage are still out there somewhere?" asked Talon.

"I guess they've died out by now, like so many clans."

"But the Silksingers were still alive all this while."

"For true," admitted Magpie. "And now there's just one."

Bertram asked, "We'll find the poor lass before the devils do, won't we, Mags?"

"Do you doubt it, blackbird?" she asked him, arching one eyebrow. "Of course we will!" She said it boldly, but in her heart she was less than certain. From what the dead Silksingers had told her, it would seem that Whisper was a skittish, helpless little creature, and if that mob of dead devils was anything to go by, Ethiag had mustered quite an army already. Magpie wondered how long she could last on her own—and how long the Azazel would last in the hands of such a monster. Under her breath she muttered, "Hold on, Whisper. We're coming."

FOURTEEN

Hirik was exhausted. Rain had kept pace with the caravan all day, and after a long, wet slog through heavy skies, they were finally making their descent toward the outpost of Poet's Curse. Far below, he could just make out its dome and stone battlements, but it was the vista beyond that held his gaze.

The Sayash Mountains.

Staring at the measureless sweep of them, Hirik felt as if the world trembled and grew bigger around him. *These* were mountains. For a moment, his awe overshadowed even the strange feeling that had been nagging at him all day, but it soon returned—it was a feeling of being watched, maybe even followed. But all day he had scanned the sky in every direction, and he had seen nothing. He concluded there *was* nothing, though he'd have felt more confident if he could have thrown off his disguise and reached out with more than mere sight.

He followed the caravan down to the courtyard. A dragonfly fumbled its landing, and the one coming in behind smashed into it and skittered sideways into a third. Hirik rushed forward as the tired skimmers went at one another with their jaws snapping, and for the next half hour he was kept busy helping Zingaro and his son Othi unburden the insects and lead them to the stables. Then, while the hobs carted off the bales to the market pavilion, he saw to the feeding and watering.

Grismal's caravan arrived just as he finished, and Hirik heard one of the hobs gripe, "Goatspit! That bandiwig of a Zingaro beat us again. Sure he'll have unstrung all the merchants' tink chains by now!"

"Leastways Fanggrin en't got here yet," Grismal observed, scratching at his wild beard. "Come on, let's go scrape up Zingaro's leftover business before he shows."

Hirik was tempted to follow the hobs into the pavilion. He could smell the cakes and simmering stews that were for sale there, but they weren't for him. Famished though he was, he had not a single roundel of tink, so he'd just have to make do with an ashcake from Anelka. He hastened into the hostelry to get it.

The sun set and the sky flushed orange, and still Fanggrin's caravan did not arrive. Nor would it. On the rocks of a tumbled slope between Shark Fin Peak and Poet's Curse lay the only clue to what had become of it. Bits of torn dragonfly wings were strewn like shattered glass, sparkling in the shine of the setting sun. Here and there lay a dropped sword or stray button. Fanggrin's tiger-fang helmet had snagged on the crest of a skinny pine, as if the tree were wearing it, and a few miles away, a raven caught a tuft of coarse beard adrift on a breeze and carried it off to its nest.

Besides a certain curdled stench, nothing else remained. Ethiag's hunters had not found what they sought, and had moved on.

"Fanggrin still en't come," Grismal told Zingaro after the trading had concluded.

"Neh?" grunted Zingaro, furrowing his brow. "What's keeping that drag-fanny? It's gone full dark!"

By the time they'd bundled up their bales, a small crowd of hobs had clustered around them—their own companies plus two others who were traveling in the opposite direction—and they were all more disturbed by Fanggrin's tardiness than they liked to admit.

"Gives me a fair shiver," said one in a gloomy voice. "Makes me think of the legends, how bands o' devils roved the mountains and no one was safe—"

"Ach," snapped Zingaro. "Shut yer gawp! Are ye mad, speaking on that? Ye trying to curse us all?"

Shamed, the hobgoblin subsided into silence, but Grismal

took up his point. "He's right though, en't he? What if something happened to 'em?"

"Plague," grumbled Zingaro. "It's a nail in yer coffin even to think such black thoughts, much less to speak 'em! Now listen up. Fanggrin's going to get here anytime, sure as a hob farts in the dark, so wipe that doom off yer mugs. Ye're ugly enough as it is! I'm going to go eat my supper, if ye don't mind. And no more talk like that! Othi?" He turned to his son, and the two of them gathered up their bales and carried them to the hostelry.

Curled up inside one of the bundles, cramped in the tight space and jarred around by the hob's lurching steps, Whisper shivered. The little gap she had made in the canvas had leaked rain all day and soaked her, but the shiver was one of dread, not cold. She knew the hobgoblins had every reason to be afraid. In her heart she had little doubt what had befallen Fanggrin's caravan and still less doubt that it was her fault.

What now? she asked herself, sick with remorse. It was she who had brought the danger of devils, but what choice did she have? If it were only her own small life at stake, she would sooner speak the words that would carry her to the Moonlit Gardens than endanger all these folk, no matter how unkind they had been to her. But this wasn't about her life. It was about keeping the Azazel safe, and nothing—*nothing*—was more important than that.

Whatever the danger, and however much it grieved her, her duty was to the Djinn.

Inside the hostelry, whichever hob was carrying her bale dropped it, and Whisper felt the impact all the way up her spine to her teeth. She stayed still as a seed, though she was stiff and chilled. She was lucky to have made it this far undetected. None of the merchants in Poet's Curse had been interested in seeing Zingaro's silks, so he had never opened up this bale.

What would he have done, laying it open to find her tucked inside? She could only imagine. But that danger had passed, for today at least. She listened through the canvas cover as the hobgoblins ate their supper. And though the sound of their smacking was not exactly lyrical, and the odor of their food not terribly enticing, it still made her so hungry she wanted to jump from her hiding place and snatch a bite right out of a big, clawed hand.

She thought that when they fell asleep she might be able to creep out, stretch, and find some food, but it seemed a long time passed, and the hobgoblin family didn't sleep. They drank brandy out of snail shells, and polished their tusks with rock salt, and about every half hour Zingaro sent Othi to see if Fanggrin's caravan had come. They murmured in anxious voices, but if anyone tried to mention the word *devil*,

Zingaro snapped and shut them up. "Must be he just went a different route and didn't say so" was his final word on the matter.

At last, their voices began to taper away into silence, and Whisper knew snores were soon to follow. Another moment and she would have been safe. She would have been out of the damp silk bale and free to roam about. But just then her stomach growled, as loud as any hobgoblin's snore, and the sounds of their breathing halted. She could feel the intent silence of their listening, and she curled up tight, her hands pressed hard against her belly to stifle any more noise it might make, but it was no use. Mutinously it rumbled, and to her ears the sound was like a roar.

"Goatspit!" Zingaro cursed.

The silk bale shook as the cover was torn off, and Whisper was caught in a wash of dim firelight. The hob chief peered down at her over the edge of the bundle.

"Hoy!" he declared. "Got us a stowaway!" He reached in a huge hand and scooped her out like a nut from a shell. Her legs kicked as he half dropped, half tossed her to the ground. She landed on her toes and skittered away from him, her kettle hugged to her chest. She tripped over another hob's tail and fell. With a lunge, Zingaro was over her, glowering. "Well, look who it is, little scampering sneak," he growled.

Whisper tried to crab-walk back, but she was trapped. There was a wall behind her, and a crowd was gathering in the opening of the alcove. She heard murmurs of "stow-away" and "waif" and saw hobs and mercenaries craning their necks to get a look at her.

"Well, what have ye to say for yerself, snippet?" Zingaro demanded.

Keeping her voice soft, she managed to gasp out, "Please, *please*, I *must* go to Nazneen—"

"I told ye neh once already! Didn't ye believe me then?"

"Aye, but—"

"But what?" he roared.

Whisper flattened herself against the wall. What could she say? That *devils* were chasing her? That even now they might be out there in the night, circling in the sky with Fang-grin's blood in their teeth, and that it was her fault? Absurd. She could think of nothing else but to whisper, desperately, *"Please."*

The hobgoblin looked taken aback. "Ach, enough of that, maidy!" he muttered. He lifted his big hand so she thought he was going to hit her and she flinched, but he didn't strike. He only grabbed her elbow, hauled her to her feet, and thrust her toward the corridor. "Git!" he grunted. He didn't push her hard, but Whisper was very light and her legs were cramped from being curled up all day, and the shove sent her sprawling. Her kettle flew out of her hands and rolled with a clatter toward the crowd of gawkers, and even as she gasped and scrambled after it, somebody was picking it up.

It was a lad. She saw his wings first and knew them at once from the silhouette in the doorway the night before—they were hawkmoth wings, with a bite taken out. And she saw his eyes next, two gleams of amber, wide with shock. He was staring at her as if she were a phantasm.

And he was holding her kettle.

FIFTEEN

Hirik stared at the lass. She was barefoot and dirty, and her long black hair was tangled around her arms like seaweed around a fin maiden. Her eyes were panic-stricken, and her eyelids were as smooth as wind-sculpted dunes. There could be no mistaking it. She was the stranger from the smoke.

"You," he breathed.

For an instant, confusion seemed to interrupt her panic. Then she darted toward him, snatched the teakettle out of his hands, and ran. Startled, he watched her flee and saw her scamper half up a wall to get around the gawkers, then disappear beyond them. He couldn't see which way she went.

"Ye acquainted with that lass, Moonshrive?" Zingaro demanded.

"What? Nay."

"Skive, greenwing!" cried Stormfoil, coming into the alcove. "Sure you are. Isn't she your smoke bride?"

"She's not—"

"Ach, don't try to deny it. I saw her myself, and so did Reaveroot, neh, Reave?"

"Aye," drawled Reaveroot. "It was her even down to that tangle of hair. I've seen monkeys better groomed than that!"

Zingaro thundered, "What is this, ye conniving scrunt? Did ye have something to do with that scrap stowing away?"

"Nay, none! I have no idea who she is! But I don't think you needed to throw her to the ground like that."

Zingaro had the grace to look ashamed of himself. He rubbed the tip of one tusk between his fingers and grumbled, "I didn't push hard. The littlething weighs no more than a bird bone!"

"Well, if she weighs so little, what would it hurt to give her passage?"

"What's it to ye, greenwing?" Zingaro asked, his voice going low and dangerous.

Hirik didn't know what it was to him. The lass seemed so helpless, but even in his confusion, he knew there was more at work in him than general compassion. There was something uncanny about her; he'd felt something akin to recognition, though he knew it was impossible that he'd seen her before the smoke. His clan was isolated, and he'd scarcely ever met a stranger until last week when he joined the caravan. He said, "Nothing. She just . . . she really seems like she needs help."

123

"How's it my problem? The scrap's got no tink, and I'm not in the business of free rides. Word gets around, every refugee from Thogong to Zandranath's going to come begging!"

Hirik knew it wouldn't do to argue with the hob chief. He'd just get himself left behind and have to find another caravan, and he had no time to waste. Ever since the news had spread about the Magruwen's reawakening, finding the Azazel was practically all he'd thought about, and surely he wasn't the only one with that dream. Even now, faeries might be exploring the caves around Nazneen, getting closer and closer to finding the sleeping Djinn.

He knew he should forget about the lass and just let the subject drop; helping her could only get in the way of his own plans. Bowing his head, he turned to walk away.

He made it three steps down the corridor before he found himself stopping and turning back. Plainly he heard his own voice ask, "What if *I* paid her passage?"

Zingaro hooted a laugh. "With what? Yer wage? Who says ye're getting one? I might throw ye off tomorrow!"

Othi chortled along with his father. "And even if ye *do* get paid," he said, "yer greenwing wage wouldn't half cover it!"

Hirik walked back over to them. Quietly, he said, "I think this will cover it." He reached inside his tunic and drew out something folded in a handkerchief. Laying back the cloth corners one by one, he revealed his clan's treasure.

Zingaro made a choking sound, and a stunned hush fell over the alcove. After a long pause, the hob chief asked in a hoarse whisper, "Moonshrive, where in plague did ye get that?"

"It's been in my clan a long while."

Zingaro didn't speak for a moment, but only stared. Then, almost shyly, he asked, "Can I hold it?"

Hirik answered, "Passage for the lass, and her food too. And . . . a hundred tink."

Zingaro agreed so quickly that Hirik suspected he could have asked for much more. "Aye, lad. I accept. On my fat granny's grave, I accept! Now . . ." When the hob held out his hand, his fingers trembled a little.

Hirik tipped the handkerchief and let the dragon scale slide onto Zingaro's palm. It was copper, dull until the firelight danced on it, then it shimmered green and bronze and violet, with red sparks and colors that no one had ever been able to set names to because they lived only in the flickers inside of light. The scale was the size of a faerie's hand—it was small, and it was whole.

"I never seen a whole scale in my life," breathed Othi over his father's shoulder. "Only slivers."

"Ooh," said Anelka, Zingaro's wife. "It's so small and delicate. Is it a face scale?"

"It's from his eyelid," Hirik replied.

"*His?* The . . . the color, lad," said Zingaro. "It was—"

"Aye. It was Fade's."

Again, silence fell hard.

A scale from the lid of the great dragon's eye. Such a treasure had not been seen in a very, very long time. In all the world of magic, there was no substance more potent than dragon scales, and over the years those that remained from the old days had gone into elixirs and spells for strength and protection. But it was another property that made them precious to hobgoblins: the merest sliver worn as a charm would keep one warm in freezing weather, and those who possessed one stood a far better chance of surviving the rogue blizzards of the Sayash than those who did not. The slivers had decided life or death for many a hob and were handed down across the generations. But dragons were long gone from the world, and no scales had been found in centuries.

When Zingaro was finally able to look up from its dancing colors, he said, "Might I have that hanky, lad, to keep it tucked?"

Hirik handed the cloth to him, and the hob bundled the scale with such care that Hirik could, for the first time, imagine his thick fingers braiding up the hairs of his beard. Watching the hob tuck it into his pocket, he steeled himself to its loss and said, "A hundred tink."

"Oh, aye," said Zingaro, fumbling a whole tink chain from the mass around his neck and handing it over. Hirik's clan had never used coin and he was surprised by the weight of the strand. It seemed like a fortune to him, though he knew the real fortune was in the hobgoblin's pocket now.

"Better go find yer little lass, then," said Anelka. "And here. Give her this." She fished an ashcake out of the big banana leaf in which it had been baked.

"Aye," added Zingaro. "Her tum roared louder than muther's snores! Must be famished, poor thing."

Poor thing? thought Hirik. This was some improvement in the hobs' dispositions! "Thanks," he said, then he set off to find his "smoke bride."

SIXTEEN

Whisper had found an incense niche and hidden inside it. It wasn't out in the courtyard—she had a horror now of the black night and the things that crept about in it—but in the corridor of the hostelry. The barrel-vaulted ceiling rose above the reach of the lantern light and she knew no one would see her up here, even though her toes did, once again, stick out over the edge.

She hugged her arms around herself, the kettle tucked beneath her bent knees. Her heartbeat had calmed since the turmoil. She felt only a queer emptiness now, as if she had already died and gone to the Moonlit Gardens, leaving only this faded imprint of her to go through the motions of failing in her clan's sacred duty. For, if she hadn't quite failed yet, certainly she soon would. No one would help her, and Nazneen was so far, the land ahead a wilderness of crevasses and black melt rivers, wolves, mannies, avalanches, blizzards, and, of course, devils.

There were so many ways to die. How few to live!

The hostelry had quieted. It was very late, and the corridor below was empty of all but one soul. Whisper saw it was the mercenary lad who had picked up her kettle. He passed beneath her once, twice, as if he were searching for something. A suspicion came to her that he was searching for *her*. But what could a mercenary want with her?

Anxiously she watched him take a third pass. He was flying slowly and peering into each alcove at the sleeping hobs and faeries. Even in its scabbard his scimitar looked wicked, and when he turned his head, his eyes shone with glints of gold that made her think of a hunting hawk.

She watched him to the far end of the corridor and saw him fold his wings and drop to his feet. He glanced around, a little furtive now, and then he did something that deepened Whisper's shiver—he extinguished a lantern, same as the devil had done, and he was immediately enfolded in darkness.

She could only distinguish the vague shape of him and couldn't tell what he did in the shadows. She only knew that when he stepped out of them a moment later he was retying the blue sash around his brow and smoothing his thick black hair down over it. And he was looking up.

He was looking right at her.

Hirik took a terrible risk removing his disguise. If he should be seen! But he couldn't find the lass, and finally frustration won out. It was such a simple thing for him, to sense somebody out—all his clan could do it. So he loosened his sash, just for a moment, and inside a heartbeat he knew where she was hiding. He looked up and got a shock.

She was tucked up in a high incense niche—who'd have thought a faerie could fit in there?—and she was staring at him! Had she *seen* him? A tremor shook him. But it was dark. Surely she hadn't seen into the shadows.

He was afraid to approach her. He'd already *been* afraid. After all, he'd scarcely ever spoken to a lass in his life who wasn't a cousin—how did one even begin? But now, struck by the terrible possibility that she'd seen what he was, he positively trembled. Some champion he'd make, he scoffed at himself, getting into a fit because of a lass!

Champion, he told himself. *Champion.* A Djinn's champion doesn't tremble, even in the face of devils, let alone lasses. He rose unsteadily to his wings and flew up to her. "Blessings," he called out softly.

She didn't answer, and seemed to shrink deeper into her tiny niche. "It's okay," he called out. "The hob chief, he changed his mind. He'll give you passage."

She shifted slightly and peered out at him. Her eyes were very black.

"It's all settled," he said. "We'll be in Nazneen in five days."

That got a reaction. Her gaze sharpened and she drew herself half out of the tiny space and stared at him intently.

130

Hirik was aware she was trying to read him, her eyes going over his face, pausing at the scar on his lip, his overlong hair, the chomp in his wing. He blushed, wondering how he must look to her, and then was angry at himself for blushing.

Whatever she saw, it must have been all right, because she came the rest of the way out of the niche and clung there for a moment before scaling gracefully down the wall with just one hand. Her teakettle was in the other. Sculling his wings, Hirik dropped down to the ground and they faced each other awkwardly.

"Uh, blessings," he said, remembering only after that he'd already said it.

"Blessings," the lass whispered, her voice scarcely louder than the sound of her breath shaped into words. He saw that there were deep shadows around her eyes, that her face was terribly pale, her lips tinged faintly blue. He wondered what had happened to her. "I'm Hirik," he said, leaving off the Moonshrive. For some reason he thought it would feel more grievous a lie than ever if he said it to her. "And you?"

"I'm Whisper," she said, still in that voice, barely audible. Hirik thought her name a fitting one. "The hobgoblin," she said tentatively. "Did he really—?"

"Oh, aye." Hirik nodded. "It's all arranged. And they gave you this." He offered the ashcake.

She didn't take it right away, and he realized how terribly

131

unappetizing it looked, a flabby circle of dough dented with his own fingerprints. Embarrassed, he drew it back and said, "But sure it's no fit fare for a lass. Maybe there's a vendor in the pavilion, still open, but I don't think so. . . ."

"Nay," she said hastily. "I don't mind. I just . . ." Her face had flushed and she was staring at the cake. Hirik handed it to her and saw her hands shake as she took it. Were those tears in her eyes?

"What happened to you, Whisper?" he asked all of a sudden. He didn't mean to; it just blurted out.

He wished it hadn't. Her tears began to spill and trail down her cheeks, thick and fast. Hirik didn't know what to do. The idea of reaching out to pat her shoulder seemed ridiculous. His hands felt useless hanging at his sides so he crossed his arms over his chest. "Don't worry," he said. "We'll get you to Nazneen. There's nothing to worry about."

As he said it, he knew he couldn't promise it. Looking at Whisper, he suddenly realized he had not only his own safety to worry about now, but hers as well.

The realization made his wings flutter, and the mountains outside seemed suddenly even wilder and more desolate. Whisper looked so fragile; he would have to protect her, maybe even from devils. He'd heard the hobs' grumbling fears, and he couldn't help recalling the sensation of being followed that had nagged at him all day. Well, he told himself resolutely, if he wanted to be champion, he would come to know plenty of devils—they would be his life, in large part, as he worked to rid the world of them like the Magruwen's champion did.

But it wasn't all about hunting and capture, being champion. A new age was dawning, and the return of the Djinn meant the awakening of wonder, as it had been awakened halfway round the world in Dreamdark. The new age would be about magic and purpose and beauty. About *building*. Not just clinging on to the tattered hem of the ancient world, but making a new world. And how he wanted that!

He uncrossed his arms and said, his voice stronger now, "I'll see you safely to Nazneen, Whisper." And then a rash urge overcame him and he added, "I swear it on the Azazel's flame."

When he said that, her eyes seemed to brighten. "Do you . . . ," she whispered tentatively. "Do you worship him still?"

"Aye. My clan never stopped. Not all these years."

"What is your clan?"

Uncomfortably, he answered, "Moonshrive."

"I haven't heard of it."

That was unsurprising, since he'd made it up as he left home. The moon had been full above him as he'd flown away, leaving his real name behind; it had been a poetical fancy, Moonshrive, as if the moon could forgive him for betraying his true name. He told Whisper, "Nay, we live remote, keep to ourselves." That at least was not a lie. "And you?" he asked. "What's your clan?"

Her face tightening with pain, she said, "My clan is *dead*."

Hirik blinked. Her voice had risen above its whisper on the word *dead*. It lifted just a little and the word seemed to influence the air, like a ripple in water. He felt it touch him. The word itself—*dead*—passed through him and a flash of grief went with it. It was the briefest instant, but in that flash he felt a wave of raw sorrow so powerful he took a step back as if he'd been pushed.

Whisper covered her mouth with her hand. For a moment neither of them spoke. She looked afraid, as if she thought he might change his mind and leave her behind.

"Come on," he said. "Let's go back to the alcove. You can eat, then get some sleep before the journey tomorrow."

She nodded, let her hand drop from her lips, and followed him.

SEVENTEEN

Two days and one more sleepless night after leaving Serendip, Magpie and company reached the Bay of Drowned Dragons. They soared over the extraordinary landscape with its jade-green water and its hundreds of jagged islands. Magpie intended to head north to Shark Fin Peak, the nearest caravan outpost. The Silksingers had said Whisper would try to reach Nazneen, and the outpost was the most obvious place to begin such a journey.

But as they sailed over the bay, Batch poked his nose out his wagon window. "Hoy! Missy!" he hollered over the wind.

With a backbeat of her wings she stilled herself to a hover until the wagon, drawn by Pigeon, caught up to her. "Hoy what, imp?" she asked.

He pointed east and said, "That way! We got to go that way!"

"What?" she asked. "Neh, but sure the lass'll have gone north—"

"East!" he snapped. "I'm feeling it fierce!"

She took a good look at him. His beady eyes were fever-bright, and his pointing finger was as twitchy as she had ever seen it. He was most certainly in the grip of the serendipity. It exerted a powerful force on him, she knew, one he was virtually unable to resist. Again she looked east. That way lay more islands and then the open sea. "Are you sure?" she asked.

"Sure as blisters!" he hissed.

"Okay then," she said, feeling a frisson of excitement. She hadn't seen Batch look this fevered since he'd led them straight to the Ithuriel's cave. Could it be the Azazel was here, close by?

They flew over the bay, and by and by Batch directed Magpie to circle down toward one of the islands. From the air it was shaped like a caldera, with steep walls rising to shelter a lagoon at its center. It fit the description the Silksingers had given Magpie of their island, and she called out, "Be alert! There could be devils here."

They set down the wagons beside the lagoon. Magpie could sense no lurking presence, only monkeys skittering around the jungled walls of the caldera, but she couldn't be certain. Leaving Swig, Maniac, and Bertram to keep watch over the Ithuriel, the rest prowled toward the Silksingers' caves with Batch in tow.

"Hello?" called Magpie. Her voice echoed through the rock rooms, and there came no answer and no movement in the air. "It's clear," she told the others.

The caves, simple as they were, were as charming and cozy as something from a tale. They had round windows of colored glass, fine silk curtains hanging in the doorways, and beautiful carpets on all the floors. It didn't take much to imagine folk here, going about their lives. There were even embroidered slippers set out in front of a rocking chair.

It also didn't take much to see what had happened the night the devils came. Here and there lay a rotten feather or a tuft of greasy fur. There had been a struggle. In the little kitchen the table was smashed, and a pair of teacups lay in fragments on the floor. But atop the woodstove, undisturbed, sat one cup still half full, a scum formed over the cold tea inside it.

After wandering for a few minutes, Magpie found a twisting stair carved down through the rock, and with Talon and the others right behind her, she descended and discovered the Azazel's dreaming place. It was a cave, but with the strong scent of sandalwood and bright rugs laid before the stone dais, it was much less desolate than the other dreaming places she'd seen. And it was empty.

She wasn't surprised. This place was abandoned.

Certainly, Whisper had not come back here, whatever the imp claimed.

"Where's Batch?" she asked suddenly, looking around.

The crows had crowded down the steps behind her, but Batch was not with them. "Skive," Magpie growled. "What's he up to?"

They fanned out to search and turned up no sign of him. But they did discover another stair, concealed by a hanging tapestry. It led up to a cavern in the island's highest spot, open to a view of the lagoon. Against one wall were racks of torn cocoons from which, at some recent time, moths had emerged and flown away. And on the floor, all overlapping, were piles of carpets.

Talon knelt and took the corner of one in his hands and stared at it. It was like no weaving he had ever seen before. He didn't know much about weaving—it was a very different art from knitting. But looking at the way the threads came together in these carpets, even he could see they weren't woven on any loom. There was no visible organizing structure, no tidy perpendicular crossing of threads that made up warp and weft in common weaving. The silk seemed simply to have grown like this, as naturally as vines, the journey of each thread impossible to trace, the interweaving far too intricate for even the cleverest of fingers to have fashioned. And the colors! He'd never seen anything like them. If forced to guess how many hues and shades were captured in one weaving, he'd fear a thousand was too low a number.

"I've never seen the like . . . ," he said reverently.

"Neh, you nor me nor anybody else for four thousand years," said Magpie, who could see the dense traceries of magic that made them up. Her voice was not reverent like Talon's, but flat, as she said, "Please tell me we did not just deliver Batch Hangnail to the world's only collection of flying carpets."

Talon only laughed and shook his head in disbelief.

Magpie groaned. "That skiving fiend! This was what got him all twitchy, not the Azazel at all."

Talon said, "Do you think he's—?"

"Oh, aye, he's gone."

"Well then," squawked Calypso. "Let's go find him, shall we?"

Batch was islands away by the time they caught up to him. Leaning forward, wind in his whiskers, he was racing through the air on a flying carpet with his eyes closed, squealing in pure pleasure, "Wheee!"

Calypso caught the carpet with his talons and gave it a jerk, sending Batch tumbling forward with a gasp, right over the edge. He managed to hold on, which was lucky for him, as Magpie wasn't feeling at all inspired to rescue him if he plunged into the bay. He did not endear himself to her further when, dangling off the carpet's fringe by the very tips of his little claws, he peered up at her with eyes narrowed to slits and hissed, "Deal's off, faerie! I don't need yer wings anymore, so go find yer own skiving Djinn!"

Of course, she didn't let him keep the carpet. When they returned to the island, where the rest of the crows were still waiting with the wagons, Magpie restored it to the weaving cave. Batch turned into a fury, as near to a rabid rat as Magpie had ever seen him, and actually tried to bite her hand when she pulled the carpet away.

"Finders keepers!" he snarled.

"Losers weepers," she snarled right back. She felt as mean as a rabid rat herself over the detour, and it was all she could do to clench her fists and keep any stray magicks from escaping in her anger. It seemed to take an extra effort this time, and when the force of her fury finally died away, her nails had dug deep half-moons into her palms.

Magpie's power was a mystery lurking within her, and she could feel it growing. From that morning back in Dreamdark when it had blurted from her and turned the fake queen Vesper's hair into worms, she had never known what it might do next. Wake the Djinn King from his torpor? Stupefy every spider in the world? Shrink a python?

Hers was the power to manipulate the very Tapestry of Creation—something no faerie from the beginning of time had been able to do. Indeed, no creature but the seven Djinn themselves had ever woven those bright threads, but Magpie did. Messily, "artlessly"—as the Magruwen told her in his simmering hiss of a voice—and unpredictably, she had many times, without even knowing it, altered the fabric of the world.

With the elemental magic steadily strengthening inside her, Magpie knew she needed to learn how to channel it. But when? It was only in sleep that her mind joined with the Magruwen's for her lessons, and over past days she had scarcely had time for sleep.

"All right, 'Pie?" asked Calypso, wrapping his wing around her shoulders. Better than anyone, the crow chief could read her moods.

With a sigh, she nodded. "I'm all right, feather. Just tired. Lock that irkmeat imp in his wagon, would you?"

The crows did, and for a long while afterward they could hear Batch cursing and breaking things within.

Weary as they all were, they decided to stay put for the night. They set up camp, ate a cold supper of stale cake and hard cheese they'd found in the Silksingers' pantry, and went straight to bed.

In her caravan, Magpie checked on the Ithuriel, then spent a few moments writing in the big book that was her almanac and journal.

Flying carpets! How my parents and grand-mother would have loved to find this place and know its magicks—when the clan was still alive, anywhich. It's just sad here now, like an empty bird's nest—where you know the eggs never hatched but got eaten by some snake instead.

The thought of her clan made her sigh. She wouldn't be able to go see them now, though Anang Paranga was frustratingly near. She'd sent a message with her grandfather, the West Wind, telling them the bad news.

Glum, she wrote in her book for a few more minutes, her handwriting getting sloppy in her fatigue. Then she pulled out flask and took a swig of Moonlight Mist. This was the cunning potion brewed by her friend Poppy Manygreen; it helped her remember her dreams. Poppy had a gift for potions, which was serving her well in her apprenticeship to Dreamdark's healer, Orchidspike, and Magpie was grateful for this particular potion. These days, it was very important that she remember her dreams. She crawled under her quilt fully clothed and fell into sleep like it was an open pit.

The Magruwen was waiting for her in the mystical space of dreaming, as he was whenever she found time to sleep. At once he began her lessons, revealing the Tapestry's brilliant threads, plucking them and naming them one by one. "Pearl, oyster, sand, serpent." His voice went on and on, teaching Magpie the weave of the world. Her mind followed his. There was so much to learn, and Poppy's potion ensured she remembered it all. "Fang, venom, ginger, wrath . . ."

Even sleep was not very restful for the champion.

Locked in his caravan, Batch Hangnail's whole lumpish body was alive with the tug of the serendipity. The nearness of all those flying carpets pulled at him with an urgency no other creature in the world could fathom. It was more merciless than a bursting bladder, more powerful than starvation pangs; it couldn't be ignored, not even for a second. Batch's mind simply could not turn away from it.

"Let me out, ye mudsucks!" he wailed at the crows, pressing his face up against the glass so that his breath steamed it and his slobber slicked it. "Let me out! Let me out!" he moaned. He even said "please," over and over like a mournful chant, but the crows just shook their heads at him.

"Clamp yer moanhole, irkmeat!" hollered Pup. "We're trying to sleep!"

He tried all his tricks to comfort himself. He snugged his toes up into his nose, but they wouldn't stop twitching. He suckled on his tail tip like a little kitten, but it didn't help, and as the night wore on, his misery turned to spite. On toward morning, red-eyed, he sang:

"Vanished Djinn without a trace;
    want to find their hiding place?
Wicked faeries, dumb and blind,
    seek but ye shall never find.
Only Batch can give the clue.
    Make me suffer? Suffer too!"

EIGHTEEN

Over the next few days, Whisper learned the rhythms of caravan life: cold sky by day, hard stone by night, with ashcakes in between. She grew used to the hum of dragonfly wings, the cheek-burning chill, and the cramped hours of riding, but not ever to the savage spectacle of the mountains.

The first evening, after a long fly from Poet's Curse upward through white peaks, they came to an outpost called Mistghost. It stood above the clouds like a lighthouse to a white sea, its namesake mists lapping at its steps. The tired dragonflies heaved toward the courtyard, spinning ice crystals off their wings, and came in to land two by two.

When her own mount came to a prancing halt, Whisper climbed out of the silk bale in which she'd been nestled for warmth. The stone was icy under her bare feet as she walked to the parapet and gazed out over it. The whole cloud sea was spread before her just at the moment that the setting sun touched it and flushed it all red. She'd never seen the tops of clouds before, and the sight filled her with wonder.

145

A voice behind her asked, "Did you fly well, Whisper?" and she turned and saw Hirik. He held water buckets in each hand, and his eyes looked almost orange in the glow of the sunset. She thought they would glow like that even without the sun, and she wondered now how they could have seemed predatory to her before.

"Aye, thank you," she whispered.

"And were you warm enough?" he asked.

She nodded, lifting her hand to clasp her new shawl close at her neck. It was green, of thick, soft silk yarn. Hirik had bought it for her that morning in the market pavilion at Poet's Curse, and it had kept her as warm in the sky as a hand in a mitten. Throughout the journey, her thoughts had turned again and again to Hirik, to his blush as he stopped to buy her the shawl. As with the ashcake, he'd mistaken her reaction. Last night, he'd thought she found the food too poor, when she had only been stunned it was offered at all. And this morning, at her surprise over the shawl, he'd said in a hurry, "Unless you don't like green. There are other colors—"

"Nay," she'd said, pressing the shawl to her face to feel its softness and hide another wellspring of tears. "I like green," she'd whispered, as if that had anything to do with it.

Tears! It was absurd to weep over kindness. She was just so flooded with relief—but that was too small a word for what this was, this feeling welling up in her. It was *reprieve.*

She'd been so near to failing the Azazel! Now, though, she had a chance. This simple shawl was so much more than a shawl, and the words "thank you" sounded so thin next to what it meant to her. She wished she knew some way to tell Hirik, but before she could even try, they were interrupted. A mercenary stopped with a cry of, "Hoy!" and slugged Hirik on the shoulder, making him drop one of his water buckets. It tipped and spilled across the stones as the mercenary laughed. He was the one with the tattoo of thorny vines around his neck, Whisper saw—the same one who had kept calling her "smoke bride" that morning, which made her blush even though she didn't understand.

He stared at her now and turned to Hirik. "Did *you* buy her that shawl, greenwing?"

"What's it to you, Stormfoil?"

"Well, she's fearsome waifish, that's what it is to me." He looked Whisper up and down with a squint and added, "Didn't you buy her shoes too? Look at her feet. It's indecent!"

Whisper saw Hirik glance at her feet and she looked down too. The sight of them, so crude and bare, blackened and callused, made her blush.

"Neh," Stormfoil went on jovially. "I jest. It was that good of you just to pay her passage. I wouldn't guess she's worth a dragon scale, but maybe you know something I don't."

"It's none of your affair," Hirik said.

Whisper heard the exchange with dismay. She looked at Hirik, who had narrowed his eyes to glare up at the taller mercenary. Had he paid her way? When he told her Zingaro changed his mind, she'd been so relieved she hadn't asked questions. It seemed ridiculous now to imagine the hobgoblin would have offered charity. But why had Hirik done it?

"Well, I say it's sweet," said Stormfoil. "You must really be in love!"

Love? Whisper's blush deepened.

"Shut it, Stormfoil," Hirik said.

But Stormfoil only laughed. "Why? It's nothing to be ashamed of, sure, even if she *is* a feeblewing—" His words were cut off abruptly by Hirik dropping his second water bucket with a clatter. His hands curled into fists at his sides.

"That's enough," he said through his teeth. "You can say what you want to me, but don't talk to the lass like that!"

"What's all that?" Zingaro hollered. With a few lunging knuckle strides he crossed the courtyard and glared around, lower tusks outthrust. "Should've known it'd be the two of ye, fighting again!"

"We're not fighting," said Stormfoil easily. "Just having a chat."

"Well, chat later! Do ye think those skimmers can drink the fog?" To Hirik he rumbled, "Get those troughs filled now, lad!"

Hirik stooped to pick up the buckets, and Stormfoil

nudged one with his toe so it rolled out of reach. He had a smug look on his face, but as he turned to saunter off, Zingaro planted a big palm against the back of his head and shoved, so he stumbled forward, arms and wings flapping to keep from face-planting into the wall. Zingaro said, "If ye've time to spill the drink ye've time to haul it, Stormfoil. How about ye help the lad."

"Me?" gasped Stormfoil. "But that's greenwing work—"

"It's whose work I say it is! And now I say it's *all* yers! Moonshrive, give him the buckets!"

Looking as shocked as Stormfoil, Hirik set the buckets down at the other murk's feet. Stormfoil was sputtering with indignation. "You can't! I'm your weatherwitch—"

"Oh, aye? And a poor one at that. Get to work!" Zingaro tossed his beard over his shoulder like a scarf and lumbered off.

Stormfoil, fairly twitching with rage, hawked and spat after him, then settled his eyes on Hirik. "Found favor with the chief then, have you, scrunt? Well, enjoy it, because before this journey's over, you'll wish you never took that dragon scale out of your pocket. This slovenly little kitten"—he jerked his chin at Whisper—"isn't half worth the trouble it's going to bring on you."

Whisper felt his words like a slap. As Stormfoil grabbed up the water buckets, she raised her hands to her shoulder, felt the tangled coils of her dirty hair and the crusted blood of the wounds that it hid. She *was* slovenly. *Low.* And to think she'd brought such trouble to Hirik! "I'm sorry—" she started to whisper.

"Nay, don't listen to him," Hirik said, shaking his head. "It's not your fault. He's rotten, and I'm sorry he talked to you like that. And I . . . I'm sorry, Whisper. I should have gotten you some shoes. I just didn't think. . . ."

Whisper couldn't believe he was apologizing for not buying her *more*. She couldn't even think how to thank him for what he'd done already! "Nay," she said, staring down at her dirty feet, abashed. "Please, don't apologize. You've done so much. If you hadn't helped me, I don't know if anyone ever would. . . ."

Discomfited, Hirik looked out over the red clouds. He said only, "Well . . . if you can stomach another ashcake, the hobmarms will be doling them out inside."

The ashcake hadn't been bad, merely flavorless, and Whisper answered that she could stomach it just fine. "But first . . . ," she said hesitantly. "Is there anyplace I might . . . wash?"

The "bath" at Mistghost was only a rough room hollowed out of the mountainside. A rust-crusted spout protruded from the wall, and a tarnished copper basin was shoved into a corner. Whisper dragged it out and discovered, behind it, a paper packet still half filled with the jasmine salts of some passing traveler. When she filled the basin and sprinkled them into the hot water, a ghost of an aroma wafted up to greet her. The simple sweetness filled her, and she closed her eyes and breathed deep.

Spelling the door locked behind her, she set to disengaging her wild hair from about her neck and arms. She was in that little room a long time.

"Look at maidy," she heard a voice rasp in the hob approximation of a whisper when she came into the hall. She looked around. Zingaro and his family were in one alcove, the mercenaries in the next, all looking at her. There were other companies gathered too, among whom she noted Grismal, squinting and staring at her along with the others. All those eyes in the firelight made her feel very conspicuous. Well, she knew she wasn't slovenly anymore. Her clothes were still frayed, but they were clean now, or nearly so, and so was her hair, falling straight as black satin to the backs of her knees. It was no longer stuck to her wounds, which she had cleaned and found to be healing, though the flesh was puckered with scabs and sure to leave thick scars. They were concealed by her shawl now as she heard Anelka say, "She's a pretty thing, after all."

Looking around, she spotted Hirik sitting by himself against the wall. He lifted a hand to her, and she went over to him. Stormfoil made a smooch sound, but one of the older mercenaries snapped, "Smooch yourself, you trouble-rouser. Can't you see they're just sprouts?"

"Smooch *myself*?"

"Who else wants to smooch your nasty mug?"

"I'll smooch your daughters, you codgerly snivel heart!"

The other one muttered something back that made Stormfoil laugh like a monkey, and Whisper tried to ignore them as she sat down next to Hirik. He handed her a cold ashcake and she took it, said, "Thank you," and again felt the woeful inadequacy of the words.

"Your hair's long," Hirik observed simply.

She nodded. The tangles had been so fierce she'd had to sing them loose. She'd sung very low, barely above a hum, and the knots and clumps had responded at once, gently unsnarling themselves. It had felt so good to sing, even low like that, *un*weaving instead of weaving, and even to hair. Hair responded, as all fibers did, but not like silk. How she missed her silks, her weaving cave, her grandparents. How she missed singing! Humming the tangles out of her hair hadn't begun to fill her need for it.

She nibbled at her ashcake for a while in silence and watched Hirik polish his scimitar. She knew nothing of weapons, but she thought the sword was very beautiful. Its hilt was of plain, ancient gold, and the curved blade itself was of the utmost simplicity but for a curious property of the steel. Though smooth and unengraved, it bore within it a swirled pattern like wood grain. It was mesmerizing to watch the firelight slip across it. "Is it very old?" she asked him.

He nodded. "It's from the Dawn Days."

"Oh," she said. "Then likely it fought devils in its time."

Hirik looked up sharply but answered quite slowly. "Devils? Aye, likely it did."

They were both surprised when Merryvenom, from the alcove across the way, asked, "Does it have a name?"

"A name?" asked Hirik, tensing.

"Aye," said Merryvenom. "Most of the ancient weapons did."

"Not that I know of," Hirik answered. Something in his voice made Whisper wonder if he was telling the truth. She looked back and forth between his face and Merryvenom's.

The other murk had a knowing smile on his face. He shrugged and said, "If you say so." After he turned away, Hirik scowled and resumed his polishing with agitation.

Whisper watched for a moment, her eyes tracing the swirls in the steel, before asking tentatively, "Have . . . have *you* ever fought a devil?"

"Not yet," he replied.

"Yet?" Whisper looked up at him. She thought the answer ominous.

"Ah, well," he said quickly, a blush coming to his cheeks.

"Sometimes the caravans meet devils, nay? That's why there are mercenaries."

"Oh, aye," said Whisper. Of course that was all he meant.

"But try not to worry," he told her, resheathing his scimitar. "The Sayash are huge, and the chances of coming across a devil are slim."

She nodded, but his words didn't reassure her, because she knew what he did not: that chance had nothing to do with it. Devils were stalking *her*. She laid her hand on her kettle and hoped fervently they'd lost her trail.

Seeing her fingers tremble on the copper, Hirik asked gently, "Is that from home?"

She picked it up and held it against her stomach. She nodded and said, "It's all I have."

And it was true.

NINETEEN

From Mistghost they went on to Evenvining, Iceshimmer, and Lost Eyelash. The outposts were all much the same, and they shared the hostelries each night with Grismal's company and others they met traveling in the opposite direction. Faeries came from the small mountain villages to trade, and the hobs laid open their bales to reveal tea and wine, kohl sticks and coffee, spices, anklets of bells, and even some magical charms. The villagers themselves brought hot bread, bundles of goose down, little rock amulets, and engraved beads.

At Evenvining, one gent was selling pure white hair yanked from the tips of foxes' tails. Zingaro snapped those right up and laughed while the gent pantomimed fleeing from grumpy foxes.

But the real treasure was at Iceshimmer, where the local clan laid out a sparkling array of tiaras and jewelry that looked to be made of diamonds and crystal but were really *ice,* spelled not to melt. There were skeins of lace knit of real snowflakes too, and magical ice mirrors that disclosed visions to the gazer.

"Can they show the future?" asked the mercenary Serefrost, squinting into one. Its surface looked like a winter pond, etched with frost flowers.

"They show you what's in your own heart," said the merchant. "They are, after all, mirrors, not crystal balls."

What was in Serefrost's heart proved to be his lady and three pretty daughters at home in Nazneen, and his gruff murk face softened at the sight of them. The hobs took turns looking in the mirrors too, seeing each other, and riches, and the big, wild skies that were their world. Whisper herself didn't step up to the mirror. She wasn't certain what was in her heart, and she didn't want to discover it here, in front of others. She noticed Hirik didn't step up either. Stormfoil did, though the mirror showed him only his own reflection, as if it weren't magical at all.

"It's broken," he protested, rapping it with his knuckles.

"Or perhaps," said the merchant coolly, drawing the mirror away, "there's simply nothing in your heart."

At each outpost, Hirik looked for shoes for Whisper, but there were none on offer in these small markets. He apologized again, and Whisper flushed and assured him, "Nay, I'm fine," though in truth, her feet were very cold, especially at night, and she had to sleep with them practically in the coals of the fire.

When they arrived at Lost Eyelash, Old Neyn surprised them by producing a pair of thick socks she'd knitted in flight. "I made 'em for myself," she told Whisper brusquely. "But I reckon ye can borrow 'em till ye get some of yer own."

Whisper wasn't fooled. The socks would scarcely have fit over one of the hob biddy's gnarled old toes, but they fit Whisper perfectly. "Thank you," she said, deeply touched.

"Goatspit," muttered Old Neyn, turning her back.

The socks were deep blue, knit from the fleece of kashmir goats, and when Whisper slipped them on, they warmed more than her feet. She was beginning to feel hopeful now, her despair fading away. Up here in this world of peaks and wind-chased snows, in company she had a few days earlier deemed "savage," she found herself smiling, even laughing.

That night at Lost Eyelash, with no roving minstrels about, the travelers entertained themselves. The hobgoblins, to Whisper's surprise, sang polyphony, weaving their rough voices together in complex melodies. The young murk Merryvenom knew an endless repertoire of ballads, especially those of the Devil Wars, and even Hirik was prevailed upon to sing a song. Nobody thought to ask Whisper, with her tiny, breathy voice, to join in.

Listening to the others, she was filled with a powerful yearning to sing too, but she resisted it. To sing would draw all attention to herself, and she didn't want that, especially with the devils out there hunting for a Silksinger. She was happy to sit in the firelight with the kettle safe at her side and let the others believe her to be a waif of no consequence.

She listened with interest when the singing gave way to a murmuring of rumors about the Magruwen's awakening in Dreamdark.

"They say the new champion's just a lass no higher than an armpit," complained Reaveroot.

"Whose armpit, ninny?" asked Anelka. "Ye're no higher than *my* armpit!"

"Fine. No higher than a scrunt's armpit," Reaveroot said, beaming a pebble at Hirik, whose hand lashed up quick as lightning and batted it back, pelting Reaveroot on the chin. "Ow!" he yelped, rubbing his face.

Stormfoil picked up his complaint. "A lass, though, as Magruwen's champion! What's the world coming to?"

"What's it coming to?" repeated Zingaro. "It's coming to *good*, mayhap, and at last. I know Magpie Windwitch and she's a force, high as an armpit or neh."

"You know her?" Hirik asked, sitting forward.

"Aye, well enough, and her folk too. They traveled with us more than once, and with all their crows and wagons. Even as a smidge she were a lively thing. Wild! Hid in my beard once to get out of a bath!" He chuckled, and Whisper found herself smiling at the thought of the tough hob chief with a sprout tucked away in his beard!

"So, what?" asked Stormfoil. "She's dirty is what you're

saying? What is it with lasses today, can't be bothered to keep clean?" He cut Whisper a look that stole her smile, but his own was wiped off quick by Zingaro's reply.

"Even knee high to a dragonfly Magpie were a better weatherwitch than ye, Stormfoil. The winds do her bidding sweet as custard, and any caravan she flies with is blessed to go piggyback to an easy breeze and show up rested and early to their next stop. I'd trade ye for her any day if only she'd turn murk. I doubt it not that she'll do the Djinn King proud."

Stormfoil scowled and some of the others laughed at him, but the talk was of Magpie and the Magruwen and he was soon enough forgotten.

"I heard tell there was faeries from the Dawn Days come out of the Blackbringer," said Anelka. "Imagine!"

"And devils too," added Othi.

"But they captured the devils and put things right," said Merryvenom. "Just like the old champions did during the wars."

"That's what we need here," declared Othi. "A champion to catch our devils!"

"Aye," added Zingaro. "If there weren't any more devils in the Sayash, then we wouldn't need murks, would we? Think what I'd save in wages and cakes!"

There was some good-natured ribbing over that, with the murks asserting they'd be lost without Anelka's ashcakes, and Anelka threatening to withhold even salt if they dared to complain. Then Old Neyn voiced what many of them were thinking. "For a champion, we need a Djinn. Do ye think the Azazel will come back too?"

"Aye, sure he must," said Gladprowl, and other murks echoed him.

Serefrost reasoned, "If the Djinn King's come, the others can't be far behind."

"Aye, a new age is dawning in Dreamdark, they say," said Gladprowl. "It'll dawn here too. It's only fair."

They all seemed quite certain of it, and Whisper looked around at all their faces, so smug, so sure they *deserved* the new age—they who hadn't spared a single blessing or incense cone to the Azazel in all these years!

Then Hirik said something that made them all fall silent. "What does *fair* have to do with it?" he asked. "New ages don't just dawn all by themselves. They're not sunrises. If you want a new age, you don't wait for it—you make it. Do you think Magpie Windwitch was sitting idle and wondering if the Djinn King would wake up and find her? Nay, *she* found *him*."

They all just looked at him, surprised by the passion in his voice. Whisper looked too. She saw a glimmer and fervor in his eyes and it made her wonder. Just who was this lad who had helped her when no one else would, and what was it that he hoped for? Surely there was something in the golden gleam of his eyes—some bright hope.

He caught her staring at him and a rush of feelings flashed over his features—suspicion, anxiety—before his face became a stony mask of secrecy.

Whisper wasn't the only one watching him. Silently, across the fire, Merryvenom cocked his head to one side and gave Hirik a look of cool appraisal. Then Reaveroot pitched another pebble and Hirik reached out and caught it cold without even turning his head.

"Skive!" cried Reaveroot. "Good catch, greenwing!"

If Whisper was beginning to suspect that Hirik was keeping secrets, Hirik was certain that Whisper was. Ever since that strange thrum of magic had passed through him when she told him her clan was dead, he'd wondered who she was and what had happened to her. It hadn't escaped his notice that she'd given no clan name, nor any information about herself of any kind.

But keeping a secret as big as his own, Hirik was not about to pry into the secrets of others, lest some landslide of questions be unleashed and catch him up in it as well. There were a dozen things he wondered, but he didn't ask them. He did, however, tell Whisper about the phantasm he'd seen in the smoke.

The evening was winding down at Lost Eyelash. The hobs were already snoring, and Hirik and Whisper were apart from the others at a little fire of their own. When Hirik described the vision, Whisper stared at him in amazement. "A phantasm . . . of *me*?" she asked in her soft voice.

"Aye, exactly you. You even had your kettle."

"But . . . *why*?"

Hirik shrugged. "I thought maybe you would know." She shook her head. Seeing that she looked troubled by this news, Hirik strove to lighten the mood and asked in jest, "You didn't send the phantasm yourself, then? Some secret fire magic of yours?"

"Secret fire magic?" she asked, drawing away from him slightly. "What makes you think I know any secret fire magic?"

Her anxiety was such that Hirik wondered if he had inadvertently hit on something. Still striving to put her at ease, he asked, "Who *doesn't* know secret fire magic?" and as he spoke, he visioned a spell that sent a flame flickering out between his lips along with his last three words. Seeing the surprise on her face, he pressed his lips together in laughter and the fire shot out his nostrils instead.

"How did you do that?" she asked, smiling.

"Phantomfire," he told her. "It doesn't burn."

"I know phantomfire," she replied, making a neat ball

of it appear in her palm, then vanish. "But how did you breathe it out like that?"

"Maybe I'm part dragon."

"Bit small for a dragon," she said. "Firedrake, maybe."

"Aye, firedrake," he agreed. He felt a stronger kinship with firedrakes anyway, since they had been companions to the Azazel. He wished it would be so again, if—*when*—he became champion, but knew it could never be. Firedrakes, like dragons, had gone extinct long ago.

"Well, I can't breathe fire," Whisper said. "But I can do this." She snapped her fingers and struck a spark from the friction. It didn't shoot and fall like a spark but floated, twinkling faintly. She snapped her fingers again and again until she had a little glittering swarm of the sparks, then she shooed them away with her fingertips so they went flitting through the air like fireflies.

"That's sharp," Hirik told her.

"At home I used to tease the monkeys with them," she said, growing suddenly wistful. "No matter how many times I did it, they always followed them! They just couldn't learn. It's funny, those monkeys were vandals and terrors, but I miss even them now."

With her mention of home, Hirik thought she had opened the door of her secrets, just a little, so he asked gently, "Where's home?"

But she only whispered, "It's forever behind me now."

They lay down on opposite sides of the fire pit, as they had each night since they met, but tonight both had trouble falling asleep. Secrets were on their minds. The next outpost was ominously called Spillsecret, and Zingaro had said it tended to live up to the name.

"Legend is it was charmed, sometime," he'd told them. "It's just got a way of bringing the truth out of folks."

TWENTY

As if Hirik wasn't unsettled enough about heading to a place called Spillsecret, the next day brought more anxiety. The caravan hadn't been in the air long when the hairs on the back of his neck began to prickle with that nagging feeling of being watched, possibly followed.

All day it stayed with him, but as before he saw no sign of trouble. Once, some shapes glimmered out of the mists and his breath froze in his throat, but they soon resolved into a V of geese and passed on their way. He toyed with the idea that it was Merryvenom's curiosity that was making him jumpy. The murk had been keeping a suspicious eye on him, and Hirik thought it must be because of the scimitar.

Does it have a name? Merryvenom had asked a few nights back.

Hirik's answer had been a lie, adding one more lie to his growing list. The scimitar did have a name, but it was none of Merryvenom's affair. It was just his own bad luck that the murk turned out to hail from a clan of scholars and knew so much about the past. Anyway, Hirik didn't really think it was Merryvenom's watchfulness stirring the hairs on the back of his neck. It felt like something darker.

They arrived at Spillsecret without incident, but his uneasiness didn't leave him. Rather, it intensified. And worse, Grismal's caravan failed to turn up.

"Plague," said Zingaro softly. He didn't rant or carry on, but he stayed out in the courtyard until well after the moon had risen, pacing and staring into the distance. There were no caravans that night traveling eastward, so in Grismal's absence the hall was empty of all but themselves. They shared no music or hand shadows or tale-telling as they had done to help pass other evenings. Everyone was subdued, and Whisper more so than anyone. She looked pale, and when Hirik said, halfheartedly, "I'm sure everything is all right," she looked at him with strange intensity, and he thought she was going to tell him something. But she didn't. She hugged her kettle and kept glancing at the high windows of the hall.

Hirik looked too, half expecting to see a face leering in, but there was nothing.

The night wore on and eventually the others nodded off, but for Hirik it was impossible. The chill had not left him, and finally he could stand it no longer. When he was certain everyone else was asleep, he rose and crept out into the courtyard. Glancing all around to make sure he was alone, he considered what he was about to do. It was more than foolish—it was mad, especially in a place called Spillsecret, but if he didn't do it, he might *go* mad. He was certain something was lurking about, something very, very wrong. And there was only one way he could find out what it was.

With deep misgivings, Hirik reached up and untied the sash that bound his brow. He wadded the cloth into his pocket and pushed aside the heavy fall of his bangs to uncover what lay hidden beneath them.

His secret.

They seemed at first to be extravagant eyebrows, but with his bangs shoved aside they began to riffle and stir. And then, suddenly, they unfurled, twitching and stretching, and revealed themselves to be not eyebrows at all but *antennae*. Bristled like bottle brushes, they were the antennae of a silk moth, with all the subtle senses that went with them. They could pick up scent plumes from miles away and trace them unerringly through the wind. They could navigate blind, in darkness or mist cover. With them, Hirik could also call to insects and make them do his bidding.

He was a Mothmage.

Feathery and probing, his antennae stretched themselves out. It was marvelous to have full range of his senses; he had felt half blind these past days with his antennae muffled under his sash. But of course, it was the only way he could leave the safety and secrecy of his clan's forest. The name

Mothmage was so despised that if he were caught, it would be a desperate situation. At least, until he became champion. Then, he was certain, he could clear his clan's name. With the Azazel on his side, he could convince the folk of Zandranath that the legend of his folk was a lie. The Mothmage had never turned traitor.

He turned his attention to his purpose. The hundreds of fine hairs of his antennae tasted the air, and they confirmed at once what he already feared: nearby, something rotten prowled. Taking at once to his wings, he rose up from the courtyard and easily traced the scent. It was like an ugly trail laid out ahead of him, smelling of dead flesh caught between sharp teeth. Hirik had never yet met a devil, but he knew this could be nothing else. He drew his scimitar.

Bijal was the blade's name, as Merryvenom most certainly suspected. It was none other than the great lightning sword of the Devil Wars, forged by the Azazel for his champion Manathakkali, Hirik's many-greats-grandfather. Magic was in every atom of the sword's steel, and as soon as he loosed it from its sheath, Hirik sensed something different about it. It seemed to hum with its own life, and when he looked at it, he saw why.

Never, in all the years his clan had been in exile, had Bijal spun lightning as it had in legend. But now, against the black of night, blue energy crackled up and down its blade, and Hirik felt the tremors of its power from his fist all the way up his arm to his heart.

Bijal had awakened. It seemed the scimitar too sensed a devil close at hand.

Hirik followed the devilish stench over the rooftop. There were bars on the windows, like at all the outposts. But the scent plume led him to a place where, he was dismayed to see, the stonework had crumbled away, leaving a large gap in the eaves of the hostelry, large enough for something to have squeezed through. Cautiously, he maneuvered inside and found himself in one of the empty alcoves at the far end of the hall. The scent trail led, unmistakably, right to where the others were sleeping.

His heart gave a thud and he reached up and hastily curled his antennae back against his brow. There was no time to tie his sash, but he shoved his bangs down and hoped they would conceal his secret. Then, on wing, he raced down the hall and rounded into the alcove where he'd left Whisper.

He gasped, and before he could fully register his shock at the scene within, Bijal jerked in his hand. A bolt of lightning streaked off the blade, lighting up the chamber like a flare. By the brilliance of its flash, in the instant before it struck, Hirik saw what had before been in shadow. A monstrous thing was poised over Whisper—a segmented carapace, many waving legs, and great pincer jaws, making little snicking sounds as they scissored open and shut.

Then the lightning hit. With a sizzle, the devil went reeling. It smashed into the far wall. The air filled with the acrid tang of burnt flesh, and Whisper—small, fragile, quiet Whisper—came awake with a jolt.

And *screamed*.

"What in plague?" roared Zingaro, leaping to his feet and whirling around. The mercenaries were awake and on wing in a bound before Whisper quite realized what she had done. She'd been having a nightmare. It had sucked her so deep. Devil teeth and devil talons, pincers opening to seize her . . .

And then she was awake, sitting up, heart pounding. Shouts filled the room, and chaos, and she saw the devil—not a nightmare, but a real devil, the one from Shark Fin Peak—and she smelled scorched flesh and heard her own scream echoing in the air.

Horrified, Whisper clamped a hand over her mouth, but the scream carried on and on, like a thing unleashed. It echoed off the vaulted ceiling and rebounded on her, assaulting her with fear. That was the glyph she had screamed—*fear*. It hit her like a dagger thrust. It hit them all, stabbing panic into their minds. They were shouting, whirling, their shadows wild on the ceiling, the fires shivering from the draft of their floundering and flight.

Did they know it had come from her?

The scream began at last to ebb away, and the panic with it. "What was that?" they were all asking. Their stares twitched back and forth between Whisper and the devil sprawled on the floor. They didn't know. They couldn't.

"Look at the thing!" Gladprowl was saying, nudging it with his foot. "It's like a giant bug! Look at those choppers!"

"Watch out—" Hirik started to say, wanting to warn them it wasn't dead. Bijal's lightning didn't kill devils, but only stunned them so they could be captured. But before he could say any more, Stormfoil hollered.

"It's still alive!" he cried, drawing his sword.

"Nay—" said Hirik and Merryvenom at the same moment, but Stormfoil ignored them. With one swift strike, he slashed the devil's throat. Black blood pooled from it and Whisper had to scramble back from its flow.

"You're supposed to capture devils," Merryvenom told Stormfoil. "Not kill them."

"Ach, shut it, snivel heart. Who made you champion?" drawled Stormfoil, leaning over his kill. He wiped the blade of his sword clean on the devil's soft underside and then proceeded to wrench off its pincers to keep as trophies. Whisper choked and looked away.

"Did ye hear its shriek?" Zingaro asked. "Plague! I never heard such a sound! Thought the roof would come down!"

Others murmured assent. Whisper watched, wide-eyed,

her hand still clamped over her mouth. They thought it was the devil who had screamed! Then she saw Hirik. He was staring at her, and she could tell the moment their eyes met that he *knew.* The knowing leapt between them like a spark.

But he wasn't the only one who knew. Old Neyn was staring too, and the look on the hob biddy's face was frightening. Her lips were drawn back over her tusks in a snarl. "Devilkin!" she hissed, lunging at Whisper.

Whisper gasped and shied back, and Hirik was there between them in an instant. "Leave her!" he cried.

"It was her!" the hob biddy growled. "Look at her. She's marked!"

They all turned, even Hirik, and looked. Whisper realized what they were seeing. Her shawl had fallen away to reveal, on her bare shoulders, her wounds crusted with scabs.

"Claw marks!" cried Othi.

"Devil marks!" Old Neyn hissed again.

Whisper raised her hands to try to cover the gouges.

"How'd ye get those?" Zingaro demanded. He shoved forward and thrust his tusks right in her face.

"I . . . I . . . ," she stuttered. "A devil . . . a devil caught me—"

"And ye got free?" he asked, skeptical.

She nodded, darting a glance at Hirik, who looked skeptical too.

Zingaro snorted with disbelief. "Ach, sure! Who are ye, maidy? Ye been sneaking around from the very start. And now look! Where did this devil come from? Is it ye it were after?"

"Not me," she whispered. The devils weren't after her. They were after the Azazel. She held the kettle close.

"It was her who screamed," said Old Neyn, at his shoulder. "She called it!"

"Eh what? Is it true? Did ye call it?"

"Nay!" Whisper said again. "I didn't! I didn't call any of them—"

"*Them?*" Zingaro demanded. "What 'them'? Ye saying there's more?" A look of dawning horror spread over his features. "Plague! Ye're saying it *were* devils that took Fanggrin? And what of Grismal?"

"I don't know—"

Zingaro roared. Whisper scampered back from him, stepped in the devil's blood, and felt it wick up into her socks, hot and sticky. She put up her arm to ward off the hobgoblin, but then Hirik leapt between them. "Leave her alone!" he cried.

Zingaro raised a huge hand, and Hirik braced for the blow. But Whisper cried, "Nay! Please!" and her voice flowed between them, pure as a bell. All felt it, and all saw their clothes shimmer and shift color, the dull grey and brown of them shimmering red, purple, black.

"What in plague—?" Zingaro gasped.

Whisper couldn't take any more shouting, any more lies. She wanted it all to stop.

So, standing there in the devil's hot blood, she sang.

Her voice filled her, and everything else went away.

It was like no singing the hobs or faeries had ever heard. At first they were only startled, expecting more of the terrifying scream that had flooded the outpost. Zingaro lunged and Hirik faced him down. The hobgoblin could have swatted the faerie away with a backhand, Hirik could have loosed lightning from Bijal, but by then Whisper's song was a presence in the room, an impossible fullness of sound.

In a daze, Hirik turned to her. Her eyes were open but unseeing, as if she were in a kind of trance. If she was singing words, it was no language he knew, but he didn't think it was words, this pure rising and falling, this spiraling and blossoming of sound. He thought—his heartbeat stuttered at the idea!—that Whisper was singing the calligraphy of glyphs, spinning their traceries into music. And if she was, that could only mean one thing.

That she was a Silksinger.

He dropped to his knees.

Around the hall, others were slower to understand, but no one made a move to harm the singer. They were still. They felt like they had become flutes, as if breath flowed through them to become this music, and they were part of it. After Hirik, it was Zingaro who next had any inkling of just what he was hearing, and that was on account of his beard, which was gently lifted by invisible fingers, and combed, and woven.

Now it wasn't fear that blossomed in Whisper's voice, but glyphs for blessing and peace, harmony and calm. The sound was ineffably sweet, wreathing round them minute after minute, diffusing all anger and suspicion. It went on and on, and by the time the singing faded away, all eyes were glistening, all jaws slack with awe.

Whisper blinked out of her trance. She looked at Zingaro, who said, "Maidy . . . ," his growlsome voice now more like a purr, and she looked at Hirik, who was still on his knees. She held out her hand to him. Then she fainted.

It was like a spell had been broken. Hirik caught Whisper before she could collapse into the pool of devil blood, and everyone seemed to burst forth at once, babbling. Othi rushed to rip open a silk bale and fashion a little cushioned bed for Whisper, and the other hobs hovered over her, waiting to offer her a snail shell of cordial when she woke.

"Are you all right?" Hirik asked as soon as her eyes fluttered open.

"My kettle—" she said.

"Here." It was right at her side, and he handed it to her. He wanted to ask her a thousand questions, but Zingaro leaned forward and thrust his tusks between their two faces.

175

"Are ye comfortable, maidy? Do ye want some cordial? Tea?"

"Nay, thanks," she said. "I'm fine."

"Indeed, ye are," said the hob, looking utterly flummoxed. "Ye're a Silksinger! Forgive me, maidy, but I thought yer clan was . . . *dead*."

"They are," she said quietly. "I'm the last."

"I'm sorry, maidy," he said. The others were there too, hulking behind him. Even the murks were peering at her with new eyes. Old Neyn gave Whisper a charm fashioned of a crane feather and a blue bead to wear for protection, and Anelka offered her a grey kashmir cloak from the trade bales, which Whisper politely refused, preferring to keep her shawl.

"You don't have to," Hirik told her. "If I'd known you were a Silksinger, I'd never have offered you such a poor kind of shawl—"

"Nay," she protested. "It isn't poor." Looking down at it, she realized that in singing she had changed its color. It was amber now, the color of Hirik's eyes in the firelight. She sang a long, soft trill that sent a ripple through it and returned it to its original green.

The hobs urged her to sing some more, and briefly she did. It was a short song, a rich moving river of sound that eddied around the hall. This time Zingaro, mindful of his woven beard, intricate with spirals and many-pointed stars, was cunning enough to untie some skeins of silk thread and set them out. He marveled as the silks came to life and flushed with color at the touch of the song and wove themselves, twisting and twining to the sound of Whisper's voice. Soon, where there had been only undyed skeins of silk thread there lay several small weavings the size of place mats, each worth the weight of a hobgoblin in gold.

After, the others retreated to the next fire pit so that Whisper could rest, but Hirik stayed by her side.

Whisper had been wondering something ever since she woke to see the devil above her. There had been, she recalled, a flare of light. It had struck the devil with a sizzle. "It was you," she whispered, "who smote the devil."

His gaze dropped to the floor. He nodded.

The words *thank you* were on her tongue, paltry as ever. Perhaps, she thought, if she truly wished to thank him, she might . . . trust him. She said, "I'm sorry I didn't tell you before, who I was. I just wanted to get to Nazneen quietly—"

He shook his head. "It's all right. You don't need to explain."

"But I want to. Maybe it's this place. Spillsecret. I guess it's had its way."

Hirik's smile was halfhearted. "I guess so," he said. "But how about your name? Seeing what your voice can do, I guess it's not really Whisper?"

"Oh, well, it isn't and it is. It isn't the name I was given when I was born. My folk only started calling me that later, when my voice . . . when it came clear that it was . . . powerful. From the first, when I learned to speak, I had to whisper or things would happen. Colors would change, hair would braid itself, or if I was upset it would snarl in knots." She smiled ruefully, recalling how her great-aunts had hated that. "My true name is Melisma."

"That's pretty," Hirik said. "Should I call you that?"

"Nay, I've been called Whisper since I can remember."

There was a pause then, as Whisper gathered her courage to spill another secret, a much bigger one. She looked at Hirik intently, wondering not for the first time who he was, what he hoped for. Her heartbeat quickened and her fingertips drummed the side of the kettle. What would he think? What would he say?

He cut into the silence to ask, "So now you're going to Nazneen . . . to live?"

To *live*? Whisper fiddled with the handle of the teakettle. She hadn't thought about what she would do after her duty was discharged. She hadn't quite believed there would *be* an after. Now, for the first time, the thought of *living* presented itself. "I don't know if I'll stay there," she said honestly. "My clan always said Nazneen was tainted."

"Tainted?"

"Aye, by betrayal."

"Betrayal." Faintly, Hirik said, "You mean . . . the Mothmage."

"Aye, the Mothmage." Bitterly she spoke the hated name. "Selling Fade's life to witches for a mound of rubies! But it wasn't only them, it was the whole city, watching from their windows while the dragon's blood fell like rain on their rooftops, and nobody flew to help but my ancestors. . . ." She was on the verge of telling him how the few surviving Silksingers, reeling from the horrors of that day, had decided to accompany the Azazel to his dreaming place.

She was ready to tell him everything, to take the lid off her kettle and show him what smoldered inside it. She was even reaching for the lid, glancing around to make sure no one else was looking, when suddenly, Hirik rose. Pale and strange, he excused himself, barely meeting her eye. "I'd better keep watch outside," he said, "to make sure there are no more . . . surprises. You can sleep soundly, Whisper. I promise I'll keep you safe."

"Wait—" Whisper said, but Hirik's wings carried him away from her.

She sat back in her little silken nest. Her secret was on her lips. She didn't want to keep it to herself any longer. She wanted to share the weight of it with Hirik. But he was gone now, abruptly, and the secret still unspoken. What had made him leave like that? Her lip trembled and she bit it, feeling all the more alone for having made the resolution to share and been prevented.

TWENTY-ONE

In his nest of bones, Ethiag shook with rage. Another of his hunters was dead, but it wasn't the death that enraged him, or even just the failure. It was the lightning. He knew the feeling of that blast. Down to his bones he knew it. His *own* bones. It wasn't only through the minds of his soldiers that he had tasted Bijal's lightning in the old days. Bijal had bitten *him*.

Bijal had conquered him.

Thousands of years had Ethiag drifted in the sea, imprisoned in a bottle, because the accursed champion Manathakkali had smote him with that sword! And now, another wielded the blade?

He hadn't seen who. Through his soldier's mind he had felt the blow, the searing pain, before blackness flooded in.

Again, maddeningly, his quarry was denied him. The Silksinger, the Azazel, they'd made it through another night, but they wouldn't last another day. All across the mountain wilderness, Ethiag's devil hunters had wheeled on their wings and were racing toward the ambush.

They would be waiting to give the caravan a stunning welcome.

"Ye snooling again, snivelskin?" demanded Num when she caught Slomby gazing mournfully at a raspberry he had just fished out of the sludge of the fruit trough.

"Neh," he said defensively, looking at the berry. It was only half covered in white mold, and if he held it just so, it looked almost fresh. If Mogorm were alive, thought Slomby with an ache, he'd give him the good half.

Out of the corner of his eye he saw that Num was readying her snapping rag, and he scrambled to his feet. "What?" he demanded, cringing.

"What? I'll tell ye what. Go feed the crone, snailmeat!"

Slomby grimaced. He hated feeding the crone. The snag whose job it was had been eaten before Mogorm, so now the task fell to him. Of course, Num never took a turn. For a slave, she did very little in the way of slaving. Slomby dared to ask her, "Why do I always have to do it?"

Num snapped him with her rag and said, "That's why. Now get to it!"

When she was out of earshot, Slomby muttered, "Who made her queen? Nasty old eyeball . . ." Then he set his raspberry on a ledge for later and started scooping rotten fruit flesh into a big wheelbarrow. When it was loaded to overflowing, he wheeled it down the passage to the main cavern.

There, all before him, was the devil army.

Not long ago, this cavern had been empty, but over the past weeks it had filled steadily, day by day, with this horde of misshapen monsters. Winged ones hovered up among the stalactites; others pawed the ground, restless, while boneless things quivered and gaped open pulsating mouths. But though they licked their teeth and eyed him hungrily, they scarcely moved. Unnatural calm gripped them like an invisible fist. They were Ethiag's puppets and did only what their wicked master willed.

Scrambling fast, Slomby made his way through them. His destination was a smaller cave off the main cavern. The black lake was at its center, where he caught fishes for the firedrakes, and on the opposite shore, barely visible in the darkness, was a mountain of silver bottles.

The lake was a portal. It was how the devils were brought here, still in their bottle prisons, by sea serpents who swam up underground streams from the sea. The serpents cast the bottles onto the shore where they lay scattered by the hundreds, and in the midst of the clutter dwelt the creature who broke open the seals to free the prisoners. It was the only sort of creature that *could* break the seals.

Long ago, during the Devil Wars, the faerie champions had crafted keen magic so that nothing alive in the world could ever unseal the bottles and free the devils. But in the thousands of years since, all unforeseen, a new species had risen: humans. No one knew where they came from, only that the Djinn who'd made everything else had not made them. And the magic of the seals did not constrain them.

That was why, along with his other slaves, Master kept the crone. She was a hunchback witch so old her hair and teeth had fallen out. In a stupor of senility, she doddered about, gumming rotten fruit and performing her one duty: opening bottles and releasing their savage occupants.

"Crone!" Slomby called. "Here, crone!" He pressed as far into the cave as he dared and tipped up the wheelbarrow. The fruit oozed out into a chunky puddle on the floor, and he spun right around, averting his eyes from the human who crept out of the shadows. He didn't want to look at her. Even knowing she was a witch and had chosen wickedness of her own free will, he couldn't help but pity her. He dashed out of the cave before she could start making slorping sounds over her small meal.

Slomby scurried back through the devil army to the kitchen. He shoved the wheelbarrow into its place and reached up to claim his raspberry off the ledge. It was gone.

Over by the stove, Num was licking her fingers, and when she bared her teeth in a nasty smile, the pulp of the red fruit was thick between them. In the lantern light, it looked a lot like blood.

TWENTY-TWO

"Trouble, 'Pie," said Calypso, poking his head into her wagon.

She was writing in her book and looked up sharply. "Devils?" she asked.

"Neh," said the bird. "Well, sure, probably someplace. But neh."

"What, then?"

"Ye'll just have to go see. I'll stay and keep an eye on the Ithuriel. Just look to the imp."

"Ach, what now?" she groaned. She closed her book and exited the wagon. It was parked with the four others in an unused rear courtyard at the outpost of Iceshimmer. She headed into the market pavilion, where a few caravans' worth of hobgoblins were ogling the ice jewels and snow lace of the local clan. Easily she spotted Batch.

He wasn't making a fuss, at least. He was gazing into a mirror while Talon and the crows stood by. Magpie approached. "What's this about trouble?" she asked Talon.

With his chin he motioned toward the mirror. It was, Magpie saw, an ice mirror, renowned throughout the Sayash for reflecting what was in the gazer's heart. She already knew what was in Batch's heart: the dream of flying. And the mirror did indeed reflect that wish.

The reflection showed Batch riding on a flying carpet.

"Skive," she said, understanding at once the nature of the "trouble."

Talon looked at her and cocked an eyebrow. "Not wings, you'll notice."

"Neh."

"That's it, then."

She scowled. "I reckon so."

The only thing that had made Batch help in the search for the Djinn had been the lure of wings of his own. But now, it seemed, he no longer wanted them. His crusty scavenger's heart was fixed on one thing: a flying carpet. And not only did he not need Magpie and Talon for that, but they were the ones who'd taken it away from him when he'd found it.

He'd been a wretched, uncooperative brute ever since they left Silksinger Island, and no help at all in tracing Whisper. Magpie had done that the non-magical way, by asking at the outposts after a scamperer lass. It turned out Whisper was with Zingaro, a hobgoblin Magpie knew well, and had a few days' lead on them.

She had still hoped Batch might come around. After the

Azazel there were three more Djinn to find, and the imp could make the search so much easier, if only he *would*. She'd already tried asking nicely.

"Suck lint," he'd replied.

"But don't you see?" Magpie had cried in frustration. "If we don't find the Djinn, it'll be the end of the Tapestry. The whole world's going to fall apart like a pair of old socks that have been walked to tatters, and then blackness will come seeping in through all the holes and we'll drown in it! Do you understand? This is the time when all the creatures of the world must use their Djinn-given gifts for the good of all. Even you, Batch. If anything happens to the Djinn, it's the end of everything. Scavenging, flying, diamonds, *everything!*"

Batch had looked her straight in the eyes, and belched.

Now, seeing his magical reflection, she had to admit there was no hope for him.

The Iceshimmer merchant was getting impatient with the imp hogging his mirror. Magpie said, "Come on, Batch," but he ignored her. Finally she grabbed his bejeweled tail and tugged it like a leash.

"Munch!" he snarled as she led him away.

They bought supper in the pavilion and retired to their wagons to make tea and get some sleep.

"Let's just leave the gobslotch here," proposed Maniac.

"Ach, can we?" asked Pup. "Eh Mags? Then I can have my wagon back!"

"I don't know if you'll want it," she said. "It's a fart stew in there. Probably nothing will ever get his stink out."

"Fart stew!" snorted Pup.

Magpie did not intend to leave Batch Hangnail in Iceshimmer, but it was purely out of consideration for the local folk. "We'll carry him on to Nazneen," she told the others. "Turn him loose there."

"At least ye won't have to knit wings for the meat," Bertram said, nudging Talon with his wing. As the two usually did whenever they had occasion to rest, Talon and Bertram were side by side, the crow sewing and the lad knitting. There had been no evidence of pixies in Bertram's box on this occasion, however, since Magpie had been too preoccupied for fun and pranks over the past days.

"Too bad there en't some way to *make* him help, though," muttered Calypso.

"Aye," said Magpie with a sigh. "But at least we got the Ithuriel. To tell true, I'll be glad to see the last of our king of scavengers. He makes everything nasty, neh? Not just his smell, either. He makes me *mean*, and he makes the magic build up in my fists till I don't know what'll happen. I reckon if he stays with us, I'll end up killing him."

"Neh, you wouldn't," said Talon with complete confidence. "Magpie, you'd never kill anything, even such a meat as that."

A momentary look of shame flitted over her face and she

looked down at her hands. She was thinking of the snags she'd slain in the Moonlit Gardens, and Talon guessed as much. Of course, she'd told him about it, and he knew how shaken she was by the killing. "That was different," he said, reaching out to take her hand, just long enough to give it a squeeze. They both felt the power of the Tapestry flowing around them and through them, always stronger when it was the two of them together.

Magpie squeezed back quickly and gave him a little smile before letting go of his hand.

"Sleep, everyone," she said, rising. "It's a long sky tomorrow."

Zingaro's caravan might have several days' lead, but Magpie was granddaughter to the West Wind, after all. At dawn, she would rally the Sayash winds to carry them the rest of the way to Nazneen in a breakneck surge of elemental speed. By this time tomorrow, she thought, they would have caught up to Whisper. They would have the Azazel.

TWENTY-THREE

Zingaro's caravan departed at dawn and flew all morning over slopes of rhododendron forests. Hirik was glad to leave Spillsecret behind, his secret still intact. By evening they would reach Nazneen. He could scarcely believe he was so close to seeing the city of his ancestors.

Toward midday, they dropped into a deep river canyon and followed it westward and downward. The long double file of dragonflies soared in a neat line between the high rock walls, and since they were angled down in gradual descent, Hirik could see them all spread out before him from his position off the left rear flank. Up ahead, a thick mist was rising off the river in billows. Zingaro and Storm-foil plunged into it and disappeared, leading the way for the rest.

Out of the blue, Hirik had a sudden pang of foreboding. He tightened his grip on Bijal. There was no clear reason for worry—the caravan often flew through fog and even occasionally blizzards. But as the dragonflies dipped into the

189

mist and vanished, it came to him that this narrowing, mist-flocked gorge was an ideal place for an ambush.

And then he heard a screech. It shivered up his spine. Shapes were rising, on bat wings and bird wings, chopping up the mist. But they were neither bats nor birds. They were devils.

Instantly, the caravan was thrown into chaos.

Bellows and howls joined the screeching. The dragon-flies broke formation and spun wild in all directions as their attackers beat up at them from below. The devils massed around the center of the file, letting the majority of skimmers escape, while trapping some dozen in a tight knot—a dozen that included the hobmarms. And Whisper.

Hirik rushed forward. His training took over and he swung his scimitar around his head in an elegant arc. He thought he could feel the air peel aside at the touch of the blade, and he watched as a zigzag of blue light streaked off the steel, shot through the air, and hit one of the devils in the back. The thing convulsed, wings twitching, and fell from the sky, plunging through the mists to the river below, where it was carried away by the current.

Then the other murks were on the mob. Serefrost and Gladprowl, slashing, killing. Merryvenom wielded a sword in each hand and took on two devils at once. Unlike the others, he didn't slay the devils, but cut the tendons of their wings so they fell away into the river. Hirik loosed more lightning. Its flash caught Merryvenom's attention and his dragonfly wings seemed to freeze in mid-air as he took in the crackling blue fire alive on the scimitar's steel. His eyes met Hirik's for an instant before he whirled back into battle, catching a horned snag under the chin with a spinning kick that snapped its foul head back and sent it sprawling.

The lightning sword sparked and spit blue fire. Mercenaries slashed. Devils fell. Dragonflies fell too, heavy as stones under their loads.

"Whisper!" Hirik yelled, searching through the chaos for some sign of her. He couldn't find her, but he saw Old Neyn. A snag opened bristling jaws, and even as Hirik leveled Bijal to strike, it bit a wing right off the hob biddy's skimmer. The scimitar flashed and zapped the devil away, but it was too late for Old Neyn. Her maimed dragonfly plunged into a death spiral, and Hirik could do nothing but watch as her tusks parted in a wail and she fell away into the mists.

Gone. She was gone.

"Muther!" Zingaro screamed.

Hirik was horrified. As much as he had trained in fighting, nothing could have prepared him for the sight of real death. A scream snapped him out of it. Another snag was charging at Anelka. Hirik dispatched it with a sizzle from Bijal. But where was Whisper? He couldn't find her in the mash of foul creatures. The devils were pressing in, still so many. *Too* many. A tail lashed, caught Serefrost across the gut, and flung him halfway to the canyon wall before he caught himself with his wings and beat back toward the fray, bellowing a fierce battle cry.

The murks were fighting ferociously, but they were sorely outnumbered.

Unless, Hirik thought with a jolt, you counted all the skimmers. He did a quick scan of the area. The dragonflies had scattered at the first onslaught and were buzzing away in all directions. A sick feeling welled up in him as he realized what he had to do, but he didn't let it slow him. He swallowed hard and pulled the sash off his brow. His antennae leapt free, and the instant they tasted the air he set to work. The fine hairs vibrated as he sent out a wave of messages that were neither scent nor sound, but tendrils of magical persuasion that only the dragonflies could feel. He ordered them to calm themselves and rally.

He ordered them to fight.

Some had already been killed, but there were still close to a hundred, and within moments the scene of chaos changed. Fleeing skimmers wheeled about and flashed back toward the battle, hurling themselves at the devils. Like a Mothmage general of old, Hirik issued silent commands. The hulking insects tore at the snags' wings with their vicious jaws and dropped them out of the sky.

At the same time that he was commanding the skimmers, his antennae were also pulling in scent plumes, telling him many things at once. They made an image like a shifting map in his mind, of snags and skimmers and faeries and . . . Whisper! He found her scent plume, cinnamon and jasmine and . . . what else? Hirik realized that Whisper's scent had the flavor of *fire*. He couldn't fathom why, and he had no time to puzzle over it. Still trying to catch a glimpse of her, he ordered a dozen dragonflies to encircle her and Anelka and protect them.

Keeping her location fixed in his mind, Hirik turned back to the fighting. With the skimmers in the fray, it was the snags who were outnumbered now. Still, they fought like creatures possessed, and the dragonflies were weighed down by their heavy bales, not agile as they might have been. The battle waged fierce. Hirik found himself overwhelmed by a phalanx of the monsters, no two of the same breed.

They were closing in. He moved to retreat. But then a voice cried, "Moonshrive!" and Merryvenom was at his side. The other murk's eyes flicked to his antennae and betrayed only momentary surprise before he said, "Back to back!" and Hirik did as he was bid. They turned back to back and fought as a team, much as Hirik had done in drills with his cousins back home, each sensing the other with his wingtips and moving as a unit to prevent any snags from surrounding and overpowering them.

And the lads were prevailing. But then Hirik sensed a shift in Whisper's position. She was falling. He glimpsed her long black hair trailing in the wind as her skimmer dropped. He had to follow—but he couldn't leave Merryvenom surrounded like this. He slashed out with Bijal, and a torrent of lightning poured from the blade, zapping a clump of devils away.

In the gap that opened up before him, he caught sight of a startled face staring back. It was Reaveroot, his mouth open in shock. Hirik cried, "Reaveroot, help Merryvenom!" and pointed behind him to where the other murk was now facing four devils by himself. Then Hirik folded his wings and dropped out of the battle, all his focus on Whisper.

Reaveroot stared after him. He blinked. Then he turned and flew. But it was not to Merryvenom's side that he went. He sought the mustard-yellow flash of Stormfoil's wings and raced to his friend, sputtering the name, "Mothmage!" while behind him, Merryvenom fought alone.

A devil spat acid at the lad and he dodged it—right into the creature's tail. Too late, Merryvenom saw it was no ordinary tail. At it tip was a *mouth*. No eyes or nose but only a gaping, circular maw, bristling with hooked teeth.

A croucher devil's second mouth.

Merryvenom's last thought, as it clamped down on his throat, was of a line from a comic ballad he'd known since he was a sprout. "A croucher devil will always prevail, if you neglect the teeth at the tip of its tail."

In seconds, he was dead.

Hirik

Whisper's skimmer was in a spin. One wing shorn at the tip, it was heading toward a collision with the canyon wall. The devil in pursuit was a vicious thing with a tail like a spiked battle flail, and it reached for Whisper, got its claws into her long, streaming hair, and jerked. She screamed. Hirik heard her and felt echoes of her panic vibrate through him.

Stretching out his sword, he blasted the devil and sent it sailing end over end into the cliff. But Whisper's dragonfly was going to hit the cliff too. Hirik sent it a sharp command to bank away. Just in time, it did. Tilting, it cleared the rock face but started to fall faster. Hirik put on a burst of speed and raced after it, reaching for Whisper.

"Grab onto me!" he screamed.

She looked up.

He saw in her eyes the precise second she perceived his antennae. She recoiled, and he felt it like a punch to the gut. The dying dragonfly was hurtling toward the rocky slope below. He had no time for her shock or his shame. He grabbed her elbow with his free hand. The dragonfly fell away from them and he struggled to keep his grip on Whisper.

"Hold on to me!" he said.

But she was clutching her kettle and wouldn't drop it to reach for him. He managed, somehow, to get his arm around her waist. His lungs were bursting from exertion. Casting a quick glance to the canyon wall, he spotted a ledge and flew to it. He set Whisper down as carefully as he could, then collapsed to his knees and sucked in a deep breath. When he could breathe again, he looked up in the air where the battle was winding down. The last of the devils were falling to the murks' swords and the dragonflies' teeth.

It was over. Hirik sent a last calming message to the skimmers and left them to Zingaro's care. He looked at Whisper. She was staring at his rippling antennae with disbelief and dismay on her face. And was that . . . disgust?

He turned away, refurling his antennae and shoving his hair back over them. But even with them covered, he didn't turn back around to face her. He couldn't stand to see her horror again.

"You're Mothmage . . . ," Whisper said. Her voice was low, but it carried a sting like chili. What glyph carried that sting, Hirik wondered. Scorn? Hate?

"I'm sorry I didn't tell you," he said.

"Hirik—" she began, but then they both heard a shout.

"There he is!"

Stormfoil, Reaveroot, and Gladprowl were rocketing toward them. Hirik put up his hands, but Stormfoil plowed into him and knocked him to the rock, and the other two seized his arms. "Moonshrive!" Stormfoil spat the name. "Indeed!" And then he reached up and shoved Hirik's hair out of the way. "Plague! Look at those foul twitchers," he said. "You make me sick!" With a look of revulsion, he grabbed the antennae. His grasp was brutal. Hirik's delicate scent receptors were ground into the heat of the murk's palm, flooding him with the tang of Stormfoil's fury.

"Did you call those snags on us, bug?" Stormfoil demanded.

"What?" Hirik gasped.

"Seems there's been a lot of devils crawling around ever since you joined the caravan. Makes sense now, you filthy traitor!"

"Nay!" Hirik cried.

Stormfoil yanked Hirik's antennae taut and raised his sword.

Hirik tried to struggle, but the other two held his arms fast, and in those seconds, as the blade flashed over his eyes, he thought of the nightmare stories of long ago, the terrible retribution faeries had exacted from his folk after the Battle of Black Rock—the frenzy of mutilation as Mothmage antennae were hacked off and even sprouts and biddies were left scent blind and groping.

To a Mothmage, it was like losing their eyes.

A black, deafening dread filled Hirik as he stared up at the edge of Stormfoil's sword and helplessly watched it come.

TWENTY-FOUR

"Stop!" Whisper screamed. Her cry buffeted them with a gust of outrage. Stormfoil whirled toward her, letting Hirik's antennae go. The relief was so great it took Hirik a moment, wrenching his arms free of the other two murks, to blink his vision clear and see Whisper standing there, trembling. Stormfoil was staring at her, his ugly lip curled in confusion.

"Leave him alone," she said. *Commanded*.

"But he's Mothmage—" said Reaveroot.

"Aye, he is," she said. She was looking at Hirik like she had the first time they'd met, like she was trying to read him. In her eyes there was still dismay. Hirik couldn't bear her scrutiny another second. He spread his wings and with a leap he was airborne, flying backward away from the ledge. Stormfoil tried to grab him but Hirik kicked away and outpaced him, while back on the ledge Whisper cried, "Hirik, wait!"

He could feel her voice curling around him, trying to call him back. But he wouldn't go back. He couldn't. Not now.

His only hope had been secrecy, and now he was exposed. With shaking hands he hid his antennae again, pulling his hair back over them with a savage yank. And then, with a single backward glance that showed him Whisper standing at the edge looking after him, he flew into the mist and left her there.

Hirik was gone. Whisper stood staring into the mists that had swallowed him. Hirik was *Mothmage*. She couldn't make herself understand. How could he be Mothmage? And how could he have left her? He had sworn on the Azazel's flame. . . . But what were such oaths to a Mothmage? They were traitors! But Hirik, a traitor? Again he had saved her. Only to leave her here on this ledge with mercenaries who had only contempt for her.

When Hirik flew away, Stormfoil leapt off the ledge as if he were pursuing him, but he soon returned, smiling. "Look what I found, lads!" he declared, swinging something over his head. Whisper saw that it was the tail of the devil that had chased her—a limp greyish lash with a bulb of spiked flesh at its tip. "Another trophy," gloated Stormfoil.

He disgusted her, but when he said with a leer, "Come on, lass, guess I'll have to carry you," she had no choice. She held herself rigid as he took her in his arms and flew her back to where the hobgoblins and Serefrost were gathered on a ridge, grief-stricken and silent.

They'd lost many skimmers, but not only skimmers. Old Neyn was gone, and Merryvenom, terribly, had been devoured in the air. When Stormfoil told the hobs about Hirik they immediately set to cursing him and blaming him for the attack. "He was the devilkin, all along!" spat Othi.

Zingaro was too anguished to speak, but the murks went on and on about it. Whisper listened with growing misery. Hirik might be a Mothmage, perhaps even a liar, but she knew he had nothing to do with the devils. These deaths were on her conscience, not his. She huddled in a little niche in the rock and wept. She looked at the socks Old Neyn had made for her. They were crusted with dried devil blood from the night before. It seemed a terrible omen now, and she peeled them off, despite the chill, and dropped them over the ledge.

While she stood there and watched them fall away, a sparkle caught her eye. Caught in a little niche in the rockface just below her was a bit of broken glass. Or not glass, but mirror. Whisper knelt to pick it up. It was a shard of one of the Iceshimmer mirrors, the ones that revealed what was in the gazer's heart. It must have shattered when a skimmer fell against the rocks. Whisper was turning to give it to Zingaro when its frosted surface suddenly cleared and gave her an unexpected vision. Of Hirik.

Seeing his face so suddenly, she almost dropped the little shard. Did the mirror show true? Was he in her heart, in spite of what he was? She knew by the answering ache in her chest that he was, but it didn't matter. He was gone. The mirror showed him flying. *Away.* Whisper didn't give the shard to Zingaro, but slipped it into her pocket. It wasn't stealing, she consoled herself. She had sung for the hob, and those little weavings would fetch more than enough to pay for this small broken thing.

While the hobs tried to ready the surviving dragonflies to carry on, she curled around her kettle and watched the sky, her eyes darting from one tatter of mist to another, heart hammering. Every sound, every movement made her jump, but no more devils came. Once Zingaro had salvaged all he could and retrieved the more valuable goods from the corpses of the fallen skimmers, they resumed their journey.

With his head hanging and his shoulders slumped, Hirik flew back the way they'd come. He thought he could retrace the caravan's path back over the high route and make his way home from there. It was risky—he hadn't a hobgoblin's navigation sense, but he would try. What else was he supposed to do?

His mad fantasy of finding the Azazel, becoming champion, restoring his clan's honor . . . it was over almost before it had begun. It had been a sprout's starry-eyed dream to think a Mothmage could ever return to the world of faeries! But when Whisper had recoiled from him in disgust, the stars had gone from his eyes forever.

If her trust could vanish so quickly, with others it would be worse. Without even having to think, Stormfoil had drawn his blade, ready to deal with Hirik as the Mothmage had been dealt with four thousand years ago. Hirik knew what had happened that day. After the battle, when the Silksingers were dead and Fade's massive corpse lay across the city, faeries had stood in the blood and the ashes and keened for the dead. Keening had given way to fury. The witches were already slain, so they turned all their anguish and blame on the Mothmage, who had done nothing to stop the slaughter.

And . . . they *had* done nothing. In this essential, the legend told true. But *why* had they done nothing? Why, when the folk of Nazneen stormed into Mothmage Castle, had they found the warrior clan gathered around a pile of rubies, blinking stupidly? Did they think they were gloating over their spoils? Anger burned in Hirik's heart when he thought of how easily the faeries of Nazneen had believed the worst of his folk.

Certainly it had looked bad, but things are not always as they seem. The warriors had been bewitched—spellbound, in the true sense of the word. Bound by some magic and held captive in a fugue state whilst all around them their city fell into chaos.

It was the rubies. They had been delivered in the morning, a fair landslide of them, dumped from burlap bags. But who had sent them? Not witches. The Mothmage, loyal guardians of the Azazel and all the lands of Zandranath, had taken no payment from witches, nor ever had dialogue with them! It was a trick. There was dark sorcery in the gems, and later, they guessed who was behind it.

He was a faerie named Onyx, and he had come from nowhere and risen to be chief scribe to the Azazel. "Black Onyx," the Mothmage called him behind his back, because though he was charming and clever, there was a taint to his scent he couldn't hide from their keen senses: a soft rot and wrongness. A "corruption of both spark and skin," the chief of the Mothmage had deemed it, and he had made it his purpose to keep watch over Onyx. Their rivalry was a quiet matter, one of watchfulness and dark looks. The chief had made certain the scribe was never alone with the Azazel, but overseen always by a guard or a firedrake.

But Onyx had prevailed, spectacularly. In that one day he had destroyed the city, the great dragon, and the lives and good name of the warrior clan. Likely it was even he who had fed the mob their idea of revenge. They had used whatever scissors and kitchen knives they could find, and even the warriors' own swords against them. At the end of the day, beside the pile of rubies, there had been another pile—one of shorn antennae.

The Mothmage fled into exile and found a forest where they could begin again, in secret. The antennae of the mutilated had never grown back, but new babes had been born as Mothmage had ever been, and they had kept up their traditions, their training, and their reverence for the Azazel. They learned only later how the Djinn had vanished after the battle. They also learned, to their bitterness, that Onyx had emerged that day as a hero. It was he who rallied the folk to rebuild Nazneen, and in gratitude, they named him king. King Onyx. A spectacular victory indeed.

Of course, Onyx was long dead now and had left no heirs. Even if Hirik were thirsty for vengeance, there was none to be had. Hirik didn't seek vengeance. He sought honor.

Or, he *had*. That fool's dream was over now.

Hirik laid his hand over his brow. He could still feel the brutal tug of Stormfoil's hand on his antennae, and his scent receptors could still taste the murk's sweaty fingers. He wanted to dunk his head in water and rinse it away; it was vile. Sour. And when he thought what might have happened—what had *almost* happened—nausea seized him and flashes of black rolled through his mind, making him dizzy. He shook his head to clear it, but other thoughts, equally unpleasant, rushed in.

How Whisper had looked at him!

Well, she would never have to look at him again. He was going home. His clan would welcome him back without shame. He would return to the simple life he had always known: working and eating, helping the sprouts master swordplay, and taking care that nobody stumbled upon their hidden hamlet in the forest. He would take his turn singing the ancient legends at firetime instead of doing what he had always longed to do: make *new* legends.

A small thought broke through Hirik's misery like a whisper. At first, he didn't want to hear it. *How could you turn your back on her?* it asked him. *How could you just leave her, to Stormfoil and Reaveroot?*

He'd had no choice, he argued with himself. She had sent him away.

But . . . she had not. Hadn't she screamed after him? He remembered the sound and the feel of her cry hitting him mid-air. There had been desperation in it. She had tried to bring him back, and he hadn't listened.

He had given his word on the Azazel's flame that he would see her safely to Nazneen, and what had made him break it? A look. If he thought he'd known shame before, the hot and miserable ache of it now sharpened to something unbearable—a whole new species of shame. It is one thing to be ashamed of a legend, and quite another to be ashamed of oneself.

It was an easy decision, after that. Hirik turned back around. He found the caravan and trailed behind it, keeping far enough back that they couldn't see him.

He had promised Whisper he would see her safely to Nazneen, and he would keep that promise, even if she didn't know it.

TWENTY-FIVE

"There's been a battle."

The words, spoken in an airy voice, sounded next to Magpie's ear. She was in the sky, coursing fast with an escort of winds, and it was one of them who whispered the ill news to her.

"A battle?" she gasped. "Where? Who?"

"Ahead, nigh Nazneen. Devils ambushed a caravan."

"Jacksmoke! Slow down please, cousins," she implored the winds. "Who brings these tidings?"

The winds eased their mad speed, and Magpie and Talon, along with the crows and wagons, clustered together in the clouds while a wisp of a breeze named Lacewing related what she had witnessed. She was an air elemental of slight power, and she told them of dozens of devils. "It had happened to the west, not far from Nazneen," she said. She'd tried to warn the caravan that they were flying into a trap, but the lead murk, a weatherwitch with yellow wings, had grunted, "Out of our path, you feeblething," and brushed her aside.

Magpie was horrified by the news. "What happened? Did anyone die?" she asked, afraid to hear the answer.

Lacewing nodded, and her storm-grey eyes were sad, but she had watched the battle from a distance and couldn't tell them any more than that.

With a shiver, Magpie told Talon, "I'd better go and see. . . ." She stopped, not wanting to speak aloud her fear that when she finally met Whisper Silksinger, it might be in the land of the dead.

Talon nodded. Magpie thanked Lacewing and gave instructions to the winds to resume their course and carry the company onward toward Nazneen. Then she slipped into her wagon, out of sight, to make use of her shortcut to the Moonlit Gardens.

She visioned the glyphs of passage and at once came the soft touch of what felt like moth wings, carrying her across the membrane that separated the living world and the dead. Within seconds she was standing at the riverbank, tense and alert. She was afraid she would find another battle like the one she'd stumbled upon last time she came, but all was serene. Looking across the moving water, she saw the dead gathered as usual, and she held her breath as her eyes sought out the Silksingers. When she spotted them, standing with Bellatrix and Kipepeo, they lifted their hands to wave at her, and she let out her breath.

There was no lass with them.

But there was an unfamiliar lad, and beside him a hobgoblin she knew well: Old Neyn, Zingaro's mother. With a heavy heart, Magpie flew to join them.

She greeted them all solemnly and hugged Old Neyn. The hob biddy was distressed to see her here, thinking she must be dead too, but Magpie quickly explained that she was not. "I can come and go," she said, chewing her lip. She did not enjoy explaining to new dead that she was, in fact, alive; it felt like gloating.

But Old Neyn didn't begrudge her her life. Rather, she muttered a blessing and pressed a bead and feather charm into her hands to keep her safe.

Magpie learned the lad's name was Merryvenom. He had the black hair and brown skin of Zandranath folk, and was wearing the usual murk hodgepodge of old armor. But though he was attired like a murk, Magpie's first impression was that he lacked their usual swagger and had a soulful intelligence in his dark eyes.

It was chiefly he who related what had happened to the caravan, and when he was through, Bellatrix added how the moment he had found himself dead, Merryvenom had launched right back into battle against the slain snags and fought until the riverbank was safe.

"And Whisper?" Magpie asked.

"I don't know," Merryvenom said softly, with a glance at the Silksingers. "I only know she's not dead."

But whether the devils had seized her, he couldn't venture to guess, as he had been killed before the battle's end. Magpie felt a deep regret for this lad's life being cut so short—he wasn't much older than she was, a few decades at most. Her regret only deepened when he told her, "It's an honor to meet you. I . . . I had hoped to be a champion too. That's why I was going to Nazneen, to search for the Azazel."

"You were?"

"I was." He smiled bitterly, resigning himself to the end of his dreams. "I didn't know he was with us all along."

"So, no one knew what Whisper carried in her kettle?" she asked.

Darkly, Merryvenom said, "I guess the devils knew."

Magpie shivered. Indeed they did. She looked at the anxious faces of the Silksingers gathered around her.

"You'll find her, won't you?" asked Whisper's mother.

Magpie nodded and promised she would, and as she returned to the world of the living, she hoped she would be able to keep her word.

TWENTY-SIX

Whisper's dragonfly crested a ridge, and all below her lay Nazneen. She could scarcely believe she was here. Little more than a week had passed since she'd stood at the edge of the Bay of Drowned Dragons with fresh devil wounds on her shoulders, her grandparents' ashes adrift on the wind. If she was honest with herself, she had to admit that she hadn't believed she would make it this far.

A state of dreamlike unreality overtook her as she gazed at the city of her ancestors.

Nazneen was built into a cliff at the knees of Cobra Lily Mountain, in a place where the rock curved inward to form a natural amphitheater safe from the Sayash winds. It faced west, with nothing but eagle-hunted sky before it and, deep, deep in the distance, the sun-flushed peaks of the highest mountains in the world.

Upcliff, the palaces of the noble clans clung to sheer vertical rock face one above another, like stacks of iced cakes. Below, the rest of the city cascaded down a sweep of stair-step tiers, making a pleasing pattern of rooftops and pavilions edged by wild orchid forests, with silver threads of waterfalls stitching them all together.

And in the heart of it, in full sun and splendor, were the golden domes of Rasilith Ev, the Azazel's ancient temple. Dreamy with wonder, Whisper murmured a blessing, and then the dragonflies were diving and the city seemed to rise up all around her. It smelled of blossoms and burnt sugar, and everywhere faeries and birds were darting and fluttering. Pigeon carts soared by, laden with apricots and silk, and there were butterflies and hummingbirds and fine carriages drawn by doves. Gliding in wide circles were plume-helmed guards riding astride peregrines, casting a sharp eye over everything.

Encircling Rasilith Ev was the Great Bazaar, its hundred lanes curved like the whorls of a seashell, and just at its south edge lay the caravan hostelry. It was far grander a place than the outposts Whisper had seen on her journey, with windows of stained glass, and courtyards laid out in octagons, all tiled in lapis and gold.

And then she was landing, her skimmer stuttering to a halt. She dismounted and slowly looked around.

Zingaro was already holding court with a clutch of hobgoblins, and she could see by their looks of gape-tusked shock that he was telling them of the attack. And over by the wall, Stormfoil was drawing a crowd by swinging his severed devil's tail in one hand and his long black pincers in the other, bragging of his kills. Whisper listened for a moment, noting how he neglected to mention both devils had already been stunned when he had slain them. He sprinkled lies into his tale like salt into soup, and his crowd ate it up. More hobs and faeries were flocking into the courtyard to hear, drawn to good gossip as if by some sixth sense.

"And what do you think . . . a Mothmage!" Stormfoil said, his voice a snarl. Horrified gasps greeted the name, but to Whisper it brought an ache. Hirik. He had saved her life. He had left her behind. He was *Mothmage*. But . . . he was Hirik! It made her head and heart hurt just to think of him.

"You should have seen the villain with his nasty twitching feelers," Stormfoil was saying. "I'd have sliced them right off and had them to show you, but the Silksinger lass stopped me—"

"Silksinger!" exclaimed many voices.

At the sound of her own name, some impulse seized Whisper and she slipped away through the gathering crowd, taking advantage of her slight stature to keep any of the company from spotting her.

"Where is the maidy?" she heard Zingaro ask just as she disappeared around the corner. "Maidy?" he called out. For a second she considered going back, but only for a second. She felt guilty, vanishing without a word after everything she'd been through with the hobgoblins, but she just couldn't get caught up in crowds and storytelling right now. She'd come to Nazneen to fulfill an ancient oath, and she meant to do it. She was so close now. She would apologize to Zingaro later.

Hugging her kettle against her chest, she ran to find Rasilith Ev.

Perched on the cliff face high above the city, Hirik watched the caravan land. It was done, he told himself. Whisper was safe. A few days ago, he might have worried what would become of her in the city, but not now. Whisper's days of eating ashcakes and sleeping on stone floors were over. The noble clans would be fighting to host the Silksinger; they'd be tripping over themselves to drape her in jewels and robes, like the lost princess she was.

Was that why she'd come here, he wondered, to claim her birthright? Somehow, that didn't feel like the truth. From the first time he saw her—saw her phantasm, even—there had been some mysterious urgency about her. The more he thought about it, the more he realized he knew nothing about her at all, not even how she'd gotten those devil gouges on her shoulders. Something told him she had more secrets than just her clan name.

He shook his head and tried to clear out all thoughts of her. Here he was, in Nazneen, with his own dreams at his fingertips. His own nightmares too. Right here, near enough to touch, was the huge black streak where Fade's dying breath had turned the rock molten and it had sagged and cooled again to this hard gloss. He put out his hand and touched it. It was almost pretty, seen up close, but its sheen had reflected his clan's darkest hour.

Could he redeem their honor? If he became champion, surely he could. But where should he begin searching for the Azazel? This whole rugged land was pocked with potential dreaming places. Where would the Djinn have gone when he left his temple? For the first time, doubt crept into Hirik's heart. Until now, all his thoughts had been bent on reaching Nazneen. Now that he was here, the search was only just beginning.

Evening fell. The sky went the color of rust as the sun sank, and thousands of tiny lights glimmered to brilliance up and down the city, making Nazneen look like a kingdom of fireflies. Sounds and smells drifted up from below. Hirik was hungry and thirsty. Did he dare venture into town? If Stormfoil and the others should spot him . . . But Nazneen was a sprawling maze of a city. From his perch he could see its serpentine lanes, its dense throngs of folk. He could blend in down there, surely.

He reached up to touch his sash and make sure it was secure over his antennae, and then he combed his hair down over it with his fingers. It would do. He rose to his feet on the little ledge and hesitated there a moment as a weird chill of foreboding crept over him. But he chose to ignore it, spread his wings, and leapt.

TWENTY-SEVEN

Whisper slipped through a silver gate and into the gardens of Rasilith Ev. There was nobody here. She passed among towering orchids and found her way into a series of cloisters, pretty enclosed gardens open only to the sky. Each was empty and very quiet. It wasn't a tranquil kind of quiet, Whisper thought. It was the quiet of *lack*—like that silence long ago that was left in the wake of her parents' death—a wrongness of stolen sound. There should have been fountains burbling, and voices and footfall, and above all, there should have been the soft nicker of flames coming from all the lanterns and niches. But there was none of it.

It felt more like a tomb than a temple.

She crept onward, and there at the nexus of the cloisters stood the great domed hall itself—a magnificent feat of white marble so grand and so vast that all the caravan outposts—which had so daunted her with their size—would have fit inside it together.

The door before her was a giant's door. Seeing it, it

became real to her that the Azazel himself had strode these paths, and a violent tremor of anticipation went through her. Would he again? With trembling fingers, Whisper pushed the door open a crack and slipped inside, into one of the eight chapels that encircled the immense central space of Rasilith Ev like petals on a great flower. It looked just as it was described in legend—except for the darkness, that is.

In the Azazel's day, the temple would never have been dark. Even now a thousand silver lanterns hung from the walls and ceilings, but they were unlit.

Whisper heard a sound. She froze. Breaking out of the desolate quiet, it jangled like some unearthly presence, but it took her only a moment to realize what it was. It was a giggle. There came another in a deeper voice—a lad's giggle following a lass's. Whisper crept across the chapel and peered into the hall. There in the darkness, right where she knew it should be, she could just distinguish the outline of the Azazel's jet-carved throne—that which she had crossed mountains and braved devils to find.

And in it were two faeries . . . *kissing.*

They broke apart and the lass giggled again and shoved playfully at the lad. Her pink wings fluttered as he pulled her up into his lap and nuzzled at her neck. So huge was the throne that the two faeries looked like little dolls posed in a grown-up's chair.

A surge of anger went through Whisper. This was the reverence that faeries showed to the Djinn?

Behind her the door creaked, and she whirled around to see another pair of young faeries come in. She ducked and watched from the shadows as they fluttered past holding hands. "Blessings, lovelarks!" they cried when they saw the others there before them.

Lovelarks? Was this what young faeries did in Nazneen—sneak into the temple to kiss? It would seem so. Over the next half hour more arrived. They were older than Whisper, long-limbed and elegant, though not yet quite grown. And they were beautiful, every one of them, with the dark hair and long eyes of Zandranath folk; they reminded her of Hirik. They lit a few lanterns, and the soft glow cast a sheen over the Azazel's throne so that Whisper could see it clearly—the chair of a giant, with three armrests on each side, one for each of the Azazel's six arms. The lasses tossed their jewel-spangled shawls across it like it was a coatrack.

One lad brought wine and crystal goblets, another a whisker fiddle, and he played reels while the others danced like this was a ballroom.

Crouched in the shadows, Whisper shook with frustration, but what could she do besides wait for them to leave? She sank to her knees and curled her feet up under her. The kettle was cradled in the crook of her arm, its shape so familiar there now, after all these days. She ran her fingertips over its tarnished surface. It was an unfit vessel for a Djinn, certainly. For generations this kettle had hung over the stove in the Silksinger caves, heating water for tea; it had even been patched once or twice. It was no fine thing. But when the devils came, her grandfather had grabbed it and run for the stairs to the Azazel's dreaming place, dumping out the water as he went.

Whisper lifted off the lid. As a sprout, she had often descended into the dreaming place to gaze at this ember and imagine that someday, in her lifetime, the Azazel would wake. Now, she wondered, what would it be like when he did? Would he stir slowly back to life, or would he explode like a flash of dragonfire?

The ember was so beautiful, like sunlight captured in the heart of a ruby. It held eternity within it, and an infinite, unguessable depth of power. To gaze into the heart of a Djinn, even in this sleeping state, was to see into the very locus of Creation.

"The wine's all gone," declared a lass. Blinking, Whisper peered out at the lovelarks, hoping the end of the wine might mean the end of their revelry. She set the lid on the floor and tensed, ready to carry the kettle to the throne the moment they were gone.

"Then let's play twirl-the-bottle!" sang another lass, and Whisper's heart sank.

It was going to be a long evening.

Hirik dropped in among the crowds of Nazneen and let them carry him like a current.

Each lane in the bazaar was dedicated to its own particular commerce: fruit, flutes, spice, dust, silk, silver, stories. By happy accident, Hirik had chanced to find his way to Sweetsellers Lane. It was very narrow, with towering, carved buildings looming on either side. Faeries lolled on balconies, and shop lads fluttered up to them with trays of mint tea. Everything was the color of sherbet and sugarplums, and every shop sold some sweet marvel, from rare wildflower nectar to nut tarts and spice cakes, coconut cream and chocolate soup to blocks of sugarcane jaggery big enough to perch on. Hirik had never imagined such a quantity of sweets, and he scarcely knew how to choose!

When his stomach rumbled, he let a biddy wave him into her shop, where he bought himself a sweet-potato tart slathered with pistachio butter. It was so much better than an ashcake he felt like his taste buds were awakening after a hibernation! A few doors down, he followed it up with an apricot ice in a tall, stemmed glass, and then, with his hunger and thirst satisfied, he wandered.

The lanes spun and twisted, converged, dipped underground, resurfaced, and spilled out into little plazas. Lutenists, fiddlers, and gem jugglers performed for tink, and Hirik paused to watch a scorpion tamer's fearsome dance. Shops sold carpets, gold, flowers, music boxes, honey. There was a lane for apothecaries and one for assassins—alarmed, he peered down that one and saw sword and dagger shops—and he even stumbled upon the mouth of Tattoo Alley. Seeing murks loitering there, he quickly backed away, right into Fortune-tellers Lane.

Fortune-tellers Lane.

Of course. Hirik had a quest, and he had a heavy chain of tink around his neck. Why not consult a fortune-teller to help him with his search? Excited, he drifted into the busy lane and discovered that Nazneen had no shortage of fortune-tellers.

Some saw the future in ancient mirrors, or still water, or the stars. Others read rune stones, or cards, or soggy tea dregs. There were dream interpreters, palm readers, and memory mages. And there was a smoke charmer. He paused when his eyes fell on a hand-painted shingle mounted on the wall.

Ask the Smoke, it read, with a shakily drawn arrow pointing down a set of cellar stairs. Most of the other parlors had rich velvet drapes or shutters painted with stars and moons. By contrast, these cellar stairs had a seedy quality. A thin curl of smoke was wafting up through a crack in a half-moon cellar window at the level of Hirik's knees, but the panes were grimed with tallow grease and he couldn't see inside. The smell of the smoke, though, was unwholesome.

He turned on his heel, resolved to try elsewhere, and nearly stumbled over a biddy standing very close behind him. "Plague!" he said in surprise, unconsciously echoing Zingaro's favorite curse.

"Plague?" returned the biddy. "That's a fine greeting if ever I heard one. Plague to you too, lad." She was unlovely for a faerie, her fat face lined with wrinkles like the crackles in stale bread. A loose flap of skin drooped under her chin in a wattle, and her eyes were tight little puckers, so lost in folds of skin that Hirik couldn't see the whites but just milky green irises. And across the fissured wrinkles of her old lips was a smear of crimson lip paint that might have been applied with a trowel. She was standing so close she was nearly under his nose, and even with his antennae bound he couldn't help catching the scent of her. It was the same scent he had disliked on the smoke—an unpleasant odor that made him think of ugly pickled roots left too long in a cellar.

"Blessings, good aunt," he said, taking a step back.

"I'm Madame Sallowpearl, if it's me you've come to see."

"Nay, thanks," he said. "Just wandering. Pardon me." He attempted to go around her, but she moved quickly and blocked his way.

"Wandering where, though? You came to ask the smoke, neh? So come down and ask."

"Nay, thanks," he said again, but she ignored him.

"The smoke can show you what you seek, wherever it lies hidden."

"How—?" he started to ask, but stopped himself. Only a fool would ask a fortune-teller how she knew what she knew! But how *did* she know he was seeking something hidden? What else, he wondered, might she know about him? Suddenly Hirik felt that the very last place he should be was a lane full of fortune-tellers!

She said, "How? Oh, every soul who comes here is seeking something, lad. Now, come. In a puff of smoke, *seeking* turns to *finding*. Isn't there something you wish to find?"

Indeed there was, but he was still uneasy. Seeing his hesitation, the biddy gestured toward the nearest street lantern, and before Hirik's eyes the smoke wafting from its wick took the form of a dragon in flight. The illusion was every bit as fine as the phantasms he'd seen back at Shark Fin Peak—the smoke dragon even breathed a spurt of real flame—and he found himself succumbing to temptation.

Madame Sallowpearl's grip was surprisingly strong as she led him down the stairs and into a shabby parlor. She started gathering things off shelves: a long-stemmed hookah pipe, a crystal goblet, an earthen bowl filled with withered leaves. "As for the matter of payment . . . ," she said.

"I can pay," Hirik assured her, jingling his tink chain.

"Ach, lad. I've coffers of tink. I've lived nine hundred years on this turning world, and every morning when I wake, my bones ask me if today's the day I'll carry them to the Moonlit Gardens to rest. So far my answer's always: neh, my good bones, not yet! But who knows? Tomorrow I might answer them aye, and then what would I do with more tink? Neh, there's something else you can pay me."

Warily, he asked, "What?"

"I'll give you two choices," she said with an unsavory smile. "A kiss . . ." She let the word linger in the air and Hirik flinched, his eyes going to her wrinkled old lips with their smear of greasy red.

"What's the other choice?" he asked weakly.

"A memory."

"A memory?"

"Aye, a simple thing, neh? Something sweet for a sad old biddy to perk up her last days. A happy memory from home, perhaps? Or you can pay me a kiss."

Hirik was frozen between the two awful alternatives. He very much did not wish to kiss Madame Sallowpearl. But a memory from home! That was a risk he couldn't afford to take. At home his folks never concealed their antennae. Any memory of home would tell her he was a Mothmage, as surely as if he were to uncover his antennae right now.

Pausing to take a gulp of air, he said, "I'll—I'll give you a . . . a kiss."

She cackled, delighted. "Ach, lad! Not many choose the kiss! Come, then, plant one on me." She gave a lusty laugh and puckered up.

Hirik stared at her lips and felt ill. He couldn't even imagine leaning into them with his own lips. He couldn't seem to make himself bend. But then, he didn't have to bend. Madame Sallowpearl came at him. Her wings looked brittle, but they worked just fine when, with a flurry of wing beats, she was suddenly upon him, her hands at his neck and her mouth on his. He felt like he was being gobbled up. Her breath reeked of onions and mildew. Her hands were hard, her mouth slick as she mashed her lips against his and left an oily smear across his face.

He tried to hold his breath as he raised his hands and pried her face off his, then he staggered back, choking. She was off him, laughing her awful laugh, and he doubled over and wiped his mouth with his sleeve. It came away stained from her paint, and he looked up, resentful. She was still laughing. "Ah, good and juicy, my tender lad. Tell me, was it your first?"

He said nothing, but she saw the truth in his eyes and clasped her hands. "A first kiss! Then sure you'll remember it forever! Come, how about another, for practice!"

He thought he might vomit. "You said the price was a kiss and I've paid it."

"That you have, that you have. Stingy! Very well. Now for your fortune. What's it going to be? Talk to the spirits? See the face of the lass you're going to marry?"

"I don't have to say it out loud, do I?"

"Ach, secret, is it? Well, that's no fun for me, but so be it." She set about crushing the dried leaves in a mortar, then packed it into the bowl of the hookah and lit it. She handed Hirik the pipe's serpentine stem. "Breathe in and think of what you wish to find," she said. "Think hard, all your mind on that one thing, and hold it in as long as you can. Then breathe out the smoke, in here—" She handed him the crystal goblet. "And see what comes."

Hirik did as Madame Sallowpearl instructed. He sucked in the smoke and closed his eyes, ignoring the bitter burn in his throat and concentrating as if he were visioning a glyph. *The Azazel. I want to see the Azazel's dreaming place.* He focused his whole mind on it.

He opened his eyes and exhaled into the goblet. He watched, breathless. The smoke roiled like a storm-brewed fog, sifting and swirling before at last settling itself into a shape. It was very clear and very simple—an object he knew well. Confused, Hirik glanced at Madame Sallowpearl.

Was there some mistake? What he saw in the smoke was, unmistakably, Whisper's teakettle.

"That's . . . ," he murmured. "That's not what I wanted to see."

227

"Are you certain?" she asked. "My smoke is honest, even if *I* am not."

He glanced at her, then back at the smoke. She reached out an old gnarled hand and waved it over the goblet so the fume shifted. The kettle was still there, but the smoke seemed to suck it in tight, shrink it, and build a vision around it. He saw then that it was in Whisper's arms and that she was in a great hall. He had to squint to make out the miniature scene inside the goblet, but he did see, and all at once he felt as if the truth collapsed on his head.

So suddenly did it hit him, so greatly did it stun him, that he gave a convulsive squeeze of his hand and the goblet shattered, spraying needles of crystal. He felt them sting his palm but pain didn't register through the shock. He stood mute and stupid as all the pieces of the mystery came together in his mind like a crystal goblet reassembling itself out of shards.

When he had first seen Whisper's phantasm, even then, the smoke had been trying to tell him, it had *shown* him . . . but he hadn't understood. But how could he have? It was absurd! In that old dented kettle, a Djinn? And . . . *Whisper,* guardian of the Azazel? But absurd or not, he knew it was true, and he understood now why her scent had tasted of fire—it had been the Azazel all along. Thinking back over all the past days, Hirik saw what he should have seen from the first: the way Whisper clung to the kettle; even when her dragonfly was falling from the sky she wouldn't let it go. Inside it was the Azazel, and right at this moment, Whisper was standing in Rasilith Ev, preparing to restore him to his throne.

He had to go there.

He turned to Madame Sallowpearl to make his excuses and saw with a shock that she had drawn all his dispersed smoke into a ball between the palms of her hands. She was watching intently as it shaped itself into a scene. With a zing of panic, he saw *what* scene. She had stolen a memory of the proudest moment of his life, when his father and grandfather had presented him with Bijal. He tried to fan away the smoke, but it was too late. There they were. His folk.

Their antennae were as clear as the wings on their backs.

Madame Sallowpearl's puckered eyes widened, and her mouth came open in a gaping O. She sucked in breath to scream, and Hirik knew what that scream would be.

"Mothmage!" she shrieked, stabbing a finger at him. "Traitor! Villain! Murderer! Mothmage!"

He stumbled away from her, groped for the door, and shot out it, slamming it behind himself and visioning a locking spell he hoped would hold her until he got well away. He flew up the stairs.

But there at the top he saw a fume was funneling itself through the broken pane of the cellar window, and it was no ordinary smoke. It was sucking itself together. . . . It was her! Flesh to smoke and back again. Still insubstantial as a phantasm, Madame Sallowpearl opened her mouth, and the voice that came out was full force. "Mothmage!" she shrieked, still pointing at him. "Mothmage!"

Hirik leapt skyward, and she came after, screaming.

TWENTY-EIGHT

From Tattoo Alley, Stormfoil heard the smoke charmer's shriek. His head snapped up. An imp was bent over his forearm, jabbing it repeatedly with a wasp stinger dipped in indigo and soot. When the scream came a second time— "Mothmage!"—Stormfoil leapt to his feet, knocking the imp backward off its chair.

His new tattoo was not finished, but he grabbed his devil's tail off the table where it had been lying for the imp to copy, and he raced out the door, hollering. Reaveroot and Gladprowl were there, a half-empty bottle of throatfire between them, and when Stormfoil said, "Come on!" they followed.

Many voices picked up Madame Sallowpearl's cry, and within seconds the hated name reverberated through Nazneen. It reached down dark alleys and up to the palaces on the cliff. It even found its way into the sanctum of Rasilith Ev.

"What's that?" said one of the lovelarks, hearing an ominous rumble and going to the door to listen. A moment later he cried out. "A Mothmage! In the bazaar! There's a stinking Mothmage in Nazneen!"

The rest rose from their game of twirl-the-bottle. The lasses grabbed their shawls off the throne and swooped like a cloud of butterflies out of the temple before their bottle even stopped spinning.

Whisper had risen to her feet as soon as she heard the name, but none of them noticed her. The door banged shut behind them, and the only sound left in their wake was the ring of glass on marble as their bottle slowed its twirl.

"Hirik . . . ," Whisper said. She had gone as white as the marble around her.

He had come to Nazneen after all! And he was in trouble.

She didn't even have to think. She didn't stoop to pick up the kettle lid but left it where it lay and carried the uncovered kettle to the door, all her thoughts on Hirik. She didn't glance over her shoulder at the Azazel's throne. If she had, she might have seen that the temple's shadows had been veiling more than herself this night. Behind her, a gust of foul breath extinguished the lovelarks' lanterns.

Whisper reached for the door handle, and something reached for her.

Hirik could barely believe how fast the mob had formed—it was like his name was a charm that conjured hate out of thin air!

"Traitor scum!" someone shouted, and hurled a lit cigarillo at him. He dodged it, turning to see menacing faces surrounding him on all sides. He hovered above the rooftops, with faeries jeering and closing in around him. He looked down. The faces of the flightless—imps, hobgoblins—were tipped up to glare at him from the ground. He glanced up. Folk were descending from the cliff palaces to join the crowd, and the Nazneen guards were circling on their peregrines. He could try to flee, but though he was fast, he knew he stood no chance of outpacing a peregrine.

"Listen, goodfolk," he called, still turning on his wings, trying to keep track of the folk all around him. "The legend of the Mothmage, it isn't true—"

Something hit him in the back of the head: a shoe. It fell with a clatter to the rooftop below, and ugly laughs and whistles came from the mob. Hirik saw the hate in their eyes, and he knew there was nothing he could say that would diminish it. They'd been reared on firetime tales of Mothmage villainy, and now they thought they had a villain trapped. They felt like heroes.

Some gents drew daggers. They were gem-crusted things, as lovely as jewelry, and by the way the gents held them, Hirik could see that the daggers might as well have been jewelry. These folk might imagine themselves heroes in the swelling of the moment, but they weren't warriors. Madame Sallowpearl was pointing at him and spitting, "He's

a Mothmage, I tell you! What are you waiting for? Get him!"
But though the gents fingered their jeweled dagger hilts, no
one made a move.

Until.

"Plague! It *is* you!"

Hirik recognized the voice at once and spun toward it.
Stormfoil was rising up from beneath the crowd. He looked
incredulous, and also delighted. "I never would have believed you'd be so daft as to come here, greenwing! Thought
I was going to have to go hunt you down myself." His eyes
were merry and malicious, as they had always been before.
But something was different now. There was new bloodlust
in him, and a swaggering righteousness. He too fancied himself a hero.

Reaveroot and Gladprowl were right behind him. As
one, the three drew their swords. Metal rang as the blades
leapt free of their sheaths, plain, unjeweled, and deadly. At
a gesture from Stormfoil, the other two fanned out to sur-
round Hirik. "Well, *Mothmage,* aren't you going to draw your
fine sword?" he asked, hissing the name like a curse.

Hirik's hand ached to draw Bijal, but he did not. No matter what happened, he could not. All his life he'd dreamed of
clearing the Mothmage name. He couldn't smirch it further
by shedding faerie blood. If he did, it would be as good as
signing a death warrant on his whole clan. They had lived
in safety all these years only because they were assumed

dead. Already he'd exposed them—he couldn't bring greater danger on them by wielding the champion's blade against faeries. Whatever the legends said, Mothmage were not traitors, nor were they killers. And Hirik wouldn't let Stormfoil make him one.

He did not draw his sword, but he did reach up, slowly, and pull the sash free from his brow. A gasp went through the crowd as his antennae unfurled. His senses opened up. All at once it was as if he could see behind himself, below, above, everywhere. He felt exactly where the two murks were positioned behind him, felt their wingbeats riffling the air, even caught the scent of throatfire on their breath. On Stormfoil he smelled blood and soot. On the crowd, excitement.

"See?" demanded Madame Sallowpearl, pointing. "Didn't I say?" To Stormfoil she barked, "I hope you're going to do something about it. That little villain kissed me. I feel sick!"

Stormfoil laughed. "Kissed? Mothmage, you devil, what will your little bridey think, eh? After just one day, already you've found a new love?"

Whisper. Hirik wondered where she was—still in the temple or down on the ground, watching along with everybody else? Was it possible that any soul in the city hadn't heard the commotion? Would she do something to help him? Might she sing? He had a sudden wild hope. Might the Azazel rise like a column of fire and turn all heads toward

235

the temple? It was too much to wish for. There would be no singing, no column of fire. Only blades and hate.

"Well, what are you waiting for, Stormfoil?" he asked through bared teeth. "A thousand on one still not good enough odds for you, coward?"

With a snarl, the murk came at him. Hirik knew when and where Stormfoil was going to move even before he did, and his own wings beat at the same moment, stronger, quicker. He shot up in the air, and as Stormfoil tried to adjust his attack, Hirik dodged the off-kilter thrust of his blade and spun to deliver a kick to the murk's hand that sent his sword spinning out of his grasp. "Oof!" Stormfoil grunted. The rooftop gawkers skittered clear of the weapon as it flashed toward them, end over end.

Reaveroot and Gladprowl launched themselves next, two on one. Hirik faced them, dodging their sword thrusts as they circled him. The fine hairs of his antennae riffled ceaselessly as he kept track of their every move—Gladprowl in front, Reaveroot behind. He guessed the coward Reaveroot would make a stab for his back, and he did. Hirik anticipated it, moving out of the way just in time so that the blade, intended to pierce his shoulder, sailed above it instead. Reaveroot pitched off balance and Hirik grabbed his forearm with both hands and twisted hard.

"Aah!" cried Reaveroot as his sword too fell to the rooftops.

With another spinning kick, Hirik dodged a slash from Gladprowl's blade, darted in close, and, by simultaneously bringing his knee sharply up and his elbow down on the murk's arm, disarmed him too.

Hirik had been training in combat since he was big enough to wave a stick, and the Mothmage way of battle was as it had ever been. Fighting, the goal was never to kill, but to disarm and capture, and Hirik had learned his lessons well. In less than a minute, three full-grown murks had lost their swords to him.

"Ach, you wastrels!" screamed Madame Sallowpearl. "Get him!"

His face crimson with rage and humiliation, Stormfoil drew a new weapon out of his belt: a long, limp tube of flesh with a spiked ball at its end. Watching him through narrowed eyes, Hirik recognized it. "You kill that devil after I stunned it, Stormfoil?" he asked. "Sounds about like you."

With a roar, Stormfoil flew at him. Hirik dodged. The murk spun around and lashed out wildly with the tail, but it didn't come anywhere near Hirik, who feinted left and darted right, easily beyond his reach. Reaveroot and Gladprowl dropped down to retrieve their swords, and the rest of the mob clung together, watching and shouting. It was just Hirik and Stormfoil for the moment.

And then came the smoke.

All the wisps fluting up from all the chimneys of Nazneen

suddenly obeyed a silent call and funneled together into a soot-clotted cloud. Madame Sallowpearl raised her arms like an orchestra conductor. The venom green of her eyes brightened, her fingers jerked and spasmed, and the cloud suddenly broke apart into myriad distinct shapes: moths.

A huge flock of smoke moths was born out of the air, darting erratically across the wind and looking for all the world like true moths. Hirik would have been able to command true moths, but these were a masterpiece of the smoke charmer's art, and they obeyed only their creator. At a mute signal from Madame Sallowpearl, they dove at him.

He was swallowed by the flock. They beat at his face, shoved their way into his mouth and nose. He choked. He was blind. He whirled to break free of them.

Then came the first blow.

The spikes of the devil's tail sank into his shoulder and he felt a seeping numbness around the wound. Venom.

Stormfoil crowed, "Got him!" and then Hirik felt another strike, this time to his leg. "Got him again!" The venom acted so fast that the stabbing pain of the spines was erased almost at once by a spreading deadness.

The smoke moths began to drift away. Hirik coughed to clear his lungs. He could see again. Stormfoil was swinging the tail over his head, and the mob was cheering. The numbness was spreading fast, down to Hirik's fingers and up to his shoulder. His arms hung limp. The poison swept across his back, and he began to lose control of his wings and drop, slowly, in little jerks and spasms, lower and lower in the air.

"Hoy, look!" said Reaveroot. "I think you've done something to him!"

"Skiving right I have," said Stormfoil. Seeing Hirik's helplessness, he closed in, grabbed him by the shoulders, and wrestled him down to a roof. The mob shifted and dropped too, all those necks craning to watch. "You two, hold his arms!" Stormfoil ordered, and Reaveroot and Gladprowl did, though they needn't have bothered. Hirik's body might as well have been a wooden weight dangling from his neck. He couldn't feel it at all.

Stormfoil drew Bijal from Hirik's sheath. He brandished it and announced, "Look, I think I just got myself a new sword, lads. You like it?" He whirled, showing off with it. Hirik clenched his teeth, hating to see Bijal in Stormfoil's possession.

But the moment the murk slashed the scimitar down in a practiced arc, a blue vein of lightning sizzled to life on the steel, as it had done in Hirik's hands when devils were near. But this time, instead of loosing a bolt to strike down a foe, the lightning leapt backward and engulfed Stormfoil's arm. He emitted a shrill wail as the force of the charge threw him hard against a chimney stack. He dropped Bijal. His wail trailed off and he stared down at his hand. Smoke was rising from his fingertips.

When he looked back up, his face was transfigured by fury, making him ugly as a devil. With a push from his wings he rushed at Hirik and grabbed his antennae like weeds he wanted to yank out of hard earth. "Reave, give me your sword!" he hissed.

And Reaveroot did.

Whisper was halfway out the temple door when something coiled around her neck and jerked her backward. Her breath choked off and her feet left the floor, and before she could even register what was happening, she was reeled deep into the darkness of the temple.

Only her habit of clinging to the kettle kept her from dropping it in shock. She grasped it tight. Her free hand flew to the thing at her throat. It was a slick, clammy coil, twining itself tighter. She tried to scream, but as soon as she opened her mouth another probing thing slithered across her face and clamped down. She gagged on the vile taste of it and writhed, trying to get free.

More coils trussed her arms and legs and dragged her over the floor.

She couldn't speak or scream, could barely breathe, but she managed to vision one of the simplest of glyphs and an orb of light glimmered up around her.

She saw what held her.

What devils had hunted her so far had been winged

monsters of the air. This was something else altogether. It was a boneless, quivering thing—a huge, pale *tube* of a creature. Its head was nothing but a pulsing sucker framed by a ruff of tentacles, and it was the tentacles that held her, strong as the banded musculature of serpents. It was slithering backward and disappearing into a hidden trapdoor in the marble floor, and as much as she struggled, Whisper couldn't get free. The devil dropped into the dark with a squelch and sucked her down with it. A marble slab folded neatly back into place, leaving behind no hint of an opening in the floor.

All was quiet in Rasilith Ev. Whisper and the Azazel were gone.

Once before, Stormfoil had brought his sword down at Hirik's antennae. That time, Whisper had been there to stop him. This time, the blade cut across the feathery stalks in one quick cut, so close to the flesh they scraped his forehead and drew blood.

Stormfoil held them up over his head, but the sad things made no proud trophy. They wilted and withered the moment they were severed and hung limp in his fingers like the dead things they were.

Hirik's senses slammed in around him, as if someone had thrown him in a grave and closed it over him. It wasn't like keeping his antennae coiled and covered. All his delicate sensitivity to the atmosphere was gone in an instant, and with it his equilibrium. With his body deadened and his senses stolen, he could have been anywhere, upside down, underground. He might even have been ripped out of his body.

The numbness from the poison had spread up his neck, and even his face was losing sensation. His tongue felt heavy. Breathing was difficult. He realized, with a dull jolt of surprise, that he was dying. Everything around him was muffled and silent, and he thought for a moment his hearing was failing. But just before he lost consciousness, he got a glimpse of the faces of the mob around him and saw they had fallen silent. They looked confused. A sprout was weeping into his mother's neck.

They had no heart for vengeance after all, Hirik saw, and he was glad. He thought one last time of Whisper and the Azazel and sent them a silent blessing. Then darkness came and took him away.

TWENTY-NINE

The devil dragged Whisper down a tunnel. It was utterly dark. Her spelled light had flickered out in her panic and she was afraid of what she might see if she conjured it again.

Besides the slither of the devil's big grub body through the mud, she heard other things: the scuttle of beetles, the drip of drains, and once a sound like a chuckle deep in some wet throat. The stench was cloying: mold, decay, guano, and worse. Horror and panic rolled through Whisper in waves, and minute slid into minute as the creature dragged her deeper underground, twisting and turning through a black labyrinth of tunnels. Sometimes she felt space open around her and heard, high overhead, the chirp and swoop of bats. Other times the beast had to squeeze itself through cracks or belly into some stream with a splash and ooze along in it, over chutes and flumes where the waters of Nazneen drained down through the porous rock. Down, and down.

And down.

And then, ahead, she saw a light. It wavered at the end

of a long black passage, and as her captor brought her nearer to it, Whisper began to see the silhouettes of many creatures. She could hear them roaring and snarling. If there was any dim hope of escape left in her, it vanished when she realized that here, directly beneath Nazneen, lay the devils' lair. All the time she had thought she was fleeing them, she had really been carrying the Azazel right *to* them.

The narrow tunnel spilled into a cavern and she saw all around a profusion of barbarous beasts. Their heads were horned and spined, their bodies abristle with jags and spikes, barbs and fangs and gnarled claws. They were crammed in such close quarters that when one reared its restless head, it speared another's eyeball with the tip of its antler, sending up a gout of blood.

The two devils snapped at each other, but they didn't fall to fighting. The one with the bloody eyeball merely squinted it shut and turned to watch Whisper with its remaining eye. In the whole cavern—and its high-vaulted ceiling was crawling with devils too—all eyes turned to her.

Her captor released her and retreated in a slow slither, each inchworm roll of its body squeezing a spurt of slime out its sucker mouth and leaving a trail. It settled back among its fellow devils and, though it had no discernable eyes, joined them in watching her. She stood in their midst, scarcely daring to breathe, but none of them made a move. The moment stretched itself out, pulsing with a sense of waiting . . . *but for what?*

"Ah, here you are at last, my little Silksinger."

Clinging to her kettle, Whisper spun to face the voice. She couldn't see who—*what*—had spoken. It was coming out of an opening in the rock, and the lantern glow couldn't reach it, but Whisper sensed something very wrong in the complicated way it stirred the darkness. There was just too much movement, no shape she could make sense of. Legs.

How many legs?

A spider, she thought wildly, though it was far too big to be a spider—perhaps half the size of a human—but then her eyes traveled upward and she saw the rest of the thing, its broad bare torso like a man's, muscle-bunched and scarred. And its hideous head. Its mouth was opening to speak—it was a mouth such as belonged to a tarantula, its fangs flexing open, unfolding. And shining black clusters of eyes, each reflecting Whisper's terrified face back at her.

"What a lot of trouble you've been, faerie. How many of my soldiers have flown to their death chasing you, and such a tender slip of nothing you turn out to be!" Its voice was garbled, thick, coming as it did from that mouth so obviously not formed for faerie speech.

"Wh-what *are* you?" Whisper stammered in a tiny voice.

"I am Ethiag," it said, and throughout the cavern, devils echoed the name in a wild chorus. "Ethiag! Ethiag! Ethiag!"

Whisper backed slowly away from him. She had no delusions of escaping; her feet simply moved of their own accord. She knew too that she couldn't protect the Azazel any longer, but still her arms tightened around the kettle.

"Give that to me," Ethiag said.

Her heart thudded. "Nay!" she cried, and this time it was her own voice that echoed through the cavern. It flowed out of her charged with glyphs, and a ripple of agitation went through the devils that seemed to shake them from their unnatural calm. They bellowed, pawed the ground, and hissed at each other, and for a moment it seemed as if they would break into chaos, but with a bark in his own devilish language, Ethiag settled them again.

He laughed. "Valiant little morsel you are, but it won't do you any good," he said, and came at her, his legs hypnotic in their rhythm, rising and falling, no two at the same moment.

Still backing away, Whisper looked down into the kettle. With the lid gone, she could see straight in to the precious ember. "Please," she whispered with a sob. "Lord, please wake!"

The ember didn't even glimmer.

Obeying a silent command, a devil reached out with a crab claw, seized Whisper by her hair, and hurled her back toward Ethiag. Her little wings fluttered uselessly and couldn't slow her momentum. Ethiag caught her. She was enfolded in his legs, their bristles scratching her like briars, and Ethiag easily prized the kettle out of her arms and lifted it away. It was so small in his hands, like a toy. He released Whisper into a heap on the ground and peered down into the kettle. "So, this is the great Azazel," he said, laughing.

Whisper's arms felt terribly empty. "What do you want with him?"

"You should worry more about what I want with *you*, Silksinger."

"Me?" Whisper hadn't even thought of herself. She looked up at Ethiag as awful possibilities crowded her imagination.

"Aye, you. Don't you wonder why you're still alive? But you must. Of course . . . you have a choice. I can't *make* you do what I wish. I can only tell you that if you won't, there's only one other use I'll have for you, and I think you'll like it even less." He clicked his fangs to demonstrate his point.

"What . . . what do you want?" Whisper asked.

"You're a Silksinger, aren't you? What do you think I want? I won't sit idle while my soldiers take Nazneen. Nor will I crawl when I should soar. I will lead my army, Silksinger, and I will *fly*, because you will sing me a carpet fit for a conquering king!"

Aghast, Whisper shook her head. "Nay, I won't."

"Neh?" said Ethiag, giving an awful chuckle that made his fangs click.

"I won't help you attack faeries—"

"The attack will go on no matter what you do. What do you think, you can prevent it? It is the eve of war. A new age is coming. Faeries might think the Djinn are returning, but we know better, you and I!" He tapped the kettle. "The new age will be a devil age. This is only the first battle. We will conquer the world!"

"You won't! There's a new champion—"

"One champion! Against this?" He swept his arm and gestured around the cave. Devils howled and grunted. There were hundreds of them, and the faeries up above had no idea. It would be a massacre.

A memory came to her then of Hirik's blade sizzling with lightning as he fought off the devils in the sky. He would come, she thought wildly. He would stop them! Then she remembered. Before the tentacles had seized her, the cries of "Mothmage!" in the city. What had happened? A new note of panic arose to join the others in her mind, like the urgent trill of a flute entering the flow of a symphony.

"You see my army," Ethiag said. "Know war will come whether you sing or not. And if you don't sing, if I have to eat you instead, the invasion will simply begin *now*."

Whisper trembled. She wasn't brave enough to surrender herself to such a death. "I'll do it," she whispered.

"Oh, I know you will," said Ethiag. "What will you need?"

"Silk thread."

"That's all?"

She nodded.

"I'll have it brought," said the devil. "Now, let me show you to your new home." He came at her and she leapt back. She stumbled ahead of his tarantula legs as he pushed her across the cavern and then down a long passage, through a filthy kitchen, into a corridor of iron-barred cells.

There were prisoners in them that Whisper could scarcely identify as she went by. Imps and such creatures as she had never seen. Miserable, lank, listless, they were so still as to seem dead, yet their eyes slowly tracked her as she passed. And then Ethiag thrust her into a cell and clanged the door shut. "Make yourself comfortable, Silksinger. And heed my words. Your voice belongs to me now. You'll use it how I tell you or not at all, and as long as you do, you'll live. Understand?"

Whisper nodded, and Ethiag laughed and left her crouched in her cell, shaking and hugging her knees. She waited a long moment, and when he was gone, she crept tentatively forward and tried to peer into the dark cell opposite her own.

"Hello?" she whispered.

No answer came. She knew she was not alone—she

could hear shallow breathing coming from the other cells and see figures in the gloom, but no one answered her. She crept back from the bars, her eyes filling with tears.

Again her mind turned to Hirik, and again that fluting panic trilled through her mind and heart. Was he okay? Had they caught him? And if they had . . . what had they done to him?

She recalled the little shard of ice mirror in her pocket. Eagerly, she fished it out and gazed into it, wondering if it would show him to her.

It did, and what she saw turned her heart as cold as the little mirror.

She saw him lying limp, his hair shoved aside to reveal his bare brow—only a smear of blood there, and no antennae. His eyes were open and glassy. Stormfoil was looming over him, nudging him with his foot, but there was no response at all. Whisper gasped and dropped the shard. It shattered into tiny fragments and melted back to water.

Hirik was *dead*.

THIRTY

"Nazneen ho!" croaked Calypso as the crow-drawn wagons soared over the ridge and the moonlit city opened up beneath them. At once they saw the crowd gathered over the bazaar.

"What's going on down there?" asked Talon.

"Flummox me," said Magpie, squinting to see. The city lay far below, but she could make out what had to be hundreds of faeries packed together, wings densely clustered and shimmering like a swarm of butterflies. "Must be every faerie in the city!"

"Looks like a feeding frenzy," observed Maniac.

"Feather, faeries don't have feeding frenzies," said Magpie.

"Well, it's some kind of frenzy," replied the bird.

"Maybe it's the Azazel," said Talon hopefully. "Maybe he's woken up!"

"That would sure draw a crowd," said Magpie. She wanted to believe that was it, but something felt wrong. Shouts and hoots were drifting up from the crowd, echoing

251

in the sheltered curve of the cliff, and though she couldn't make out the words, she detected an ugly edge to them. Maniac was right. It *was* some kind of frenzy.

"Talon, Calypso, Swig, with me," she said. The other five crows were hitched to their wagons, and she directed them to continue to the hostelry. "We'll meet you there."

"What about me?" demanded Batch, who was hanging half out the window of Bertram's wagon.

Magpie bit her lip, considering. Then she looked at Bertram and said with resolve, "Feather, when you set down, turn the irkmeat loose. Blessings, Master Hangnail! May our paths not cross again!"

His beady eyes widened. "Flotch!" he cried. "For true?"

Deeply relieved to have done with him, Magpie folded her wings, gave him a wave, and dropped straight out of the imp's line of sight. She let herself fall a long way feetfirst before tipping back her head and arching her back to flip gracefully over to a dive. A few more seconds of fast falling and she flicked her wings to slow her descent. Talon and the crows were right behind her.

The noise of the crowd rose as they descended, but they still couldn't see what was at its center. It was just too dense, with hovering faeries closing off any aerial view. When they reached the outer edges, they dove in and darted through the fluttering folk. There seemed to be a lot of confusion as faeries struggled to see around each other.

"What happened?" folk were asking.

"Can you see?"

"Did they get him?"

Magpie exchanged a worried look with Talon, and they abandoned any attempt at politeness and just shoved their way through, the crows squawking behind them. They reached the inner circle of gawkers as the shouting gave way to a weird hush that was more unnerving than the shouts had been.

And then they heard, in a stage whisper that carried the unmistakable tone of gossip, "I think he's *dead*." Magpie thrust the rest of the way through the throng and saw at last the scene on the rooftop.

A lad lay on the glossy roof tiles, eyes open and unseeing. A mercenary stood over him, sword in hand, and nudged him with one foot, but the lad's body was limp and the nudging evoked no response. Two more mercenaries stood by, watching. Magpie felt ill. In all her life, she had never seen one faerie slay another. Strong grown gents, the three of them towered over the lifeless lad, and the sight shocked her deeply.

Dropping to her feet on the rooftop, she cried, "What happened here?"

The mercenary in the center whirled round and took her in with a disdainful up-and-down glance. She disliked him on sight. He looked sly, with cruel eyes and an upper lip that curled somewhere between a smile and a snarl. He drawled, "Who's asking?"

"*I* am!" she snapped, stalking toward him.

"You? Well, I don't answer to sprouts," he said dismissively, and started to turn back around.

Calypso squawked, "Show some respect, ye sad murdering excuse for a faerie! This is the Djinn King's champion!"

"Skive! Really?" To his two fellow mercenaries, he said, "Reave, she really *is* no higher than an armpit!"

"Shut it, Stormfoil," muttered the other, shifting uneasily from foot to foot.

Overhead, a chorus of gasps had gone up in the crowd, and a murmur began to build like a drone of bees, but Calypso was louder. "Ach!" he squawked. "Clamp yer gossipholes up there! Did ye just flitter there and watch him do it? Ye should be ashamed!"

A stuttering silence redescended. Brushing past the murk, Magpie dropped to her knees beside the lad. Talon knelt at her side. "Is he really dead?" he asked.

"I don't know." She scanned him up and down with her eyes and saw no sign of a wound. What had happened, then? "Lad?" she said, leaning over him. "Can you hear me?" She put her hand up to his throat and held her thumb under the curve of his jaw to feel for a pulse. His throat was warm. She felt no immediate throb of blood against her thumb but she didn't give up. "What did you do to this faerie?" she growled over her shoulder.

"Faerie? He's *Mothmage!* That hardly counts."

"Mothmage!" said Magpie, swinging back around to stare at the lad. She didn't know what she would expect a Mothmage to look like. Some hulking gent with beetle-black eyes and the taint of treachery on him? This lad looked just like any faerie. She said, "Whatever his clan, to kill a faerie—"

"I didn't kill him. I don't know what's wrong with the scrunt. I only cut off these."

He held up a scraggly bundle that vaguely resembled limp feathers. Magpie saw what they were at once, and she realized why the lad looked like any other faerie. She knew what silk moth antennae should have looked like, proud and alert. These were nothing like that; they were dead. Fury built in her, tingling down to her fists so she had to draw her hands quickly away from the lad and clasp them hard while she willed herself to contain it. She said, "You cut off his antennae."

Smirking, Stormfoil said, "Aye, is there a reward?"

"There's no reward for mutilation!" Magpie cried, leaping to her feet.

"Mutilation!" he spat. "Call it a haircut!"

The rage escaped her fists. Some traceries of magic collided harmlessly with the roof tiles and dissipated. She had a powerful urge to aim them at the mercenary and see what happened. But Talon, who had put his own fingers to the lad's throat, said, "There! I feel a pulse, real thin."

Blessings, thought Magpie. But she still didn't know what was wrong with him. Eyes flashing, she faced the murk and commanded, "Tell me what you did to him, *now!*" The air came alive around her and crackled like an electrical storm.

Feeling the overflow of her power, Stormfoil took a step back, his sly surliness vanishing. "I—I just hit him with that—" he stammered, pointing across the roof.

Magpie's eyes followed his finger. She saw the severed devil's tail and recognized it for what it was. "Skive!" she hissed through her teeth. She turned quickly to Talon. "He's poisoned the lad with fugu venom. If it's not too late already, this glyph—" She visioned the glyph Bellatrix had taught her when she'd been poisoned with the same venom, then reached out and touched Talon on the brow, passing it into his mind. They closed their eyes and focused on the Moth-mage lad as Bellatrix and Kipepeo had focused on Magpie, and together they poured a flow of healing into him to strain the poison out of his blood.

When the crowd started to murmur, Calypso and Swig flapped their wings and flashed menacing looks around at all the peering faces. Stormfoil was casting furtive glances around as if looking for some escape route. Calypso told him, "Don't think ye'll get very far if ye try it, coward."

At last Magpie sat back and opened her eyes, giving Talon a light touch on the shoulder to indicate they were finished. Anxiously, they watched the lad.

His eyes, open and glassy, shifted. His lashes fluttered and he drew a sudden, ragged breath. Magpie breathed out a long sigh of relief and let her shoulders slump. Talon squeezed her hand.

The lad looked up at the two unfamiliar faces bent over him and blinked in confusion.

"It's okay," Magpie told him. "Just stay still. We're going to get you to an apothecary."

He parted his lips and managed to murmur, "Whisper—"

"Whisper!" Magpie repeated, eagerly leaning closer to him. "Aye, lad?"

His eyelids were fluttering as if he were struggling against unconsciousness. Delirious, he whispered, "Kettle."

Magpie and Talon exchanged a significant glance. So somebody *did* know Whisper's secret—a Mothmage, no less. "What about it?" Magpie asked, but to her dismay, the lad's words made no more sense after that.

"Calypso," she asked, "can you carry him?"

"Course, 'Pie," said the crow, hopping forward.

"Then let's get him out of here."

She rose to her wings and flew across the roof to the fugu tail. "Swig, do you mind carrying this awful thing?" She handed it to him, warning, "Be careful with it."

"Hoy, that's mine," protested Stormfoil.

Magpie looked at him. "To my way of thinking, using devil venom to kill a faerie makes you a devil yourself."

"How was I supposed to know it had venom in it?" he asked peevishly. "And anywhich, he's not dead, is he?"

"For which you should be very glad!" It occurred to Magpie to wonder how he'd come into possession of a fugu tail. Might he be the same yellow-winged murk who had ignored the breeze Lacewing's warning of a devil ambush? "Are you with Zingaro's caravan?" she asked him.

"Aye," he said. "So?"

"The Silksinger lass," she snapped. "Where is she?"

"How in hollerbelly should I know?" he asked. "Do I look like her mammy?"

Magpie's patience was spent. Even clenching her fists could not prevent the sudden surge of her fury from escaping. This time it did not cascade harmlessly down onto the roof tiles but spurted out between her fingers and flew straight for a collision with the murk's sneering face.

In a twinkling, his sneer was wiped away. His lips bulged out, and right before Magpie's eyes, four tusks grew from his jaws, just like a hobgoblin's. They began small and sprouted fast, two curving down, two up. His eyes crossed as he watched the sharp ivory points come straight for his eyeballs. He gave a terrified squeak, and just in time, the tusks stopped growing.

"Jacksmoke," muttered Magpie, cringing as she surveyed her accidental handiwork. The murk's lips were stretched out of all shape, pulled tight and bloodless across the expanse of his newly gaping mouth. With a guttural holler, he reached up and seized the ivory spikes and tried to wrestle them off, jerking his head forward with each tug. The tusks didn't budge, but the effort knocked him face-forward on the roof, and Magpie noticed the tusks were not his only new body part. From his backside sprouted a long, tufted hobgoblin tail.

A clamor had risen in the mob, but over the noise she could still hear the murk shouting. His voice was made mushy by his huge new teeth, and it sounded something like, "Ud id oo oo oo ee?"

What did you do to me?

Magpie didn't know. She never knew. Her power blurted into the Tapestry and made messy knots in its threads and creation was . . . rearranged. Sometimes the knots were useful—indeed, the Magruwen had said that without them the Tapestry would already have fallen apart. But sometimes they were like this: wild and ridiculous.

Shamefaced, she looked over at Calypso. If she thought the crow would scold her, she was surprised. "I wouldn't make 'Pie mad, if I was ye," he was saying to the other two murks. "If ye know where the Silksinger lass is, now's the time to speak up."

The answer came very quickly. "Last we saw her was at the hostelry!"

The hostelry. Magpie felt a fist unclench in her chest as the worst of her fears abated. Whisper had made it to Nazneen.

"But," the murks went on to say, "she went off. Nobody's seen her."

Of course, thought Magpie, the anxiety clenching back up in her chest. Nothing could be easy.

Stormfoil had managed to turn over onto his back and was still wrestling with his tusks, giving short, panicked shouts.

"Listen," she said, kneeling beside him. "I'll ask the Magruwen to undo that spell, but for now you're just going to have to live with it, you ken?"

He blubbered an unintelligible reply, tears streaking his red face, and Magpie felt the tiniest bit sorry for him. Then she spotted the wilted antennae still clutched in his fist and her pity evaporated. "Give me those," she said, grabbing them and tucking them into her pocket.

She helped Talon lift the Mothmage lad up onto Calypso's back. They were about to fly off when a small voice said, "Wait!"

Magpie turned to look up at the crowd, both scornful of them and ashamed of her own loss of control. What a way to present herself, the first Djinn's champion in twenty-five thousand years! It was a sprout who had called out. His face was streaked with tears, and his hand shook as he pointed and said, "You forgot his sword."

A scimitar was lying on the roof. Magpie went to pick it up. With a shock, she recognized it. The wood-grain pattern of its steel—the result of an infinite number of folds in the forging process—was unmistakable. Bellatrix and Kipepeo had taught her about the champions' ancient weapons, each with its own unique magic, like her own Skuldraig. And here was none other than Bijal, the lightning sword of Manathakkali. Curious about its owner, she slipped it back into the sheath at his side.

THIRTY-ONE

Apothecary Lane was a prosperous avenue of the bazaar where all the shops had tall windows displaying shelf upon shelf of jars full of herbs and seeds, petals and powders, bits of bark and knobs of roots. Shop signs all depicted the mortar and pestle that were symbols of the medicine makers' trade, and they bore names like The Serpent's Gall, and Ashes & Dust, and Eldritch's House of Cures. Magpie guided Talon and the crows to one called The Dragon's Scale.

The windows were dark, the door locked. She gave it a hard thumping with one hand and tugged on the bell chain with the other, then leaned close to peer through the glass. In spite of all her tension, she felt a little flush of warmth at the sight of the familiar shop. There were times and places from Magpie's sprouthood that stood out brighter in her memory than the rest of her family's gypsy wanderings. Seasons spent hither and thither, faerieholds and folk she recalled with a special fondness for the feeling they had given her of belonging someplace, even for a little while. Dreamdark and pretty Poppy Manygreen were among them, and so were The Dragon's Scale and the apothecary who owned it.

Some fifty years ago Magpie and her folk and crows had come to Nazneen searching for the Azazel, and though they had found no trace of the Djinn, they had made a very good friend.

"En't he there, 'Pie?" asked Calypso.

"Probably back in that mob, like everybody else," said Talon.

"Neh, not Dusk," Magpie said. "If he was, he'd have stopped it!"

"Dusk?" asked Talon. "You know this apothecary?"

Swig made a smooching sound and said, "Know him? He's her sweetheart."

Instantly a blush rose from Magpie's neck to her hairline. "Jacksmoke, spatherbeak!" she cursed. "He's no such thing!"

"Neh? Seem to recall ye saying ye were going to *marry* him."

"Ach, hush!" she replied hotly. "I was just a sprout, wasn't I?"

"Still a sprout," said Calypso.

"Neh, I'm not," she said, giving the bell chain a sharp, jangling pull. With a quick glance at Talon, who had remained silent, she said, "And anywhich, he's old enough to be my father!"

"I don't think he's here," said Talon.

"Maybe he's downstairs. That's where his library is." She knocked on the door again. Another moment passed and there was still no movement within. Magpie frowned and looked over at the Mothmage lad. He was astride Calypso, slumped forward against the crow's neck. He was breathing, blessings be—he was *alive*—but there was a ghastly pallor to his brown skin, giving him a yellowish hue, and his eyes were closed and underscored by blue bruises. She'd been able to dilute the venom, but she guessed he was far from well. He needed an apothecary.

"Maybe we should try somewhere else," suggested Talon.

Magpie chewed her lip and glanced around. The lane was still pretty empty, but since the mob had started to break up, faeries were fluttering back down to land. She fancied she could hear the malignant spread of gossip reaching its way to every corner of the city, expanding now to include news of her own dramatic arrival. She was proven right when, a few doors down, a pair of ladies in shimmery dresses caught sight of her and started pointing and whispering. Magpie had no difficulty hearing them with her sharp ears.

"That can't really be the champion, can it?" one murmured under her breath.

"Nay, surely not. She's so . . . *dirty.*"

Magpie shot them a glare and turned away, only to catch her reflection in Dusk's window. Her chestnut hair was wind-frazzled, half pinned in a braid many days old, and the rest of it sticking out in tufts so she could barely tell which was her foxlick. Add to that her faded and much-mended green leggings and too-big firedrake-scale tunic, and she saw all too well what the ladies were staring at. She thought she looked like a very small hobgoblin—though unlike a certain mercenary, she lacked the tusks and tail.

So be it, she thought belligerently, giving the bell chain a tug so hard it tore away in her hand. "Skive," she grumbled. Clearly, Dusk wasn't in. She was just about to concede defeat and take the Mothmage to another apothecary when a light flickered on in the back of the shop. "Coming, coming!" called a deep voice, musical but unmistakably irritated. "This had better be an emergency!"

A key rattled in the lock and the door swung open. The apothecary was a tall, broad-shouldered faerie with massive butterfly wings of velvety black and palest green. His face was strong and striking, with elegant cheekbones and full red lips. His hair was the glossy black of young crow feathers, and his skin shone like dark copper. Against that rich coloring, his eyes, pale green like his wings, were luminous.

"Ah, it *is* an emergency, as it happens," said Magpie, finding herself suddenly shy. She hadn't seen Dusk in so long, and it occurred to her now that he might not remember her. In an uncharacteristically small voice, she said, "We've need of an apothecary."

Dusk took in the sight of the crows and young faeries on his doorstep. His eyes lingered on Talon's pale hair—a rare sight in this part of the world—and facial tattoos and crow wings—rare anywhere—and then on the lad slumped over on Calypso's back. Last, his gaze settled on Magpie, and in a blink, vexation turned to amazement. "Little Terror!" he declared, and the green of his eyes seemed to brighten, like jade struck suddenly by the sun. "Is it really you?"

Magpie's cheeks turned the color of strawberries. He did remember her. "Aye, it's me," she said with a shy smile. "Blessings."

He took a step toward her and she outfaced her palms to him in the faerie greeting, but he swept her hands aside with a low laugh and grabbed her up into a crushing hug that lifted her right off the ground and made her sleek wings flutter.

Talon's jaw clenched. The hug, he thought, went on longer than it had to, and when Dusk set Magpie back on her feet, he kept his hands on her shoulders and smiled down at her in a way that reminded Talon, with a flash of irrational resentment, of the marveling look Magpie gave *him* whenever he did something fine.

Laughing, Dusk said, "I can scarcely believe it. Little Terror Windwitch! But . . . I suppose it's disrespectful to call you Terror now? What should it be? Lady Champion?"

"Neh, I don't mind Terror," said Magpie.

"Little Terror, Magruwen's champion! I wondered when I might see it for myself! And now here you are in Nazneen, standing on my step."

His clear delight at seeing her made Magpie a little giddy, and she had to remind herself this was not a social call. "We just arrived this minute," she said, glancing over her shoulder at the Mothmage lad.

Dusk followed her look. "And here is your emergency," he said. "What's happened to him?"

"Fugu venom," said Magpie.

"Fugu!" he exclaimed. "Nay, I'm sure you're mistaken—"

Magpie cocked her head at Swig, who held up the severed tail and let it sway back and forth.

Dusk's eyebrows shot up. "As I said, I'm sure you're *right*. Bring him in at once." He drew aside to let Calypso pass, and the crow bore his passenger through the doorway.

The front room of The Dragon's Scale had a ceiling three times the height of a gent, with shelves all the way up to it. There were brass instruments, gold-leafed books, and all manner of potions in bottles and flasks. Everything sparkled, and behind an elegant marble counter was the store's namesake, framed in gold: a large, copper dragon's scale.

"How long ago was he struck?" Dusk asked. The lad

was still on Calypso's back, eyes closed, while Dusk felt his pulse.

Magpie said, "I'm not sure. Maybe fifteen minutes ago?"

"Surely not. He'd be dead by now."

She told him quickly about the healing spell she and Talon had visioned, and a look of awe came over his face. He murmured, as if to himself, "That spell was lost," then asked her, "Where did you learn it, Terror?"

She was about to tell him when Talon's elbow jabbed into her side. "Ow," she said, giving him a scowl. "It's okay, Talon, we can tell *him*." To Dusk she said, "I got it from Bellatrix and Kipepeo."

"The champions?" he asked, looking puzzled.

"From *a book* that belonged to them," said Talon, shooting Magpie another elbow.

She glared but didn't correct him. Dusk looked back and forth between them, his expression unreadable, then said, "Well, that sounds like a book I'd very much like to see." He pointed Calypso through a doorway. "In there with him, please . . . *Calypso*, if I'm not mistaken?"

"Aye," said the crow, giving Dusk his cracked-beak grin. "Blessings. I'm pleased ye remember."

"Of course I do! And I see Lady Kite's long-life potions are in excellent form. You look fit and fine after all these years."

The arched doorway led into a parlor, and as Dusk followed Calypso through it, Magpie turned to Talon. "What's with the elbows, hooligan?" she whispered, rubbing her side.

"It's supposed to be a secret, neh, about you and the Moonlit Gardens?" he asked. "You going to go bragging to everybody how you're friends with Bellatrix?"

"Bragging!" she exclaimed, stung. "When did I ever?"

"You were just about to tell *him*, weren't you?"

"I've known *him* a lot longer than I've known *you*," she said, then turned on her heel and followed the crows into the parlor. Looking surly, Talon followed too.

They eased the Mothmage down onto a velvet chaise, where he lay back with his eyes closed. His breathing was shallow, his color almost green now. Dusk examined him, his full lips pinched thin with concern. He lifted his hand to feel the lad's temperature, but his palm paused and hovered when he got a good look at his brow. "Magpie," he said quietly.

She peered over Dusk's shoulder at the lad's forehead. The amputation was not dramatic. The antennae had been delicate, their stalks very fine, but it was clear that they had been there. There was some swelling around two small nicks with just a smear of blood. "He's Mothmage," she told Dusk, giving him a nervous sideward glance. "You'll still help him, won't you?"

"Mothmage," Dusk repeated, sounding surprised but not

hateful. He brought his palm gently down to the lad's brow. "This day is spilling out legends. Earlier I heard there's a Silksinger in Nazneen."

"You did?" Magpie asked. "Did you hear anything else?"

Dusk shook his head, his attention fixed on the Mothmage. "Nay, I haven't been out all evening."

The lad stirred and half opened his eyes. He mumbled, "Whisper."

Magpie knelt down at his side. "Lad?" She touched his shoulder. "Do you know where she is?"

Very faintly, he replied, "Rasilith Ev."

A little shiver coursed down Magpie's wings. "She is?" she said, her eyes brightening. "Of course she is. That's where I'd go if I was her."

The lad lost consciousness again, and Magpie turned to Dusk. "Is he going to be all right?"

"Aye, he should be. He's running a fever and his pulse is weak, but you saved his life with the spell you did. I'll mix a potion to purge any residual venom out of his blood, but mostly he needs rest."

"Thanks," she said. "We'll come back later to check on him—"

"Come back? But you're not going to leave him *here*," Dusk said.

"Oh," said Magpie. "I have to. I'm sorry about it, but we have to find the Silksinger lass right away. We've been

270

tracking her all the way across the mountains and we've finally caught up to her."

Dusk gave her a penetrating look. "What's this about, Magpie? Mothmages and Silksingers suddenly turning up in Nazneen, back from the dead? Who's next, Fade?"

"Neh, Fade truly is dead," she said. "But . . . the Azazel isn't."

"The Azazel!" exclaimed Dusk. "What, here, in Nazneen?"

She nodded, taking pleasure in being the bearer of such wondrous news. "You'll never believe. The Silksinger lass has him in a *teakettle*. We've been tracking them all the way across the Sayash. That's my task now, for the Magruwen, to find the rest of the Djinn in their dreaming places. Well, the Azazel's here—"

"But . . . where?"

Talon answered before Magpie could. Tersely, he replied, "We don't know yet. That's why we have to go."

Dusk looked at him. "Magpie," he said. "I don't believe you've introduced me to your friend."

Talon said, "This isn't really the time for introductions." Giving Magpie a look, he cut his eyes sharply toward the door.

"Jacksmoke, Talon," she said, taken aback by his rudeness. "How long does it take to say blessings, pleased to meet you?" To Dusk she said, "This is Talon—"

"Rathersting," Dusk finished for her. "Aye, I know the tattoos. Fine clan."

"He's prince of 'em," said Calypso.

"Well then, my blessings, *Prince*." He outfaced his hands.

Talon's eyes were cool as he replied, "And mine." They pressed palms, and Magpie saw that Talon was studying Dusk's fingers as if he truly were examining them for possible devil disguise. She frowned. During the Devil Wars, it was true, some of the more cunning snags had mastered a dark kind of glamour that let them pass as faeries, but even at its best that magic had been crude, especially about the hands and feet—hence this greeting had been born as a show of good faith. But those glamours were a thing of ancient days, and the greeting now just a formal remnant. In fact, to be taking it seriously like that was just plain rude of Talon. It was her turn to elbow him.

Talon didn't acknowledge her nudge. He said to Dusk, "You have scars on your hands."

"So have you," returned Dusk, dropping his hands.

Magpie had forgotten Dusk's scars, though not Talon's, which he had gotten by hanging on to her tether and reeling her out of the darkness of the Blackbringer. Dusk's were burn scars, which, she now recalled him telling, he had sustained by catching bluefire flung at him by a mad witch doctor.

"Well, you two can start a scar club sometime," she said.

Dusk

"But not right now, all right, Talon?" She turned to Calypso. "Feather, stay here with the lad?"

"Sure, 'Pie," said the crow.

"Nay, that's not necessary," Dusk interjected. "Truly. Just leave him with me. I'll see to him."

But Magpie shook her head. "We don't know what we're dealing with. He is a Mothmage, after all. I'd rather Calypso keep an eye on him till he wakes up. Anywhich, this way you can get back to your work, and you don't have to sit with him. Calypso can just call you if he needs you."

Dusk surrendered. "No arguing with the Djinn King's champion, I suppose. But you will come back and talk to me? I want to hear everything, Terror. The Magruwen, the Blackbringer, all of it, from your own lips."

"Of course," said Magpie, smiling. "Once this is all over, we can tell firetime stories in your library like we used to."

"Except you probably won't want to sit on my lap anymore, like you did when you were a sprout."

"Still a sprout," said Calypso, as he always did, and as Magpie imagined he always would.

Shaking her head, she followed Talon and Swig out the door.

THIRTY-TWO

Nazneen had quieted in the aftermath of the mob. The crowd had dispersed, but many faeries were gathered atop pavilion domes and down in the plazas of the bazaar, and as Magpie, Talon, and Swig flew over the city, they felt eyes on them and heard everywhere the hush of gossip-charged whispers.

Ignoring it, they flew to Rasilith Ev, circling its golden domes once before descending into the interior cloisters. "Blessings," said Talon. "It's in a lot better shape than Issrin Ev was all these years."

"Aye," said Magpie, recalling how the Magruwen's temple had looked as she had first seen it, all tumbled with broken statues and utterly forlorn. Rasilith Ev, by contrast, had been rebuilt by King Onyx after the Battle of Black Rock and preserved like a museum. Though tidy, the cloisters were empty and dark, and Magpie decided this was just a neater kind of ruin.

They came to the immense door and pushed it open, fully expecting Whisper to be inside the hall. It was really the only thing that made any sense—that the lass would have brought the Azazel here directly and put him on his throne. So they were dismayed to enter the temple and find it dark and still.

Swig and Talon followed Magpie through the small chapel and into the vast central hall. Magpie visioned an orb of light and sent it floating up to the ceiling so the whole of the interior was illuminated. There was no one here. Her disappointment was profound. She turned in a slow circle, peering into all eight chapels that ringed the hall. She saw the pillars, the throne, and, on the floor, an empty wine bottle that had rolled to rest against a pillar.

"Where *are* they?" she asked a little irritably, as if Whisper were late for an appointment.

"Hoy, Mags," called Swig from one of the chapels. "Here's something." He fluttered over, holding a copper lid.

Magpie took it. "It's from a teakettle!" she exclaimed.

"Proof she *was* here, anywhich," said Talon. "Do you think she did it? Set him on his throne?"

"Well, if she had, sure we'd know it, neh?" said Swig.

"Aye," agreed Magpie. "Djinn aren't such subtle beings."

The crow asked, "Do ye think it didn't work? Maybe he didn't wake up."

"Flummox me."

"Should we try memory touch?" suggested Talon.

"Aye," said Magpie, looking at the lid and wondering

276

what secrets were contained in the copper. Talon reached out and laid his fingertips on it, and simultaneously the two of them visioned the glyphs for memory and touch. It was a spell that would reveal what Whisper had seen the last time she had held the lid. At once, her thoughts surged through their minds, and Magpie and Talon peered into a vanished moment.

Whisper had crouched in the chapel with the kettle in her hands; she had stared into the burning heart of the Djinn and imagined what it would be like when he woke. Magpie and Talon strained to see what would happen next, but the vision ended abruptly.

"Skive," Talon swore. "Then what?"

Equally frustrated, Magpie said, "It's like reading to the end of a book to find the last chapter torn out!"

"What did ye see?" asked Swig.

"She was going to set him on his throne," she said.

"And?"

"And nothing. She put the lid down."

"But if she did put him on the throne, ye could tell by touching it, neh?" asked Swig.

She nodded. Talon was nearest the throne, and he was the first to vision the glyphs again and lay his hand on its polished surface. After just a second he snatched it back as if the throne was hot.

"What?" asked Magpie. "Did you see something?"

"Neh, nothing," he mumbled.

"Skive nothing," said Magpie. "Are you blushing?"

"It was just some faeries, um . . . kissing."

"Kissing?" Magpie repeated skeptically. "Let me see." With a flick of her wings she was over to the throne, laying her fingers on it. A second later, she yanked them back just as Talon had. Her cheeks went hot. Seeing a kiss was one thing. Memory-touching it was another. It had been like being in the kiss herself, and it was nothing like the smooches she planted on the crows' beaks or her parents' cheeks. It was *a kiss*, and it was . . . *wet*.

"Ick," she muttered. She had to resist the impulse to wipe away the phantom spit of the unknown faerie love-larks who'd been perched here slobbering on each other. She knew there was none on her, but she still felt the pressure and moisture of that memory kiss, the feeling of arms around her waist in passionate embrace, though of course it hadn't really been her waist or her embrace. "What were they doing, smooching on the Azazel's throne?" she demanded. "Is nothing sacred?"

Talon didn't reply. He was still blushing with the memory of the kiss.

"Well, what the skiffle?" Magpie asked in exasperation. "Let's go search the cloisters."

She took to her wings and started for the door, and the crow followed. Talon hesitated a moment, and after they were across the hall, he reached out to the throne, visioning the memory-touch spell once more. This time he let his fingers linger and only pulled them away when Magpie called back, "Coming, slowpoke?"

He leapt to his wings to follow her, a new blush creeping up his neck. So *that*, he thought, is how kissing is done.

The cloisters disclosed no more clues. Unhappily, Magpie said, "Let's go see if the birds have heard anything."

Pup and Pigeon were waiting on a rooftop of the caravan hostelry, and led the way to the private chamber the crows had engaged. It lay down a fountain-lined walk from the landing courtyard and through a double door large enough for the wagons to pass through. It was a big, bare room with a vaulted ceiling made entirely of stained glass in a motif of suns and orchids. There was a fire pit in the center of the chamber, with just enough space to fit all five wagons in a circle around it.

The crows had made camp. A fire was flickering in the pit, and the cushions had been tossed out in a ring around it. Bertram was standing by Batch's wagon, fanning the door to air it out.

"Imp's gone?" Magpie asked.

"Aye, and good riddance," said Bertram.

"I guess," said Magpie with a wistful frown, thinking how useful the serendipity would be right about now. She wished she had it herself. If only she could make the magicks she *needed* in the Tapestry, instead of wild spurts, she'd give herself this gift! She told the crows what they had found—and *not* found—in Rasilith Ev. "No lass, no Djinn," she concluded. "You find out anything around here?"

"Aye, darlin'," said Bertram, and Magpie's heart leapt. "Old Zingaro was talking about her down in the courtyard and griping and grumping how she just upped and vanished soon's the skimmers set down, without so much as a thanks or blessing."

"I call that bad manners," added Pigeon.

Magpie's heart sank again. She was getting a bad feeling that they had not come to the end of their trail after all. Staring into the fire, she murmured, "Whisper Silksinger, where the skiffle are you?"

THIRTY-THREE

Whisper's face was hot, her eyes swollen from weeping. The Azazel was in the hands of a monster, and she was trapped in a dungeon. The enormity of her failure welled up inside her, filling her and seeming to crowd out any room for breath or heartbeat. And that was only the beginning of her sadness. Hirik was dead. She dropped her head onto her knees as a new rush of tears came.

She saw his face so clearly in her mind, as he'd looked when he blushed buying her shawl. He was dead. And still, *that* wasn't the end of the horror.

Devils were readying an invasion, and like a captive bird on pain of death, she was supposed to *sing*.

She sat in her cell for a long time, face on her knees, crying. More than once she thought of the words that would carry her to the Moonlit Gardens. She didn't have to stay here. All she had to do was speak those words and she would be with her folk. She would see her parents again, and she could see Hirik and tell him she was sorry for the way she had looked at him. But she kept remembering the last thing her grandmother had said to her. "The clan's duty is yours now, Whisperchild."

As long as she was still alive, there was a chance, even a tiny chance, that she could still do something. Much as she might wish it, she couldn't succumb to the lure of an easy death. She wouldn't speak the words.

At a sound outside her cell, she looked up. Two red orbs seemed to hover at the bars. Eyes! She gasped and scurried backward. The eyes bobbed and blinked in the dim. Whisper could just make out the creature they belonged to. He had immensely long, rubbery arms and was kneeling, face pressed up against the bars, staring at her with what seemed to be . . . *wonder*.

He was a devil, he had to be. He was ugly, his flesh fish belly white against those awful, bulging red eyes. His face was narrow, he had no nose to speak of, and only a thin line for a mouth—but that thin line was turned up at the corners, giving the odd impression of a smile. A smile? Whisper stared at the thing. If he was ugly, he was not at all the same kind of ugly as Ethiag and his soldiers. She thought, rather, that he was *homely*.

He was a hunchbacked kind of thing, and it took Whisper a moment to realize his hump had a hard sheen to it. It was white with delicate stripes of pink, and it was a shell.

The snag was gripping the bars on either side of his face and just staring at her with that hapless, dazed smile, and she found it hard to be afraid of him.

"All right, maidy?" he asked, his voice high and reedy.

All right? She could almost have laughed at the absurdity of the question, but there was no laughter in her, and besides, he had asked so solemnly. She shook her head. "Nay, I'm not all right," she said. Her voice came out as a rasp and she realized how thirsty she was.

The devil held out a tin cup to her. "Water?" he asked.

She had never thought she would see the day she would willingly take water from a devil's hand, but she didn't hesitate. She was so thirsty, she took the cup and sniffed it. She smelled nothing, and the water looked clear. Tipping it up, she drained the cup. Immediately her throat felt soothed and even some of the fever heat of her face subsided. "Thank you," she said, not even thinking until after she said it how ridiculous a thing it was to say, here in this dungeon.

But the snag didn't seem to think so. The little upcurl of his mouth, which had seemed possibly to be a smile, now positively became one. He beamed at her. "What's yer name, maidy?" he asked her.

"It's Whisper," she said. "What . . . what's yours?"

"Slomby, maidy."

He made a sudden move with one long arm. Whisper flinched, but she saw she needn't have. He was holding something else out to her. At first glance she thought it was a flower, even more absurd in this place than a thank-you. But it wasn't a flower. It was a plume.

"Th-thank you," she said again, reaching out to take it. "It's beautiful." She gazed at it, turning it over in her hands. It was of the most brilliant crimson, feathering out to orange on the tips, rather like a flame. Whisper had never seen a feather of such vivid color.

"It fell off Ryawy's tail," Slomby told her, talking fast and nervous. "She's nicest, usually. If it was Vesrisath, he'd probably torch me trying to take it. He's always mad. He hates the leeches, but so do I. He doesn't have to scorch me." He gave her a woeful look and held up his hands so she could see the angry red blisters on them.

Whisper stared at him. "Did . . . did you say Ryawy? And Vesrisath?" The names were legend. Ryawy and Vesrisath were the firedrakes who had been companions to the Azazel.

"Aye," said Slomby. "They're down there." He pointed to the far end of the row of cells.

"They're alive!" Whisper exclaimed, rushing up to the bars to try to see down the aisle. The word *alive* slipped out like a chime, bright to the ears as sunlit copper to the eyes, and carrying all the magic of the glyph for life with it. Slomby went still as the sound wreathed around him. His lipless mouth dropped open and the shine in his red eyes seemed to brighten as *life* thrummed through him. He wasn't the only one. All along the row of cells, prisoners stirred in the shadows. Dull eyes blinked and brightened, and sad, caged creatures crept slowly forward to peer out at the lass who had unleashed that sound, beautiful as a bell, and somehow pierced their long misery.

Whisper didn't notice them at first. She was trying to see the firedrakes, but it was dim at the end of the corridor. She murmured, "I thought they were dead!"

Slomby snapped out of his daze and said fervently, "Neh, not dead!"

Vesrisath and Ryawy would have come away with the Azazel and the Silksingers when they left Nazneen but for one thing: they had been incubating a clutch of eggs. Their plan had been to follow and find their master after the young hatched, but the years passed and they had never come. As a sprout, Whisper had daydreamed that they might still arrive at the island, four thousand years late, but as she'd grown older, she'd resigned herself to believing they were dead.

"But how did they come to be here?" she asked.

"They always been here," said the snag. He was pacing

back and forth, and Whisper saw he was dragging heavy iron shackles between his feet. She also noticed the faces peering at her from the other cells—an imp, a fox, a slim, pale maiden with green-tinged hair, a griffin, a gnome.

"But why . . . ," she whispered. "Why are you all here?" She had been brought here to sing Ethiag a flying carpet, but what of these others? "What does he want with you?"

A few cells down was a thing that seemed to be a toadstool until it tipped up its fleshy cap and revealed its pinched face hidden beneath. An agaric! Whisper had heard of the mushroom folk of the forest but never seen one. In a voice that creaked like hinges on a door that has not been opened in ages, he said, "We're . . . *ingredients*."

"Ingredients? I don't understand."

Across from her, the fox gave a low growl and said, "Ask him," jerking its head toward Slomby. "He's Master's leech lackey."

Slomby's line of a mouth, so recently curled into a smile, now quivered into a frown. "It en't my fault," he said piteously.

The fox growled, "Lackey!"

With a whimper, Slomby protested. "If I don't leech 'em, Master'll beat me and worse!"

"*Leech* them?" Whisper asked. "But what do you mean, *leech* them?"

Trembling, he explained. "The firedrakes, I . . . I put the bloodsuckers on 'em, here—" He pointed to a spot beneath his own chin. "And when they're fat, I take 'em to Master."

"But . . . what for?" Whisper asked. "What does he *do* with them?"

"He eats 'em," he said. "For the blood. He's older than old, Master, and it's their blood that keeps him alive."

Firedrakes, as blood slaves to that monstrous thing out there! Whisper shuddered. "Without their blood, he'll die?"

"That's what Vesrisath says. He wants me to . . ." Slomby hunched, looking as if he could barely support the weight of his shell. "He asked me to . . . to kill them, but I won't do it!" He looked quickly around at the other prisoners. "I won't kill the beauties!"

"Kill them?" Whisper shivered. "Nay, nay. Not them! But Ethiag *must* die. Slomby, there must be another way—"

"Ethiag?" repeated Slomby, cocking his head at her. "I hate that nasty devil, but what's it to do with him?"

"What?" Whisper didn't understand. "You . . . you said he'd die without the firedrakes' blood—"

"Ach!" Slomby slapped his forehead. "Neh, not *him*! He's just a devil, en't he? Master lets him eat the slaves, but he'd never let him taste firedrakes' blood!"

"But Ethiag's not master?" asked Whisper, perplexed. "Then . . . who is?"

The fox slunk into the light, and Whisper saw its form go blurry and shimmer into that of a lady, bent double, with dirty red hair dragging over the floor. "Master," she said, spitting out the word, "is a faerie, like you."

THIRTY-FOUR

It was very late by the time Magpie and Talon returned to Apothecary Lane. Dusk let them in and followed them into the parlor. Calypso was perched beside the Mothmage lad, who was now awake, sitting up with his head in his hands so his hair fell over his face, obscuring it. He looked up quickly when they entered, and the sudden movement seemed to make him dizzy. He squeezed his eyes shut and clung to the edge of the velvet chaise, but still managed to ask, "Did you find her?"

Magpie regarded him warily. Could you tell if someone was wicked, she wondered, just by looking at them? Wickedness curdled the soul—certainly it showed in the eyes. When he opened his again she saw a burning intensity in them. As for wickedness, she couldn't tell. She asked, "And just what business is it of yours?"

"It's my business," he said, "because I swore an oath to keep her safe. And I swore it on the Azazel's flame."

"On the Azazel's flame? And what do you know of the Azazel?"

"I know he's in Whisper's teakettle. So—"

She cut him off. "Seems you're the only one in Nazneen who knows that. In all that gossip out there, not one word about the Djinn. How do you know what nobody else does?"

"So you haven't found her," he said, rising. He was unsteady on his feet and had to hold on to the edge of the chaise while a look like seasickness washed over his face. "You looked in the temple?"

"I'm asking the questions," said Magpie. "And I want to know what you know about the Silksinger."

His golden eyes bored into her. "You think I did something to her."

"Well, did you?"

Bitterly, he said, "I'm surprised you even bothered saving my life if you think just like the rest of them! I'm a Mothmage, so I must have hurt her? Is that it, or is there some other reason you suspect me?"

Magpie realized that, in fact, there was no other reason. Was she just as bad as that murk, cutting down a lad for something his ancestors did four thousand years ago? She glanced at Talon, who stepped up to her side and asked Hirik, "Can you give us a reason to trust you?" In Talon's calm voice, the question didn't sound like a jibe. It sounded as if he were genuinely hoping Hirik would give them a reason.

Hirik said, "I'm telling you, I swore to protect Whisper,

and I followed the caravan to Nazneen and made sure she was safe. She was. She was at Rasilith Ev—"

Magpie asked, "Do you know what happened there?"

Hirik shook his head and was beset once more by dizziness. "Nay," he told them. "I was going there when . . . when they caught me. I'd seen her in the smoke charmer's smoke—"

"Smoke charmer?" asked Dusk, leaning forward. "You consulted one?"

Hirik nodded. "Madame Sallowpearl." He spat the name and told them of the smoke charmers, both of them, the first vision of Whisper that he had not understood, and the one in Fortune-tellers Lane. "That's when I realized what was in her kettle. The vision was so clear, and I finally understood. I was going to find her. But—" His face clouded with the memory of what had followed. "Madame Sallowpearl saw what I was. . . ."

The rest, they could guess. "I'm sorry, lad," said Magpie. She was still trying to read him. He seemed earnest in his concern, even distressed. She decided it was past time to stop calling him lad. "What's your name?"

"Hirik."

"Hirik, I guess you recognize this." She held up the kettle lid.

"Aye. But where's the rest of it?"

"We don't know," she admitted. "No trace. Nobody's

seen her. This was on the floor in the temple, but nobody was there." She watched as Hirik swayed on his feet, closed his eyes from the dizziness, and sat back down. "Are you all right?" she asked him.

"Nay, I'm not all right! My antennae have been hacked off. If they hadn't . . ." His voice trailed off and he swallowed hard. "If they hadn't, I could go to Rasilith Ev and I could track her. I could find Whisper and the Azazel too. But now I'm useless. I can't find anybody, and now I'll never be champion. . . ."

There was silence in the little parlor. Champion. Like Merryvenom, this lad had dreamed of becoming champion. Magpie looked to Talon, Calypso, and Dusk. They were all somber. After a moment, she said, "I'm real sorry we got here too late." She remembered she'd put the severed antennae in her pocket, and she took them out now and gave them to Hirik. He stared at them.

"They don't grow back," he said softly. Then, with a sudden glimmer of hope, he turned to Dusk. "Unless . . . unless there's something you can do?"

Dusk shook his head and answered sadly, "I'm sorry, lad. I know of no medicine or magic that can regrow what's been severed."

"Nay, I thought not." Miserably, he raised his hand to touch his brow.

Magpie felt an ache of sympathy for him. She would

almost have sworn now that there was no wickedness in him, Mothmage or not. She asked, "Do you swear you're loyal to the Djinn?"

He didn't hesitate. "I would give my life," he said. His eyes burned. "For the Azazel and for Whisper. We have to find her. I was so stupid not to see. Twice she was attacked by devils. Nay, *thrice,* by the wounds on her shoulders, and I never realized it was her they were after."

"Jacksmoke. They're sure stalking her fierce," said Calypso. "Ye don't think they could've got her here, in Nazneen?"

"Devils in Nazneen?" said Dusk. "Certainly not. I think such a thing must surely be noticed."

It did seem highly unlikely, thought Magpie, imagining devils out in the lanes of the bazaar. "We don't know yet it's anything so dire," she said. "Could be the Azazel just didn't wake. If he's anything like the Ithuriel, I can imagine it."

"The Ithuriel!" said Dusk. "Have you found him?"

"Oh, aye," said Magpie. "He was easy to find, just stayed in one place. Of course, we had the imp then."

"Imp?"

Magpie told him about Batch. "Anywhich, we turned the irkmeat loose," she finished with a sigh.

"But you thought a scavenger imp would *help* you?" Dusk asked. "I seem to recall your parents had difficulties with such an imp once."

"Aye, but we bribed Batch," said Magpie. "And he *did* help. The way he led us straight to that cave? Skive, but I wish I had his gift!"

For a moment Dusk just looked at her, wearing that same marveling smile he had favored her with earlier.

"What?" she asked, growing self-conscious. Was he looking at her messy hair?

"Nothing," he said. "I'm just amazed by the young lady you've become, Terror. Chasing Djinn and devils all over the world! I always knew you were an uncommon sprout, but this. . . ." He just shook his head.

She blushed. He reached out to tousle her hair, and Talon watched the apothecary with narrowed eyes. Could it be considered showing off, he wondered peevishly, to be that skiving handsome?

"And the Ithuriel, where is he now?" asked Dusk. "Has he awakened?"

"Neh, he's still sleeping—" Magpie said.

Talon coughed. "I wonder if we might get some tea?" he asked. "We been flying for . . ." He thought about it and turned to Calypso. "How long, crow?"

"A long sky, for true," agreed the bird. "I'm parched."

"Forgive me," said Dusk, rising. "Where are my manners? I got so caught up in the intrigue. I'll make some tea at once."

He went to a large silver samovar in the corner and

started to set cups out on a tray. Magpie gave Talon a quizzical look behind the apothecary's back. "Tea?" she said. "You want some crumpets with that too?"

"At least I didn't elbow you that time," he said.

"Ach, lad," she said, rolling her eyes. "I told you, we can tell Dusk—"

This time Talon did elbow her. Dusk returned with the tea tray and said, "Now, you were saying, the Ithuriel—"

Talon said, "On second thought, Magpie, don't you think we should get back to the search?"

"Aye," agreed Hirik at once. "Whisper's out there somewhere."

Magpie looked at the tea, and at the deep velvet chairs in the parlor. How inviting it was, and what memories it brought back!

Right here, when she was a tiny thing, Dusk had held her in the crook of one arm and read dragon histories to her off ancient scrolls penned by the Azazel's own scribes. He had taught her how to grind up forgetting dust and giggling powder in her own small mortar, both of which she had tested on the crows. He had shown her how to measure the breath of serpents, which was an ingredient in many powerful potions, and how to catch a shadow, extract the very essence of a hibiscus petal or a rose thorn, draw venom from an unwilling spider, and gather pollen from the legs of butterflies.

But her favorite times in The Dragon's Scale had been firetime, when she and her parents and her grandmother Sparrow had gathered with Dusk in the library beneath the shop. How many wonderful tales he had told, about his adventures with witch doctors, traveling the world to learn new cures and dust spells. He was a kindred spirit, a scholar and an adventurer, even if by the time they met him he had set up this shop and become respectable. And now Magpie had stories of her own adventures to tell, and things *she* could teach *him,* and he would keep on giving her that smile that made her feel like a marvel of the Djinns' creation.

But the lads were right. There was work to do. She sighed. "Aye, we got to keep searching. But Hirik, are you well enough?"

He tried to look stoic. "Aye, it's just my balance, it's gone, like I've been spinning circles and made myself dizzy. Only, it won't go away."

"That," said Dusk, "is something I can help you with." He fetched a bottle off a shelf in his shop and decanted some of the pale golden liquid into a flask for Hirik. "Take a sip of that when it gets bad," he said.

Hirik thanked him, and they all bade him good night. Dusk tousled Magpie's hair again and said, "Good luck with the search, Terror. Come and see me as soon as you can. I'm going to hold you to those firetime stories."

"Aye, sure," she said, and went out smiling. Dusk locked

the door behind them and watched them leave. Only after they disappeared over the rooftops did he unlock it again and exit. It was very quiet in Nazneen. All the shops of the bazaar were shut up tight as he set off, whistling, to run a quick errand before the sun came up.

THIRTY-FIVE

Dusk flew along the empty lanes, cut across Storytellers' Plaza, and followed a fragrant alley of perfume shops until it spilled into Fortune-tellers Lane. There he set down on his feet and strolled, still whistling a low, sweet trill. The windows were shuttered and draped. None of the fortune-tellers' parlors were open for business, but when he spotted a shingle that read *Ask the Smoke*, he went down the cellar stairs and rapped on the door.

When there came no immediate answer, he rapped again. "Hello?" he called. "Madame?"

Finally, a grumbling and grunting could be heard within, and the door cracked open to reveal the fat, squinting face of Madame Sallowpearl. "What in the name of all that's blessed—?" she croaked.

"A thousand pardons, good lady," said Dusk. "I was hoping to ask the smoke."

"I'm closed!" she declared. "Sleeping, like all decent folk—"

"It's an urgent matter, or I wouldn't dream of disturbing your slumber. I do apologize for the trouble," he said, giving her the dazzling smile that had made him the most popular apothecary among Nazneen's ladies. "Please?"

"Ach, very well," she relented, standing back from her door to let him in. She was dressed in a nightgown and cap, with her hair dangling in a long, white braid between her wings. "Come in, come in, but it'll cost!"

"That's not a concern," he replied.

"Neh? You haven't heard yet *what* it'll cost," she replied. "I'm not interested in tink."

"Oh?" Dusk asked, intrigued. "What, then?"

With a salacious chuckle that set her wattle swaying, she said, "Why, a kiss, my handsome lord, or . . . a memory. The choice is yours, but I know which *I* hope for."

Dusk laughed. "I think I'll have to choose the memory, good lady."

"Ach, well, they usually do," she said. "Make it a good one, then."

"Oh, I can promise you that," he replied easily. "But . . . after, if you please. I'm most anxious to see a vision."

Yawning and muttering, Madame Sallowpearl set about gathering her hookah pipe and leaves and preparing her spell. Dusk looked around the squalid little shop, reaching out now and then to run his finger over a dusty jar or book.

His handsome face was alight with eagerness as he remarked, "I've heard your magic is quite extraordinary, Madame."

"Oh, aye? So it is, too. There's precious few left with the gift of it, that's certain. Up there in the lane," she said with a jerk of her chin, "they might be pretty things and have shiny crystal balls, but it's weak magic at best and sometimes none at all. There's not another fortune-teller in Nazneen that can show you what I can, my lord, and that's the truth."

"I'm glad to hear that," he said softly.

"Well, then," she said, handing him the pipe. "Here you go."

Dusk sucked in the smoke and held it for a long moment before he leaned over the goblet and loosed a thin spout of fume from between his red lips. It poured like liquid into the glass, and he watched keenly as it stirred. "Extraordinary," he murmured, turning his shining gaze on Madame Sallowpearl.

A flush rose to her wrinkled old cheeks. "It is, if I don't say so myself," she replied, flustered by the flattery. Then, when the vision settled, she blinked at it and said, "That's strange."

"Is it?" Dusk asked.

"Aye. It's the same thing that filthy Mothmage saw. I could swear."

"That *is* strange," he agreed, peering at the vision. It was a teakettle, lidless, sitting on a slab. "Look at that," he said.

"Truly astonishing. Every bit as clear and true a vision as the lad said." He upturned the goblet so the smoke spilled out. Favoring the biddy with another charming smile, he said, "Magic such as yours could chase all mystery from the world, Madame."

"Indeed it could," she said, bragging.

"But . . . who would want to live in a world without mystery?"

Sallowpearl cocked an eyebrow at him. "Eh? Well, now for that memory, lord."

"Certainly."

She gathered his dispersed smoke between her hands and formed it into a ball. It began to swirl and draw itself into a complex scene of the city in miniature, with all its domes and spires. She squinted at it. Something was happening in the sky, and her mouth fell slack when she realized what she was seeing.

It was a dragon, thrashing in death throes. A wild burst of flame escaped him and he reeled and fell, and the vision dispersed with a sudden puff, buffeting her face and making her cough.

"What was that?" she whispered, taking a step back.

Dusk said, "I promised you a good memory."

"But that was . . ." She faltered, then demanded, "Who are you?"

"I'm your new master, Madame," he said.

"Master!" She spat the word. "I've no master. I'll abide no master!" Her voice was brash but there was fear in her eyes. Taking another step back, Madame Sallowpearl transformed, very suddenly, to smoke.

"Extraordinary," Dusk said again. Quick as a flash, he grabbed a silver flask off the shelf and splashed out its liquid contents. The smoke that was Madame Sallowpearl was swirling up toward the cracked windowpane, trying to escape, but Dusk put out his hand and the fume seemed to freeze in place until, with a quick curl of his fingers, he summoned it back. It roiled, trying to fight him, but his magic was stronger. The smile never left his face as he funneled it down into the neck of the little flask and clamped on the lid. "Good," he said, slipping it into his pocket and patting it. "Very good."

He was whistling again as he went back up the cellar steps, but when he saw by the pallor of the sky that night was already tipping toward dawn, his whistle trailed away. "Sunrise," he said, startled. He had a certain sunrise ritual that could not be delayed. Taking to his wings, he hurried back toward Apothecary Lane.

By the earliest gleams of dawn, the city seemed still to sleep, but not every creature in Nazneen had chosen to dream away the night. Murks stumbled out of taverns and made their way back to the hostelry. In the alleys, mice rooted in the trash, and in the sky, thousands of bats coalesced into twisters and siphoned back into their caves in the rock. There were other creatures too who sought sanctuary from the day, slipping away into sewer grates and tunnels.

Batch Hangnail had a jaunt in his step as he made his way into one such tunnel. "Scurry scurry, little furry, find the darkness, better hurry," he sang to himself as he scooted along, his diamond-strung tail leaving a slither trail in the muck of the underground world.

He was just winding down his first nighttime frolic in weeks, and he was exhausted. Nazneen was a scavenger's paradise! Everywhere, hidden pretties were calling out to him with the silent voice of *impulse*. Bones and teeth and old meat, diamonds and sapphires and buried flakes of ancient dragon scale. There was the Azazel too. He felt that presence like a sore tooth, and with a grin of savage glee, he ignored it. He was his own imp again, and no faerie's stooge!

He was not perfectly happy, though, because there was not, in all Nazneen, the thing he craved most: a flying carpet. He'd know if there was; he'd be drawn to it by a compulsion of pure sweet certainty. But all he felt was the muted cry of the carpets he'd left behind on the Silksingers' island.

He wondered how he could ever make it back there, all the way across mountains and bay to that marvelous island. He cursed Magpie again for tearing his treasure right out of his grasp. "Flotching mudsucks," he muttered, then gave a little coo when he found an abandoned rat's nest where he could curl up for the night, cozy as a flea in a hobgoblin's belly button.

Not far off, in Silk Alley, a pair of lean weasel-like devils came up out of a sewer grate on a mission from their master. The shops in the alley contained bolts of silk in every color. The devils forced doors open and plundered the wares with filthy paws. They knew nothing of silk, nor did Ethiag, who was watching through their eyes, controlling their every prowling move. Silk, everywhere silk. Carpets and cloth, ribbons and robes. But what he needed was *thread,* and when his devils broke into a cavernous warehouse, he found it in the form of cocoons, hundreds of them, spaced on wide wooden racks.

"This will do," he said, and the devils gathered them into sacks to carry back down to the dungeon.

Aboveground, the sun rose, but down in the dungeon, there was no such clue to the passage of hours. To Slomby, born and raised in this world of black tunnels, the words *day* and *night* held no meaning. Ryawy, the queen drake, sometimes let him listen in when she told stories to the young drakes, who'd hatched in the dungeon and knew no more of the outside world than he did. Though he'd heard her explain about day and night, Slomby's imagination couldn't stretch itself around such a notion. When she described the

Slomby

sky, the best he could picture was a higher kind of cave ceiling, and the sun, only a very, very large lantern. Stars he couldn't imagine at all.

To him, the only meaningful division of time was the flip of the big sandglass hanging in the kitchen. When it ran down, it meant it was time for a fresh leeching.

"Get to it, fishwit," grunted Num. "Sand's almost up."

"Aye," he said mournfully, taking up the bowl. He fretted all the way to the leech trough, where he fished out five black squiggles. They looked so different before they gorged themselves on blood—just little shiny worms. Taking care to keep them from sucking onto his own pale flesh, Slomby trudged down the corridor to the firedrakes' cells.

The faerie maidy was asleep as he passed her cell, and he was glad. He didn't want her to see him doing this nasty work. Maybe she would stay asleep until he finished, and then she wouldn't start hating him like the others did. "Blessings, my beauties," he said, like always, though he whispered it today so as not to wake Whisper, and he hoped the drakes might go easy on him. Giving them a lipless smile, he approached Ryawy's cage.

She took one look at him and snorted out twin whips of fire from the slits atop her beak. Slomby ducked with a squeak. So much for going easy. He sighed and set to work.

By the time he headed back up the corridor with the

leeches in his bowl, his knuckles were freshly blistered, and every prisoner, including Whisper, had been awakened by the ruckus of flame spurts and Slomby's yelps.

"Slomby?" Whisper said as he passed her cell.

Hearing his name spoken in that sweet little voice made his heart melt. "Aye, maidy?" he asked.

With a glance at the leech bowl, she asked, "You're going to *him*, to . . . to *Master*?"

Shame-faced, he nodded. "I *got* to, maidy."

She put her pale, pretty face up against the bars and looked out at him beseechingly. "But when you're there, can you look for a . . . a teakettle?"

"A teakettle?"

"Aye, a teakettle with an ember inside. It belongs to me. Slomby, if you see it, can you get it for me?"

"Get it?" he squeaked. "*Take it,* ye mean? From Master?"

She nodded. "It's important, Slomby. *Please.*"

Slomby started trembling all over and edged away from her. "I can't, maidy! It's too dangerous! And I'm late, I got to go—"

"Wait!" she cried. "Slomby, the ember, you're the only one who can save it—" Slomby was skittering down the corridor now, away from her voice, which was rising and seemed to carry with it a whirlwind of desperation. His shackles made a terrible racket as he stumbled away. As he rounded the corner, he heard her cry out, "It's one of the seven who made the world! It's the Azazel, and the world needs him! *Please!*"

Her *please* echoed and echoed through his head, and it was a moment before another word she had shouted cleared its way through his thoughts. *Azazel.* He knew that name from Ryawy's stories. The Azazel was the firedrakes' master, their real master. One of the seven who made the world? Like thoughts of the sun and the sky, it was too big for Slomby's poor head. He started to hyperventilate.

Num was waiting with her hands on her hips when he rounded the bend. "What took so long?" she demanded. Then, seeing the state he was in, panting and gulping for air, she gave a hard rap to his forehead with the spoon in her hand. "Breathe, guppy!" she commanded. "Ye want to git yerself killed, leave me to do yer job too?" Slipping the spoon into the leech bowl, she took his shoulders and spun him toward the corridor. "Now, scramble. Ye're late! *Run!*"

As fast as his shackles would allow, Slomby did. Master got so mad when he was late. He raced across the devil-thronged cavern without even pausing to suck himself into his shell like he usually did. He thought he felt the flicker of a tongue tasting the nape of his neck, but he just kept on going, right past the opening to Ethiag's nest, all littered with bones and shackles. He glimpsed the devil's hairy black legs as he passed and he just kept on going. Before he knew it, he was on the black stair that wound round like a corkscrew, up and up and up.

He got dizzy going round and round, and he was wheezing, slumped over with one hand on the rail as he mounted the seemingly endless stair. In his haste he wasn't watching where he was going, and he gave a loud squeak when he suddenly collided with someone coming the other way.

He bounced back and teetered on the edge of the stair. Though his eyes were fixed on the leech bowl in dread dismay lest he drop it, he knew who he had bumped into, and his blood froze. It could only be Master, coming down to get the leeches for himself. As Slomby balanced on tiptoe for that brief moment, the weight of his shell starting to topple him backward, it ran through his mind that it might just be better to tumble down the steps and die than face whatever punishment Master would mete out.

Just as the thought flitted through his mind, a hand shot out and caught him by the wrist.

"You're late!" hissed Master.

Slomby collapsed into a quivering heap on the steps and Master grabbed the bowl out of his hand. Seizing the spoon, he shoveled a leech into his mouth, caught it between his back teeth, and chomped down hard. Slomby heard the bloodsucker's body pop like a grape. A dribble of blood oozed out the corner of Master's mouth and his tongue probed out after it and licked it up hungrily, careful not to lose a single drop of the precious elixir.

He was in a bad way. Slomby knew from Vesrisath that if Master didn't get the blood, he'd wither right away to his true age, and it looked as if the withering had begun. His coppery skin was grey as putty, his face waxen and starting to droop. His eyes, usually brilliant gem green, were yellowed like ancient paper, and the glossy black of his hair had dulled to ash. His hands were wrinkled and shaking as he scooped the next leech out of the bowl and devoured it with gusto. Pop! Then the next, and the next. *Pop, pop.* By the time he scooped up the fifth and final leech—*pop!*—his hand had stopped shaking and the withering was beginning to reverse itself right before Slomby's eyes.

His eyes cleared, his skin tightened, the sheen came back to his hair. Within seconds he was, once more, the handsome, green-eyed apothecary whom the faeries of Nazneen knew as Dusk.

THIRTY-SIX

Dusk shuddered as vitality flooded back into him. The leech slave had cut things very close this morning. Briefly, Dusk considered killing him but decided against it for the simple reason that, with Ethiag in the dungeon, his slaves were disappearing fast.

When he'd freed the devil general from his bottle several months ago, he'd laid out the conditions of their association: chiefly, that Dusk would help Ethiag build up an army, so long as the army would be at Dusk's disposal when he needed it. A more minor condition had been that Ethiag not eat all the slaves. "I've need of them," Dusk had said, but last he'd looked, there had only been a handful still scurrying about the place. He supposed Ethiag couldn't be accused of defying him; he'd merely told him not to eat them *all*, and he hadn't. Yet. And Dusk couldn't blame him for his hunger—twenty-five thousand years the devil had gone without a proper meal.

Soon, however, he and all his army would have a feast.

And very soon, Dusk would have no more need of leeches or slaves. He smiled. That era of his life was most certainly drawing to a close.

Slomby, mistaking his master's smile for a reprieve, started to slink back down the stairs.

"I don't think so, slave," said Dusk. "Up you go."

Slomby whimpered but did as he was told, creeping past him on all fours. Dusk followed. His voice almost genial, he said, "You know I can't abide tardiness." He was feeling the flush of power that always overcame him in the first few minutes the firedrake blood mixed with his own. It was calming, knowing the onslaught of age was held at bay for another day. It put him in a generous mood, so when the slave reached the top of the stair and crept into Dusk's laboratory, he told him, "You can choose your own bone. How's that?" He gestured to the rack on the wall in which a selection of long bones—mostly nice solid femurs from various creatures—was displayed.

Slomby was familiar with the bones, having been disciplined with them before—though if memory served, thought Dusk, he hadn't used a bone the last time, but a bit of antler that had been lying handily by. His laboratory was full of such bits and parts of creatures. This wasn't the laboratory his clients knew about, the one with sparkling windows and white marble where he dispensed wrinkle creams and love potions to rich, stupid faeries. This was his real laboratory. It had no windows, for it lay belowground, and it didn't sparkle and shine, because no eyes but his own and his slaves' ever saw it.

The smell was that of a catacomb: an overripe fug of flesh gone nasty. There were bones bundled like kindling and tied with twine, buckets of hooves and toenails and teeth, jars of eyeballs floating in liquor, and little packets of crushed skeletons that had been regurgitated by serpents and owls. Hair, eyelashes, whiskers, and vials of breath were tucked away in hundreds of tiny apothecary drawers, all carefully labeled with their species of origin.

Such ingredients would never be sanctioned by faeries, with all their indignant belief in the sanctity of life. And certainly, faeries would shudder at the thought of Dusk's primary ingredient. That was one that could not be stored, but had to be collected fresh and warm as it was needed: blood, and not just firedrakes' blood. Blood was the very essence of life, and very little of Dusk's work could be accomplished without it.

He had spent his life—many lifetimes—in an exploration of magicks largely unknown to other faeries. Repulsive to them, in fact, though if they knew the power they shunned in not wanting to stain their hands and souls, Dusk thought, they would change their tune. He was in no hurry to enlighten them, however. The secrets contained in his dozens of black-bound journals had taken him millennia to compile, and he was not about to share.

To Dusk alone was revealed the full scope of dark magic and all the power it could bestow.

Faced with the rack of bones, the slave Slomby quaked, and Dusk's brow furrowed. He said, "What is it, snag? I'm letting you choose, aren't I? I believe the proper response is *thank you.*"

"Th-th-thank you," whispered Slomby, creeping toward the bones. His chose the smallest one he could find, the ulna of a fruit bat.

"Very well," Dusk said with a smile. "Now, don't go shrinking into that shell of yours. That's right. Stay where I can see you."

He proceeded to administer the snag's beating. The ulna was light and very thin, but Dusk still managed to make him wail. When he finished, he slipped the bone back into the rack and said, "All right, snag, that's all," and Slomby slowly picked himself up off the floor. "Don't be late with my leeches again," Dusk told him mildly. "Go on."

"Aye, Master," whispered Slomby, wrapping his arms around himself in a pathetic hug. They were so long they went all the way around and met again in the front, where he clasped fingers. As he was slinking toward the top of the stairs, Dusk saw his big red eyes fix on the teakettle that was resting at the corner of his worktable. The sight of it set Slomby's eyes into a frantic swivel.

"What is it, slave?" Dusk asked.

Slomby's eyeballs darted toward him and away, whirling like tops. "Nothing, Master!" he blurted, slinking backward down the stair. His face was frozen in terror, as if he feared Dusk would stop him, but Dusk was anxious to get back to the work that had been interrupted by his evening visitors, so he let him go.

He turned his attention to the kettle. Sitting there on the worktable, it looked just as it had in the smoke vision. Madame Sallowpearl's magic was indeed fine. He patted his pocket for the flask in which he'd trapped her. It would have been dangerous to leave her free—he couldn't have anyone else making use of her arts to trace the Azazel here, or the lass Ethiag was keeping in the dungeon.

The Silksinger. It had come as a surprise to Dusk to learn that all these years Silksingers had been guarding the Azazel, but he supposed it shouldn't have. They had always been brave—and foolish. He perfectly remembered the day four thousand years ago when they had risen on their flying carpets to join Fade in battle.

Of course, he hadn't been called Dusk then, but Onyx, chief scribe to the Azazel. He had watched the fight and seen the cyclone of dragonfire that engulfed everything when Fade spasmed and finally died. He'd had to shield his eyes against the dazzle and almost missed seeing the dragon fall. He'd have hated to miss that!

He'd dreamed too long of Fade's death—*schemed* too long—to blink and miss his moment of triumph.

Fade had come to Nazneen to kill him and had died instead. Dusk had bested his old enemy and gotten rid of the interfering Mothmage all in one day, and he had not known a single threat since. These millennia had been good to him—a time without honor or Djinn, without dragons or guardians to interfere with his work! And now the Magruwen thought to return and reclaim the world, just like that? It was like the arrogant old scorch to think it would be so easy. Well, Dusk had his own plans, and they did not include the return of the Djinn.

Never again would he kowtow to elemental masters. *He* was master now, and soon the world would know it. What little resistance faeries might muster would be demolished by Ethiag's army, and now that Dusk had a Djinn under his power, nothing could stop him.

He peered down into the kettle. That this was the Azazel . . . it almost beggared belief! With a pair of tongs, he reached into the kettle and removed the ember. He held it up before a cloudy, ancient mirror propped on a shelf above his worktable and said, seemingly to his own reflection, "So what do you think, Mistral? Would you have known him?"

Like a creature rising from a sea, a face came to the surface of the mirror. It had broad cheeks and a stern brow and eyes the grey of a storm at sea. It was the face of a wind, a powerful air elemental imprisoned inside the glass.

"A far cry from his old self," said Dusk. "Couldn't even toast cheese on him."

"So you've done it," said Mistral coldly. "Now you have all the elements. Winds, water spirits, earth elementals, and now fire. Your collection is complete."

"Complete?" said Dusk. "Nay. When I have *all* the Djinn, then it will be complete."

"All?" said the wind with a gust of breath that fogged the inside of the mirror. "One Djinn isn't sufficient for your purposes?"

The apothecary laughed. "Aye, one Djinn is 'sufficient,' as you say. This pitiful ember is all I need." He regarded the Azazel with something akin to affection. "Blessings, my old master," he said to it. "It's fine to see you again after all these years, though you *are* so very changed."

The last time Dusk had seen him, the Djinn had been a fearsome sight: three heads on a broad neck, three arms on either side of his powerful body, feet split into the hooves of a bull. That was the skin he had worn over his fiery essence, before he had fallen into this deep sleep—this sleep from which he wasn't ever going to wake. This slumbering state suited Dusk's purposes perfectly. It would be much more difficult to steal his power if he were awake.

That was the essence of dark magic: *stealing*. It was the theft of life force, immortality, magical gifts, power. And of course, there was no greater source of power than a Djinn. Long ago, Dusk had tasted it. That sweet fire of perfect power had raced all too briefly through his own veins. He'd been punished for it—severely—but he'd never forgotten the feel of that surge of might. Of supremacy. He would have it again, and not for a brief instant this time, but forever.

By stealing the Azazel's power, he would perform no less a feat than to plunge his fingers into the weave of the world: the Tapestry! What had until now belonged to the Djinn alone, the threads of Creation, would be his. Every glyph and every life, every leaf, rock, and rainbow on Earth, every fang and phantasm, dream and dread. Even the stars in the sky would be his to rearrange.

Feeling drunk with power, Dusk said to the Azazel, "Sleep on, Lord. Dream deeply. Don't bother yourself about a thing." He turned once more to the mirror. "As for the other Djinn," he told Mistral, "it simply wouldn't do to leave them loose. Somebody could awaken them, and I won't have that. I shall rule the new age, not Djinn."

Mistral laughed at him. "Getting a little ahead of yourself, aren't you? If you're going to find them, you're going to have to leave Nazneen. Haven't I been captive for thousands of years, watching you work and seeing you fail, time and

318

again, in the one thing that matters to you most? You're as much a prisoner as any of us—"

"You're right," Dusk said, "I have been a prisoner. But not for much longer, my old friend." He looked at the long rows of shelves above the worktable. Alongside Mistral's mirror there were coffers, jars, crucibles, and even seashells. Each held prisoners: river spirits, pixies, breezes, echo maidens, shadow imps, mist creepers. He took the flask containing Madame Sallowpearl and set it up with the rest. There were plenty more prisoners down in the dungeon with the firedrakes too.

Dusk was not like them, trapped behind bars or mirror glass, but he *was* trapped. He was held captive by *need*. His sunrise ritual, the salty pop of leeches between his teeth. He couldn't do without it. Thus, he couldn't venture far from the firedrakes.

In his very, very long life, Dusk had used every long-life spell and elixir that had ever been dreamed up in the minds of witch doctors, healers, and apothecaries. Long ago, he had traveled the world searching out those magicks, and they had sufficed for a time. But as he grew ever older, their potency wore out, so he had invented his own potions, grisly things that no other soul in the world had ever tasted. And for millennia he had thrived. But faeries were never meant for immortality, and age had built up like a tidal force against him. The only thing that held it back now was the firedrake blood.

Four thousand years ago in the aftermath of Black Rock, Dusk had known exactly where to find the firedrakes' nest. Queen Ryawy had been sitting on her clutch of eggs, Vesrisath protecting them. The king drake had fought fiercely—that was the true provenance of the burn scars on Dusk's hands, not some witch doctor hurling bluefire at him, as he claimed—but Dusk had won, and the firedrakes had been in his dungeon ever since.

Once he had been more genteel in his consumption of their blood—he had extracted the juice from the leeches and put it into wine. Now he couldn't be bothered and just ate the bloodsuckers alive. The practice would sustain him indefinitely, he believed, but he had never viewed it as an ultimate solution. It wouldn't do to remain leech-addicted and at the mercy of firedrakes and dull-witted snag slaves.

The ultimate solution was something Dusk had long sought and never discovered in any ancient manuscript, nor even in the archives of the Djinn. So simple a thing and yet so secret!

It was the glyph for immortality.

"I'll soon have what I need," he said.

"What do you mean?" asked the wind. "If you think you'll draw the glyph from the Tapestry—"

"Nay," said Dusk dismissively. He knew it could take

months or years of studying the Tapestry before he discovered the one glyph he sought. He didn't wish to wait—and now he wouldn't have to. "I've had a very interesting visitor today," he said.

Mistral glowered at him through mirror glass.

"Several, in fact. A Mothmage, for one. What a shock! If his antennae hadn't already been cut off, I'd have had to do it myself. Do you know, he asked if I could regrow them!" Dusk laughed softly at the absurdity of it. Of course he could, but would he? The last thing he needed right now was a Mothmage sniffing around! Even after four thousand years he remembered the way the guardian chief had looked at him, those antennae riffling ceaselessly as they took in the corrupt scent of Dusk's unnatural life.

"You smell maggoty," the old Mothmage had told him once, speaking through clenched teeth. "Like something too putrid even for a vulture to eat."

Rather an unflattering description. Well, Dusk had had the satisfaction, not long after that, of seeing the fellow's antennae shorn from his brow.

But the young Mothmage was not the "interesting visitor" of whom he spoke. He told Mistral, "But the other was even better. I could scarcely believe my luck. I opened the door, and there she was! Magpie Windwitch."

"The champion . . . ," breathed Mistral. The despair in his airy voice told Dusk that the wind grasped the fine point:

that which Dusk craved most had just turned up on his doorstep!

The only faeries who had ever been privy to the glyph for immortality were the Djinns' champions. They had used it in the seals they placed on devils' prisons as they captured them. It was cunning magic—to keep their prisoners alive forever in their bottles so that they might never die and terrorize the Moonlit Gardens. Dusk had studied many of the seals his human crone gouged off devil bottles, but he had not been able to extract the secret. And the champions, Bellatrix and the others, were dead before his time, fools that they were. They'd given immortality to devils, but nary a one of the seven had used the glyph for themselves!

Dusk had despaired of ever getting it. He had never imagined that a new champion might rise, let alone that of all faeries it should be a little blue-eyed lass who worshipped him and who would, he had little doubt, tell him anything he wished to know.

At least, she would if he could separate her from her Rathersting friend, which he had every intention of doing.

THIRTY-SEVEN

After Slomby left with the leech bowl, the echoes of Whisper's final desperate cry died slowly away in the prison corridor. *The Azazel.* She had said his name, here in this place. She had screamed it, loosing a torrent of desperation on the dungeon's poor prisoners that plunged them even deeper into misery than they had been before. In the aftermath of the echo, the silence was haunting.

It was broken by a melodious seethe of a voice. "*What* did you say?"

Whisper peered down the corridor. She saw the golden eyes of a firedrake, glowing in the radiance of the fire he was exhaling. Vesrisath. He was magnificent. The size of a large lizard, sleek and scaled, with a mane of crimson plumes and a deadly hook of a beak.

She said, "The Azazel. It's true."

"In the hands of that fiend?"

She nodded. Behind Vesrisath, craning their necks to see, were the younger firedrakes, who had still not attained their full size even at four thousand years of age. Whisper could hear them murmuring.

"The Azazel, *here*?" asked one.

"Is he going to free us?" asked another.

Their mother hushed them. "Nay, precious," she said gently. "He's a prisoner now too."

The firedrake queen's soft words thrust a spear of guilt into Whisper's heart. It was her fault. She hadn't been able to keep the Azazel safe. Around her in the gloom, the eyes of the other prisoners stared at her, flame orange and sea green, shimmering silver and beady black. They had all been here so long—decades, centuries; in the firedrakes' case, millennia.

They were creatures who despaired of ever again seeing the sky, and after only hours in their midst, Whisper felt the despair infecting her too. Her one small hope had been Slomby. Devil or not, she was certain there was goodness in him. She had seen it in his pitiful smile and those rolling eyes that had gazed at her with such wonder. But though there might be goodness in him, there was no bravery.

If the fate of the Azazel rested in that devil slave's poor, scorched hands, then the Azazel was most certainly doomed.

Whisper slumped against the bars of her cell, and like all the other prisoners, began to subside into mute despair. She could not have said how much time passed before she heard a voice, taunting, at the end of the corridor.

"Silksinger . . . ," crooned Ethiag. A chill horror went through her. All the other prisoners scrambled back into the shadows and she wanted to hide too but she knew it was no use. The devil was here for her. He shambled into view on his restless legs, two devils slinking along behind him, low as weasels. They were dragging burlap sacks that Whisper knew must have her silk thread inside.

"I've brought you a present," Ethiag said. He gestured, and the devils emptied their sacks. She stared at what tumbled out. She had expected bobbins of reeled silk, but here were white silken spheres of cocoons, each about the size of her head. And . . . they weren't spent cocoons from which the moths had already emerged. They were *live* cocoons.

What did Ethiag think she could do with live cocoons?

"Wait," she said, but the devils kept emptying their sacks and the cocoons tumbled toward her, mounding up against the bars of her cell like a snowdrift. She said, "Nay, but you've brought the wrong thing."

Ethiag unfolded his fanged mouth to say, thickly, "Wrong? Did you not say silk thread? And is this not silk thread?"

Whisper said, "Aye, it will be, but it isn't ready yet. These are living cocoons. There are moths in them."

"And what should be in them? Slugs?" he snapped.

"Nay, there should be *nothing* in them."

Whisper knew well the process of preparing silk. She

had always raised her own silkworms, and she knew how long it took for the caterpillars to weave their cocoons and how many days they slept inside them, undergoing their extraordinary transformation. After the moths emerged and zigzagged away on their newborn wings, she gathered the torn cocoons and boiled them to loosen the threads. Then came mending the torn threads and reeling it onto bobbins, and only after all that was done could she begin to sing a carpet.

She told Ethiag, "After the moths have emerged, these can be boiled and reeled, but if you want a carpet now, I need reeled thread or, at least, spent cocoons."

Ethiag laughed. "Is that what this is about? The moths inside? Do you think I care if these bugs are born and flutter their useless lives away? I'll just have them boiled now."

"Now? *Alive?* Nay! You can't!"

"I assure you, I can."

Whisper was aghast. All those lives, all those moths, their new wings ready to unfurl and feel the air riffle across them. Instead to die unborn, and horribly. She said, "But . . . they only need another day or two and they'll emerge, and then I'll sing your carpet. Or . . . or . . . you can bring reeled thread. But I can't sing *dead* thread!" The very idea was abhorrent. It would be akin to painting a picture with blood.

"Might I remind you that if you refuse, you cease to be a Silksinger and become nothing more than a faerie, and the only other use I have for you will not require that you remain alive. Do you understand?"

Whisper clenched her fists, staring in horror at the drift of cocoons, and gave a tight nod.

Ethiag summoned Slomby from the kitchen. Whisper noticed the bruised and split skin on the snag's arms and legs at once, and the way he cowered and slunk, not meeting her eyes as he did Ethiag's bidding. He brought in a cauldron and scurried around with firewood to build up a blaze, and all the while Whisper had to sit in her cell and watch as the water slowly came to a boil. Around her she felt the cocoons emitting a hum of life that was soon to be extinguished.

When the time came, she watched with tears rolling down her cheeks as Slomby scooped up an armful of the snow-white cocoons and dropped them into the simmering cauldron.

Tears were streaming down his face too as he gathered another armful. His expression was one of purest misery, and he wouldn't meet Whisper's eyes. As the cocoons plunged into the cauldron, Whisper thought she felt a disturbance roll off the water with the steam—pain, panic, death, billowing up from the cauldron like a nest of ghosts. She stood numb as Slomby stirred it with a paddle.

When it was done, Ethiag reared up and, with his big tarantula legs, tipped the cauldron so it spilled into Whisper's cell. She leapt back as scalding water sluiced over the floor.

Cocoons tumbled out and Slomby shoved them through the bars until they formed a sodden mound in the center of the cell. Then he dragged the cauldron away with a forlorn look, and Ethiag peered in at Whisper. "There you are, Silksinger. Silk. Now sing me my flying carpet. Sing it big and sing it fine, as befits a conqueror. But above all, sing it *fast*. I want that carpet!"

He whirled away down the corridor, but he left the two weasel devils there to watch over her.

She was up to her knees in the litter of cocoons, facing the task of unwinding all the silken shrouds from around these many little corpses. The aura of death was so thick in her cell she felt she was inhaling it and exhaling it. She knelt and gingerly touched a cocoon, rolling it until she found the end of the thread. She ran it between her fingers. It was a thing of exquisite beauty. But though it looked perfect, Whisper could feel that it was . . . polluted. It was beautiful but corrupt.

What sort of carpet could she weave with such silk?

Even as she wondered it, she had her answer. All around her she felt the surge of the invisible guiding force that always led her through her weaving when she was deep in her singing trance. She saw a pattern of glyphs in her mind's eye—unfamiliar shapes giving themselves to her from some mystical place beyond her own mind. These were ugly glyphs, powerful and dangerous. Her eyes narrowed, no longer vague with horror, but hard as flakes of obsidian. What sort of carpet could she weave with dead threads?

A carpet unlike any other ever sung, in all the days of Silksingers.

With a plan taking shape in her mind, she set to clearing the cocoons to one side of her cell to give herself space to work. Nobody was going to rescue her or save the Azazel. No one was going to find this dungeon or stop the devil army. But even if she never left this cell, there was something Whisper could do. Ethiag wanted to fly? So be it. She would sing his carpet, and when he climbed onto it and rose into the air, he'd wish he had been content to crawl.

THIRTY-EIGHT

Whisper prepared herself to sing. Her whole body resisted, as if her voice did not want to emerge in this terrible place. All around her was darkness and stench, the misery of the prisoners, and the knowledge that an entire army of devils was waiting for her to fulfill her task.

She wasn't just afraid of what was around her. She feared what was *in* her and what she was about to do. It was wrong—as wrong as the death-polluted threads themselves. She wondered if the ugly glyphs would burn her throat, if they would scorch her very voice and render her unable to ever sing beauty again. Her whole body trembled as she laid the patterns out in her mind and readied herself to sink into her singing trance.

Slomby brought her food—some slippery fruit with the tang of ferment about it—and whispered, "I got the best ones I could." He brought water too, and Whisper ate and drank. She would need her strength for what was to come.

She took a deep breath, closed her eyes, and let her voice pour forth in untried magic. Like the cocoons themselves, made up of a single unbroken thread, Whisper's song was a continual skein of sound, flowing from her with no audible pauses for breath. It lifted and dipped as it went down the passages, flowing through all the tunnels of the dungeon, eddying around the prisoners in their cells, the firedrakes. Out into the cavern, the devils heard it. In his nest, Ethiag smiled.

And the skeins of death-polluted silk heard, and responded. Dozens of threads rose and danced, swaying with the tide of her voice, and merged, weaving themselves together to make the edge of a carpet. Color flushed into them as she sang, blues and reds mostly, the colors of bruising and dried blood, deepening at the edges to black.

In her trance, Whisper knew nothing but the intricate pattern of interwoven glyphs that moved through her mind. The sound of them—her own voice—she heard as if from some small place deep within herself, and it seemed not to come from her but through her.

For every bright note she sang, every glyph for strength and flight, there lurked an underlying *dark* note, treacherous as a beast hiding beneath a bridge. In a wily feat of song, she sang them together, and the bright disguised the dark so that the river of her voice did not carry her intentions to Ethiag's ears. Without the disguise, her song would have poured forth undiluted glyphs for transmutation, ensnarement, flesh, blood, and vengeance. It would have battered the senses of all who heard it and even Ethiag, ignorant of her art, would have known something was wrong.

As it was, only the firedrake king and queen detected the dark undercurrent. Vesrisath and Ryawy had lived in the age of Silksingers and knew the proper sound of their song. This—rich and sonorous as it was—was also *wrong*. It was as if the music cast a shadow.

The carpet took shape. It was exquisite, but it was not beautiful. Its decorative border was designed with a harsh geometry. Here were no delicate leaf motifs, no flowers, but dagger shapes and jagged-edged stars. The only curves were like the curvature of scythes and talons, all tapering to points.

In the center of the carpet was the beginning of a portrait. So far only bristled legs were picked out in thread, but they were so realistic that the soft rise and fall of the silk made them seem to prance.

Whisper sang, and the carpet grew.

In the sewers, Batch Hangnail was awakened by a pang of pure, sweet compulsion. For a moment he thought it must be a dream, but as he shook off the haze of sleep, it didn't fade away. It sharpened. His fingers started to twitch. His mouth filled up with saliva. The serendipity seized him and pulled, as surely as if a crow were dragging him by the tail.

With greedy eyes and a glad heart, he followed where it led.

THIRTY-NINE

After a scant hour of sleep, Magpie woke and tumbled out of her bunk. "Good morning, Lord Ithuriel," she said, peeking into his cook pot. Then she opened the door of her wagon to a dazzle of color. Morning light was streaming down through the stained glass ceiling, making the chamber look like the inside of a kaleidoscope. The crows were up, lounging in their dressing gowns, blowing smoke rings, and sipping their strong coffee.

She joined them but opted for tea. An hour of sleep had done little to shake off the heaviness from her limbs, but even that hour was time stolen from the search for the Azazel. Sleep was a luxury they could ill afford. Whisper's whereabouts remained a mystery. They'd asked around the hostelry late last night but learned nothing.

Zingaro's family and crew were the only ones who knew what the lass looked like, and they hadn't seen her. They'd greeted Magpie with blessings but bristled at the sight of Hirik. "He called the devils down on us," the hob chief growled, to which Magpie replied, "Oh, blither!"

"Ney, for true, maidy. It were a swarm of the dastard things! We'd all have been killed if the skimmers hadn't fought like lions!"

Magpie cocked an eyebrow. "The skimmers fought like lions, did they?"

"Like lions."

"Zingaro, you old goatloaf," she declared. "What do you think might make skimmers suddenly up and fight like that? Just the love in their hearts?"

Zingaro stroked his beard—which was woven, Magpie noticed, into a pattern of stars—and cast a glance at Hirik, who stood back amid the crows. "What? Ye don't mean—"

"I *do* mean," said Magpie. "Only a Mothmage could've done that. The lad saved your life. Now that's some gossip you might want to spread around town, neh?"

In the end, Zingaro had apologized to Hirik, and when Magpie told him how Stormfoil had spurned the warning of the wind and flown them heedlessly into the ambush, he'd vowed to dismiss the murk from his company.

The sky had already been brightening by the time the faeries and crows laid their heads down for their too-brief sleep. Magpie yawned. "Guess I should wake up the lads," she told the crows. "Get back to the search."

"Talon's up already," Calypso told her. "He went with Bertram to get breakfast."

"Ach, good," said Magpie. "I'm starved."

Bertram and Talon returned with a huge sack of glazed rolls, still hot from the oven, and an earthen pot of plum jam. They woke Hirik, who'd slept in Talon's wagon, and he joined them at the fire for breakfast.

"Are you feeling any better?" Magpie asked him.

"Not like I'm dying, at least."

"That's always a good way not to feel."

"Aye. I'm not so dizzy as I was. I think I'll be able to fly some."

"That's good. We got to get back to it. It shivers me we haven't found any hint of Whisper yet."

"We should try Rasilith Ev again," suggested Hirik. "Maybe she'll go back there."

The others agreed. Finishing up breakfast, the lads stood and brushed crumbs off their fronts while the crows shrugged out of their dressing gowns and hung them on hooks. Pigeon and Swig, it was determined, would stay behind to guard the caravans and the Ithuriel, while the rest went out to search.

Headed for the door, Magpie caught sight of her reflection in a wagon window and halted, chewing her lip. "Hang on," she said, and zipped into her wagon.

When she didn't emerge within a few seconds, Talon went and peered in the open door. He found her with her comb woefully ensnarled in her wind-whipped hair. "What are you doing?" he asked, having not once spied Magpie with a comb in all the weeks of their journey.

"What's it look like?" she grumbled, trying to free the comb from her tangles.

"It looks like you're primping, since you ask."

"Primping!" she cried, shooting him a scowl.

Crows appeared behind Talon. "What ye doing, Mags?" piped Pup.

"She appears to be . . . tugging some sort of tool . . . through her hair," Talon told them in a bewildered tone, as if he were describing a bizarre ritual.

"What?" squawked Pup, perplexed. "Why?"

"Why indeed?" asked Calypso with mock suspicion. "Who is that really, and what's she done with our 'Pie?"

"Skive!" Magpie exclaimed. "I'm the Magruwen's champion now! I can't go around like a scrubby sprout, can I? I don't want the folk here to think I'm a barbarian."

"Neh," agreed Calypso seriously. "We don't want *them* to think *that.*"

Swig made a smooching sound and crooned, "Nor a certain apothecary, neither. . . ."

Magpie flushed red and cursed, "Jacksmoke!" finally yanking the comb so hard it snapped in half. "You'd think I was taking a bath in perfume, the way you spatherbeaks carry on!" Her hair as wild as ever, she stormed past them.

"You still got half a comb in there," said Talon, pointing at her head.

She glared at him and tried to remove it.

"Want me to?" Talon offered.

"Neh!" she replied, giving it a hard tug that pulled out a hank of hair with it. Abashed by the attention, and because she *had* been thinking particularly of Dusk, Magpie turned away with a haughty lift of her chin. "What's so wrong with looking halfways respectable?" she grumbled.

Bertram was behind her. He caught her with his wingtips and held her still to look her up and down, squinting over the rims of his spectacles.

"Well, I reckon ye *could* use some new clothes, Mags," he said. "There's clothes for hunting and there's clothes for town, neh? Nothing wrong with looking sharp. But don't ye worry, neither. Ye're beautiful, darlin'. Any eejit can see that plain as day."

"Thanks, Bert," she said, softening. Looking back over her shoulder at the others, she called, "Let's go, then. Why are you all standing around like eejits?"

Rasilith Ev was as empty as before. This being Hirik's first sight of the temple, he turned in a circle, awed by its splendor. He tried to ignore the tide of dizziness that swelled at his every slight movement, but when he tipped back his head to look up at the dome, it proved too much, and he staggered and squeezed his eyes shut. Calypso was right by his side, ready to prop him up.

"Okay, lad?" he asked.

"Aye, thanks," said Hirik, steadying himself against the crow and fighting down the rising nausea. He wondered if it was possible he would ever adjust to this new state of being, or if he would feel seasick for the rest of his life. And then there was the intense frustration of not being able to do what a Mothmage should! Magpie showed him where they'd found Whisper's kettle lid, and for an instant, in the little chapel, he forgot himself and tried to reach out with his senses to trace her scent. Of course, there were no such senses.

He gritted his teeth. He was useless. He recalled the first time he'd seen Whisper, how frail and desperate she'd looked, pleading with Zingaro for passage. How alone she must have felt! And now? Was she alone again? Where? He couldn't stand not knowing.

"I'm sure her scent plume must be here," he said, turning in a slow circle, knowing the clue to Whisper's whereabouts was lingering in the air all around. "I . . . I would have been able to pick it up."

At his side, Magpie felt his frustration. "Skiving irkmeat murks," she muttered.

Hirik cocked an eyebrow. He'd never heard a lass curse like Magpie Windwitch. "There's one thing we might try," he said reluctantly.

"What's that?" Magpie asked.

"Madame Sallowpearl," Hirik said. At the thought of the biddy and her vile kiss, he thought he might lose his ongoing fight against nausea.

Magpie screwed her lips to one side and considered it. "But wasn't it her who called the mob on you?"

He nodded. "Aye, she's horrible, but she's powerful. The smoke, it knew where Whisper was."

Talon said, "Hirik doesn't even have to see her. We can go in."

"It's a plan," said Magpie.

They flew for Fortune-tellers Lane. At the sight of them in the air, faeries swung round and flew backward to watch them pass. They ogled Hirik, whom they all recognized as the Mothmage, and Magpie, who was champion. Talon got his share of stares too, with his pale hair and his cheekbones covered in a glyphlike pattern of tattoos. His feathered wings drew the most murmurs, but he ignored them and stared straight ahead.

Magpie returned the stares, though. Nazneen folk were known for their elegance, and she looked around, taking in their shining hair and gorgeous robes. There were ladies with their eyes painted in flourishes of kohl, gents with jeweled daggers at their hips, and sprouts as tidy as little lacquered dolls. Magpie couldn't help feeling a little like a fly that had buzzed into a flock of butterflies. She thrust out her chin and gave them all flashing looks as she flew by, as if challenging them to judge her messy hair.

She heard the murmurs of "champion—" and "bird wings—" and her ears perked up at "Mothmage!" This last exclamation was followed by, "—rallied the dragonflies to save the caravan!" and she was glad that, for once, the speed of gossip was working for good.

When they arrived at Fortune-tellers Lane, Hirik directed them to Madame Sallowpearl's cellar stairs, though he himself stayed well away and waited with Bertram and Mingus while the others went inside. They weren't inside long. The smoke charmer was not in. They inquired with the neighboring parlors, but no one had seen the biddy. She had not, apparently, emerged for breakfast as she usually did. Standing with her hands on her hips, Magpie said, "This hunt is starting to feel cursed."

"Maybe we should try other fortune-tellers," said Talon, looking down the lane at the many brightly painted parlorfronts.

"Aye," agreed Magpie. "Let's split up, see how many fortune-tellers we can consult."

They dispersed. By the time they reassembled an hour later, it was immediately clear from all their faces that they had had no luck.

"I'll tell ye what I learned," said Maniac. "That palm readers know skive-all about crows' feet."

"Maybe a palm reader wasn't the best choice since ye en't got *palms*, blackbird," quipped Calypso.

"Neh? Well, what did ye see then, if ye're so wise?"

"I got a message from my old granddad Dizzy in the Moonlit Gardens. He sends his blessings, 'Pie. Oh aye, and my lucky number is eighteen."

"Well, that's mad important," said Magpie. "Me, I did find out something interesting." They looked momentarily hopeful until she told them what it was: the Azazel's ancient skin, the three-headed one with bull's hooves, was folded up in a trunk in the attic of Nazneen's opera house.

"That might be useful *after* we find the Azazel," said Talon. He himself had been told by an astrologer in a turban that the crow star shone on him. Pup had seen something in his tea leaves that looked like either an octopus or a mop, and Mingus had learned he would fall in love within the year. The others made smooch sounds and Pup snorted, "Mingus in love?" but Mingus just shrugged and said calmly, "Ye never know what life's got in its basket for ye."

Bertram, when questioned, would reply only vaguely, "Ach, just some blither from a card reader. Naught to do with naught." He tapped the ground distractedly with his peg leg and avoided meeting anyone's eyes. "And ye, lad?" he asked Hirik, deflecting attention from himself.

Hirik blushed. "I saw . . . in a crystal ball, I saw Whisper," he said.

"What? Skive! Where is she?" they all demanded.

He blinked and said hastily, "Oh, nay. Nay, not like that. It was just a vision of her. . . . But it wasn't now."

"How do ye know?" Calypso asked.

"It was the future," he said. "She was . . . grown. She was a lady."

"Ye sure it was her?"

"I'm sure."

"I reckon that means she's still alive, anywhich," said Pup.

That gave Hirik a start. He hadn't let himself consider she might not be. And though he had indeed seen a vision of her grown, he didn't trust it was a true vision. More like it was a future that could never be. He didn't tell the details to the others, but in the crystal ball he'd seen Whisper dressed as a bride. She'd looked beautiful, her long hair dressed in tiny orchid blooms, and by her side had stood . . . himself, also grown. It gave him a very curious feeling inside, to see himself as a gent, not to mention the thought of marrying Whisper, which made his face grow hot. But that wasn't all. In the vision he'd had his antennae, full as feathers and not hidden by hair or sash. That was how he knew it couldn't be a true vision, but just some kind of a cruel taunt. The whole thing gave him a new ache in his heart.

"Well, skive," Magpie muttered. "What a lot of useless nothing."

They checked Madame Sallowpearl's again and found it still empty. They were standing in a cluster, slump-shouldered with new frustration, when a lady beckoned to Hirik from a doorway. She was clad in a sequined robe and turban, and her dark eyes were very sad as she said, "Lad, I'm so terribly sorry for what happened to you yester-eve. I'm ashamed to have watched with the rest and done nothing. Please, let me read your cards to make amends."

Hirik wanted to say he didn't know what amends a stupid card reading could possibly make, but she looked so sad and pleading he just shrugged and said, "All right."

The others all gathered behind him as he sat down to her table. They watched him shuffle the deck of painted cards, draw five as instructed, and lay them facedown, one by one. The lady flipped over the first card. It showed a moth. "Ah," said she, smiling. "An auspicious card. The moth means metamorphosis, lad. You are entering a new stage of your life, and nothing will ever be the same again."

No one spoke. They were all thinking that the new phase of Hirik's life was one of sense blindness and the death of all his dreams, and nothing auspicious at all, and then the lady turned over the next card.

It showed a flame. "Fire," she said, her voice dropping to a whisper. She fluttered a surprised glance at Hirik. "It's a very rare card. It's the Djinn's card. It stands for strength and for creation . . . and *re*-creation, like metal smelted in a furnace and made pure. *Forged,* as it were."

Hirik stared at the card and listened to the lady's words. A few days ago, he would have believed it to be a sign that his dream would come true, that he would be champion. But now, it seemed just another taunt.

In quick succession, the fortune-teller flipped over the remaining three cards. They showed a poppy, an orchid, and the moon.

None of these meant anything to Hirik, nor to the fortune-teller either, who started in on a meandering augury of love and luck, but to Magpie and Talon, they did mean something. Their eyes met over the top of Hirik's head, and all the morning's frustration was temporarily forgotten.

They knew what to do.

FORTY

Back in her gypsy wagon with the door closed, Magpie visioned the glyphs of passage and took herself to the Moonlit Gardens. She paused just long enough to wave to the dead across the river. She saw the champions and Merryvenom and the Silksingers, clustered together and anxious for news. She waved, feeling guilty for not going to talk to them, and then drew new glyphs in her mind that would carry her to Dreamdark.

Usually, when Magpie used her mystical shortcut, she visioned herself straight to the courtyard of Issrin Ev, the Magruwen's temple. This time, she aimed for the healer's cottage on the far side of the Deeps.

She found Poppy and Orchidspike in the garden.

"Magpie!" cried Poppy, leaping to her feet and then to her wings and sailing up to meet Magpie in the air. She was dressed for gardening in a plain chemise and wide-brimmed hat, with her red hair hanging straight in two plaits. The simple attire did nothing to dull her beauty, however. She

346

was as lovely as ever. Her brown eyes sparkled, and so did the golden veins of her tremendous butterfly wings. "I didn't hear you coming!" she said.

It was difficult to sneak up on Poppy Manygreen, what with the trees and ferns acting as her lookouts and telling her everything that happened in the forest. Poppy was possibly the last faerie in the world with the ancient gift of speaking with plants. Magpie said, "I guess I finally figured out how to surprise you! I came straight from the Moonlit Gardens."

The two lasses hugged, and when they drew apart, Poppy asked, "How goes the search?"

Magpie just grimaced. She dropped down to the ground to greet Orchidspike, the old healer of Dreamdark. Orchidspike was some two thousand years old, a whole lifetime older than most faerie elders still alive in the world, and Magpie couldn't help but notice that she looked as if her age was catching up to her.

Orchidspike had lingered in the world past her time, hoping to find a suitable apprentice to carry on her knowledge. Now that she had Poppy, her yearning for the Moonlit Gardens had grown sharp. Magpie knew that as soon as Orchidspike had passed on the last of her arts to Poppy, she would sigh with relief and bid the living world farewell.

She hugged her gently and gave her a parcel. "This is from Nazneen," she said. "Talon sends his blessings and wishes he could come too."

"Aye, and so do I. I miss him terribly," said Orchidspike, opening the little parcel to find a packet of Nazneen's finest masala chai, a fragrant tea mixed with ginger, cardamom, pepper, and cloves. The old healer inhaled the exotic spices and shook her head in wonderment. "What scents!" she said. "I should have gone to see the world! Thank you for bringing it to me in spice."

"You're welcome," Magpie said, breathing deeply too, but not of the chai. The green woodland scent of Dreamdark gave her a sudden feeling of home.

Poppy said, "But what brings you, Magpie? Can you stay awhile?"

"Neh," Magpie said. "I wish I could, but I come begging, I'm afraid. What would you say if I told you that all the way in Nazneen, a fortune-teller's cards just turned you two up?"

"What do you mean?" asked Poppy.

Magpie told them about Hirik, keeping her story quick and winding it up with, "So, I'm hoping it was no coincidence in those cards and that there's something you can do for him. Dusk the apothecary knew nothing for it, so I thought mayhap there was no magic for growing back what's been cut, but seeing those two flowers alongside the moth and the moon, it made me hope."

Poppy and Orchidspike turned to look at each other. "Are you thinking what I'm thinking?" Poppy asked.

"Well, it's not exactly the same. . . ."

"Nay, but the *idea* is the same. . . ."

"It just might work—"

"What? What?" Magpie asked, fairly bouncing up and down. "What might work?"

Poppy said, "Well, there's a poultice to regenerate lost limbs on trees. The healers of Dreamdark have used it for ages."

"Do you think it might work for antennae?"

Orchidspike said, "It's never been tried on a creature."

"But I think it could," said Poppy. "I think if I . . ." She trailed off. Her eyes went dreamy as she sank into her thoughts, working out the magic in her head—carried, as Magpie knew, by the guiding pulse of the Tapestry. Even in excitement Poppy had an aura of serenity that soothed Magpie. She found herself feeling absolutely certain that Poppy would be able to help, and she was unsurprised when, after a moment, her friend said, "I'll want to make a few substitutions, but I think I can do it."

It took Poppy some time to mix a new version of the ancient regeneration poultice, and Magpie had no choice but to practice patience, which she did not number among her virtues. At last, Poppy finished and troweled the paste into a little jar. She asked Magpie hopefully, "Can you stay for tea?"

"I wish I could, but I've got to get back. Hirik's antennae might be our best chance of finding the Azazel."

"Well, I hope it works," Poppy said. "He needs to put this on the wounds, thick, and then wrap his brow in something silk to spur the metamorphosis, and then sleep for at least twelve hours."

"Twelve hours!" exclaimed Magpie.

"Aye, I'm sorry, but it's crucial to the spell, Magpie. Here's a sleeping draught for him so he'll be sure not to wake and disrupt the magicks." She decanted a small bit of an emerald-green solution into a vial, corked it, and handed it over. "Okay?"

Magpie nodded. "Thank you," she said earnestly, hugging her friend.

In parting, Orchidspike gave Magpie two kisses on the forehead. "One for you and one for Talon." With a twinkle in her eye, she said, "You won't mind passing his along to him, will you?"

Magpie wrinkled up her nose and said, "I'll *tell* it to him, and that'll have to do!"

Orchidspike laughed, and Magpie vanished out of Dreamdark.

When she glimmered back into her caravan, she scarcely waited until she had fully materialized before she burst out the door. The lads and crows were waiting for her on the scattered cushions around the fire, and she took note that Bertram scrambled to hide something from her in his sewing basket, then blinked at her innocently through his spectacles. Hirik, who had no idea that she hadn't been inside the wagon the whole time, looked confused when she thrust the little jar and vial at him and said in a rush, "This might work, lad. For your antennae!"

"What?" He leapt to his feet. He took the little containers. "But how—?" He looked at her wagon, then back at her. "Did you *make* these?" he asked.

Magpie frowned slightly. She couldn't tell him where she had gotten the medicines without telling him about her otherworldly shortcut, so she just said, "Eh, sure."

Hirik wasted no time opening the jar and, at Magpie's direction, smeared the paste onto the nicks where his antennae had been. Magpie fetched a silk scarf for him to wrap around his brow and said, "Now you better take the sleeping draught and go lie down. We'll wake you up in twelve hours and see if it worked. Okay?"

"Okay . . . ," he said, starting toward the wagon where he'd slept the night before. He turned back and said, his voice hoarse with emotion, "Thank you."

"Thank me if it works," she replied with a hopeful smile.

Once Hirik was gone, Magpie turned to Talon and said, "Oh, I almost forgot. I have something for you too." She made a show of kissing her fingernail and then, with a flourish, flicked him on the forehead with it.

"Ow!" he said, rubbing his brow. "What was that for?"

351

She shrugged and said innocently, "I don't know. It's not from me, it's from Orchidspike."

"She told you to *flick* me?"

"Neh," Magpie said, rolling her eyes as if it were a ridiculous suggestion. "It was the kiss part that was from her. The flick was just the only acceptable means of delivery."

"Oh, well," Talon said, kissing his own fingernail. "Next time you see her, give her a kiss for me too." She twisted and the flick landed on her ear.

"Ow!" she cried, darting away on her wings. "Crows," she complained. "Talon just kissed me on the ear!"

"I did not!" he said. "My fingernail did."

The crows shook their heads and clucked their tongues. "And she claims she en't a sprout," said Calypso with a chuckle.

It was evening by now. Mingus and Swig had cooked up a pot of curry while Magpie was away, and Pigeon had flown into the bazaar to buy savory bread to dunk in it, so they all sat down together to eat. After they were through, Pigeon said, "And look what else I got," and produced a little pink box filled with chocolates.

"Chocolate!" Magpie declared, pretending to fall into a swoon. Faerie hands and crow feet darted toward the box as they each grabbed a piece and ate with gusto.

"Mmm, mine's got coconut in it!" Magpie exclaimed.

"Mine's got nuts," said Talon.

"I think . . . ," ventured Pup, smacking his beak, "mine's got *radish*."

"Radish! Glad I didn't get that one," they all agreed.

After the box was empty, which didn't take long, Talon said, "It reminds me of the first night I camped with you feathers, in the school attic outside Dreamdark. Remember, Ming stole some chocolate from the mannies?"

"I remember," said Magpie. "You'd never seen chocolate before, or mannies, or much of anything! Funny to think that wasn't so long ago, and now look at you. You been to Rome, Ifrit, and Serendip, the Bay of Drowned Dragons, the Sayash."

"Aye, lad," said Bertram, patting him on the back with his wingtip. "Seems like ye been with us a long time. Ye're just one of us is all."

Talon smiled, and a warmth crept up his cheeks. "Thanks," he said softly. When he stopped to think about it, he could hardly believe how much his life had changed since that day in West Mirth when Magpie had tackled him in his falcon skin and held Skuldraig to his throat. What a meeting it had been! If somebody had told him that day that in scarcely more than a month he'd be camping in a dragonfly hostelry in the Sayash Mountains with the wild lass who'd almost cut his throat, he'd have laughed. But here he was, with Magpie at his side. She was like a spark of pure energy, he thought, stealing a glance at her.

She looked back just then and their eyes met, and Talon felt the surge in the Tapestry, as if the very threads of creation were dancing in their weave.

"Aye," she said, her blue eyes sparkling. "You're one of us for true, Talon. And as such, it's your turn to do these dishes!"

Talon's groan was just for show; he didn't really mind at all. Back home where he was a prince, he never had to wash dishes, but here, having his place in the mundane rotation of chores made him feel like part of this small, strange family. "Fine," he said, and stood up to collect the tin cups and spoons.

He was up to his elbows in suds when a knock came at the chamber door that disrupted the harmony of his evening.

"Dusk!" said Magpie happily when the apothecary poked his head in.

Talon watched him smile his preposterous smile, come inside, and hug her. "Enough with all the hugging," he grumbled under his breath.

Dusk greeted all the crows, and when his gaze came to rest on Talon, he laughed and said, "They've got you doing all the work, have they?" His voice was jovial, but there was a mocking twist at the corners of his smile that made Talon feel like a scullery maid.

"Neh, it's just my turn is all," he replied defensively.

Dusk smiled and looked around. "Where's Hirik?" he asked.

"Oh," said Magpie. "He's asleep."

"How is he? Is the dizziness improved?"

"He says so," she replied, smiling mysteriously. She was looking forward to sharing Poppy's spell with him and revealing Hirik's antennae once they were all grown back. She was sure he'd be surprised.

"I'm glad I could help," he said. "It's such a terrible thing, what those mercenaries did to him."

"Ye want some tea, Dusk?" Calypso asked.

"Thank you for the offer, Calypso, but I came to lure Magpie out to the bazaar. I thought we could get caught up, just the two of us." He winked at her and added, "I'm prepared to offer chocolate as a bribe."

"We just had chocolate, in fact," said Talon.

"Well, you can never have too much, can you?" Dusk returned evenly.

"Actually, ye can," said Swig. "I've seen Mags do it. She had to lie on the ground for a good three hours once when she ate so much her wings couldn't lift her."

"That was only because you dared me!" said Magpie.

Dusk laughed and offered her his elbow. "Shall we?"

Talon bristled, but when Magpie sighed and said, "Ach, I can't. Talon and I were about to go out searching again," he smiled a gloating smile into his dish suds.

Dusk rallied. "Ah well, if it's all work and no play, then perhaps I have another inducement to get you to spend some time with me. I have gossip that may relate to your Silksinger."

"Oh, aye?" asked Magpie. "What?"

"Last night," he said, lifting an eyebrow dramatically, "Silk Alley was plundered."

"Silk Alley? But what was taken?"

"That's the interesting thing. No cloth was stolen, only cocoons. When I heard that, I wondered if your lass might not have taken them, to sing herself a flying carpet."

"Jacksmoke!" said Magpie. "Do you think so?"

"I'll take you to Silk Alley," said Dusk. "You can see the warehouse where the cocoons were stolen."

"Okay," she said. "Let's go." Dusk offered his elbow again, but his smile was cut short when she looked over her shoulder and called, "Talon, you coming?"

FORTY-ONE

Batch Hangnail found nothing of interest in the gleaming front room of The Dragon's Scale. Roots and flower petals—not at all his sort of plunder. He didn't even pause there. The serendipity had him in its undertow, and once he'd slipped inside the apothecary shop, he scooted straight to the staircase that led down.

He'd lurked in the lane for what felt like hours waiting for the apothecary to leave, and at last, he had. It had taken another half hour before the lane emptied enough for Batch to risk picking the lock, but now he was in, and he glided down the steps with the utter certainty of one in the grips of a higher power.

Somewhere down here he would find a flying carpet. He could feel it.

At the bottom of the steps was a library. Rows of bookshelves receded in darkness, but Batch's eyes were made for the dark. He had no trouble picking out the grand fireplace, its heavy stone mantel all covered in candles, years' worth of wax drippings seeming to form strange figures like the gargoyles on a manny's cathedral. Before the fire were a pair of armchairs and, between them, a carpet.

Batch didn't have to sniff or search. With the genius of his gift, he went straight to the carpet and tossed it back to reveal the trapdoor beneath. Even this was disguised to ordinary eyes to look simply like flagstones, but Batch reached instinctively for the edge of the stone where a latch was hidden. When he pulled it, it gave a satisfying twang and the flagstone popped open.

Golden light glimmered up into the library. The room below was lit by candles, and it wasn't only candlelight that beckoned Batch down; it was the unmistakable whiff of bones. He smiled. *This* was his kind of plunder.

There was a problem, though. The floor lay quite far below, and there was no staircase or ladder betwixt it and the trapdoor. Of course, a faerie like the apothecary would simply bridge the distance with a whoosh of wings, but Batch had no wings. He leaned down, his nose quivering with the smells. He could jump, he thought; it wasn't getting *down* that was the problem. It was getting *up* later on. But by then, he told himself, it wouldn't be an issue.

By then he'd have his flying carpet.

With gleeful abandon, he leapt. He landed hard with a wheeze of, "Munch!" and looked around. Drool gathered in the divot beneath his tongue when he saw what manner of place he had discovered. It could have been a paradise dreamed up just for him. Jars of teeth! Baskets of vertebrae! Tusks, skulls, eyelashes! His nose was in overdrive, taking it all in.

But as much of a wonderland as this laboratory was, Batch didn't even pause there for long. The serendipity was still tugging at him, so he scampered through it and found the corkscrew stair that coiled straight down into the rock. Humming to himself, he descended in darkness.

"No place is too dark—the dark is my pleasure!
No danger's too great, to keep me from treasure."

But when he got to the bottom, he took one peek at the army of devils that lay between himself and his flying carpet, and he turned right around with a squeak and scurried back up.

After all, perhaps some dangers *were* too great.

Magpie and Talon poked around in the warehouse where the cocoons had been stolen, but they found no evidence to suggest Whisper might have been there. They tried to memory-touch a few spots but got only disjointed fragments that clearly belonged to the proprietor, a portly codger named Figwort.

"I think he likes prunes," Talon whispered to Magpie after he'd experienced three separate memories of the faerie eating them out of a paper sack.

They shrugged to each other and joined Dusk at the door. "Nothing?" he asked.

"Nothing," Magpie answered.

Brightly, he said, "I've had another idea. Didn't Hirik mention a smoke charmer in the bazaar? You might try her—"

Talon said, "Now why didn't we think of that?"

Catching his sarcasm, Dusk said, "You tried her already."

"Well, we *tried* to try her," said Magpie. "She wasn't there."

"Perhaps she is now. Shall we go and see?"

"Aye, sure."

When they got to Fortune-tellers Lane and found Madame Sallowpearl's shop dark and empty, Dusk said simply, "Curious." Then, since they were so near Sweetsellers Lane, he proposed they go for a nectar. "Come, my treat. If you keep resisting Sweetsellers Lane, I'll have a hard time believing you're really Little Terror Windwitch and not an imposter."

"Well, okay," Magpie said with mock reluctance. "If I *have* to."

"But we should—" Talon began.

"You needn't come along, lad," said Dusk. "Truly."

Narrowing his eyes, Talon came along. As soon as they were sitting down in a shop with tall glasses of nectar ice,

360

Dusk started asking Magpie questions. "Tell me about capturing devils," he said, leaning forward and fixing her with all the stunning intensity of his green gaze. "Have you fought many?"

Magpie nodded, spooning mango ice into her mouth. "I used to know how many exactly, but after that whole horde in the Moo—ow!"

Talon kicked her under the table, and she glared at him and muttered, "*All right.* Skive." Turning back to Dusk, she said, "It seems like a lot sometimes, but it's nothing compared to how many the old champions caught."

"Aye, but that was during the wars. Surely there will never again be so many devils to fight."

"I hope not."

"And the seals," Dusk said, all fascination. "Tell me, Magpie . . . you were capturing devils before you became champion, so how were you sealing the bottles?"

"Oh, that," she said. "You mean the champions' seal? I used to worry about it. My father never could find the sealing spell in any books."

"Nay," said Dusk. "Nor I. So, what did you do?"

"I made up my own."

"Aye, you always were making up your own spells. But such a spell, surely, goes beyond your ability."

Talon made a snorting sound into his tamarind ice, and Magpie said casually, "Neh, my spell works."

"But how do you know?" Dusk persisted. "Inside those sealed prisons could be dead devils. Without the proper sealing spell . . . without the *glyph for immortality* . . . the devils must die in their bottles and go on to the Moonlit Gardens. And you couldn't have known that glyph before you became champion."

"Neh," Magpie acknowledged. "I didn't know it. At least, I didn't *know* I knew it. But it was in my spell just the same. The Magruwen looked at it and he said it was fine."

That was just what the Magruwen had said: that her sealing spell was "fine." But it was the way that he had said "fine" that had made her blush with pride. It hadn't been the sort of fine as in, "How are you, I'm *fine*," but more like a startled, smoky exhalation of, "Little bird, this spell is a very *fine* thing." It had been one of their earliest lessons, and he'd gone on to tell her the spell was "extraordinary." She really would have liked to tell Dusk that part, but recalling how Talon had accused her of bragging, she kept it to herself.

Dusk looked confused. "But . . . how is that possible?"

"He says I'm intuitive," she replied with a shrug. In an effort at humility, she added, "He also says I'm messy and wild, though. When I weave the Tapestry I make awful tangles, but some are *good* tangles—"

"When you *weave the Tapestry* . . . ," Dusk repeated, his voice flat with incredulity.

"Oh," said Magpie, biting her lip. Perhaps, she realized too late, mentioning that she could weave the Tapestry of Creation was not the best attempt at humility. She glanced at Talon, and she could tell by his half-lidded look that he considered this a brag. Still biting her lip, she mumbled, "Aye. I can . . . do that."

Dusk was looking at her in that marveling way of his, but she thought there was something different about it now, something slightly squinting and dubious. "You can weave the Tapestry."

She nodded.

"And you *intuited* the champions' seal."

"Oh, well, not exactly. Mine's a little different." Besides the glyphs for eternity, invincibility, and immortality, Magpie had included a glyph that had never been a part of the champions' seals: the sixth glyph for sleep.

It was the sleep of the unborn, the unformed—the dreamful rest of creatures in cocoon and egg. "And you have gifted it to your prisoners," the Magruwen had said in amazement when he examined the tangle in the Tapestry that was responsible for the spell. "All these thousands of years these prisons have drifted since the Devil Wars, their occupants were alive, immortal, and *awake*. In the hatred spawned by war and the Astaroth's betrayal, my brethren and I did not think to give the devils peace, though their wickedness was none of their own doing. You have

363

done what we were too cruel to do. You have given them not only eternity, but eternal *peace*. Little bird, this spell is a thing of beauty. Your intuition is an exquisite, unguessable thing. In truth, I am growing accustomed to the new, wild Tapestry you have been weaving up in bursts and starts. In some small ways, like this one, it is *better* than it was before."

It was by far the nicest thing the Magruwen had ever said to her, and there was just no way to tell Dusk about it without sounding smug. She said only, "I used a glyph for sleep in mine, to give the devils peace."

Dusk said, "Perhaps you can share the spell with me so that I can write it down."

Magpie chewed her lip uncomfortably, but it was Talon who saved her having to refuse. "She can't," he said. "The sealing spell's only for champions, as you surely know."

"Then I suppose *you* don't know it," said Dusk.

"I'm not a champion, am I?"

Dusk gave him a thin smile and replied, "The champion's own champion, perhaps. It's so nice that Magpie has you around . . . constantly. She always wanted a brother. Didn't you, Terror?"

Talon replied stiffly, "I'm not her *brother*."

"Ach," said Magpie, watching the ever-growing animosity between her best friend and Dusk. "I got seven brothers

Batch

of the crow kind, and that's plenty. Talon's more like a . . . *sidekick.*"

He turned to her to protest but saw the mischievous twinkle in her eyes. "Sidekick," he grumbled. "I'll side kick *you*," but his eyes were twinkling too. He stood up from the table and said, "If you're done flibberting around with nectar and conversation, Lady Champion, your sidekick thinks it's time to go. We can do a sweep of the city." With perfect politeness that still somehow came across as insolence, he thanked Dusk for the nectar ice. Turning back to Magpie, he said, "Race you to Rasilith Ev," and leapt into the air.

Magpie barely had time to call goodbye to Dusk before she leapt too. Talon knew how she hated to lose a race.

Back up in the laboratory, Batch caught his breath from the long climb up the stairs from the devil-infested cavern, then started poking around in the bins of teeth and oddments. As he scavenged a few choice finds, like a lock of dryad's hair and the knucklebone of a selkie, it occurred to him to wonder what a faerie was doing with such grisly goodies, not to mention access to a devil army.

It was then that he realized what was right in front of his nose, smoldering away in a lidless copper kettle.

The Azazel.

"If only missy faerie could see me now," he said with a

wicked chuckle, picking it up to peer at the fire elemental inside. It wasn't much to look at, just a little glimmery ember that could hardly set a whisker ablaze. "She'll never find it down here," he gloated. "Faeries can't find their nose with both hands!" He set it back up on the worktable and said, "Ach, well, it en't my worry!" And he got back to plundering. But to his very great surprise, his mind kept turning to the Azazel.

It wasn't desire. He didn't want the thing. Quite the opposite. He'd had enough of Djinn! That ferocious old scorch of a Magruwen had sizzled him good back in Dreamdark. The fur on his rump had barely grown back! Batch would be happy if he never saw another Djinn. It was just that he started to recall some of the things Magpie had told him. He hadn't *meant* to listen to her, but some words must have slipped into his head anyway, like letters under a door. What was it she'd said? Something about old socks. The world falling apart like old socks, and the end of everything?

The end of diamonds, and flying, and everything.

Whiskers twitching at the thought, Batch turned back to the kettle. It would be easy enough for him to take it, he supposed. There it was, right there! He could take it and hide it someplace and not tell her where until she got him a flying carpet!

And . . . all those devils down in the cavern . . . he supposed he could tell her about them too . . . but probably not. Batch had always had a fantasy about plundering a ghost town where the folk were all gone or dead, with everything right how they'd left it—like back in the Silksingers' caves, but a whole city's worth! Neh, he wouldn't tell the faerie about the devils, and maybe he'd get his ghost town.

But the Azazel, he'd better get him out of here if he didn't want to see the world end before he could finally fly. He tucked the kettle under his arm and turned to go. He stopped and stared up at the trapdoor high overhead.

He had forgotten that he couldn't get out.

A few minutes later, Dusk, coming home from Sweetsellers Lane, entered his library to find his trapdoor thrown open. He was already in a foul temper to be returning without the glyph for immortality. He had believed, setting out this evening, that he had bitten his very last leech. But instead he would welcome the dawn with his usual blood breakfast, and he would have to try again to separate Magpie from that tattoo-scribbled little bodyguard of hers.

So, when he saw his trapdoor open, his thinly concealed rage erupted. With a snarl, he dropped down through the opening and landed hard on his feet, his wings sending a gust through the laboratory that riffled the pages of open books and unsettled dust from the bundles of bones.

Immediately he set eyes on the intruder and knew it for a scavenger imp. "Well," he said in an acid voice. "What have we here?"

Very faintly, the imp squeaked, "Munch."

FORTY-TWO

It was dawn in the hostelry. Maniac, the crow on watch, perched atop the stage caravan, while within it Magpie was snug in her bunk at the end of her first real sleep in days. While her body rested, her mind was with the Magruwen, exploring the Tapestry.

Smoldering in the cook pot, the Ithuriel dreamed his own unguessable dreams, and in the next wagon, the lads were sound asleep too.

Hirik's was no ordinary sleep. Brought on by Poppy's potion, it was the sleep of metamorphosis, the same as that of a moth chrysalis, and the same, for that matter, as that of the devils sealed in Magpie's prisons. His dreams were as vivid and real as if he entered a new country and met other dreamers there—things unborn, preparing themselves for life. Cricket and frog song curled around him, and the air was thick with the green perfume of new leaves uncurling to the sun. A heron flew past and was followed by a school of fish, swimming in air. It was a curious sort of dream in which he knew that he was asleep and that he was waiting, as if to be reborn.

The crows all slept too, except for Maniac, and it was he alone who heard the soft scrabbling that came just after sunrise at the big wooden door. It sounded like claws. And was that a feeble moan? He glided down off the caravan roof and went to investigate.

He thought it might be the murk with the hobgoblin tusks, who'd been hanging around the hostelry, chugging throatfire and pleading with Magpie to undo her spell. When the crow unlatched the door, the weight of a creature on the outside forced it fully open. Maniac squawked and leapt back, ready for a fight, but it wasn't the murk. It was Batch Hangnail, swaying on his feet. The imp took one staggering step forward, wheezed a pitiful, "Help," and collapsed across the threshold.

"Jacksmoke!" croaked Maniac. "Mags! Feathers! Come quick!"

Blood-drenched, the imp looked to have been savagely beaten. When Magpie raced to his side, she saw Batch's eyelids quivering as he struggled to maintain consciousness. "What happened to you, imp?" she asked him.

"Help," he repeated in a tiny, forlorn voice.

He whimpered in agony when they tried to carry him to the cushions, so Magpie floated him there and set him gently down. "Batch, can you talk?" she asked. "What happened?"

Moaning, he managed to say, "The Azazel . . ."

"What? What about him?" Magpie demanded.

"Found him. . . . He's . . . he's . . ." His voice was growing ever fainter.

"Where, Batch? Where?" Magpie prompted.

Whispering now, Batch said again, "He's . . ." and then he fainted dead away, and nothing Magpie did would rouse him.

"Skive," she said after shaking him, splashing water on his face, and the exclamation "Look! A flying carpet!" failed to wake him.

Calypso suggested she try memory touch, and she did. But the way the spell worked, she could see only the imp's most recent thoughts—in this case the dream he was having at that very moment of himself upon a flying carpet.

"I'll have to bring him to Dusk," said Magpie. "He'll know how to wake him."

Talon said, "Hirik will wake up soon—"

"Aye. You stay here until he does," Magpie said. "I'll come back as quick as I can. If Batch knows where the Azazel is, I have to be there when he wakes up. *If* he wakes up." In spite of her contempt for Batch Hangnail, she felt a surge of tenderness to see him in such a condition. "I wonder what did this to him."

"It doesn't bode well for Whisper, does it?" said Talon quietly.

Magpie realized he was right. If whoever—or *whatever*—had the Azazel had done this to Batch, what might have become of Whisper by now?

"Calypso, come with me," she said. She floated Batch once more into the air, and with a care he'd never taken when he'd hauled the imp before, the crow chief took hold of his tail and guided him gently through the air.

They flew over the bazaar. It was quiet, with only the bakeries open this early. The air smelled of dew and hot bread. In Apothecary Lane, all the shops were still dark, but blessedly, Dusk answered on the first knock.

"Terror," he said with a broad smile. "What an unexpected pleasure. . . ." His voice trailed off when he saw the imp. "But what—?"

"I need your help again," Magpie said. "He's unconscious. I need you to wake him up."

"I don't often have . . . imp clientele," he said with a frown of distaste.

"Please," Magpie said. "He knows where the Azazel is."

Dusk raised his eyebrows. "Does he now?" he murmured. "Well, bring him in."

Magpie and Calypso entered with Batch floating between them. Dusk peered past them into the street and asked, "And the Rathersting lad? Isn't he coming too?"

"Neh," said Magpie. "He stayed behind."

Dusk smiled and locked the door.

Hirik opened his eyes and sat up. The movement did not make him dizzy. As he reached up with steady hands to unwind the silk scarf from around his brow, he was filled with calm certainty that he was healed. That he was *whole* again.

And he was.

The scarf fell away and two antennae uncurled from his brow like young ferns, perfect, new, and alive. Joy bloomed in Hirik's chest, swelling to fill him. His heart felt huge with it; a lump formed in his throat; tears came to his eyes. He couldn't contain it all, but sat there quietly as joy flowed out him.

A tear spilled over his lashes and streaked his cheek—the first true tear of his journey. He remembered Stormfoil's wager, and even the thought of the murk wasn't enough to dampen his joy. He rose and walked out of the wagon. The crows and Talon turned at the sound of the door and broke out into cheers when they saw him. They surrounded him, laughing and patting him on the back with their wings.

"It worked!" trilled Pup. "Blessings, those are handsome feelers! Can ye smell me?"

Indeed he could. Their scents swirled around him: cheroots, coffee, rain, dirt—a wonderful combination, he thought. Smiling, he asked, "But where's Magpie?"

"She's not here," Talon told him. And then he explained about the scavenger imp.

Hirik felt all his joy freeze within him. "He was beaten?" he asked.

"Beaten bloody," affirmed Swig. "Looked partways dead to me."

Hirik's mind made the connections. The imp had seen the Azazel. The imp was beaten bloody. "Whisper—" he said.

"It doesn't mean—" Talon began, but Hirik cut him off.

"I'm going to Rasilith Ev," he said. "Now."

"I'm coming with you."

Side by side, the two lads flew out the door and raced toward the temple domes, where they circled and went down.

Hirik entered first and darted straight to the spot where Swig had found the kettle lid. The small hairs of his antennae were moving in waves, like harp strings played in scales. He turned in a slow circle, then the antennae twitched and he moved, quick and fluid, to sail across the whole breadth of the great hall with one powerful wingbeat. He knelt and flipped up one of the marble tiles in the floor. Beneath it lay a tunnel. Talon was right behind him, and even without antennae he could smell the rank odor that wafted up from below.

"A devil took her," Hirik said. "It took her down there."

"We need to go get Magpie," said Talon.

"Nay." Hirik shook his head and drew his scimitar. A crackling filigree of lightning coursed up and down its blade.

"I'm going in. If she's still alive, I'm going to make sure she stays that way. Are you coming with me?"

Talon hesitated. He wished one of the crows had come with them so he could send Magpie a message.

"I'm going," said Hirik, and he dropped down into the tunnel.

Talon unsheathed both his arm-holstered knives in one swift movement, then jumped into the darkness after Hirik.

"He's alive, isn't he?" asked Magpie, holding a hand out in front of Batch's massive nostrils.

"He is," Dusk said, and Magpie felt the soft touch of air as the imp exhaled.

"Well, good," said Calypso. "Though I never thought I'd root for this varmint's life."

But alive or not, Batch could not be awakened. Dusk had tried various smelling salts, and with Magpie's assistance he had poured several potions down the imp's gullet. They had even tried pinching him, all to no avail. "I can't imagine why nothing's working," said the apothecary, putting his hand to his chin in a pose of consternation. "There must be a spell that's holding him under."

"A spell?" said Magpie. "But who could've done that?"

"I don't know." Dusk lifted up one of Batch's eyelids and peered into his beady black eyeball. He let the lid snap back into place and said to Magpie, "I may be able to lift it, though."

376

"Oh, aye?" she asked.

He nodded. "I've a magical gem," he said. "It was a gift years ago from a witch doctor in the Skyrn Tangle. I've never had to use it, in fact, but its reputed magic is that it frees victims from sorcery."

"That's a fine trick," said Magpie. "Can you try it on him?"

He nodded. "Let me get it," he said, and went out of the room.

They were in the parlor where a few days earlier Hirik had lain ill, and Batch was sprawled on the same velvet chaise. He was covered in blood, scarcely breathing, and his diamond-decked tail was worm-limp. He looked like a dead thing. Magpie couldn't sit still, but paced the room while Dusk was gone.

He returned holding up a chain from which dangled a large ruby. It was a very red gem, of the precious grade of ruby called "pigeon's blood," and when the light hit it, it threw off red starbursts like fireworks. As for it being magical, that was not in doubt. Magpie saw at once that its surface was crawling with traceries and glyphs.

"Its name is Mogok," said Dusk, holding it up over Batch's head. He turned to Magpie. "Are you ready?"

She nodded and leaned forward. At her side, Calypso leaned in too. As Dusk began to speak in Old Tongue, they watched the gem. It seemed to pulse with an inner light.

"Skelau ethbane en ysak y rakath," said Dusk. Magpie's gaze was fixed on Mogok, and she didn't notice that Dusk closed his eyes midway through his utterance.

On *"rakath,"* the red jewel pulsed, shooting out sparks of light, and pinpoints of red appeared dead center in Magpie's and Calypso's pupils. Dusk opened his eyes and looked at them with satisfaction. They were sitting perfectly still and staring unblinkingly at Mogok, whose trick was in fact not to *free* victims from sorcery, but to *enslave* them to it, as it had the Mothmage warriors four thousand years ago, preventing them from flying into battle. Its name, Dusk had failed to explain to Magpie, meant *thrall.*

"Magpie?" he asked softly. "Can you hear me?"

"Aye, my lord," she said, her voice eerily flat.

"And you'll tell me anything I wish to know, won't you, my dear?"

"Aye, my lord," she repeated in the same tone.

Dusk smiled. Had Magpie been fit to remark on it, she would have seen it was the same beautiful smile that always sent a little thrill through her. "Wonderful," he breathed.

On the chaise, Batch suddenly shifted his bulk and sat up on his elbows. "Are we done yet?" he asked petulantly. "I itch."

"Nay, I'll tell you when we're done, imp," said Dusk.

"But that blood you poured on me is all sticky," he whined, scratching his rump.

"Shut up and lie back down," Dusk instructed.

"Ye got to admit, though, I'm a flotching fine actor."

"That you are, Master Hangnail, and you shall have your reward. Now, if you please, play dead."

With a grumble, Batch resumed his lifeless pose. "Fine, fine," he said. "But hurry up, would ye? And no more pinching!"

FORTY-THREE

Slomby crouched in the dungeon kitchen, listening to Whisper's song. It seemed to twirl the very air into patterns, and when he closed his eyes he saw bursts of color against the insides of his eyelids. All throughout the night, this river of sound had poured through the dungeon. Whisper had sung without respite, and all the prisoners and slaves, even heartless Num and the whole horde of devils in the cavern, had held themselves still to listen.

Ethiag paced restlessly in front of Whisper's cell, watching his carpet take shape. If it wasn't for that, Slomby would have been there himself, kneeling at the bars and watching the maidy sing. Just before dawn he had gotten a glimpse of her, when he'd gone to leech the drakes. She'd looked very delicate, head tipped back on her slender neck, eyes closed, lips open to release her haunting song. Beautiful as it was, that song, it made Slomby's skin creep, just a little, like it was alive and—he had a queer feeling—like it was *hungry*.

The silken threads had been unwinding themselves from the cocoons and dancing into the magical weave of the carpet. And as each cocoon exhausted its thread, disclosing the moth corpse within, another spun forth to replace it. Corpse after corpse was unveiled, and Whisper sang on.

Slomby sniffled, thinking of that sad litter of little corpses. He had done that. He had dropped them by the armful into that boiling water and killed them. The pretty maidy would hate him now, and he didn't blame her. His heart, which already felt like a wrung rag, twisted itself even tighter. Everybody hated him, and they should. He was just a low snag and a coward, an ugly, craven sniffler of a suckfish who did the bidding of his wicked masters no matter what he really wanted to do. And what he wanted to do was *help*.

Maybe if he did help, he thought, Whisper wouldn't hate him after all. At the thought, the tight twist of his heart eased just a little. Could he help, low thing that he was? He wanted to go and talk to the firedrakes about it, but he couldn't, not with Ethiag pacing the prison corridor.

When it came to Slomby what he should do, he started shaking so hard his shackles rattled and caught Num's attention. "Hoy, fishwit," she said. "Go feed the crone!"

Slomby lurched upright and faced her, his hands balling into fists. "Feed her yerself, ye nasty . . . *eyeball*!" he cried.

Num gaped at him and readied her snapping rag, but Slomby reached out one long arm and snatched it from her before spinning around and heading down the corridor to the devil cavern. Of course, he thought, even the worst of rag snaps would seem but a tickle next to what he was about to face. He fought down his terror and thought of Whisper.

Then he shrank into his shell and picked his way slowly around the scores of devils toward the stair.

There were two ways out of the dungeon and two ways in—not including the underground river by which the devil bottles had been brought here. The short way was the corkscrew stair that led to Dusk's laboratory, and the long way was the labyrinth of tunnels that wound their way up to the city.

The stair was too narrow for a mass devil exodus such as Ethiag had planned; plus, Master Dusk would stand for no such rampage through his work space. The army would attack Nazneen through the tunnels. They would roil up and into the sewers, burst from grates all throughout the city, as well as through the marble floor of Rasilith Ev. They would devour everything—faeries, pigeons, hobgoblins, hummingbirds. It would be a proper meal, the first of many, and it would begin soon.

Ethiag watched with his clustered eyes as Whisper's

carpet progressed. The portrait of himself in its center was whole now and pleased him immensely. It was as realistic as a reflection in a mirror, down to the bristles on his legs and the shine on his many tiny eyes. Now there remained only the border to complete, with its pattern of bruise-hued spikes.

Ethiag paced and waited.

"Do you see that?" Talon whispered, aghast.

"See it and smell it," replied Hirik, who had traced the devils' scent through the tunnels to arrive at this place.

They knelt in the dark and peered into the cavern ahead. Wavering torchlight threw devil shadows against the walls, making them seem even more monstrous and numerous than they were. There had to be hundreds of the snags, of more shapes and breeds than either lad could have imagined to exist. There were gelatinous devils like tubes of slime, and big, prowling reptilian things so huge they could surely not fit up the tunnel. The flying ones winged around the stalactites, and some climbed the walls with sucker-tipped fingers.

There was a deafening din of roars and howls—and another sound, smooth as water, that undulated softly through it all: singing.

"Whisper's alive," said Hirik, feeling a powerful flush of

relief followed by one of dread. She was there, somewhere, alive, but between them lay this horde. How was it possible that all these creatures lurked beneath the city?

"*Now* we need to go get Magpie," said Talon.

Hirik agreed.

FORTY-FOUR

Dusk's fingertip was resting lightly against Magpie's skin, in the space right between her eyebrows. Her blue eyes were open, with points of ruby red still burning in her pupils. Dusk held Mogok swaying on its chain. Magpie and Calypso were under its spell, and if the Rathersting lad had come along, so would he be, and anyone else who laid eyes on the ruby.

Dusk loved the gem. It was a dark sorcery of his own creation, but he had not exactly been lying when he told Magpie it came from a witch doctor in the Skyrn Tangle. In a manner of speaking, it did. That is, Dusk had forced the codger to swallow the ruby before he'd killed him, and then he'd extracted it with a curved knife. It had been an ordinary ruby going in, but blood, murder, and magic had rendered it into Mogok. Such were Dusk's abominable arts.

"Show me the glyph for immortality," he said to Magpie.

"Aye, my lord," she said in the featureless voice of thralldom, and into her mind sprang the glyph.

Dusk was surprised by its simplicity. In all the years he'd searched for it, he'd built it up in his mind into something complex, but in fact, it was only an elegant twist of light. As he gleaned it from Magpie's mind, he was filled with exultation.

He was free now, and best of all, he was *safe*.

This was Dusk's secret: he was terrified to die. The afterworld, which was to other faeries a land of peace, was the stuff of nightmares to him, because Fade was waiting for him there.

Dusk had defeated the dragon once, but he'd had the element of surprise that day, and he knew that Fade's thirst for vengeance would be undiminished by the passage of millennia. Dusk knew him well enough to be sure of that. They had a long history together, going back much farther than the Battle of Black Rock—back, indeed, to the days when Dusk had truly been young.

In Dreamdark.

Even before Dusk had been Onyx, before he had come to Nazneen and become scribe to the Azazel, long before all that, he had worked in the archives of Issrin Ev in Dreamdark, a bright, ambitious young faerie and a favorite to none other than the Djinn King himself. But never *the* favorite. That honor had always belonged to the dragon. The Magruwen's pet. Dusk's enemy.

They hadn't begun as enemies, but they had ended that way, and Dusk was determined never to meet Fade in the Moonlit Gardens. Now, thanks to Magpie Windwitch, he never would.

He had what he wanted, but he didn't draw his finger away from Magpie's brow. He would be a fool to stop now. "Show me the champion's glyph," he said.

"Aye, my lord," intoned his little thrall. The glyph for immortality fell from her mind as she visioned a new one. This one *was* devilishly complex, formed as it was of all the Djinns' secret sigils. Dusk committed it to memory.

Now he was not only immortal, but as near to invulnerable as it was possible to be. Only a Djinn could breach the champion's glyph. Magpie would have done well to use it more often, he thought; it could have protected her from Mogok.

He took his finger away from her brow and stroked her messy, glossy hair. "Thank you, Terror," he said. "Now, just one last thing. Magpie, and Calypso too. I rather wish that young Prince Rathersting was here to share this moment with you. I'd like you to hold your breath until you die."

"Aye, my lord," they said in unison, and then they simply ceased to breathe.

Dusk watched, anticipating the blue tinge that would soon creep into Magpie's face. But it never came.

The doorbell jangled and a fearsome pounding sounded on the window. It jolted Dusk and he jerked Mogok, and at once Magpie and Calypso were released from the spell. They blinked. To them, no time had passed since Dusk had spoken his incantation in Old Tongue. They looked at Batch, who still lay as if dead, and then in the direction of the ringing and pounding.

"Magpie!" came Talon's voice. "Are you in there?"

She leapt up and flew out of the parlor to the front door of the shop. Talon and Hirik were there, breathing heavily. At once she saw Hirik's antennae, fully restored. Unlocking the door, she started to say, "Lad—" but he cut her off.

"We found Whisper," he said.

"And a devil army," added Talon, pausing for a breath before adding, "Underneath Nazneen. Hundreds."

Hundreds of devils, under Nazneen? The information penetrated Magpie's thoughts slowly. Her mind felt slightly thick, like honey left too long in the crock. "What?" she asked.

At her side, Calypso uttered a likewise flummoxed, "Eh what, lads?"

Impatiently, Hirik said, "Come on, we have to go now."

"But the imp—" Magpie gestured behind her. "He hasn't woken up."

"Magpie!" Talon said, giving her a strange look and

darting a glance at Dusk, who stood behind her. "It doesn't matter about the imp! We *know* where Whisper is, and the Azazel must be there too." Enunciating clearly, he repeated, "There's an army of devils under the city."

"Oh," said Magpie, shaking her head to clear it. "Oh!" Her heart lurched as the full weight of the revelation sank in. "Let's go, then." She went out the door without looking back.

Dusk, watching from the doorway, caught sight of Hirik's antennae and blanched.

The lad's eyes widened. He said nothing, but his antennae leaned toward Dusk, rippling, and ever so slightly, his lip curled as he caught the apothecary's scent. It was rancid and wrong. But Magpie, Talon, and Calypso were already airborne so, casting a confused glance back at Dusk, he took off after them.

Dusk's face darkened with displeasure as he watched them go. Then he turned on his heel and strode to the parlor, where he hauled Batch off the chaise by his tail.

"Ow! Watch it!" Batch exclaimed.

"Shut up," said Dusk, pulling him to the stairs and down them so his rump bumped over each step. "Ow! Ow! Ow!" Batch squawked, all the way down. In the library, Dusk threw open the trapdoor and hurled the imp through it, then dropped down after him.

Sprawled on the stones, Batch was spitting with outrage. "Ye mudsuck! What was that all about?"

"Shut up," Dusk said again. He reached up to one of his shelves and plucked down an urn with handles on both sides. He looked Batch over, sizing him up. "This should do," he concluded.

"For what?" Batch demanded.

"For you, creature," Dusk said, his voice thick with disdain. "You didn't think I'd let you scamper around free, surely. A wicked, backstabbing vermin like you? Come here."

"What?" Batch's eyes bulged with fear. The urn was scarcely the size of his head, but he had a terrible foreboding that the apothecary meant to fit his whole body in it. "Neh!" He tried to scuttle away. There was nowhere to go, and Dusk yanked him back. "But we had a deal," Batch squealed. "My . . . my flying carpet! You promised!"

Dusk just laughed. "Master Hangnail," he said, "I'd think a liar like you would be a little wary of promises, seeing as you don't keep your own."

"Let me go!" snarled the imp.

"Not a chance. I need your services to find the Djinn."

"Eh what? Neh! I'm through with Djinn and through with faeries! I won't help you!"

"But you will, and do you know why? Because unlike

Magpie Windwitch, I won't hesitate to bleed you dry if you disobey me. It's a powerful incentive, wouldn't you agree, the desire to keep one's blood *inside* one's body?"

Batch screamed for help, and when he thought of help, he thought of Magpie Windwitch. Choosing to forget how he'd just conspired to kill her, he had a sudden hope that she would appear and save him. Indeed, he fumed, where *was* the flotching faerie when you really needed her? "It en't fair . . . ," he blubbered, despairing.

"Fair!" spat Dusk. "Fairness is the plea of the weak." He made a sudden gesture with his fingers and Batch jerked like a puppet. Powerless, he was pulled toward the tiny neck of the urn and *into* it, nose first. His flesh reshaped itself with an agonizing ache as his bones went to jelly and he was stuffed into the little prison. And then only his pink tail was hanging out the neck of the urn. Dusk swept the diamond rings off it with a flick of his fingers and they tinkled to the stone floor. The urn swallowed Batch's tail like a slurped noodle, and Dusk set on the lid.

"There," he said, content. He turned to Mistral, who was watching somberly from his mirror. "You'll be interested to know, old friend, I have the glyph for immortality, and the champion's glyph too. So you see, I am not a prisoner, not to anything, not to time, or Djinn, or blood."

"You're going, then," said the wind.

"I've lurked and studied long enough. It's time to claim the world."

He took a moment to gather some things off shelves. There was the row of handwritten journals containing his life's work, and Mogok, which he looped on its chain around his neck. He took three receptacles: Madame Sallowpearl's flask, Batch Hangnail's urn, and lastly, he took his tongs and picked up the smoldering ember from within the kettle. He peered at it; if possible, it seemed even dimmer and less impressive than before. Still, Dusk had more respect for his old master than to transport him in that shoddy kettle. He selected a golden coffer crusted with rubies and deposited the Azazel inside.

He was ready.

Mistral said, "Someday you will die, and when you do, Fade will be waiting."

Dusk snarled, "I'll never die! I'll see the world dissolve, and the Moonlit Gardens too, before I let that happen! Now, just one thing to do before I go."

He didn't wish to linger in Nazneen to kill Magpie himself, but he had to ensure it would be done. As luck would have it, there was an army of devils standing by, just waiting to get their fangs in faerie flesh. He said, "I must let Ethiag know to expect company."

Through a crack in a cupboard door, Slomby saw Master disappear down the stair. A violent tremor went through him, rattling his shackles, and he hugged himself tight to suppress it. He'd just managed to skitter into this hiding place when he heard the howls overhead, and he'd barely pulled the doors closed before the imp plunged down through the trapdoor, with Master right behind him.

He hugged his knees to his chest and moaned low in his throat. His bravery was spent.

FORTY-FIVE

Ethiag's carpet was nearly finished. Only the final edge remained to be bound off, and as Whisper sang her last notes she let the dark glyphs fall from her mind one by one. Her voice fluted softly away, and she came out of her trance. She didn't know how much time had passed since she'd begun the carpet, only that it was complete. It lay before her, vast, with its jagged patterns and blood and bruise colors. She shrank from Ethiag's likeness staring up at her from its weave. She was so weary; darkness was creeping in on her, ready to steal her away from consciousness.

"Give it to me," she heard the devil's voice say, and she spun around. He was right there, a glut of greedy saliva dripping off his fangs.

Have it, then, thought Whisper, and she sang a last trill that rolled it up as the devil groped through the bars for it with his spider legs. He laughed his loathsome laugh and drew it through the bars. "It's a shame you won't be able to watch, Silksinger, as the devil age dawns!" he said, and then he whirled away down the passage.

It was done. Whisper's heart felt as dark as the death-polluted threads and the thing she had made with them. "Blessings fly with you," she whispered, then she could fight off the weariness no longer. Her eyes fluttered closed and she swayed on her knees before collapsing onto the soft litter of moth corpses, where she lay still.

Out in the devils' cavern, Ethiag laid out his carpet. His army was arrayed around him in all their glory.

But . . . not quite *all* their glory. Some he'd sent up the tunnel. Thanks to Master Dusk's warning, they were lurking there now, sunk up to their eyeballs in the filthy slurry of bat guano so the Mothmage wouldn't smell them. Long ago, Ethiag had fought the Mothmage. He knew a few tricks, and he'd always been partial to an ambush. He climbed onto his carpet and waited for his guests to arrive.

Magpie's face was fierce and pale as she told the crows a devil army was massed beneath Nazneen.

"So what do we do?" asked Pup. "Do we fight?"

Magpie took a deep breath and let it slowly out. Hundreds of devils! She wasn't ready for a battle like this, but here it was, ready or not. Trying to keep her voice even, she said, "We fight if we have to, and we probably will, but it's a lot more snags than we've ever faced before, so right now we'll creep in quiet and see what we see. Stealthy, birds, until we have a real plan.

"Bertram," she said, turning to him. "You stay here and guard the Ithuriel, all right, feather?"

Bertram opened his beak to protest but clicked it shut again. With his peg leg and poor vision, he knew he was the weakest fighter. "Aye, Mags," he said glumly.

On her way out the door, she paused to give him a hug. She said, "Don't feel like we're leaving you out, Bert. Remember, it's just as important the Ithuriel stays safe as it is we find the Azazel, and I'm trusting you to it."

Puffing out his feathers, he said, "I'll see to it. Be careful, darlin', neh?" She nodded, and Bertram stood at the door and touched wingtips to the other crows as they filed out. As they took flight, he called after them, "Be fierce!"

When they were gone, he got out his sewing basket and flipped open the lid quick, but no pixies darted out. He drew out the thing he'd been hiding from Magpie—it was of pale blue watered silk, just the color of her eyes. To his dismay, he discovered there were no threaded needles ready for him in the basket. There hadn't been for a while, and he wondered where the pixies had gotten to; had they been left behind on this wild journey, someplace in the cold mountains, mayhap? The thought troubled him. Squinting through his spectacles, he threaded his needle himself.

The others flew to Rasilith Ev. Inside the temple, Hirik led the way to the trapdoor, and they plunged into the darkness one by one. Magpie and Talon spelled up orbs of light, and Hirik guided them all down the tunnel, his antennae stretched ahead, ceaselessly tasting the air. It was a long and labyrinthine descent, down countless branching passages and through caverns thick with the eye-stinging stench of bat guano. Besides the guano there was the funk of rot and snags, and Magpie marveled at the sensitivity of Hirik's senses to be able to trace a trail through the odor.

Passing through a large bat cavern, his antennae twitched and he spun to look around but saw only stalagmites emerging from the slop of the guano, with cockroaches and centipedes scuttling through it. There was an eerie quiet disrupted only by trickling water and the rustle of the bugs. Warily, he proceeded down a tunnel, and the others followed.

The passage narrowed. The illumination of their faerie light made the darkness ahead and behind seem all the blacker. "A few more bends in the tunnel," Hirik told Magpie in a low voice, "and we'll reach the cavern."

She nodded. And that was when the quiet burst like a dam.

The tunnel behind them erupted with an echoing cacophony of howls. Snapping around, Magpie spurred her light back the way they'd come, desperate to see what was there.

A horde of devils came charging out of the dark.

"Ambush!" cried Maniac.

In that instant of shock, they tried to make sense of their attackers. Magpie had never seen such devils—they looked like monsters forged of excrement!—and she realized they were crusted with guano.

The beasts lunged, mouths open in shrieks and howls. Hirik got off a few hot blasts with Bijal and several devils fell and were trampled by the ones coming behind. But he couldn't repel the whole tide of them. The faeries and crows could do nothing but whirl on wing and race down the narrow tunnel. Magpie knew that was what the devils wanted, that they were being herded toward the cavern, but there was no other choice.

Hirik's lightning strikes strobed in the tunnel. Devils screamed as they were struck, and a scent of scorched flesh filled the air. The passage brightened and then they were surging out into a vast cavern, filled to bursting with devils.

The faeries and crows halted and hovered in a flurry of wings and stared at the scene around them.

Ethiag's army.

It was arrayed in formation. On the ground, blocks of devils were grouped in phalanxes, one after the next. Others hovered on wing, and more hung from stalactites or crouched, poised to spring from the rough walls. They were very still, the only movement the dart of tongues and the roll of eyes.

In the space between one pounding heartbeat and the next, Magpie scanned the cave for escape routes and saw several tunnels snaking out of the cavern and a smaller cave scooped off one side. The devil troops made all of them inaccessible, and the ambush force was blocking the way they'd come so there was no possibility of an easy retreat that way.

How quickly her plan for stealth had fallen apart!

She and the others crowded together in the middle of the cave, wingtip to wingtip in a small phalanx of their own. There were devils above and below, devils on all sides. This was not a fight her small company could win.

"Listen, 'Pie," Calypso said urgently. "If it comes to it, ye glimmer yerself right out of here, get yerself safe to the Moonlit Gardens, ye hear me?"

"What? And leave you?" she shot back, her eyes glinting. "I'd never!"

"Ye better! Don't ye dare go and die, whatever happens to the rest of us."

"Quit talking of dying, blackbird! I'm not going anyplace!"

"Well, I hope at least ye got the sense to vision yer champion's glyph," muttered the crow chief.

"I have!" said Magpie hotly, though in fact, she had not thought of it. She summoned it up now, and its brilliant pattern leapt gleaming into her mind. So long as she could hold it there, no devil would be able to harm her. She wished the others could be protected by it too. Clutching her knives in her fists, she looked around, her eyes sweeping the masses for a glimpse of the devil general. From the legends she knew only that Ethiag had spider's legs, but she couldn't see any such creature among the multitudes.

Then, from below floated a voice. "Blessings," it said. "We've been expecting you."

Ethiag! But the devil that spoke was an horned thing with a gold ring in its flat nose. It was nothing like a spider. It was not Ethiag's body, Magpie knew, but the words were his. The general was speaking through one of his soldiers.

"Expecting us?" Magpie repeated, turning in the air and scanning the phalanxes for the true Ethiag. How could the devils have known they were coming?

This time the voice came from a slime-coated snag. "Aye. We were expecting a champion. . . ." It lingered over the word, its tongue sweeping a rope of drool back into its mouth. "And . . . the champion's own champion . . . with seven crows, though I count only six. And best of all, a Mothmage!"

The voice shifted again and came out shrill from the lips of a hag. "Twenty-five thousand years I've dreamed of vengeance on the Mothmage, but I didn't think I'd get it!"

Magpie heard, but her mind was stuck on what the slime devil had said. She looked at Talon. *The champion's own champion.*

It was Dusk who'd called him that.

Taunting, the voice moved again. Always it was Ethiag who spoke; these soldiers were just puppets to him. "I thought there were no more Mothmage left for revenge," snarled a fugu devil. "The Master told me he took care of them long ago—"

"The master?" Magpie called out, turning, searching the horde. Hundreds of eyes glittered back at her. "I thought *you* were the master."

"Oh, I am, faerie," came the answer. "Master of my army. But I owe a debt for my freedom, and killing you is the least I can do."

"Killing me?" she said. "If it's me you want, then show yourself and fight me, and let the others go!"

"Neh, champion. It's the Mothmage *I* want. You are only a duty. And the others will be . . . a taste before the feast."

The feast. The devils were going to invade Nazneen. Twenty-five thousand years ago it was just such an invasion that Manathakkali had thwarted, and now, here it was again—this time to rise as a surprise from beneath, with no warning and no warriors in the city but a handful of mercenaries and peregrine guards. It would be a bloodbath—unless they could stop it.

But how?

And then, as Magpie wondered how on earth she could possibly capture all these devils, they attacked.

Winged snags launched themselves at the faeries and crows, and Magpie, daggers in motion, had good cause to recall how, in the Moonlit Gardens, she'd wished for long swords. The beasts came from all sides, and as many snags as Skuldraig dropped paralyzed out of the fight, more devils just sprang up to fight in their places.

The crows were overmatched against such foes. Their only weapons were their beaks and claws, and fiercely Magpie wished the birds were anywhere but here. She gasped when she saw a whip tail coil around Swig's neck, but before she could move to help him, Talon was there, slashing it away. Swig flew free, and Talon fought on, his knife blades silver blurs in the air.

Hirik was fighting fiercely too. As Magpie whirled and lashed out with Skuldraig and her second knife, she could see him out of the corner of her eye. Lightning flew from Bijal's blade, slapping devils back.

Skuldraig, by contrast, needed contact with its victims for its paralyzing magic to work. When Magpie saw Mingus grappling with a croucher's tail, she wished furiously that Skuldraig could project its magic and stun foes over distance!

No sooner did the thought flicker through her mind than she felt a powerful pulse in her fist and saw light unwinding from the dagger's blade.

It wasn't lightning, but the soft traceries of magic that

unwound from her fingertips when magic escaped from her. They were coming through Skuldraig itself, and when they came in contact with the croucher it went limp and plunged to the ground, leaving Mingus free.

Magpie's heart leapt when she realized what she had done. She had made magic with intention. The Tapestry had never felt so alive all around her. It was flowing through her, flooding her with strength. With a kind of delirious abandon she sliced the air with Skuldraig and set a pulse out to meet a wave of soldiers. At once, they fell away. She sliced again. More traceries spun across the cavern, and more devils fell.

Bijal was flashing in Hirik's grip, and Talon and the crows were fighting hard, gouging at devils' eyes and wings in an effort to disable them. Magpie believed, for a moment, that they could overcome even this many foes.

But the devils were only stunned. Neither Bijal nor Skuldraig were magicked for murder, and down where the zapped snags fell to the cavern floor, they picked themselves up and regrouped, only to come at them again.

And again.

How long could they last against such an onslaught?

A bat-winged monster grabbed Pigeon; it gripped him tight and squeezed, and Magpie saw the crow's eyes bulge as his breath choked out of him.

She lashed out with a flare of magic from Skuldraig, but

she couldn't get to him. A wall of devils reared up in her way and surrounded her. Tails lashed out and clawed hands reached for her, but they couldn't touch her.

"The champion's glyph!" hissed a devil, voice sharp with wrath, as the magic knocked him backward.

The wrath, like the words, was Ethiag's. He couldn't get Magpie, the one he was charged to kill, but he could get the others.

Maniac fell. A pair of snags wrestled him to the ground where a serpent beast lay waiting to coil around him. Seconds later a tentacle caught Hirik's wrist and wrenched his sword arm wide. Another snag clamped onto his hand with its teeth and Hirik screamed, dropped Bijal, and was reeled down by the tentacled beast. Magpie, fighting a slew of devils, could do nothing as the rest of the crows were seized one by one. Besides herself, only Talon was left free.

Then a gape-mouthed thing shot out a long, sticky tongue and dragged the lad to the ground.

Fury and panic built in Magpie. Helpless, she looked around at her companions. A bug devil held Mingus, and its pincers were open around the crow's neck like scissor blades. All it had to do was bite, and Mingus's head would . . . She couldn't consider it. With one swift wing beat, she knew, she could get there and free him. But she couldn't get to them all.

"Ethiag!" she screamed. "Where are you?"

"I am here," said a voice.

"And here," said another.

"Here . . . here . . . here . . ." Taunting, laughing, Ethiag called out with his soldiers' voices, and Magpie spun and searched, her fury building and building. She clutched the hilts of her daggers so tight she thought she might dig finger-prints into the metal.

"Show yourself, Ethiag!" she snarled.

And at last, he did.

There was a shifting in a phalanx in the rear of the cave. They were especially huge slabs of snagflesh, and they parted to reveal the creature Magpie knew at once must be the devil general. He had the legs of a tarantula and the bare, pow-erful chest of a man. He was standing atop a shimmer of colors—a carpet.

He snarled, "Make a move, champion, and you'll watch all your friends die one by one. Or you can surrender your-self. Die first and spare yourself the sight."

"Fine, I surrender," she hissed. "Come and get me!"

"Drop your weapons!" commanded the devil general.

"Neh, 'Pie!" squawked Calypso, but his voice choked off as his captor throttled him.

"Now," said Ethiag. "Or the crow dies."

Magpie let both daggers clatter to the floor below.

She glanced at Hirik, hoping he might be able to get off a blast with the lightning sword, but she saw he'd been disarmed and was bound tight by tentacles. He couldn't move, but there was a look of ferocious concentration on his face and his antennae were rippling in waves, fast and steady. What was he doing? Magpie felt a flutter of hope.

"The glyph too, faerie!" said Ethiag. "I know the feel of that magic. You think I haven't fought champions?"

"Aye, and *lost!*"

"Not this time. I've sworn to kill you, and I mean to keep my oath. Surrender the glyph, or watch your friends die."

"Magpie, don't do it. Fight!" Talon cried.

No sooner had the words left his lips than the devils on either side of him took ahold of his black, feathered wings and ripped them brutally from his body. Magpie gasped. They weren't his true wings, but the devils hadn't known that. The feathers turned instantly back to spidersilk, and although Talon's true moth wings still fluttered at his shoulders, the violence left Magpie breathless. It might have been one of the crows, and those *were* their true wings.

Ethiag said, "It will be his arms next," and the two soldiers gripped Talon by the wrists and prepared to pull.

"Neh!" Magpie screamed. She let the glyph fade from her thoughts. She held out her arms and let the devils grab them and wrestle her toward the abomination of a spider beast.

Behind her, she heard the crows shrieking. Again, Talon screamed, "Magpie, fight!" and devils howled, victorious. Her mind spun, trying to think of some way she could save her friends. To save herself would be easy—she could do as Calypso had urged and vanish right out of here, but she never would. She couldn't go on living if she left her friends to die!

"Come to me, champion," said Ethiag, flexing open his fangs as the devils dragged her nearer.

She clenched her teeth and curled her fists around her mounting fury. She could release all her anger in a flare of magic, but she couldn't predict what would happen. One snip of a devil's pincers and Mingus's head would roll. And Talon's arms, and all the others . . . Could she gamble on wild magic when the lives and limbs of her dearest friends hung in the balance?

In an agony of indecision she watched as Ethiag bid his carpet, "Fly!" It rose up off the floor and came toward her, and the devil gave a triumphant cry.

FORTY-SIX

Ethiag expected the carpet to sweep forward toward the faerie, but no sooner had he uttered the word "Fly!" than a crawling sensation broke out over his flesh. Within seconds it intensified to pain—stinging, furious pain over every inch of his body, even the shining surface of his many eyes.

The carpet did not fly, but only floated in the air while agony engulfed him like fire.

Once before, Ethiag had been captured. The Mothmage champion had forced him into the prison in which he had drifted, alone and in the dark, for thousands of years. And there had been pain in the stinging magic that sucked him into the bottle, but it was nothing like this. This wasn't capture. And it wasn't death.

Ethiag was . . . unraveling.

His flesh, his blood, the bristles on his legs, every fiber of his being screamed with anguish. He looked down at the carpet and what he saw filled him with horror. The silken threads had crept free of their weave and risen to clutch at him. Like tiny vines they climbed inside his flesh, leeching at him, *transfiguring* him. Already his legs were enmeshed in the silk, and the threads climbed. They wreathed round him, ensnaring, sucking. The carpet was devouring him. Ethiag wailed as his flesh melted away, inch by inch into the weave of the carpet, becoming something else, something dead. Becoming *silk.*

He battered at the carpet with his arms but he couldn't dislodge it, and as he wailed, his soldiers wailed too. Many times had Ethiag known death in the flesh of his devils—he had felt their agony as they were captured and killed, but never before had they felt his. They did now. Every devil in the cavern writhed, screaming with the torment of their master as his pain pierced the many minds enfolded in his own.

Their screams shook the rock. Stalactites splintered. The sound poured out of the cavern, into the dungeon on one side, the tunnels on the others. As it moved up the tunnels, it met a vast collection of creatures coming the other way. Centipedes, beetles, millipedes, crickets—a swarm of cave-dwelling troglobites, pale and eyeless, they were an insect army, like those of old. They mustered in answer to Hirik's call, and the screaming of devils stirred their antennae, and the trembling of the rock jostled them, but they didn't slow. In a seething mass of thousands, they came.

Overhead in the city, birds burst from their perches

and folk paused in the lanes to look around as the ground trembled and a muted roaring sounded under their feet.

And in the cavern, Talon, Hirik, and the crows struggled in the grips of their pain-ravaged captors. Mingus jerked his neck out from between the pincers just before the devil convulsed and snapped them shut. Talon and Calypso shook off the snags who held them. Magpie, breaking her gaze from the sight of Ethiag's transmutation, flew to retrieve her knives and quickly slashed the tentacles that bound Hirik. Shaking out his wings, he darted for his scimitar.

Magpie turned to Talon. His lips moved as he shouted something to her, but she couldn't hear even her own voice over the din, let alone his. It was just such a relief to see him safe. She reached out and touched her fingertip to his brow.

His eyes went wide with surprise when he saw what she passed into his mind. It was the champion's glyph, and only the champions were supposed to know it.

"I can't lose you," Magpie told him, but he didn't hear her words over the squall of snags.

He committed the pattern to memory and nodded, mouthing the word, "Thanks."

Turning to Hirik, she gave him the glyph too. It was hard to imagine the Djinn would mind, under the circumstances.

Ethiag's change was nearly complete. Only his head was

410

still flesh, mouth splayed open in a scream. The threads kept working, sucking, until that too sank away.

The devil was no more. Neither alive nor dead, he had been translated into silk. Magpie didn't have to go to the Moonlit Gardens to know he would not be there. Whatever deep magic was in the threads, it had unmade him.

The carpet drifted down to settle on the cavern floor, and with that, the soldiers' agony was ended. Their minds were released from their master's grip. They were their own masters now, and they cared nothing for order, or even for vengeance.

They cared about just one thing: hunger.

"Stay close, feathers!" Magpie screamed to the crows as chaos erupted around them. The devils broke from their phalanxes the moment their minds were freed, and within seconds they were at each other's throats. It was a feeding frenzy, and though the soldiers were no longer focused on the faeries and crows, the whole of the cavern had become a maelstrom of teeth and claws.

They had to get out of the thick of it.

"There!" hollered Talon, pointing to the smaller cavern; it was at their backs, dark and seemingly empty.

"Go!" cried Magpie, and she and Talon, protected by the champion's glyph, covered the crows' retreat. Hirik remained in the heart of the battle, Bijal loosing torrents of lightning at the devils and trying to stun them before they could slay each other and send dead monsters to the Moonlit Gardens.

"Look, 'Pie!" cried Calypso when he reached the cave.

Magpie tensed, fearing there were more devils within. Then she saw where Calypso was pointing with his wingtip. In the depth of the cave was a mountain of silver bottles. Of course. Those devils had to have come from somewhere, and here were their prisons, just waiting to be filled again!

"Well, blessings for that!" she said. "Bring 'em here, birds!"

And they set to the familiar work of capturing snags.

The crows grabbed bottle after bottle and hauled them to the front of the cave. "Vortex!" Magpie called to Talon, and together they visioned the glyph. It was the same glyph Magpie had used to suck the weakened Blackbringer down into his prison in Dreamdark. Then, she had been working the spell on her own, clinging to the edge of consciousness in utter black exhaustion. Now, her spell joined with Talon's and the Tapestry quickened around them, the union of their magic creating something greater than the simple sum of their power. Cyclones sprang to life in the necks of the bottles, so strong the faeries and crows had to brace themselves against stalagmites so as not to be caught in the undertow of the powerful magic.

Devil after disoriented devil was caught in it, and lurched through the air, powerless to resist. Beasts far too large for

412

the narrow bottle necks were warped out of shape as the magic sucked them in. They bellowed and writhed, claws scrabbling against silver but each in its turn succumbed, and vanished from sight. Magpie sealed the bottles as they were filled, holding the sealing spell and the vortex spell side by side in her mind.

When the first bottles were filled and sealed, the crows brought more, and again Magpie and Talon magicked devils into them, sucking them out of the chaos of the cavern. Magpie visioned a third spell, the glyphs for floating, to carry devils nearer so the vortex could seize them. Overhead, Hirik's lightning flashed and broke apart snag battles, preventing devils from slaying each other.

There were some devils who managed to slip out by the tunnel and break for the city above, but none of them made it very far. They met Hirik's troglobite army, and like a tide the insects swept them back the way they'd come.

Some devils did inevitably turn up on the riverbank of the Moonlit Gardens, where Bellatrix, Kipepeo, and Merryvenom were waiting to dispatch them into nothingness.

The small cavern was aflutter with crow wings as the birds brought more bottles to the fore, and more. Magpie and Talon filled them, the glyph for vortex scorched across their minds like a light that has been looked at too long. The mass in the main cave thinned, and Hirik's lightning strikes tapered off.

At last, it was all over.

The weird blind troglobites melted back to the cracks and fissures of their underground world, and the faeries and crows stood amid rows of silver bottles, exhausted. They were gouged and bruised, covered with devil slime, flakes of dried guano, and even snag blood and phlegm. Talon had lost his crow wings, Maniac suffered some cracked ribs from the serpent's crushing coil, and Pup was bleeding freely from a gash to his neck, but they were all alive.

Magpie looked at the bottles and remembered how, until very recently, she had proudly tallied her captures. The Blackbringer had been only her twenty-fourth, and here already, little more than a month later, she had gone beyond counting.

So many devils! How had it happened? Certainly, Ethiag had been here to grip their wild minds in his own and bend them to his will, but first . . . something had to have released them, here, beneath Nazneen. It occurred to her for the first time now to wonder just who had opened up this mountain of bottles. She jerked her head at Talon and Calypso to follow her and they went cautiously deeper into the small cave, skirting the black lake at its center.

Soon enough they had their answer.

A human, hideous and ancient. She was slumped over in the midst of the bottles, and Magpie knew at once she was dead. Small mercies, she thought. What would she have done with the big, ungainly creature if she were alive? But how had she come to be here, deep beneath a faerie city? This was not Ethiag's doing.

A dull anxiety was buzzing in Magpie's brain. Ethiag had spoken of a master. She chewed her lip.

"What is it, 'Pie?" asked Calypso.

This short lull to catch their breath was fine, but they hadn't yet done what they came to Nazneen to do. She said, "We still haven't got the Azazel."

"Or Whisper," added Hirik.

"Aye, or Whisper," she agreed. "Come on."

FORTY-SEVEN

They agreed to split up. Besides the tunnel by which they'd come, there were three rough portals off the central cavern. Inside one was what must have been Ethiag's nest. It was filled with iron shackles and chewed bones, and the smell of it made Hirik stumble back. The next was a corkscrew stair straight up, and the third, a corridor. Hirik stood at both of these with his antennae riffling. He tasted the smoky scent plume of the Azazel going up the stair. It wasn't fresh, but it was distinct. And down the corridor, he scented Whisper.

"The Azazel's up the stairs," he told Magpie. All his life he had dreamed of finding the Djinn, but now, poised between the two scents, he surprised himself. "I'll take the corridor."

"Be careful," Magpie said.

"And you."

Pup and Pigeon came with him. First, they came to a filthy kitchen, thick with the stink of rotten fruit. There was a figure cowering in the corner and Hirik almost lashed out at it with Bijal. But the snag, when it looked at him with its single rolling eye, seemed so pathetic that he held off. Its ankles were trapped in heavy iron shackles, he saw, like the ones in Ethiag's nest. A slave? With a shudder, he signaled to the crows and continued on.

From then on, the misery only deepened. Before he even turned the corner into the aisle of prison cells, Hirik had to furl his antennae and cover them with his hair in an effort to mute the overwhelming aura of long captivity and despair. He passed cell after cell. Things cowered in the shadows and drew slowly forward when they saw him.

A small voice whispered, "Are you here to save us?"

Tears came. Blinking them back, Hirik said, "Aye . . . aye. I am."

He wasn't champion yet. Perhaps he never would be, but he could do this. Leveling Bijal, he blasted the locks off the cells one by one. The shocks of lightning illuminated the sad corridor as no light ever had, and by its flash, he found Whisper. She lay as if dead on a bed of moth corpses. He blew the lock off her cell and sank to his knees beside her. He touched her cheek.

Alive.

He squeezed his eyes shut in relief, but his tears kept coming. He gathered her up in his arms, and briefly, she flickered open her eyes. When she saw him, color flooded back into her pale cheeks. "Even dead," she whispered, "you came for me."

"Dead?" he said. "I'm not dead."

"I'm glad," she whispered with a weak smile.

He carried her from the cell and continued down the row, blasting off locks, and at the end he just stood and stared.

Firedrakes, five of them, more beautiful than he had ever imagined. He released them from their imprisonment, blasting off not only the locks but the shackles. The drakes rushed into the corridor, where they were able to touch each other for the first time in four thousand years.

"Thank you, faerie," Vesrisath said.

"It's—it's an honor," Hirik stammered.

They followed the other prisoners out to the main cavern, where little remained but stench to prove a devil army had been there. Whisper looked around. "They're all gone," she whispered.

"Because of you," Hirik told her. "Because of your carpet."

"Where is it?" she asked, and he carried her to where it still lay on the stone floor. She shuddered when she saw Ethiag's likeness staring up at her. In the portrait she had woven, the devil general had stood battle ready. The picture had changed. Now his awful mouth was open in a scream of agony.

When one of the young firedrakes moved forward to sniff the carpet, Whisper said quickly, "Don't. Don't touch it. It's . . . dangerous. *Dark.*"

"What should we do with it?" Hirik asked.

"Burn it," she said at once.

And the firedrakes obliged.

At the top of the long spiral stair, Magpie, Talon, and the rest of the crows emerged into a laboratory. They didn't need Hirik's senses to be overwhelmed by the stink of old flesh and bones. "Skive!" said Magpie, choking. "What is this place?"

"It looks like . . ." Talon hesitated. "It looks like an apothecary shop."

The tall shelves were covered with books, brass scales, vials, and mortars, as in Dusk's workshop. But there were other things: eyeballs, skulls. A tremor went through Magpie, and a small voice inside her tried to deny what in her heart she knew to be true. It wasn't possible. . . .

"The kettle!" squawked Calypso.

She saw it too and sprang toward it. But . . . it was empty. She picked it up and held it in her hands, and before she was even fully aware she was doing it, she drew the memory-touch glyphs in her mind. She wanted to prove that her suspicions were wrong. There had to be another explanation. Another villain—

The kettle clattered to the stone floor. Magpie staggered back, her eyes wide. For an instant she had been plunged into Dusk's thoughts, and they *festered*.

"What is it, Mags?" asked Swig, at her elbow. "What did ye see?"

Her eyes cut across the crowd of crows to meet Talon's. She whispered, "Dusk." The crows started squawking in disbelief, but Talon didn't even blink.

"Ye sure, 'Pie?" asked Calypso.

She gave a tight nod and swallowed hard. "I'm sure. He's . . . he's wicked. And . . . he's got the Azazel."

"Well, let's find the scoundrel! We'll go to his shop—"

"You're too late," said an airy voice.

Magpie looked up at the mirror on the wall just as a face appeared within it. It was broad-browed and bearded, so similar to her own grandfather she thought for a moment it was him, but it was another wind. Startled, she said, "Cousin, what do you there?"

"Dusk's gone, and he won't be back. He's free now."

"Free?" Magpie didn't understand. She was reeling from the betrayal. She'd known Dusk half her life, trusted him and believed he was a kindred soul—one of the few faeries besides her own folk who took an interest in the world, old magic, the lore of the Djinn. . . . "We . . . we have to find him," she said. "He has the Azazel. . . ."

"Neh, maidy, but he doesn't," spoke another unfamiliar voice, and they all spun to see a creature emerging from a cabinet.

"Mags! A snag!" cried Swig, launching himself at the creature, who gasped when he saw the crow coming and sucked himself up inside the big snail shell on his back so

420

that the only things left visible were his long arms, cradling something that looked like a bird skull.

"Wait, Swig," Magpie said. She approached the snag. "What do you mean, he doesn't have the Azazel? Come out and speak up."

A thin face with bulging red eyes slowly emerged from the shell. The snag blinked, terrified, and said in a shaking voice, "He doesn't. . . . I mean . . . I tricked Master. He's got a coal from the fire, but . . . but . . . the Azazel is . . . *right here.*"

He held out the skull. It was upside down, and there in its brain pan reposed an ember. Magpie saw at once that it was a Djinn. Like the Ithuriel, this small glowing thing was nothing to the common eye, but to Magpie it was like a window to the Tapestry, alive with glyphs. She crouched before the snag and gently took the skull from his trembling hands.

Relief overcame her. It was okay. By some miracle of a snail-shelled snag, the Azazel was safe. Whatever Dusk had done or tried to do, whoever and whatever he was, he hadn't gotten his hands on the Djinn.

Hesitantly, the snag asked, "Did I do good, maidy?"

"Aye, you did real, real good."

He beamed a big smile at her and she smiled back. She almost felt like laughing. Talon knelt beside her to peer into the skull, and the crows drew in around them. Pup gave the snag a wing hug, and Calypso trod on a little pile of diamond rings lying on the floor, scattering them. They caught Magpie's attention for just an instant before, at her side, Talon said, "It's a good thing you never told Dusk where the Ithuriel was."

"Aye," she agreed, taking a deep breath. "I would have, if it wasn't for you. Thank you."

The wind in the mirror said, "He knew."

"What?" Magpie asked quietly, turning to face him.

"The scavenger imp told him. As I said, you're too late."

FORTY-EIGHT

After that, everything was a blur. Magpie was barely aware of thrusting the small skull into Talon's arms. The pulse of the Tapestry carried her straight up to the trapdoor and she was through it, right in the very library where as a sprout she had spent some of her happiest evenings. Then, a blur of rooftops as the bazaar sped under her, Rasilith Ev just a golden smear. When she thought about it later, she would realize she had scarcely thought of the Ithuriel during that flight. Though the world balanced on the Ithuriel's safety, she thought only of Bertram.

She flew over the stained glass ceiling of their chamber with its suns and orchids and swooped down to the door, thrusting it open with her shoulder and darting into the center of camp. The fire had burned out. That was the first thing she saw. The doors to all the caravans stood open. That was the second thing.

Bertram's spectacles were the third thing.

They were lying on the floor, and when she stooped to pick them up, she knew.

She knew before she saw the bird foot that protruded from behind a wagon wheel, and the ebony peg reposed beside it. She was cocooned in silence. The air had been sucked out of the world. She didn't breathe and wasn't aware of moving, but her wings must have pushed her onward because the next thing she knew, she was standing in blood and Bertram was stretched out before her, his eyes wide, beak hanging open.

Blood soaked her slippers, and she didn't feel the hands and wings on her arms as Talon and Calypso came up behind her. She didn't hear their voices in her ears, or the cries of the rest of the crows arriving from the sky. She felt only that the blood seeping through the weave of her slippers was cold, already congealing, and the thing that caught her eye was a dazzle at Bertram's chest, looking like a silver brooch set against black feathers.

But it wasn't a brooch. It was the hilt of a knife, protruding from his heart, and Bertram was dead.

The world swung in an arc around her so only Talon's arms kept her standing. She shrugged him off. She dropped to her knees and fell across Bertram, her fingers in his feathers, her face against his throat.

She stayed like that a long moment and still she didn't breathe, and as long as she didn't breathe, the world stayed silent, but then a dizzy blackness rose and threatened her and she had to gasp, and when she did, sound came roaring back. Cawing and curses, the grief of the crows, and Talon's sobbing behind her. She couldn't bear it.

And so she vanished.

In the Moonlit Gardens, Bertram had not yet crossed the river but stood waiting. Magpie saw him and flew to him, and he opened his wings to catch her and then folded them around her and held her close. She buried her face in his feathers as she had done with his dead body back in the living world, but here there was no dagger protruding from his heart; murder weapons did not cross the threshold of the worlds. She was enclosed by his feathers, breathing the tobacco and rainy-sky scent of him as she finally released the sob that had been building and building inside her like held breath.

She wept into his feathers while he rocked her, and when her sobbing quieted, he asked her in a low croak, "Ye're all right, Mags? Ye're not . . . ye're not dead too?"

"I'm not dead," she said into his feathers, "and I'm not all right."

"Well, I mean, ye all got out okay and all? I guess all the others are well or they'd be standing around here griping, sure."

Magpie stood back and tried to swallow her sobs. She whispered, "They're okay."

"And the devils?" he asked. "Did ye get 'em?"

She nodded.

"Good, good," said Bertram. "Now Mags, listen, darlin', I've something to tell ye, and it's a strange and hard something, but who killed me . . ."

"I know," she said, her voice going sharp.

"Ye do? Well, I'm fierce flummoxed by it. He just came in and I offered him tea and he . . . he did it."

"He was after the Ithuriel," she told him.

"What?" he squawked. "Neh, sure! And did he . . . ?" he asked. When Magpie nodded, his beak quivered. "Skive, Mags, that was all I was supposed to do was guard the Ithuriel and I failed—"

"Neh!" she said fiercely. "It's not your fault! How could you know? It's my fault for not seeing what he was!" Tears spilled down her cheeks. If she had seen Dusk for who he was, Bertram would be alive, and the Ithuriel would still be burning in a cook pot in her wagon. "I'm going to get him, Bertram," she promised.

"I know ye will," he said.

Remembering his spectacles, she held them out to him. "Here. You dropped these."

"Oh." He took them but didn't put them on. He blinked

and looked around, peering across the river to where Bellatrix and Kipepeo were waiting arm in arm. "I don't guess I need 'em here, pet. And . . . skive! Look at me!" He looked down and noticed that his peg leg was gone, his true foot restored.

"Oh, aye," Magpie said, noticing too. "The Moonlit Gardens makes you whole again."

"Well, I wish it didn't," said Bertram. "Of all the interfering! Ye made me that peg yerself, and it had yer initials carved in it. That was *me*, that peg, not this old foot that got itself eaten by a croucher."

"Oh, Bert!" said Magpie, burying her face in his neck again. Even here while she was with him, she felt his absence from the world as an unbearable ache. "You'll be okay here," she said, "and you'll wait for all the rest of us, and someday—"

"Now listen, Mags," said the crow sternly. "The day ye come to live here is a long way off. Hundreds and hundreds of years, and don't ye do nothing to make it any sooner, ye hear me? As for the others, keep 'em by ye as long as them long-life potions'll let ye. Don't go sending me any company. I'll make friends here, and I'll be just fine waiting. Now." He took a deep breath. "Let's see." He surveyed the land around him. "That's one skiving big blare of a moon up there. And . . . hoy!" he cried. "Dragons!" At once, he was as excited as a hatchling and gave a little skip. "Can I fly up and look closer?" he asked her. "Can I meet Fade?"

Smiling in spite of her sadness, she said, "Maybe first you should come meet Bellatrix and Kipepeo? They can introduce you to the dragons later."

"All right," he agreed. "I think I'd like that."

FORTY-NINE

Back in Nazneen, the first thing Magpie did, besides give each one of the crows a long, tight hug, was go right back to Dusk's secret laboratory. She smashed the glass on the mirror and freed the wind who was trapped in it. His name was Mistral, and he had much to tell her, though he insisted she fly with him into the sky for the telling. He had been a prisoner far too long to stay indoors another moment.

With every new thing Mistral told her, her heart grew colder:

That Dusk had been ancient even when he was Onyx, which was not his true name any more than Dusk was . . .

That he had orchestrated the slaughter of Fade and used the gem Mogok to frame the Mothmage for it . . .

That he had spent his unnatural long life in the study of dark magic, and that with a Djinn in his power, he could weave the Tapestry . . .

And lastly, that Magpie, in her trance, had given him the glyph for immortality, and the champion's glyph too.

That she had made him virtually invincible.

"Who *is* he?" she asked in a small, desolate voice.

"Ask the Djinn King, child," said Mistral. "Before he was scribe to the Azazel . . . long before, the one you knew as Dusk was in the Magruwen's employ."

"The Magruwen!" exclaimed Magpie.

Mistral nodded. "He was exiled long ago from Dreamdark."

"Why?" she asked breathlessly.

"I don't know," said Mistral.

Thoughts wheeled in Magpie's mind. Dusk had been exiled from Dreamdark. Could this have something to do with the betrayal that had driven the Djinn from the world? She thought it must. Mistral was right—she would have to ask the Magruwen. She shuddered at the thought of bearing him the news that Dusk had taken possession of the Ithuriel.

And worse, Dusk had Batch Hangnail with him, and no doubt even now he was winging his way to finding the rest of the Djinn. She and Mistral asked the Sayash winds which way he had gone.

"East," was the answer.

"I have to go after him."

"I'll hunt him with you," said Mistral. "I'll speed your journey."

She nodded. "We'll leave tonight."

"I'll await you here."

When she came back down out of the sky, Magpie told the others, "We go tonight, and we fly fast. We'll leave the wagons here."

"Aye," Calypso agreed. He was staring at the spot on the floor where the crows had tried to scrub up Bertram's blood. "The sooner we catch that dastard, the better."

Talon heard their words. Leaving tonight, and without the wagons? He shrank in on himself a little. His wings were destroyed. He held his knitting needles in his hands; already he had begun a new skin, but the last one had taken him more than a week. His needles fell still and he stared at the chain of spidersilk in his lap, defeated. It was no use. There wasn't time.

Magpie saw his hands go slack and she realized at once the problem with her plan. "Jacksmoke," she murmured, then she went and knelt at Talon's side. She said quietly, "I know that sad look on your face is just for Bert and not because you got some blither-brained notion I'd go off and leave you here."

He looked at her. "It'll take me days to knit a new skin, and you've got to go."

"Skive, lad, didn't you hear what Bertram said yesterday? You're one of us. I'm not going to leave you any more than I'd've left *him* behind!"

"Neh?"

"Neh."

Overcome with relief, Talon pretended to study his knitting.

Magpie said, "So we'll bring one wagon, and you can ride in it and work until you're done. Okay?"

He nodded. "So long as it's not Batch's stink wagon . . . ," he said, meaning to make a joke but realizing as he spoke that the imp would never again be a joke to them. The next time they met him—as they surely would—they would treat him as a villain, just like Dusk. Batch Hangnail was the enemy now.

"Neh," said Magpie. "Not that wagon."

"Magpie?" Talon said. She looked up at him, and her grief was plain in her eyes. Talon wished he could do or say something that would make her feel better, but what? He did the only thing he could think of. He kissed his fingernail and flicked her softly on the cheek with it.

"Ow," she said, though it had been hardly a flick at all, and then she kissed her own and flicked him back. And, Talon was glad to see, she smiled, just a little.

Turning to Calypso, Magpie relayed the new plan. But

there were things to do before they could leave. First, they would bury Bertram in a cloister in Rasilith Ev.

Then they would set the Azazel on his throne.

Kneeling, Magpie picked up the bunched blue silk off the floor where Bertram had dropped it, and her heart ached when she saw what it was. Hugging it to her chest, she made her way to her wagon.

Whisper was inside. She and Magpie had not yet met. Since Hirik had brought the lass back here, they had been careful not to intrude on the company's grief. Now, they set eyes on each other for the first time. Whisper rose from the trunk on which she'd been perched. Hirik stood beside her. Crouched beneath Magpie's bunk, the snag Slomby gave Magpie a shy smile. The Azazel was still inside the upturned pigeon skull in which he'd placed it, and Whisper was cradling this to her, unwilling to let the Djinn out of her sight again.

"Blessings," the lasses said, blue eyes meeting black. A day earlier, Magpie might have given a crow squawk of a laugh and chided Whisper for being so hard to find. But too much had happened. It was hard to imagine ever laughing again.

"Thank you," Whisper said. Her voice was low, but not a whisper, and Magpie felt gratitude thrum in the words.

"Neh," she said. "It's we who should thank *you*. That

carpet . . ." She shook her head, recalling the sight of Ethiag being transmuted to silk. That such magic as that had come from this slight lass!

"He did it to himself," said Whisper. "If the silk hadn't been polluted with death, I could never have made that magic."

"Well, if it wasn't for that carpet, I don't know what would have happened. I'd have lost more than one crow today, that's sure."

"I'm sorry about your friend," Whisper said.

"Aye," added Hirik.

"My brother," Magpie corrected. "And . . . thanks."

They looked at the Azazel. "Do . . . do you think he'll wake?" Whisper asked.

"One way to find out," Magpie replied. "Shall we go and see?"

"Now?" asked Whisper. A little thrill of anxiety went through her as she considered that after everything, the Azazel still might not wake. Her hand trembled on the skull.

"It's okay," said Magpie. "We're with you now. The Azazel's safe, and so are you."

With a deep breath, Whisper nodded. She said, "Okay, let's go meet him."

Magpie looked down at the blue silk in her arms. She said, "I'll be just a moment," and the others left to give her privacy. When she came out to join them a moment later, she was wearing not her hunting garb, but loose, flowing trousers in shimmering blue, and a fitted, sleeveless tunic in the Zandranath style. It came to her knees, with slits up the sides for movement, and a high collar fastened with a moonstone button. There were even new slippers to match.

"Ye look lovely, pet," Calypso told her, wrapping his wing around her shoulders. "Ye'll have to go let Bert see ye wearing it."

She nodded. "Aye. Now, if only I could get a comb through my hair without breaking it in half, maybe I could pass for a civilized faerie." Frowning, she held up half a comb.

Whisper said, "Let me," and before Magpie could ask what she meant, she started to sing. It was a simple song, and lovely, and as its notes wove round her, Magpie's hair seemed to come to life and unwork itself from its tangles. It made her scalp tingle, and within moments, instead of a nest of snarls, her hair was streaming smooth and loose to her shoulders, with the front gathered away from her face in small, neat braids.

"Skive," said Magpie, looking at herself in a wagon window. "That was much nicer than combing! Thanks."

"You're welcome," said Whisper, smiling. "I couldn't do anything for that piece, though," she said, pointing at Magpie's foxlick. "It just won't lie down."

Though Magpie had only minutes earlier found it hard

to imagine ever laughing again, a bubble rose in her like magic and came out sounding like a cross between a hiccup and a laugh. The crows chuckled too. Magpie said, "Your magic is strong enough to defeat Ethiag, but not my foxlick. I like that!"

FIFTY

They walked in procession to Rasilith Ev, bearing Bertram's body on a litter. The firedrakes were with them, trailing their crimson plumes, and the citizens of Nazneen fell into step behind and followed them through the winding lanes of the bazaar. Folk were on the rooftops too, and watching out windows, but the city held silent as they passed, and Magpie's sharp ears heard not one utterance of gossip.

When they reached the temple, as if by mute understanding, the crowds waited quietly outside.

The firedrakes dug Bertram's grave with their powerful claws, and the crows gently lifted their brother down into it. Magpie climbed in with him and gave him a last hug and a kiss on his beak, though she knew this body was no longer Bertram. She said a silent thanks for the hedge imp's blessing that allowed her to cross between the worlds to see the real Bertram. With a snap of her wings she lifted herself out of the grave.

Whisper sang and Calypso said a tearful blessing as the

firedrakes filled in the grave. It was in a beautiful spot, with the tinkling of a fountain not far off, and the heavy heads of orchid blooms bending over a sunlit wall. Another day, they would return and put a stone here that described how much they'd loved him. Now, there wasn't time. Bertram would understand.

The drakes dug one more grave, and into it Slomby placed a bundle containing the chewed slave bones from Ethiag's nest. Atop the grave, once the dirt was mounded over it, he placed a single, perfect raspberry.

They all went into the temple and crossed the great circular hall to the throne, where they gathered in reverent silence.

Whisper went forward. With shaking hands, she tipped the pigeon skull so the ember rolled out onto the throne's polished seat. It lay there for a long, breathless moment and they all began to fear that nothing would happen.

Then it flickered. Flared. Its light gleamed in all their watching eyes as, out of the small seed of fire, the Azazel grew and kept growing, as if his full, massive form had been contained within it all along. His fiery figure stretched out two arms and those arms split each into three. His head trebled, the single flickering shape splitting and becoming three, and he kept on growing.

Hirik reached out and wrapped his arm around Whisper's shoulders. He said in her ear, "You did it." One of his antennae brushed her temple, and it was as soft against her skin as a firedrake plume.

"*We* did it," she said, feeling the weight of duty suddenly lifted. She had fulfilled her clan's oath. Now, all before her, lay her own life, whatever she might choose to do with it. The thought made her giddy.

The Azazel exhaled smoke through his three mouths, his heads turning from side to side, six eyes blinking as he surfaced from his long, long sleep. It was good that the fire-drakes were here so that familiar faces greeted him, but after looking around at them all, it was on Whisper that his gaze settled.

She stepped forward and said, her voice strong and pure, "Welcome home to Nazneen, Lord Azazel. Welcome back to the world."

Sparks cascaded out of the Djinn's three mouths as he replied, "Thank you, daughter. I have dreamed much of you."

He fixed his gaze on Hirik next. "And of you," he said.

Hirik dropped to one knee before him. "My lord, as my many-greats-grandfather Manathakkali once did, I offer my life to your service."

All in the temple held their breath. The Azazel stared at the lad for a long moment, and Hirik felt a slight prick-ling sensation on the back of his neck and right between his eyes. He sensed that the Djinn was looking inside of him, reading his heart and his mind. He wasn't afraid. He knew the Djinn would find the purity of his clan's commitment to their master.

The Azazel said, "Hirik Mothmage, will you take the oath to become my champion?"

He answered, "Aye, my lord Azazel. With all my heart."

The ceremony was brief, as Magpie's had been at Issrin Ev not two months before. There was no time in the world for rituals now, but only for action. The Azazel took Bijal's hilt into his flaming hand and brought the flat of the blade down to touch Hirik on both shoulders. "I name thee, Hirik Mothmage, Azazel's champion," he said.

The four young faeries all felt a powerful pulse ripple through the Tapestry, but Hirik himself felt more than that.

When Bijal touched his shoulders its steel lit up with a brilliant lace of lightning, and he felt it enter him. It snapped him upright as outward from his heart raced a pulse of heat and light, branching, burning, all his veins lit like fuses. Out through his fingers and feet, out through the top of his head, in a space of snapped fingers it passed through him, leaving him . . . *bright.* Conscious, more fully awake than he had ever been, and blazing, not with the pain of fire, but with radiance, as if he were lit from within. His blood was more than blood; his heart pushed light and life through him, funneling it from the Djinn's greater pulse.

Gradually the feeling subsided. Hirik's heartbeat slowed to normal rhythm and he was himself again, almost. The pulse ebbed away, but he still sensed it, invisible and everywhere, and knew that he would never be the same again.

He was champion.

By moonrise, it was time for farewells. Magpie, Talon, and the crows would fly east with Mistral. They were tense and went about their preparations with few words. Whisper wished she could give them a gift in parting—some kind of thanks—but she had nothing to give. As if she were newly born into the world, she possessed nothing—no longer even the copper kettle that she had once held so tightly in the crook of her arm.

The Azazel would not fit in a kettle ever again, she thought, looking at him. They had gone from Rasilith Ev to the opera house to retrieve the ancient skin Magpie had seen in a fortune-teller's vision, and the Djinn was clad in it now. Rather than a being of wild flame, he was an exquisite beast of fur and flesh. The skin of his six arms and three heads looked as real as her own, and his legs were of velvet brown fur as soft as a horse's throat. Only his eyes gave away his fiery nature, sparking and flaming through the six vertical eye slits of his skin.

Magpie made her farewells to him, then turned to face Whisper.

"Blessings and safe skies," Whisper told her.

"You too," Magpie said. "I'll see you in Dreamdark one of these days soon."

Dreamdark.

Not tonight but soon, Whisper would begin a journey too. She was to accompany the Azazel halfway around the world to Dreamdark, where the Djinn would be reunited with the Magruwen, and hopefully soon with the rest of their brethren.

Hirik was coming, of course, to make sure they made it safely, and the five firedrakes would join them too. Hirik could fly, but since none of the others could, Whisper would sing flying carpets for them all, and she would share her own with the ninth and unlikeliest member of their party: Slomby.

She glanced at the snag at her side, hunched under the heavy whorls of his shell, and smiled to see the wonder on his face as he took in everything, drinking the world with his big red eyes. "What are all those lights up there in the sky?" he asked her in a hushed tone.

"Those are stars, Slomby. They're like the sun, but much farther away."

He stared at the sky and beamed. Seeing him all lit up with joy, Whisper wondered how she could ever have thought he was ugly.

He had begged to serve her, and she hadn't been able to refuse. After all, he had saved the Azazel. He deserved a place in the world. She reached out and linked her arm through his and told him, "We're going to see a lot of stars, Slomby. We're going to see millions."

"I'm glad I'm not the only champion anymore," Magpie told Hirik. "It's like . . . a weight shared."

"I'm proud to share it," Hirik said with quiet intensity. "I wish I could help you find Dusk, though. It was he who ruined my clan's name."

"Aye, well, you've unruined it," said Magpie. "And now Nazneen will have a guardian clan once more, with your folk coming back. I know you want revenge, Hirik, but it's better you see the Azazel safe to Dreamdark, and protect the last five firedrakes and the last Silksinger in the world."

"And the last snail-shelled snag too?" he said in jest.

"Aye, him too," Magpie said. "You never know about someone by looking at them, do you?"

He knew she was thinking of Dusk. He said, "Not always, maybe, but sometimes you do. You trusted me."

"That's true," she admitted. "Good thing too. The world needs champions fierce."

Talon came up. "We'd better be off," he said.

"Aye, the wind awaits. Hirik, you'll make sure Dusk's

prisoners get wherever they need to go? Zingaro said he'd help any way he could."

Hirik nodded. "I'll see to it."

"Good. And one last thing. I'll leave it to you whether you want to ask the Azazel to make that meat Stormfoil normal again."

Hirik considered it. "Maybe the tusks, but I think I'll let him keep the tail. It suits him."

Magpie nodded. "It might help him remember any lessons he learned."

The last thing Hirik said was, "Thanks for . . . everything. My antennae, my *life*—"

"Ach, sure," said Magpie awkwardly.

The moon was high, and it was time to go. Swig slipped into the harness of the one wagon they would haul, and Talon climbed up onto its roof with his knitting needles sticking out of his pocket. Then, with a blur of wings, they lifted off.

"Blessings fly with you," called Whisper, waving as they grew smaller in the distance. She realized then that, though she owned nothing, there was one gift she could give, and so she did.

She sang. Her voice climbed the sky, and it carried with it glyphs for luck and speed, and a low, soothing note that was a balm for grief. It rose in a sweet crescendo around the travelers, and as they paused for a moment before the moon, a flash of light streaked up from the city—a bolt of lightning like a salute, rising skyward with Whisper's song.

Music and lightning, beauty and strength, magic and legend, Silksinger and Mothmage, alive again in Nazneen.

Magpie, Talon, and the crows basked in the wonder of it for just an instant, then Mistral came in a great gust and they were gone, following a trail of treachery into the dark.

Acknowledgments

Hugs to all the readers of *Blackbringer* who've sent me e-mails. Seeing Dreamdark through your eyes has the power to make me fall in love with my own characters and world again and again, and many times those messages buoyed my spirits when the writing was rough.

Thanks to Jehsyka and Lexi, who are thirteen and destined to write brilliant books themselves. To ten-year-olds Miriam Saperstein and Owen Netzer: I am indebted to you for your astute feedback on the second draft of this book. Your teachers and parents should be very proud of you! To ten-year-old Rachel in Michigan, who has read *Blackbringer* eleven times: thank YOU!

Many grown-up readers deserve thanks too, notably Patti and Jim Taylor, Alexandra Saperstein, Chary Deutsch, Amy Hughes, Heather Cohen, Stephanie Perkins, Amber Lough, Debbie Meyers, Lauren Widtfeldt, Marianne Elliott, Daanon DeCock and Michelle Aron, and Jennifer Fox (with Stephanie and Debbie getting the award for most detailed positive feedback and reactions). Many of you I met through blogs, and I am so grateful for that alternate world where we share our love and terror of writing and our general bemusement about life.

Speaking of blogs, my dread devil general would be named something quite different were it not for the word-verification function of the Disco Mermaids site, which offered "ethiag" up to me one day in lieu of something like "gfqlix" or "vbruyyt" as I was leaving a comment.

The biggest thanks of all are reserved for three people:

—my wonderful husband, Jim Di Bartolo, for constant support and brainstorming help with the story; for running all errands while I was buried in revisions; and for bringing my characters magically to life with your artwork.

—Timothy Travaglini, my editor, for being more deeply immersed in the world of Dreamdark than anybody besides me, down to the tiniest matters of faerie pronunciation and the relative size of a dragonfly to a hobgoblin.

—Jane Putch, my agent, for unstinting moral support, cheerleading, and all the wearisome work behind the scenes.

Thank you!

About the Author

Laini Taylor is a writer and artist living in Portland, Oregon. Her debut novel, *Dreamdark: Blackbringer*, was published to much acclaim, including stars from *Booklist*, the Bank Street College of Education, and *KLIATT*. *Blackbringer* was also a Book Sense Children's Pick, winner of the Baker & Taylor/PYRG Teen Readers Sweepstakes, and on the Sequoyah Book Awards Master List. It has received glowing praise from such luminaries as Newbery Honor winner Shannon Hale, and *New York Times* bestsellers Holly Black and Brandon Mull. A Fuse #8 Production states, "If you read only one fantasy book this year, read this one." *Blackbringer* is followed by the companion volume *Dreamdark: Silksinger* and an unrelated short-story collection, *Lips Touch*.

Laini Taylor is also the creator of Laini's Ladies, a gift-product line she began making by hand to sell at a local art fair, which has expanded to seventeen product lines—from stationery to garden objects to holiday ornaments to jewelry—that have been sold in over 5,000 gift and specialty stores throughout the United States and Canada.

Laini Taylor lives with her husband, artist Jim Di Bartolo, and her elderly dog, Leroy, in a bright yellow house filled with lots of books and marionettes and robots. They spend their time drinking coffee and making stuff up, and are currently awaiting the birth of their first child.